D0411470

THE DROWNING PEOPLE

THE
DROWNING
PEOPLE

Richard Mason

MICHAEL JOSEPH

LONDON

MICHAEL JOSEPH LTD

Published by the Penguin Group
Penguin Books Ltd, 27 Wrights Lane, London w8 5tz, England
Penguin Putnam Inc., 375 Hudson Street, New York, New York 10014, USA
Penguin Books Australia Ltd, Ringwood, Victoria, Australia
Penguin Books Canada Ltd, 10 Alcorn Avenue, Toronto, Ontario, Canada m4v 3b2
Penguin Books (NZ) Ltd, Private Bag 102902, NSMC, Auckland, New Zealand

Penguin Books Ltd, Registered Offices: Harmondsworth, Middlesex, England

First published 1999
1 3 5 7 9 10 8 6 4 2

Set in 11/14pt Monotype Garamond
Typeset by Rowland Phototypesetting Ltd, Bury St Edmunds, Suffolk
Printed in England by Clays Ltd, St Ives plc

ISBN 0-718-14365-5

For my parents, Jane and Tony

Acknowledgements

My great thanks, first of all, to my parents and my family: to Jane, Tony, Jenny, Kay, William, Terry and Matthew, without whose faith, love and encouragement this book could not have been written. My thanks also to my friends: to Rod, Christina, Marina, Victoria and Lycia Parker, for their seemingly endless generosity; to Lord Joicey for commissioning the diary which first sent me to Prague; to Adelyn Jones, Randy Watson and Holly Golightly who were my partners in crime there; to Daph and Shells Borkum for their tireless talk and tequila; to Chris Ogden for being at the end of a 'phone when needed; to Fremmers, Thierry Morel, Eleanor Rees, Joy LoDico, Jani Loder, Sophie Orde, Kate Harris, James Hardy, Emma Dummett, Dougald Hine, Will Poole and my uncle Arthur Schoeman, amongst others, for all their affection, conversation, criticism and coffee. From a succession of fine teachers I am particularly grateful to Karen Le Gros, John Evans, Nicholas Kaye, Dennis Hunt, Nick Welsh, Angus Graham-Campbell, Richard Pleming, Chris Davis and Jeffrey Branch; and I could not have asked for better agents than Peter Robinson, Kathy Anderson and Diana Mackay, nor for better editors than Jamie Raab at Warner, Tom Weldon at Penguin UK, or Hannah Griffiths at Curtis Brown. My thanks to them all.

'I leaped headlong into the Sea, and thereby have become better acquainted with the Soundings, the quicksand, & the rocks, than if I had stayed upon the green shore, and piped a silly pipe, and took tea & comfortable advice'

John Keats, from a letter to J. A. Hessey, 8 October 1818

Prologue

My wife of more than forty-five years shot herself yesterday afternoon.

At least that is what the police assume, and I am playing the part of grieving widower with enthusiasm and success. Life with Sarah has schooled me in self-deception, which I find – as she did – to be an excellent training in the deceiving of others. Of course *I* know that she did nothing of the kind. My wife was far too sane, far too rooted in the present to think of harming herself. In my opinion she never gave a thought to what she had done. She was incapable of guilt.

It was I who killed her.

And my reasons were not those you might expect. We were not unhappily married, you see; far from it. Sarah was – until yesterday – an excellent and loving wife, for she was conscientious, in some respects, to her core. It's funny that, isn't it? How completely contrasting standards can coexist in a person without seeming to trouble them. My wife was, at least outwardly, never anything but dutiful, correct, serene. 'She gave of herself tirelessly in the true service of this island and its people'; that's what the chaplain will say of her when the time comes; and he will be right. Sarah had many virtues, chief amongst which was an unflinching sense of duty made graceful by serene execution. That is what she will be remembered for. And her serenity was not only for herself: she had a way of making the lives of those around her serene also: serene; ordered; and secure. It was security on her terms, of course; but I would have welcomed it on anybody's terms when I married her, and that has held true over forty-five years.

If you knew me, you wouldn't think me at all the murdering type.

Indeed I don't consider myself a violent man, and I don't suppose that my having killed Sarah will change that. I have learned my faults over seventy years on this earth, and violence – physical, at least – is not amongst them. I killed my wife because justice demanded it; and by killing her I have at last seen a sort of justice done. Or have I? Doubts trouble me; old wounds reopen. My obsession with sin and punishment, laid to rest so imperfectly so long ago, is returning. I find myself wondering what right I had to judge Sarah, and how much more harshly I will be judged for having judged her, too; judged her and punished her in a way I have never been judged or punished myself.

It might not have come to this; I might never have known. But Sarah's inexorable sense of wifely duty exposed her. If only she'd been slightly less considerate, slightly less conscientious, she might not be dead now. She was organizing a surprise party for my seventieth birthday, you see; not that the arrangements for it could have remained secret for long on this island. Nor did they. I've known that something was afoot for a month or more. And I was touched. But I'm particular about parties. I don't like the tenants invited; and I don't like some of Sarah's more fawningly agreeable friends. So it was only natural that I should want to consult a guest list so that by hinting at least I could have made my wishes known.

I chose last Monday afternoon to search her desk because my wife was out, supervising the extension to the ticket office. And quite by chance I found the drawer she has kept it in all these years.

Even now, with her dead and nearly buried, the arrogance of it chills me.

I

I am in the little sitting room (in days gone by a dressing room) which connects my bedroom to Sarah's. It is the warmest room in this icy house because it is the smallest. With both doors closed and a fire blazing and the radiators on under its pointed Gothic windows, it is almost cosy. There is no desk in here, only a sofa and two chairs and a small table covered with books. Old books; my favourite books; their inscriptions faded, their givers dead. They have sat on that table for more than forty years, I should think: a bible, calf-bound, from my mother; my grandfather's *Fowler's*; Donne's love poetry, an old edition of Ella's borrowed long ago. There is a music stand in the corner too, hardly used now; a graduation gift from my parents. From where I sit I can see my initials engraved on its base: *For J. H. F. June 1994.* June 1994; almost fifty years ago. That stand was mine before I ever knew her.

It seems suddenly important to me that I should have explained myself to myself by the time everyone arrives. I need clarity. The coroner's inquest is set for tomorrow; then there'll be the funeral and the interment and the house will be full of people. From this evening on I shan't have a moment's peace for weeks; no time to myself in which to think. If ever I am to put the events of my life in some sort of order I must begin the sifting now; I must try, I know, to understand what I have done; to understand how I, at the age of seventy, have come to kill my wife and to feel so little remorse over it.

It is curious, my lack of compunction; not complete, perhaps, but almost. Now that Sarah is gone, now that I know the truth, I feel very little. Hardly any outright regret. Just a curious, empty, almost

3

eerie, calm: a numbness that shows me, perhaps, quite how much I have learned from her. Quietly, detached, I sit here alone; and it strikes me that in some ways I should be glad, though I am not; that the absence of gladness is a striking one, for years ago this knowledge would have freed me. It would have given me what some call a new lease of life; I might have gone back. So it is odd that I should feel nothing now, or at most next to nothing. The events of those weeks and months long ago, in which the seeds of it all were sown, have a play-like quality. I know the plot and can empathize with the characters; but the young man of twenty-two who plays such a central part is a stranger to me. He bears little relation (beyond a slight, decreasing, physical similarity) to the image that confronts me as I pass the looking glass by the fireplace; as I stare at the books, at the music stand, at the waves and the gun-grey sky.

My life seems to have slowed. The present takes up so much time. I see myself as I was at twenty-two. Young, very young, a certain physical gangliness characterizing my movements (I was tall, with long legs) and a small nose, delicate like my mother's. My mouth is thin-lipped; my eyes a pale brown; and all are set in a regular oval face with small ears and a slightly pointed chin. Hardly handsome, I suppose; and at that age undignified by the lines of age. My face is more careworn now; the years have creased and folded it. But that is at it should be.

I suppose that my family life and upbringing must go some way to explaining why my adult life has turned out as it has, why I have turned out as I have. Ella's shoulders are too fragile to bear the complete weight of the responsibility, as are mine. Perhaps it is time to exhume old ghosts, to see my parents as they were in their forties and fifties: my mother, with her dark hair greying and her piercing blue eyes, so shrewd and voluble; my father with his powerful shoulders and huge veined hands. He was a man of deliberate gesture and unshakeable self-belief, a quality I don't think he ever succeeded in passing on to me. What he did give me, and it is this for which I thank my family most, is stubbornness: for it has sustained me when all else has failed, when arrogance and self-belief have deserted me.

What did my parents want for me? What were they like? It is so difficult to know, so difficult to give complete answers to any questions like these. We were not rich, I know that much, but we knew rich people (which my mother felt, and once or twice almost said, was enough). And I suppose that my parents, like any parents, hoped that their son would go far in the world. In *their* world, I should say; for they lived, like so many of their class and generation, in comfortable, unquestioning calm, unruffled by external change. My parents did not look outwards. They never ventured beyond the range of their own ambition, being serenely confident – in a way which frequently infuriated me – of their place in the order of things. Their gods were tradition, propriety, the maintenance of the social hierarchy. They looked both up and down; were deferential to those above and polite to those beneath. They read *The. Times*, voted Conservative and held unchanging and predictable views on the events of the day. The revolutions of the 1960s had done nothing to unsettle their values or to disturb their quiet hopes; and because they were kind they insisted on planning my future on their own terms and with all the tenacity of challenged sincerity.

My own private plan of becoming a concert violinist, flatly and sullenly expressed in my last year at Oxford, could have met with no favour in their eyes; nor did it. And my late adolescence was punctuated occasionally, but always dramatically, by the slow build-up of family tension, its explosive release, and its subsequent subsidence over long days of icy politeness.

It is ironic that I should end my life in a house like this one, with a titled wife whose family history is as weighty as any to which her parents-in-law could ever have aspired. It is ironic that, having made so much of following my own lights, I have succeeded ultimately in achieving only what my parents wished for me all along. My musical career died gradually as my marriage progressed, for Sarah could not hope to fuel it as Ella had done, nor did she try to; and my reserves of emotion have dwindled unavoidably over time. My talent lay in translating private passion into public performance, and as the private passion stopped flowing, dried, and finally turned to a dust so fine that the slightest wind scattered it to nothingness, there was no longer anything to be translated. Technically I remained pre-eminent, for I have always been diligent; but I stopped playing when I could hope for nothing more than mechanical brilliance.

But I am wandering, losing the flow of my narrative. It is only to be expected from a man of my age, I suppose.

My education was unremarkable. I was clever enough to join the majority of my public school fellows at Oxford, a great relief to my parents; and until the age of nineteen I made a creditable enough return on their investment in me. But over the three years of my separation from my family at university I was encouraged by those I knew and the books I read to cultivate a certain detachment from home life and its aspirations for me, a detachment which made me critical during term-time and superior in the holidays. It was then that I turned with real determination to my secret love, the violin; and it was then, comparatively late but in time enough, that I had the leisure and the teaching to discover that I might be really good; good enough to matter. Good enough, certainly, to use my music as the basis for my first serious confrontation with my parents, one that raged the whole of the summer following my graduation and which centred around my stubborn insistence that I was going to be a musician.

But I digress in my attempt to make my twenty-two-year-old self more real to me now, an attempt in which I have been only partly successful. I remember once more what he looks like, that is true; I see his half-smile and his rosy cheeks and the hair tumbling over his forehead into his eyes. But I know him no longer; I have no empathy with his tastes and only a little with his enthusiasms, surprisingly few of which have remained. I struggle to remember the people with whom he filled his life, the friendships he made: curiously intense, for he was a young man of extremes, inclined to manic sociability and profound gloom by turns. Of course, a few stand distinct from the tableau. People like Camilla Boardman, the girl my mother always hoped I would marry: pretty; bubbly; well-connected; more substantial than she liked to seem. But I was insular at twenty-two. Indiscriminately friendly, I shared myself intimately with great discrimination; I still do. Perhaps I had little to share; certainly my life up to that point contained nothing very remarkable. I had made the progression from preparatory school to public school to Oxford with as few jolts as possible; I had not forced myself to think much or to examine the world. Life was as it was and I accepted it on its own terms, much in the way I would later accept my marriage to Sarah: with a sort of dogged determination which I would not admit to myself.

Unthinking, unseeing, unknowing, I drifted through life until I met Ella. It was she who baptized me; it was she who threw me into the sea of life. And she did it quite unthinkingly, little caring or even knowing how much good or how much harm she might do. It was in her nature, that wild abandonment, that driving need for experience and explanation. It was she who made me swim, she who pushed me from the safety of the shallows; it was she with whom I floundered, out of my depth. It is to her, and to my memories of her, that I must turn now in seeking to explain what I have done.

In memory she is a small, slight girl, my age, with tousled blonde hair and green eyes that sparkle back at me complicitly, even now. She is in a park, Hyde Park; it is an early morning in mid-June: birds sing; keepers in green overalls are setting up deck-chairs; the air is sweet with the scent of newly-mown grass. I can hear myself panting.

I had been running, up early and out of the house to escape the frosty conversation that had become habitual since my acceptance to the Guildhall. My father had strict views on the desirability of merchant banking; my mother, usually a useful ally (for my own happiness figured more in her plans for me than it did in my father's) had sided with him, saying that no grandchildren of hers would grow up in Hounslow because their father was an impoverished musician. I had begun, in vain, by telling them that musicians weren't necessarily impoverished; later I had openly called them snobs and sworn privately that nothing could be said to deter me from my course. The atmosphere at home had not yet recovered from the latest scene (unusually venomous on the parts of all concerned), staged two days previously. I had no wish for another meal of silent recrimination.

So I went running in the park. I can hear myself panting, can feel the pulse of the blood beating in my head, can see what I wore: a white T-shirt; school rugby shorts; the socks of my College Boat Club. I can see what Ella wore, too, because I noticed her long before she saw me. She was sitting on a bench, in a black dress that pulled tight against her slender hips. Her eyes were dazed from wakefulness; coffee steamed in a Styrofoam cup on the bench next to her; a pearl necklace (which I have since, on another's neck, come to know well) was in her closed hand, which was shaking a little. She was a dramatic figure in the half-light of the early morning: sitting on that bench; hardly moving. I ran past her twice before she noticed me, each time shortening the route by which I doubled back unseen and passed her again. The third time I passed her she looked up at me and her eyes focused. She smiled.

I stopped, panting, a little distance from the bench, regretting my last circuit of the carriage track. When I turned to look at her, she was still smiling.

'Tough run,' she called out.

'You could say that.'

We nodded politely to each other.

'Tough night?' I asked, looking at her clothes. She saw my eyes hesitate on her hand and the shaking stopped.

'More of a long night,' she said. Her accent was American, but lilting and musical with anglicized vowels. She was softly spoken. We smiled at each other as I wondered what to say, but it was she who finally broke the silence. 'I'm sure I know those socks,' she said.

'Really?'

'They're College socks, aren't they?' She paused. 'Although, know-ing my luck, they're going to turn out to be school socks or some other kind of sock – there are so many kinds in England – and I'll feel a right arse.' Her pronunciation of the word 'arse' was self-consciously rounded; here was a person who had trained herself not to say 'ass'.

Glad to have been offered a neutral topic of conversation, I told her that they were college socks, as a matter of fact. 'The socks of my College Boat Club,' I said with adolescent pride.

Remembering it now, I find it curious to think that the course of my whole life might be said to have hung on something as inconsequential as my choice of footwear that morning. Ella would not have noticed different socks; and without her remarking on them as she did do I would probably never have known her. In that case I would not be the person I am today; I would not have killed my wife yesterday afternoon; I would not be in this smoky room, trying to keep warm, listening to the waves of the Atlantic crash on the rocks beneath my windows. It is curious, the way in which seemingly innocuous details like the selection of a pair of socks can set in motion a chain of events which, as one leads to another, build up such momentum that they become a guiding force in your life. I find it strange; strange and slightly unsettling. But the evidence is there, I suppose; and who am I to refute it?

I watch myself saunter over to the bench where she is sitting, a question on my lips. Ella remains absolutely motionless, the fine bones of her neck and shoulders showing clearly through her pale skin. She is sitting a little hunched, which contributes to the effect of her fragility. She would look innocent but for the cut of her dress and the stylish parting of her short hair, which a hand pushes back from her eyes occasionally and ineffectually. Getting close, I see that pronounced cheekbones make her face almost gaunt, as do pale blue rings which undercircle her eyes. But the eyes themselves are bright: sharp and green, they move swiftly up and down me as I approach and seem to indicate a place beside her on the bench. I sit down.

'These are the socks of my College Boat Club,' I say again.

'I know,' she says. 'Oriel, Oxford, aren't they?'

I nod, impressed by her accuracy. 'How do you know?' I ask, smiling.

There is a pause while the smile on her lips fades and she looks serious once more. Her fingers become conscious of the string of pearls in her left hand, which she puts into a small square bag at her feet with an unconscious gesture of protection.

'That's a complex question. More complex than it sounds,' she says. But realizing my awkwardness, she continues: 'Let's just keep the answer brief and say that I know someone who has them.' She takes a last sip from the Styrofoam cup and discovers that it is almost empty. She seems surprised and faintly irritated.

'Who?' I am eager for her to define herself to some extent by her acquaintance with someone I can judge.

'You wouldn't have known him, unless you're older than you look.'

Since she doesn't seem disposed to say anything further, I question her more closely, telling her that one never knows.

'His name's Charles Stanhope,' she says, uttering a name I indeed do not recognize. I say this and she looks up at me and smiles. 'I'm sorry to have interrupted your run,' she says. 'But I've been sitting out here on this bench for so long I think I'd've stayed here for ever if someone hadn't disturbed me and broken the spell.'

'What spell?' I am bold enough to ask.

'The spell of wakeful hours.' She looks up at me, eyes twinkling. 'The rut of question-answer-same-question your brain gets into when developments take a turn you didn't really expect.'

I see her fumble absently in her bag for a cigarette, watch her light it and follow silver-grey smoke circles upwards to a pale blue sky. The park is noticeably warmer now; people are trickling in, and as they pass they cannot help but look at us, an odd pair under the trees. I can smell the faint odour of sweet perfume and soap and stale cigarette smoke that surrounds her; can hear the click of her lighter flint as she makes a flame; can see, as she holds her cigarette, that one of her nails is bitten to the quick.

'Have you been out here all night?' I ask.

She nods, with a little tightening of pale lips. 'Oh yes,' she says. 'This bench and I are old friends. It's heard more of my secrets than it cares to remember, I suspect.'

'And has it offered good advice?'

'Well that's just where benches have the advantage over people. They don't offer advice; they don't sympathize. They just sit, listening, reminding you by their very immovability that nothing in your life can be that earth-shattering. I think benches are a good guard against melodrama.' She looks up at me. 'I suppose you think me very melodramatic.' She says this more as a half-murmured musing to herself than as a question to me. 'Sitting here in these clothes,' she goes on. 'Smoking. Drinking coffee. Forming crazy relationships with benches.' She looks up at me again, shyly this time, and we both laugh.

'Not at all,' I say, itching to ask her more but being constrained by . . . what? By twenty-two years of being told that it is rude to pry; by a certain social reserve which is characteristic of me to this day; by a fear that she is troubled by love for another, whom I instinctively hate and whose existence I want to put off confirming until the last possible moment.

'You are very polite,' she says eventually, in a tone which sows doubt in my mind about the sincerity of the compliment.

I nod, and as I do so her words sound in my ears like an accusation. I feel that something is required of me, but what it is I do not know, and as I am not experienced in talking to pretty women I say nothing.

'I wonder if that is your personality or your education,' she goes on. 'This admirable respect you seem to have for my privacy. In your place I should be curious to know what prompts a fully grown woman to sit up all night in a lonely park and grow garrulous with the larks.'

This sounds like an invitation, which I cautiously accept. 'Would you tell me if I did ask?' I say quietly.

'Five minutes ago I might have done,' she says, closing the clasp of her bag with a click. 'But your presence has cheered me too much for confidences. And of course this old bench is still just where it was last night, a fine example to us all.' She pauses. 'Constancy in a changing world.' She smiles and pats the worn wood of its seat. 'I feel better now,' she says, 'and less inclined to . . . bore you with my troubles. All of which, I should add, are purely of my own making.'

'They wouldn't bore me at all,' I say, now wanting to know more than ever what is troubling this beautiful, fragile woman with the softly foreign accent and the bitten fingernails.

'Well I'm glad to know you're human,' she says and we both laugh again.

'Could I ask your name, at least?' I say, braver now that I sense she is about to go.

'You could. A name is the least private thing about a person.' She gets up and leans over to stub her cigarette on the ground. She puts the butt into an empty carton in her bag. I hear the click click of the clasp unclosing and closing. I see that she isn't wearing any shoes and watch her pick up a pair of black satin pumps which have been collecting dew under the bench. There is a pause.

'Well, then, what's your name?'

'I'm Ella Harcourt,' she says, standing, and offers me her hand.

I shake it.

'And you are?'

'I'm James Farrell,' I say.

'Well, James . . .' There is a slight awkwardness between us, born of intimacy almost attempted and just missed. 'It was a pleasure,' she says at last.

'Now whose education is dictating what they say?' I think to myself, irrationally annoyed at her leaving. She sees my irritation and laughs.

'Goodbye,' I say, getting up too.

'Enjoy the rest of your run,' she says and turns to go, bare-footed, her shoes in one hand, the empty Styrofoam cup in the other. I see the redness on her heels where the pumps have been chafing her.

She walks delicately, but purposefully and quickly. She does not look back. I sense that she knows I am watching her. It is a long time before she is gone completely from my view, for the carriage track is straight and almost empty. I stand looking after her shrinking form, hearing the thud of my pulse once more, aware of tiny sounds usually lost: the scratch of squirrels' claws on bark; the rustle of a breeze in the oak leaves; an indignant magpie.

2

I have said that I struggle to recreate myself as I was then in any way that makes sense to me now. At twenty-two one labours under the delusion that one knows everything; at seventy, I find to my regret how little I hold certain. I am mistrustful of myself; of recollection; of feeling. And my memory, long disused, is imperfect; that I freely admit. Yet certain images, as I am discovering, remain with one always. Ella sitting in the park that first morning is one such image; it has returned to me, with very little effort on my part, as complete and perfect as if I had observed her yesterday. And it has brought with it a host of other images: the sights and sounds and smells that surrounded our second meeting; the weight of the people crushing in on every side; the manic tinkle of their purposeful laughter; the sweet taste of brandy in champagne. Rising above it all I hear the cadences of Camilla's voice, the shrill, rapid emphases of her speech, the fantastic elongation of her vowels. '*Daahling!*' For the scene that now flickers into life is the scene of Camilla Boardman's twenty-first birthday party, and I can see Camilla, her auburn curls framing her face with all the elegance that coiffeurial skill can impart, leaning on the present table, smiling at no one in particular and fingering the silk bow of a large striped gift. The 'intimate dinner' for 'a few of her *closest* friends' is over, a dinner to which I have not been invited, and I am arriving with a horde of others to join the 'crush'.

I am tired. I have spent seven long hours practising in a cramped, airless room at the top of my parents' house; an endless trill from a Beethoven violin sonata drums in my head and my fingers twitch involuntarily at the stimulus. A difficult passage of pizzicato, frequently repeated, which joins the trill as I say my first hellos, has made the tips of the fingers on my right hand ache. I want nothing more than to go to bed, to dream of my music in peace; but Fate and my mother have decreed otherwise and sent me, bathed, brushed and faintly bemused, to the birthday party of a highly eligible girl who scares me a little but whom I like and who my parents think is someone 'one should know if one can'.

My fellow guests and I are under the high ceilings of the Boardman drawing-room in Cadogan Square; bewigged, darkly painted gentlemen stare down from the walls; the furniture has been cleared from the centre of the long room and most people are standing. Younger sisters and their friends, in black skirts and white blouses, circulate with trays of champagne and count the hours until 2 a.m. and the presentation of a cheque for their pains.

In remembering the friends of my early twenties Camilla Boardman stands pre-eminent. Not for any special intimacy on our part (although, in a purely platonic way, that did develop later) but for the absolute panache with which she did things. Camilla took herself from the realm of the cliché and into that rarefied space beyond parody. Her curls were curlier, her dresses tighter, her breasts rounder, her vowels longer, her use of the exclamation mark in conversation more indiscriminate, than anybody's I had ever met. My mother was delighted that I knew her and harboured secret hopes, I am sure, of just such a daughter-in-law. I, needless to say, was thoroughly in awe of the great auburn-haired beauty who flung her arms around me on the slightest provocation (a compliment she paid to all the men she knew) and who, that evening, took her present from me with a squeal of delight and dragged me into the centre of the room to 'mingle'.

'Darling, you look *fabulous*,' she cooed, tweaking the lapel of my dinner jacket and reminding me with the subtlety for which she was famed that I had not yet complimented her on her dress.

'So do you, Camilla,' I said feelingly, looking with frank pleasure at the swathe of tight white silk, like a second skin, which covered just the polite minimum and offset the gentle glow of her tan so admirably.

'I bet you say that to *all* the girls,' she whispered slyly into my ear, but I was spared the inevitable '*naughty* boy' by our arrival at the centre of a group I did not know, all the members of which seemed to be on terms of easy familiarity with each other. Hastily, for streams of guests were arriving, Camilla performed the introductions.

The faces of the people to whom she introduced me are faded now. Their names have collided, blurred and finally commingled with the names of countless other drinks-party guests with whom I have spoken for ten minutes and then never seen again. I remember black dresses and gleaming shirt fronts; curls; hopeful sideburns; occasional laborious attempts at dishevelled Bohemian chic; mono-grammed cuff-links. These were the people my parents had educated me to know and whom it pleased me privately to despise. I have said that my mind at this age was beginning to take its first tentative steps towards independent thought; and these steps, naturally enough, were leading me away from the received ideas on which I had been brought up, away from the unquestioning observance of social form which an education in the 1950s had instilled in my parents. I now viewed such concepts with extreme, and to my mind enlightened, distaste.

It had not always been thus; indeed even then (for all my superiority) I was conscious of looking much like my fellow guests and of making conversation much like theirs in accents just their own. This made me wonder, as the trill continued its endless tattoo in my head, if perhaps they were judging me as I was judging them. Perhaps this was a charade for us all; perhaps we each, individually, appreciated the absurdity of the ritual we were forced to act out; perhaps it was only collectively and outwardly that we submitted to it in such numbers and with such apparent willingness. In my superiority I was not overly hopeful.

One has such thoughts at that age. I had not yet learned the advantages of complete conformity, preferably unconscious, to a given code of behaviour; or the benefits to be derived from the subjection of self to a social system designed to keep both people and feeling in check, unruffled in the smooth maintenance of social hypocrisy. You don't kill for good manners. Had I never considered any system of values beyond that of the drawing room, I would certainly never have killed Sarah. But then Sarah deserved to die; and had I never strayed from the confines of polite morality, from the limits set by sermons preached in school chapels to tweed-suited audiences, I would never have been able to punish her as she deserved. Odious word, 'punishment'.

I little knew, as I stood at Camilla's party that evening, how soon my eyes were to be opened to a truer reality, to an infinitely more varied and correspondingly more dangerous range of moral possibility than that to which I had hitherto been exposed. My mind was too obsessed by its habitual worries about how other people saw me and I saw them to see beyond the confines of its own social rebellion, which (because it was only ever stated privately or, very occasionally, in the ugliest of the scenes with my parents) was hardly rebellion at all. That evening I was preoccupied – as I have said – with the possibility that some amongst my fellow guests might despise me for the same reasons that I despised them; might think that I, too, talked only of holidays in the south of France, or of weekends in the country, or of parties in London that I had been to or pretended to have been to. And all the while I talked animatedly of someone's villa in Biarritz, lacking the means, the courage, and perhaps even the inclination to give my criticism voice.

Oh, yes, it's all flooding back now. The bundle of contradictions that passed, in my own mind, for self-knowledge: the desire to break from the mould but to prove to myself how admirably I could fit it if I chose; the formation of social theories I lacked the nerve ever to articulate, and used only in the long struggle with my parents over my future; the blend of arrogance and humility which made me by turns delighted and appalled by my hypocrisy. I had, in those days, an ability to think and not to think; to convince myself that I was living when I was not; that I was feeling when I hardly knew what feeling was. I thought I knew everything: my own mind; my own opinions; my own values. I was smug in a way which cried out to be put to the test, though I had no idea that this was so; and because I did not know I was ripe for it, the test (when it came) was unexpected and its results disastrous.

But that belongs to a later part of this story.

I stood, that evening, as I say, talking of someone's villa in Biarritz. I smiled, I drank the champagne cocktails, I discovered that I had been at school with someone's brother and told an amusing (and not altogether kind) anecdote about his time there. Occasionally the high notes of Camilla's conversation drifted towards me: the string of superlatives with which she greeted the arrival of each guest and gift; hasty introductions; loud exclamations over dresses. I was nearing the end of anything useful I could say (or invent to say) about villas in Biarritz when I felt her nudge my arm and push into the centre of the group a lean, rather pale young man, tall, with floppy blond hair and small hands which belied his great height.

'James, darling,' she said, addressing the entire group, 'this is an old friend of yours.'

I had never seen the man before in my life. But the complete assurance with which Camilla made this pronouncement encouraged me to think that I must have done and I racked my brains for his name.

'Hello,' I said, shaking his hand warmly. It was moist.

'Hello,' he said, a searching look in his eyes too. It occurred to me that neither of us knew the other. I said so to Camilla.

'But you *must*, darling. You were at Oxford together. At the same College. Charlie's also an Oriel man.'

'I don't think we were there at the same time,' I said.

'No, we weren't,' said the increasingly uncomfortable Charlie.

'Well, then I see I'm going to *have* to introduce you,' groaned our hostess, as though the weight of the world had been placed on her shoulders while Atlas went to find himself a champagne cocktail.

'James Farrell, Charlie Stanhope. Charlie Stanhope, James Farrell.' This was said very quickly, with much waving of her well-manicured hands. The rest of the group seemed to know Charlie well, and I had plenty of time to examine him while he submitted to the kisses of the women and the handshakes of the men.

A week had passed since my meeting with Ella Harcourt in the park, and I had resigned myself to the fact that I would never see her again. Yet here, completely unexpectedly, was a link that might take me to her. She had recognized my socks because they were the socks that Charlie Stanhope wore, so she must know him; and if she knew him, he must know her and might, if prevailed upon, tell me how I could contact her. The thought that this might be a different Charlie Stanhope from the one she knew crossed my mind, but I was unwilling to think so ill of Fate and I dismissed the possibility of such a trick. Watching Charlie's small hands grasping the shoulders of the women he bent to kiss, I felt a rush of barely containable excitement.

When he was completely upright once more, I saw how very tall he was. Taller than I and if possible even more gangly, with hair the colour and consistency of straw and pale, watery blue eyes. A large, aquiline nose sat awkwardly on his gentle face; and I could tell by the strangled movements of his Adam's apple that his collar was too tight. I considered my options deliberately, methodically, delighted by this unexpected opportunity but cautious of it too. I decided to establish the groundwork of acquaintance before probing him for details of his friends; and so I did not renew my conversation about French villas but turned instead to Charlie and began the conversation which Camilla had doubtless intended that we should have.

'How did you find Oxford?' I asked, politely.

And Charlie, with equal politeness, began a tried-and-tested response to a tried-and-tested question, thinking no doubt of something else as he spoke to me. His replies to my questions suggested a familiarity born of repeated practice; and in an understood progression we moved from College to course to general university life, his elegant narrative punctuated occasionally by well-mannered promptings from me. But his anecdotes belied the smooth delivery of their accounts and were, I noticed with something like relief, unremarkable. Charlie Stanhope had done all the things expected of an undergraduate enjoying the best days of his life: conscientiously he had jumped into the river on May Morning; conscientiously he had made the Survivors' photograph at his last Oriel Ball; conscientiously he had come away with a 2:1. Conscientiously, with the faintly bored good manners of someone overused to such conversations, he described each incident to me. Now he was working at the family bank and living in Fulham. He played tennis at the Hurlingham Club; he went to Ascot on Ladies' Day with his grandmother; he had recently become engaged. He nodded his thanks at my congratulations. 'A splendid girl,' he said absently. 'Splendid. But don't say a word to anyone. We haven't made it official yet.'

I warmed to Charlie as he spoke, with the warmth that comes from dissipated hostility; for if Ella Harcourt's troubles involved another man, as I suspected they did, they did not involve him. Though I knew nothing of Ella beyond what she had said in the park, and though I had no way of knowing whether I would ever see her again, I knew enough to know that someone as blandly unobjectionable as Charlie Stanhope could have no hold over her. He was not a potential rival, and as I decided this with increasing certainty I began to warm towards the innocuous, obviously bored young man who spoke with such practised ease at my side.

With dismissive nonchalance I asked him, once the topics of university and career were exhausted, whether he happened to know anyone by the name of Ella Harcourt.

'I know her well,' he said, looking down at me through white, almost invisible lashes. And since he did not seem disposed to say anything else, I asked him how long he had known her.

'Oh, years,' he said.

'Really?' I paused, wondering how to phrase my next question.

'Yes.' His small hand reached towards a passing tray for another champagne cocktail.

'You wouldn't happen to know how I could contact her, would you?' I decided eventually that the direct approach would be the least awkward one.

He raised a quizzical eyebrow at me.

'You see,' I continued, feeling myself about to lie and not quite sure why, 'I have something of hers. She left it at a party we were at together last week. A bag. I wanted to return it.'

'How kind of you,' he said. 'But why don't you arrange its return now?' And I followed his glance to the door, through which Ella was just entering.

I can see her quite clearly: standing under the heavy gaze of a patrician Boardman ancestor; smiling at Camilla but not looking at her. She is wearing the dress I first saw her in; or no, it can't be quite the same one, because I can see her knees and the other dress was long. It is, at any rate, black with tiny straps. There is a gauzy scarf tied tight around her throat and knotted at the nape of her neck, from where it falls in two thin strands down her back. The scarf is cream, and makes her look pale although her cheeks are glowing. She is shorter than Camilla and not as immediately pretty. I wonder suddenly what the hollow under her collarbone would feel like to touch. I can see Camilla taking her present and deliberating for a moment over where to put it on the table already over-heaped with gifts. She eventually elects the uppermost summit, where Ella's package balances because it is so small. Its wrapping paper is brown; it is tied with a gold, gauzy bow; I wonder what it is.

'I'll tell her about it, if you like.' Charlie's voice, insistent in a way I had not yet heard it, broke through the delicious chill of my excitement. Already he was moving through the crowd in Ella's direction. 'The bag I mean,' he called out as he disappeared.

'It's all right,' I muttered, hoping that my lie, my unnecessary lie, would not be discovered; but other thoughts crowded my head and before I could say anything further he was gone. Through the crush of people I walked slowly towards Ella, brushing against elbows and shoulders, smiling my apologies; I watched Charlie tap her on the back and saw her turn, smile and kiss him; I watched them both move out of the flow of arriving guests and altered my course accordingly.

'Hello Ella,' I said when I was finally standing behind her. Hearing her name she turned and seeing me, smiled. It was an awkward smile, its awkwardness expertly concealed; clearly she was surprised.

'Hello James. How unexpected.'

'Isn't it?' I said.

'Absolutely.'

'For me, too.'

For a moment we looked at each other, she trying to remember precisely what she had said to the stranger she had never thought to see again, I taking in every detail of her delicately-boned face: the straight parting of her short, rather boyish blonde hair; the blue rings still under her eyes; the glow of her cheeks; the vividness of her green eyes. It was she who remembered her manners first.

'You remember we talked of Charles Stanhope,' she said.

I nodded, enjoying Charlie's slightly mystified look. He was standing slightly behind her as she faced me.

'Well here he is.' She turned half round to him so that she was standing between us. 'Charlie, I want you to meet a friend of mine, James Farrell. He was at Oriel, too, though a little after your time I think.' The lilt of her voice was music to my ears.

Charles smiled at me, slightly uncertain. 'We know each other already,' he said. 'We've been talking for the last hour, while Your Ladyship has been frizzing her hair to make sure she's fashionably late for the party.' He gave Ella's shoulders an affectionate tweak. 'James here has something to return to you.'

Ella looked at me as Charles continued.

'A bag,' he said, 'which that pretty little head of yours forgot to take home from some party last week.'

I met the look of her unflinching eyes, trying not to blush. I saw her expression change from surprise to comprehension, from comprehension to – I thought – a slight mischievousness. 'Yes,' she said eventually, eyes sparkling, 'how silly of me. But you know how forgetful I can be.'

'Don't I just,' said Charlie, smiling.

Ella turned to him. 'Would you be a dear and get me some champagne? No brandy in it, please. I can't bear the stuff.' Charlie nodded and disappeared obligingly. Together we followed his blond head bobbing through the crowds, a good half-foot over everyone else's.

'So, James. We meet again.'

I nodded. 'Thank you for sparing me just then.'

'That's all right. I'm rather flattered, as a matter of fact. And I'm glad to see that you have more audacity than you showed the first time we met.'

'Is lying so audacious?'

'Lying to Charlie for information about me is. I applaud you.'

We smiled at each other.

'How are you?' I asked eventually.

'Oh, much the same as when I saw you last. Nothing has changed. A different dress; new make-up; new shoes. Unfortunately problems are more difficult to solve than questions of wardrobe or lipstick.'

'So the problem remains, does it? The one you wouldn't tell me about?'

'You are forthright tonight, aren't you?'

But before I could answer, Charlie had returned with a glass of champagne for Ella and a tumbler of orange juice for himself. 'Driving,' he said to me as he raised it. Beaming, he surveyed the room and we heard a voice begin to sing 'Happy Birthday'. Soon everyone had joined in a spirited chorus, and the lights dimmed as a large, white birthday cake with twenty-one candles was rolled in on a tray.

Camilla, in the middle of the room, blushed becomingly.

'Isn't she miraculous?' whispered Ella in my ear.

3

The arrival and distribution of the birthday cake took up the next half-hour or so and I lost sight of Ella while the guests separated into those who intended to make a night of it and those (very much in the minority) who would use this as their opportunity to leave. She had disappeared from my side before the end of the singing; Charles I could see in the distance, actively procuring a slice of creamy sponge cake. I found myself talking once more to the girl with the villa in Biarritz, whom I suspected of toying with me in the hope that I would make a play for an invitation. I took a perverse pleasure in doing nothing of the kind.

It was not until I had a slice of birthday cake in my hand and was telling Camilla what a lovely party it was that I saw Ella, standing alone, looking out over the sea of bodies. At whom? For whom? For me, perhaps. It was small encouragement, but it was enough; and I disengaged myself and made my way to the small recess in which she was standing. It was lined with books, never read, whose rich red spines made her pale in the half-light of the alcove.

'Hi, James,' she said at my approach.

'Hello.'

In another room music had started, loud and monotonous. We stood together for a moment watching people move off in search of the sound. I saw the girl with the villa in Biarritz talking distractedly into her mobile phone.

'I would give a lot to know what's going on in all those minds out there,' Ella said suddenly, not facing me but continuing to stare out at the room, dense with dinner jackets and skimpy dresses. 'If, of course, there *are* any. A possibility which the behaviour of their owners makes me doubt.'

This so closely mirrored the spirit of my own thoughts earlier that I was taken aback. It also confirmed what I had spent this and other evenings worrying about: that I was not alone in my criticism of this world of heavy social ritual and display; and that I myself was not immune from the censure I so liberally dealt out to others in the privacy of my own mind. It was not a comforting thought.

'I think everyone has a mind,' I said. 'It's a question of whether they choose to use it or not.'

'Well put.' She smiled at me and took a mouthful of cake. There was silence between us. 'I suppose I owe you some sort of explanation for such a piece of arrogance,' she said quietly.

'Only if you care to give it.' Relief at my apparent exclusion from her criticism made me magnanimous.

'Oh I'm happy to explain myself. God knows I've had enough practice over the years.' She smiled at me. 'You see, James, my problem is not the absence of a mind, though sometimes I wish it were. My problem . . .' She paused.

I waited.

'My problem . . .'

'Yes?'

Ella hesitated; and as she did so she seemed to think better of her intended confidence.

'My problem is that I talk too much,' she said at last. 'I shouldn't be telling you any of this. We hardly know each other. You've no need to listen to my ramblings. I'd better go and find Charlie.' She leaned down to pick up her bag.

'No, don't.' I said quietly; and the unintended urgency in my tone made her stop. 'Don't go. Tell me.' There was a pause. 'I'm interested.'

'Really?'

I nodded, touched by the unexpected vulnerability of the question.

'You can't honestly be interested in the random ramblings of a girl you hardly know.'

'I am. Tell me.'

There was another pause.

'Well,' she said at last, looking out of the alcove at the streams of guests beyond it, 'my problem is that I have a mind but that I choose to use it so bloody infrequently. I'm only ever goaded into self-control when events have long since overtaken me. That's my trouble. I'm rude about the people out there because, I suppose, I want the comfort of knowing that I'm not alone in my world of fools.'

'You have at least one fellow citizen in me, if that's any consolation.'

'You're very kind.' She fumbled in her bag, the same one I had seen a week before. Again I heard the click click of its clasp; again I watched her take out a packet of cigarettes; again I followed the first silver rings of smoke upwards, though this time they rose to a white ceiling and not to a blue sky streaked with rosy dawn. 'My hope,' she continued, 'is that the fault doesn't lie so much with me as with that ocean out there.' She paused. 'Society is like an ocean, don't you think?' she went on, waving her cigarette towards the swirls of people beyond our alcove. 'I find myself hoping against hope that it's not really my fault I've washed up where I have. The currents of people's expectations are strong. Who am I to try to swim against them?'

'You forget that I have no idea what your particular island looks like.'

'No you haven't, have you?' Her tone was almost tender, I thought. She took another long drag on her cigarette. 'And I won't bore you with its geography. It's not very interesting.'

I waited, not knowing what to say.

'But you do agree with me, don't you,' she began again, almost anxiously, reverting to her former theme, 'that Society is like an ocean?'

'I'm not sure.'

'Look at all the people at this party, for instance. They're all swimming dutifully with the current; dutifully and easily through their particular sea. They don't need to plan their direction, they don't need to give a thought to where they're going. I wonder how many of them do. Give a thought to where they're going, I mean. I wonder if any of them try to swim by themselves for long.' Another drag on the cigarette. 'People move in schools, like fish. It's safest that way.'

I listened, fascinated by the holistic insouciance with which Ella could express what I could not.

'But does it make them happy?' I asked.

'What?'

'This moving in schools.'

'After a fashion, I imagine. If they've never known anything else, they can't want much more than what they have. Ignorance *is* bliss, sometimes. For some people.'

'And for you?' Secluded in the alcove, I was bold and only half surprised by my boldness.

'Unfortunately I possess just the wrong amount of knowledge: enough to know how little freedom I have; not quite enough to know what to do about it. I think that perhaps, just perhaps, I should've swum harder, because in the past I have intended to . . . swim for myself. It's just so darn difficult. So tiring.' She stubbed out her cigarette with an air of finality.

'Well it's not too late now, whatever you've done. How old are you? Twenty-two, twenty-three?'

'Twenty-three.'

'Well there you go. You have your entire life ahead of you.'

'Don't say that. The prospect isn't a particularly appealing one. And in any case . . .'

Her words were drowned by the arrival of Charlie Stanhope. He put his arm around Ella's waist and apologized politely to me for snatching her away.

'Let's dance,' he said to her. 'Sorry to be such a bore,' he murmured vaguely in my direction.

To my surprise, I saw that Ella allowed herself to be led away without protest. But I stayed where I was, content in the afterglow of her frank green eyes. Languidly, leaning against the books, I watched her retreating form with Charlie Stanhope's arm draped awkwardly over her shoulders. Further and further from me she swayed, but through the crowds my eyes remained on the back of her small blonde head, fixed there, for I felt the moment ripe for a sign. And sure enough, when she reached the far end of the room I was rewarded for my pains with a brief backward glance. But far from wearing the smile I had expected, the face she turned to me was drawn and pale, and it woke me from my reverie and called to mind the glazed, wakeful eyes I had seen in the park and the shake of her hand as it held its Styrofoam cup.

Before I could move she had been led through the door and was lost in the crush of people who lined the passage beyond it. I heard the thump of the music once more and pictured the grace of her swaying body in the darkness; and as I did so I caught a faint sweet whiff of lemon soap, cigarette smoke and expensive perfume.

I remember how I felt then; I remember that curious sensation of frustrated pleasure which made me so impatient for her return. Even from a distance of almost fifty years that memory has a certain power over me; even now, in my armchair by the window, the mere recollection of the speed, the grace, the infinite possibility of that moment, is enough to make my breath quicken with excitement. It was like the first kick of a powerful drug, inexpertly and incompletely administered; it broke the boundaries of previous sensation and made me determined for more.

Naturally enough, my immediate impulse was to follow her and to snatch her back from Charles; but I waited, wondering how to effect her recapture more subtly, anxious not to anger her. How was I to know that she would welcome my intrusion? I wondered whether she might feel that she had overstepped some sort of mark; and I thought delightedly as I did so that our conversation had hardly been the talk of strangers, though strangers we were. I wanted to tell her this, to share my excitement; but I lacked a pretext to seek her out and I knew that I must wait for her to find me.

It was then that I saw her bag: square; velvet; compact; lying on the floor at my feet. It had been left, forgotten by its owner; and slowly I leaned down to pick it up, hoping against hope that she had left it on purpose, my thoughts running to all kinds of wild implications. As I straightened with it in my hand I put it quickly, almost furtively, on the shelf by my side in case anyone else should see and rescue it. Deliberately I waited: five minutes; ten; fifteen; relishing the intrigue of it. Then I reached for my prize and, threading my way through the thinning throng, I went to find her.

A quick tour of the room I was in convinced me that she was not in it. Nor was she in the passage. Nor in the room set aside for dancing, where the DJ and his turntables looked strangely incongruous by the Adam fireplace. I waited for a while outside the most obviously-located girls' loo, thinking that she might emerge from it; but instead I saw Camilla come out, rubbing her nose with self-conscious vigour, and smiling. Our eyes met.

'God, darling, I haven't *really*,' she whispered in my ear, deftly slipping her arm through mine. 'But pretence at *least* is *de rigueur* nowadays.' And it amused me to see that Camilla's attitude to cocaine, as to everything else, was acutely proper in its social observance.

My hostess guided me back into the room from which I had come and I saw Charles Stanhope dancing, rather badly, alone in the corner. Quickly, I moved on, for I had no wish for him to join me in my search. And it was then, as I heard Camilla tell someone how *hysterical* something was, that the thought occurred to me that Ella might have left without saying goodbye; and a momentary pang hit me in the throat. Steadying myself, I whispered silently that she couldn't have gone; that she must be here. And I went again into the passage, now emptying, and checked once more, wading through the first flurries of goodbyes and thanks. She was nowhere to be seen. With irrational tears pricking my eyes I looked towards the staircase and began to climb it, for if she had left without saying goodbye, if all my excitement had been founded on nothing, if that was how she spoke to all the men she knew, I wanted a small dark space in which to be alone:

Camilla Boardman was not someone to be faced in any but the most expansive of moods. So I climbed the wide slope of the Boardman stairs, up to a dark landing and up again, past another landing and another, the broad sweep of the staircase getting narrower with each flight. By now my ascent was slow, cautious, in a dark so black that I had stood on Ella's hand before I even noticed she was there. She was sitting on a step, her back to the banisters; and her cry was sharp and her alarm real. Apparently she had neither seen nor heard me.

'Who is it?' She spoke shrilly, aware for the first time, perhaps, how it might look to be discovered, so high above the party, by one of the Boardman guests.

'Just me,' I whispered.

'*You*? James? What on earth are you doing here?'

'I could ask you the same question.'

'You could, but you won't. You'll wait for me to tell you, all bound up in that English reserve of yours. But I won't.' This last was almost petulant. 'I don't see what business you have following me around this God-forsaken party. It's enough having to deal with Charlie . . .'

I cut her off by pressing her bag into her hand. 'I came to find you and give you this. You left it by the bookcase.'

There was a pause. I heard a click and the rummaging of fingers; then a flame flared up and cast an orange glow briefly over us as the cigarette was lit. I saw, in the short life of its glare, that Ella had been crying; and she saw that I had seen.

'Girls,' she said as the flame went out, by way of explanation. 'Don't take any notice. We all enjoy a few tears occasionally. Me more than most.' There was a pause, as I settled myself two steps below her, my back to the wall. When our eyes grew accustomed to the dark I wanted to be facing her. 'I'm sorry for snapping at you back then,' she said at last. 'I suppose this is one of those nights. Thank you for bringing this.' She rattled the contents of her bag. 'Don't take any notice of me.'

'That's the second time you've said that,' I said quietly.

'Then you'd be doubly well advised to pay attention.' She took a long drag on her cigarette but was careful to blow the smoke away from me. 'I tend to mean what I say.'

'I can imagine.'

There was another pause.

'Why are you doing this?'

'What?'

'Why are you still here? Why haven't you gone back downstairs? Isn't it obvious I want to be alone?' Another pause. 'Thank you again for bringing the bag. In my very weak way I need cigarettes now more than a world of conversation.'

'So you would have me rejoin the fish?' I felt a thrill, as of fingers touching, in my appropriation of her terms.

She leaned towards me and I could make out the dim line of her nose in the darkness. 'No,' she said in a different tone, 'I wouldn't have you rejoin the fish. I'm not sure that a life of swimming with the current would altogether suit you.'

I felt a glow of pride. There was silence again. 'I agreed with what you said, incidentally,' I ventured at last.

'With what? My little monograph on oceans and currents?'

'Yes.'

'I'm apt to let my metaphors run away with me a little. Particularly when I'm trying to explain my actions to myself. It was kind of you to have listened.'

'We share many views.'

'Do we?'

'Yes.' I waited, sensing that something more was required of me. 'I've spent the whole evening despising myself for being so like all the other fish,' I said at last.

'Oh, I don't think you are, really.'

'I hope I'm not. But I dress like them; I speak like them; perhaps I even think like them. My convictions aren't very strong or well formed, at least not by comparison with yours.'

'A fat lot of good my convictions are doing me *now*,' she said drily. And through the darkness I could sense that she was smiling. 'The thing is, James, you just have to accept a certain amount of social pressure. It's part of what it means to be human, I guess; we're social animals, after all. The danger comes when you feel yourself giving way to that pressure, when you feel it pulling you under. Control over your own life should rest with you, but in practice it doesn't. We allow our views on religion, gender, class, sexuality, politics, anything that's important, to be dictated to us by others, by the particular school we happen to swim with. You think like your friends do; like your family does; like your class or your background tells you to. How many people do you know who act outside the boundaries of their own little set, their own particular group? Very few, I think. And even fewer in the school we happen to be in.'

'Which school is that?' I asked, fascinated, not wishing to disrupt the smooth flow of her words.

'You have to *ask* me? After spending an evening with those people downstairs, talking inanely about Biarritz and the Berkeley Dress Show, you have to *ask* me?' She was indignant now. 'Money should give you liberty; education should free you. But they don't. Privilege is a chain that binds us to the world of our great-grandparents in a way in which other fish in other schools aren't bound. You've no idea,' she finished wryly, 'how high family expectations run if an ancestress happened to seduce Charles II and get a title out of it for her disgruntled husband.'

'Did one of yours?'

'Oh yes. You may think I'm American because I sound it. But that's education. I'm English to the core. Family tradition is so tangled up with who I really am that sometimes I wonder how much of me is real. How much of me can I really claim as my own?' She took a last draw on her cigarette. 'Sometimes I think that most of my psyche belongs to the generations who have gone before me. They're the ones who really control my life.'

She finished this speech with her cigarette, and I heard the rustle of cardboard as she put the butt in an empty box.

'Filthy habit,' I remarked.

'Isn't it?'

We sat in silence.

'Do you think me very odd, James?' she said at last.

'I think you remarkable.'

'Thank you.'

I almost felt for her hand, but I hesitated too long and the moment passed.

'What does your island look like?'

'My island?'

'The one the tide's washed you up on.'

'Oh one of my metaphors again. I see what you're talking about.'

'Then tell me what it looks like. So far you've only said it's uninteresting, though it hardly seems so.'

There was a pause. I could now see the faint outline of Ella's nose and jaw opposite me. When she opened her mouth to speak I saw a tiny flash of white teeth.

'Forget islands,' she said. 'I've done something I shouldn't have done, something I certainly shouldn't be telling *you* about.'

'Go on.'

'I've allowed events to overtake me, I suppose. And I don't know what to do about it.' She waited, lulled by the darkness, and then moved abruptly. 'I should be going down now,' she said quietly and I heard the rustle of her dress as she got up to leave.

'Aren't you going to tell me what you've done?'

'If you really want to know, you haven't got long to wait.' And I heard the creak of the banister as she felt for it and began her slow descent of the narrow staircase.

I didn't hold her back; I didn't think it right to do so. Instead I sat in the dark, completely still, listening to her cautious retreating footsteps, smelling the smoke from her cigarette, giving her time. I heard the door of a bathroom two flights down open and close and open again after a few moments; and I imagined her, radiant once more, walking down the final broad sweep of the staircase into the Boardmans' hall, tranquil above the chaos of dancing and farewells.

I myself was not tranquil. The incomplete feeling of curiosity almost but not quite satisfied burned in me. But I waited, as I had waited earlier in the alcove; I waited until I was certain that she had had time to lose herself in the crush of guests and then I got up and made my own way gingerly downwards. Ella had told me that I didn't have long to wait, that I would find out soon enough; and I was content with that, content and interested in the precise way she would choose to tell me.

Remembering it now, I see myself on some kind of vantage point, presumably the stairs. In front of me is a narrow hall, black and white marble, highly polished. Through a set of double doors, jammed open, I can see the drawing room and the groups of tired, laughing people ranged on its chairs, drinking the last of the champagne cocktails. It is past two. The younger sisters have disappeared with their friends to the basement, where their own slumber party is presumably in progress. The door to the dancing room is closed, but the music is clearly audible nevertheless: loud; frenetic; insistent. It dies suddenly and I hear a raised voice I recognize, cheerful, excited, asking everyone if they wouldn't mind moving into the drawing room, for it has an important announcement to make. The closed doors open soon after this and I watch a stream of people, flushed with exertion, flood the hall and then the drawing room. Among them I see Ella, with Charlie Stanhope still in attendance. Excited ripples of exclamation spread outwards from Camilla Boardman, and I see her tapping her nose with her finger in a gesture of complicity. She is beaming; the party is going *fabulously*; it is past two and almost nobody who matters has left. She is delighted by the forthcoming announcement: delighted because she has been told all it is to contain in advance. She looks forward tomorrow to telling everyone that she could barely *control* herself last night but that she knows when a secret is a secret. I read all these thoughts clearly in her unwrinkled brow and in the victorious gleam of her brown eyes. I see the girl with the villa in Biarritz smiling vacantly, a little drunk, her champagne cocktail in one hand, the other anxiously touching the back of her hair to make sure that a vital clip is still in place. She sees someone she knows, forgets the hair, and throws an arm around him. It is only when I hear the same loud, excited voice that spoke before asking everyone for a moment's attention that I realize that it belongs to Charlie Stanhope. It surprises me momentarily that he should have something to say, but then I remember that his engagement has not yet been announced and instead of going into the drawing room I stay where I am on the stairs in order to get a good view of the proceedings. I scan the women near him as I hear him tell the crowd that as a collection of his greatest friends he wants it to be the first to share his happy news.

It is only when I see his hand in Ella's that I know the worst; and even then I struggle to believe it. The proof is conclusive, however, when I see Charles lean down and kiss her long and publicly and I watch her return his kiss as everyone's glasses rise in a heartfelt toast and someone starts singing 'For They're Two Jolly Good Fellows'. Both pull apart, flushing with happiness; and Ella looks up, smiling her thanks, and sees me on the stairs.

Our eyes meet, I think.

4

The details of how I left that over-large house; of how I submitted to Camilla's fervent embrace as I said my goodbyes; of how I avoided Ella and Charles in the crowds of guests, kissing and coating each other in the hall; all are blurred. What I remember after all these years is the exhilarating sensation of clarity I took away with me that night, the complete understanding of a situation which I felt myself uniquely equipped and placed to change.

I knew now what Ella's island looked like: dutiful; untroubled; endless; the security of a loveless but socially acceptable marriage. Barren indeed. I could see the current that had washed her up on it, could picture the subtle stages by which she had succumbed to the tides dragging at her feet, could imagine the gradual weakening of her strength to resist. How nineteenth-century her dilemma was, I thought; but then how nineteenth-century she was herself in some respects. And I remembered her talk of ancestors and tradition with the fascination of the uninitiated. My own family might know families which had such things, but we had no direct experience of them ourselves, however much might be implied to the contrary.

I could speculate about the intimate conversations which Ella had endured with her mother; about the number of times she had been asked whom she liked best of the young men she knew; about the delighted way in which her family would have pounced on so blandly well-bred a young man as Charles Stanhope. And to please them she would have begun to see more of him; would have allowed him, perhaps, to imagine that she felt more than she did.

And then events, as she had told me herself, had overtaken her in a spectacular fashion and before she knew what was happening her engagement was being announced by a high-spirited Charles and she was being subjected to the congratulations of her friends and the rejoicings of her family. It was a romantic dilemma and one that held for me the romantic role of Ella's saviour. I clung to it in the weeks after Camilla's party and nursed romantic plans of private rescue like the schoolboy I was.

Had I had any idea quite how far wide of the mark my conclusions had fallen, my feelings would doubtless have been very different. As it was, I threw myself into my day-dreams with a vigour which carried over into the rest of my life and surprised my parents, for no longer was I a sulky companion at the breakfast table. On the contrary, I now had a goal which was quite distinct from my battles with them and I was prepared to be conciliatory. Instead of warring with my family I focused my attention on a more immediate goal: the liberation of Ella from the clutches of convention. And I dare say that had I had any opportunity to execute my long-pondered-over designs, I might have embarrassed myself seriously. Even now, as I look back on that time, I shudder with embarrassment. But I also chuckle at my own naïveté. I cannot bring myself entirely to pity the earnest figure I was, with the shuffling gait and furrowed brow. I envy that lost self his passion; for he was in love, and in hopeless love at that. It is not an unpleasant sensation.

It was not a sensation which persisted long either, at least not in its initial form. For six weeks my mind was filled with daring plans but little action. My one concrete success was in obtaining Ella's telephone number from Camilla Boardman on the pretext that I had had no opportunity to congratulate her friend on her engagement. 'Jamie *darling*,' Camilla cooed at me down the telephone, 'it's *just* like you to be so sweet. Wherever *did* you get such *perfect* manners?'

But the gruff voice that answered the telephone at the Harcourt house in Chester Square regretted to say, on each of the weekly occasions on which I scraped together the courage to call, that Ella was not at home. Thus thwarted, I considered writing and rejected it; considered waiting and accosting her on her pavement and rejected that too, at least as an initial measure; considered flowers; a dramatically-phrased telegram; an engagement gift with a meaningful card; and rejected them all. For days I was in the sweetest of black despairs as I imagined the date of Ella's wedding drawing ever nearer, with me helpless to do anything about it.

I was brought down to earth with a jolt one afternoon by seeing the object of these dreams, her nose in a book, sitting under a wide-brimmed straw hat on a deck-chair across the water from me. I was in Hyde Park once more, having walked from my own home and made the long detour via Chester Square in the hopes of seeing her. They had not been realistic hopes, I knew; and I had settled myself by the Serpentine to enjoy the sun and to indulge in idle contemplation of how things might have been. Confronted so unexpectedly by the reality of my musings I was taken aback. Then I thought that I must have been mistaken and looked again, my pulse quickening. Over the water sat the girl on whom my thoughts had focused exclusively for more than a month, which at that age is an eternity. There was no mistaking the delicate oval of that face; the slightly upturned tilt of that small nose; only the glow in her cheeks was new. For a damsel in such distress, she looked irritatingly healthy.

Slowly I got up and made my way around the lake and through the crowds on the bridge: stalking her; wondering what she would say when she saw me. As I approached I saw her reach into a large basket at her feet and extract a packet of cigarettes and a small silver lighter. I paused and watched her fingers as she attempted to light the long, thin roll of tobacco in her hand. Her lighter needed to be refilled, I noticed; I noticed too that she was smoking a different brand from the one she had smoked before. When I was sufficiently close but still behind her and so out of her view I stopped, coughed and called her name. The pale blue of the eyes that turned to face me warned me, though no other feature did, of my mistake. They were eyes I did not know then, but which I have come to know intimately since.

'I'm afraid that I'm Sarah Harcourt, not Ella,' the girl said, turning towards me and taking off her sun hat, shaking out a wave of dark brown hair. 'There's no need to be embarrassed.' She smiled at me, sensing my awkwardness. 'We were often mistaken for each other as children. Until my hair darkened, in fact.' There was, nevertheless, an embarrassed silence. 'We both look like our grandmother, you see,' she continued, filling the void between us before it reached unpleasant proportions.

I nodded. Privately I thought this a strange fact to offer, but a moment's reflection convinced me that it was precisely the sort of allusion which Ella herself might have made; so I responded to it, thinking as I did so that Sarah's accent, very English, betrayed no trace of her cousin's American lilt.

'You're almost identical from a distance,' I said. 'Apart from the hair, of course.'

The faintest suggestion of irritation passed over the face that looked up at me from under its wreaths of hair; but Sarah's thin lips composed themselves hastily into a polite, if slightly chilly smile. 'I'm told it's unusual for cousins to look so similar,' she said.

Again there was a pause, which she seemed to expect me to fill this time. I mumbled something about her grandmother probably having had very dominant genes.

She nodded at this. 'Yes, she was a remarkable lady. She affected a great many people. I never knew her, but I've read some of her letters. She was terribly funny about the English.'

'But wasn't she English herself?' I thought that polite enquiry was the best course to follow in this unlikely situation.

'Oh no, she was American. My family's long had American connections. But then you must know that if you know Ella. She's one of them, in a way.'

'I thought she was English,' I said.

'By birth, yes,' said her cousin. 'But by education she couldn't be more foreign. And I think you'll agree that it's education which counts in such cases.' She spoke of foreignness as she might have spoken of a benign but unsightly growth: one of life's little unpleasantnesses, regrettable of course, but not seriously threatening. Such things as having a virtual American in one's family, Sarah's tone implied, had to be taken in one's stride.

As she spoke I looked closely at her and saw that she was not quite as like Ella as I had at first thought. Her hair, which fell in a neat shiny sheet to the middle of her back, was the most obvious point of difference between her and her cousin. But Sarah's face was different too: it was longer; her lips were thinner and more set than Ella's; the bridge of her nose was more severe than her cousin's. She belonged, I thought, to a different generation; and although I took her to be about my own age, I felt instinctively deferential towards her without quite knowing why. Sarah Harcourt, it seemed to me (and in this I was correct), was not a person with whom liberties could be taken lightly.

'Can I do anything for you, or will only Ella do?' She looked up at me politely.

I hesitated.

'I'll tell you where you can find her if you'll buy me an ice-cream.' Clearly Sarah was feeling conversational. 'I'm completely out of change,' she went on, still looking up at me from the striped canvas of her deck-chair. The note of command in her voice, though faint, was unmistakable; and I complied. To make conversation as we walked towards the kiosk on the bridge, I asked her how she came to have an American grandmother.

'It's a long story,' she said.

I nodded.

'But I'll tell it to you, if you like.'

'I should like that very much.'

She looked at me searchingly, apparently assessing my sincerity. I must have passed her test for once we were re-established by the Serpentine, ice-creams in hand, she began her story; and as she talked she convinced me, as perhaps no one else could have done, that Ella Harcourt was unlike anyone I had ever met. If, in my day-dreams, I thought I might have magnified her beauty, her image taught me that I was wrong. But Ella's charm went deeper than that; and a certain similarity in gesture and manner between the cousins served only to emphasize, for me, the superiority of one in subtle respects which I tried silently to define as I listened to the other. The regal, slightly stiff set of Sarah's angular shoulders reminded me, I thought, of the natural grace of Ella's; the detached ice of Sarah's blue eyes made me think of her cousin's, green and sparkling in my memory; the absence of hand movement in Sarah's conversation recalled the occasional but effective use that Ella made of her hands. Yet Sarah was not without a certain compelling air of her own, though her methods were subtly authoritarian and Ella's were not.

'My grandfather,' she said, 'was a very poor man with an illustrious name. And my grandmother was a very rich woman with no name at all, to speak of. She was also American.'

'I don't see the connection.'

'Oh it's a simple one, really. My grandmother's father felt that a title for his daughter was just the thing to ensure the respectability of his money; and his future son-in-law had an ancient, weather-beaten house with a leaking roof and no electricity to run.' Sarah looked at me, assessing my reception of her anecdote. I smiled. 'So a match was arranged,' she went on. 'A bargain was struck. Each side got what they wanted: titled grandchildren for my great-grandfather; central heating for my grandfather. The only person they neglected to consult was my grandmother, Blanche, who arrived in England at the age of eighteen, was married at nineteen, and had conceived a complete and not entirely irrational aversion to her husband by the time she was twenty.'

I nodded.

'That didn't stop her from producing four healthy children for him, though,' Sarah continued. 'An heir and three spares if you like. She understood that that was her end of the bargain.' Ella's cousin paused. 'But she was one of those compelling women who need people and life about them. The decaying house, a castle in fact, was in Cornwall. And her father wouldn't finance a house in London that befitted the status of the new couple, so in Cornwall she languished, painted once by Sargent, but otherwise left undisturbed by the fashionable world.'

'And what did she do with her time?' I found myself surprisingly interested by this forbidding young Englishwoman eating ice-cream at my side, and found further to my surprise that my interest was independent of her similarity to her cousin.

'Well, she wrote letters; she redesigned the garden; she saw to the upbringing and education of her children. She ran the house smoothly, presiding over the small army that was needed to keep the place going; she got in the way, as much as she could, of her husband's philandering.'

'I see.'

'But her mind needed more of an outlet than such activities could provide.' Sarah smiled at me. 'Blanche, you see, was not at heart a domesticated woman. That was the thing. And she was highly gifted, which made things worse.'

'So what happened to her in the end? What did she find to do?'

'She didn't really find anything at all. That was her tragedy. And there's only so much solitude, by which I mean so much isolation from her equals, that a woman of that kind can bear.'

'What happened to her?'

Blanche's granddaughter was quiet for a moment, looking silently out over the cheerful, boat-filled lake. 'She killed herself eventually,' she said at last. 'Jumped out of a window on to the terrace. Caused a huge scandal at the time, as you can imagine.'

I could imagine. 'How awful,' I said quietly.

'Isn't it? I think it affected her children profoundly.'

'It must have done.'

There was a pause.

'And there,' she said briskly, looking directly at me once more, 'you have the story of how I come to have an American grandmother. I hope I didn't tell you more than you care to know.'

'No, not at all. I found it fascinating. And tragic.'

'Yes,' she said thoughtfully. 'It certainly has both of those qualities.' She turned to me, confidential suddenly. 'I have an idea, you know, of writing Blanche's biography one day. She was a woman who gave to everything she did the kind of glamour one usually finds only in fiction. I think hers would be an excellent story to tell. And I think, too, that she would have wanted it to be told.'

'She certainly chose a very public way of ending her life.'

'Yes she did. She was also, of course, in an interesting position historically.'

I nodded.

'One of the emancipated young women from America sent to prop up the ailing feudal system with democratic gold.' Sarah smiled. 'It's funny to think, isn't it,' she went on, warming to her theme, 'that young women like Blanche helped to sustain all from which the Pilgrim Fathers had fled so far?'

'Very.'

There was silence, though this time it was not an uncomfortable one.

'Well,' I said at last, 'I'm sure it would make a very interesting book.'

'Do you really think so?'

'Yes I do,' I said rising. 'But I've kept you from your reading for far too long. I nodded towards the deck-chair and the novel lying on it. 'What is it?'

'It's *The Buccaneers*. By Edith Wharton. A friend of my grandmother's incidentally.'

'And of Henry James,' I said.

'Precisely.'

'Well goodbye,' I said.

'Goodbye.' She held out her hand.

'You couldn't pass on a message to Ella, could you?'

The same flicker of irritation which I thought I had observed earlier reappeared, and was, as earlier, modified at once to a polite smile. 'Of course,' she said, 'though I'm not sure when I'll next see her. We don't see very much of each other.'

'And why is that?'

'Frankly, we don't get on. Oh you needn't be embarrassed,' she continued after a moment, sensing my discomfort. 'It's an open secret. I find her rather crass; she, I dare say, finds me too English and reserved. But doubtless she'll tell you her criticisms of me herself when next you see her.'

'I doubt that,' I said, doubting too whether I would ever see Ella again. Obviously an acquaintance with Sarah was going to bring me no nearer my goal.

'Oh she will, I'm sure. Very sweetly but very deftly. That's her way. But do you want to give me a message for her anyway, just in case I run into her before you do?'

'Tell her you saw James Farrell,' I said, realizing that until now I had not offered my name to Sarah and she had not asked for it. 'Tell her that you saw James Farrell and that he wondered how life on her island was suiting her.'

'Is that all?' Sarah eyed me quizzically.

'That's all. She'll understand.'

'I hope so.'

'Well, goodbye again.'

'Goodbye.'

And with that I left her and walked once more over the bridge and down the carriage track. I felt Sarah's cold blue eyes on me as I went and I turned on the far side of the bridge to wave. But she was seated, her nose in her book once more. If she saw me, she gave no indication of having done so.

5

As it happened, none of the Harcourts gave any sign of acknowledging my existence in the days which followed my meeting with Sarah, days which I spent practising my violin and thinking of Ella. I found to my delight that I was able to transform the bitter-sweet frustration which hopeless love produces into the energy which serious work requires, and even my parents were impressed by the resulting ardour of my diligence. Throughout that hot August I was never far from the airless room at the top of the house where my violin was kept; and as I practised I played to an imaginary audience of one, hoping as I did so that the sheer dexterity of this or that scale would impress her, or that this or that sonata would make her smile. I played a good deal of Brahms at that time, I remember; and I remember finding in the drama of the music a fitting accompaniment to my own secret dreams of rescue and of valour.

Youth is foolish and youth in frenzied love is worse. Even now I smile to think of those heady days in that stuffy room; I smile but am glad to have lived through them, hot and dusty though they were, young and foolish though I was.

But Ella, the unwitting object of all my thoughts, remained nowhere to be found or seen. She was never at home to my telephone calls; she never gave any sign of having received a message from me; the forbidding Georgian portals of the house in Chester Square never yielded up her slim frame when I happened to be passing, as I frequently was. But the effortless way in which she had entered my mind; the strange, unlooked-for meeting with her cousin; the occasional photographs of her and Charles which appeared in the magazines I read while having my hair cut; all fanned the flames of my interest in her. I continued to play and dream and be disappointed.

But even the interest of an unusually impressionable boy begins to wane. With no encouragement from the unknowing object of my devotion, without so much as a note or a look from her – either of which might have conquered me for ever, I felt – the intensity of my enthusiasm could not be maintained indefinitely. And it might, I suppose, have faded and finally died, consigned to history as a last memory of fiery adolescence, had Fate, if indeed such a force exists, not decreed otherwise.

The instrument that Fate selected to bring Ella and me together once again was chosen with exquisite taste: it was Camilla Boardman; and she telephoned just as I was deciding that there was nothing to be done, and that if Ella wished to waste herself on Charles Stanhope she was welcome to do so.

'*Daaarling*!' cooed the voice I had not heard since it had given me Ella's telephone number many weeks before.

'Camilla. How are you?'

'How are *you*? That's *far* more to the point.'

'I'm well, thank you.'

'So why have you been hiding away? Positively *ignoring* all your friends.'

I knew Camilla well enough to be suspicious of her tone of mock injury. Cautiously I replied that I had not been hiding away, but that I had been practising hard in preparation for the Guildhall.

'Oh I forget you're off to be a famous musician,' she said. 'You'll still remember me when you've made it, *won't* you darling? Even with all those terribly glamorous women throwing themselves at you.'

I sensed that a compliment was appropriate. Hesitatingly, I attempted one. 'They couldn't possibly be more glamorous than you, Camilla . . . darling.'

'Oh Jamie, you're *so* sweet. *So* lovely. You *always* are.' The frequency of Camilla's emphases prepared me for her inevitable climax. 'In fact that's *just* why I've called you. Ed Saunders has left me *completely* in the lurch, like he always does.' Ed Saunders was Camilla's current man, I gathered, and I pretended to recognize his name.

'Oh Ed,' I said.

'Yes, the *toad*.' A petulant Camilla was even more alarming than usual. 'And Ella Harcourt's engagement party starts in an hour, would you believe?'

'Ella Harcourt, did you say?' I caught my breath, hoping against hope.

'Yes, her parents are giving a lunch for her and Charlie. *Everyone's* going to be there. Pamela (that's Ella's stepmother) is a *fabulous* entertainer. And that *toad* Ed has just rung me up and told me he's got laryngitis and can't possibly come. *Laryngitis*. Honestly!' said Camilla, as though it numbered amongst the rarest of tropical diseases. 'In August! And *so*,' her voice changed tone, 'I wondered whether you might *possibly* be free. I couldn't *bear* the thought of going alone. And,' realizing that this probably sounded selfish, 'I haven't seen you for *ages* and I remembered how well you and Ella got on at my party.'

I wondered privately how many people she had called before trying me. Aloud I said, 'I'm not sure, Camilla. Of course I'd love to see you, but it's very short notice.'

Camilla respected few people as much as she did those with multiple engagements. 'I *know*, darling,' she said. 'And if his laryngitis doesn't kill Ed you may be sure that I will. But I would *so* like to see you. And if it's any consolation, I'm sure it'll be a very brilliant affair. Wonderful food . . .' Camilla was tenacious in pursuit of her social goals. 'And there're bound to be *lots* of Oxford people there,' she went on. 'And . . .' She considered what further inducements she could offer. 'Ella's cousin will be there, of course. She's *very* pretty. An odd fish, by all accounts' – for Camilla was a strictly truthful person – 'but *very* pretty.'

'I know,' I said, thinking of Sarah's cold beauty.

'So you'll take me, then?'

An hour later I found myself on the steps of the house in Chester Square, past whose black door I had so often walked in the hopes of meeting Ella. Camilla, beside me, squeezed my hand with relief and smiled a practised and perfectly-formed smile of red lips and white teeth, expensively arranged. 'Darling you're a *saviour*,' she whispered in my ear as I rang the bell.

We were late, for it was part of Camilla's creed always to be missed, and we entered the drawing room just as the other guests were beginning to shuffle hungrily and glance at their watches. There were perhaps thirty of us in all: a dowdy but respectable pair in tweeds whom I took, correctly, to be the Stanhopes; several people my own age, amongst whom I recognized the girl with the villa in Biarritz; and the Harcourts themselves, tall and stately, precisely as I had imagined them, talking to Sarah by one of the long windows that gave on to the square. Neither Ella nor Charles were anywhere to be seen.

Camilla moved straight towards her host and hostess, her arms flung out in a gesture of greeting. Trailing in her wake, I noticed that conversation had died. 'Lady Harcourt,' she said, embracing a tall, angular woman with red hair scraped off her face and piled in complicated wreaths on her head. 'How *lovely* to see you.'

The voice that replied asked her, in the drawling tones of a Bostonian, not to stand on ceremony. 'My name is Pamela,' said the angular woman with a certain emphasis, extending a bony, bejewelled hand to me as she did so. 'We're just waiting for the happy couple. They're upstairs putting down the engagement presents.'

As she spoke I felt how empty my hands were, but on cue Camilla produced an extravagantly-wrapped parcel from her handbag and gave it to her hostess. 'This is from us both,' she said with her sweetest smile, as she turned to kiss her host.

Alexander Harcourt had the same colouring as his daughter, although on him the blond hair was thinning and the cheeks were ruddy rather than rosy. His eyes were blue, like Sarah's, but shone like Ella's; and he moved with the confidence of a handsome man who has always been thought one. His hands were large; his shoulders broad; his manner frank. I liked him.

'Here they are now,' he said, nodding amiably at and past me, towards the drawing-room doors. His wife, very erect in a green dress which did not suit her, went forward to greet her stepdaughter. 'How lovely you look,' I heard her say as she kissed her cheek.

If Ella did look lovely, I could not see it. The skilful hands of a hairdresser had fluffed away the sleek lines of her short hair and almost persuaded it into a bob for the occasion. The work of the make-up artist was visible, too, in the pink of the lips and the sparkling blue of the eye-shadow. The circles beneath her eyes, if they still existed, had been expertly concealed. In a pink floral dress with puffed sleeves, she looked like an Edwardian doll and moved with the stiffness of one. She did not appear to see me.

'You look *fantastic*, darling!' Camilla, as ever, was the first in the impromptu line that formed to greet the engaged pair. Charles, standing behind Ella in a dark suit, his hair severely parted, glowed with pleasure as his fiancée submitted to the embraces of his friend. I waited with the other guests as he and Ella, relinquished with reluctance by Camilla, came down the line, receiving the congratulations of their parents' friends and their own.

Ella saw me while three people still separated us. She was kissing Sarah formally on both cheeks when her eyes, straying down the line, met mine. Instantly she looked away, and I thought that I detected evidence of a real blush beneath the blusher. I glowed at this secret triumph.

'I didn't know you'd be here,' she said as she reached me, and made a point of offering her hand rather than her cheek.

'Camilla invited me,' I said. 'And in any case I haven't had an opportunity yet to congratulate you and Charles.'

She looked at me for a moment, more embarrassed than hostile, and passed on.

Charles, when he reached me, greeted me as an old friend.

'So this is the splendid girl I wasn't to talk about?' I asked, smiling.

'This is the girl,' he said, looking down the line at Ella. 'And she is splendid, isn't she?'

'Congratulations,' I said quietly.

He moved on. The afternoon proceeded. Lunch was served on a long, silver-laden table in the dining room, a lofty, red-papered space with a large reproduction chandelier and a view of the garden. Outside it was raining. I sat between Camilla and Sarah and opposite the girl with the villa in Biarritz, who was sitting next to Charles. The food, as Camilla had confidently predicted, was excellent; the wine, too, was good; tubs of freshly-picked roses, pink like Ella's dress, filled the room with their scent. Occasionally I heard snatches of Ella's conversation, three places down on my left, tantalizingly close.

But it was only as the meal progressed and I heard more that I realized that every phrase I caught was precisely as it should have been; that my love was speaking with precisely the same thoughtless, practised ease of which she had been so critical a few weeks before. Her thanks for people's presents were pretty; her enthusiasm for the wedding plans nicely put; her secrecy about her dress conventional. Nowhere could I detect any trace of the woman with the gaunt face who had spoken to me of drowning in the darkness of the Boardman stairwell; and this transformation infuriated me. Ella, it seemed, had decided to swim with the current rather than against it; and she was swimming with a rehearsed grace which reminded me of Charles's and impressed me as little as his had done.

Yet I did not despair of her wholly. Something in her voice reminded me of the voice I had listened to in the park and in the alcove. I heard again the confusion of her words then, the sincerity with which she had railed against the forces which were ... How had she put it? 'Pulling her under'. And Ella pulled under had resolved to put a brave face on it. So I thought, and in so thinking I was half right; I came closer to the truth in that conclusion than in any of my flights of nineteenth-century fantasy. I was wrong only in thinking that I knew what had pulled her down.

Tantalizing though Ella's presence was, however, I did not forget my duties as Camilla Boardman's partner; nor was I allowed to. The infectious laughter of the woman who had brought me, the intimate way in which she confided other people's indiscretions, the complete and gratifying attention she paid to my responses, all combined to put me in an agreeable mood. Ella was not the only one, I thought, who could conceal her feelings behind a flow of seemingly effortless social patter. I would show her that I was as adept as anyone. And so I talked: to Camilla; to Sarah; to the girl with the villa in Biarritz; all the while wondering how to get Ella to myself for a moment and resolving not to leave the house without at least making an attempt to do so.

Sarah Harcourt, rigid in blue linen on my left, spoke to me of her distaste for pink roses. Her criticism, inaudible to her hostess, was more for Pamela than for Pamela's flowers, I suspected; and I thought that I understood where the disapproval came from. Pamela, for Sarah, was an invader. To begin with, her accent was American and thus hardly to her credit; but what was more to be deplored was her self-conscious attention to the anglicizing of every other personal detail. Pamela's hair, piled above her head, was impressively Edwardian; her jewellery was heavy and old-fashioned; she addressed the caterer's maid who waited on her with just the correct amount of polite disdain. All this, I could see, irritated Sarah almost as much as her cousin's charming conversation irritated me. And although she said nothing, I felt within her the hostility to foreigners, particularly usurping foreigners, which is latent in certain English souls. She sat by my side, hardly touching the food which was put before her, splendidly regal. I noticed that no one spoke to her but that her presence was very much felt, and I thought again that she was someone to be treated with deference but no intimacy: an outsider by choice and circumstance. Even Camilla, though nothing and no one could upset her iron self-assurance, seemed disinclined to engage Sarah in conversation, sensing her to be a difficult conquest. And I, looking at the set lines of Sarah's mouth and wondering how I could ever have found in her an exact likeness of Ella, felt sorry for her in a way I would never have dared to express. Sarah was the prisoner of her own self-control, I thought; and today, thinking back on her then, I see that I was right.

Only once did the girl with the villa in Biarritz attempt conversation with Sarah, and her choice of opening was unfortunate.

'Do you know,' she said from across the pink roses, 'I never knew that Ella had a sister. Are you very close?'

There was the slightest suggestion of a pause; but it was frosty enough to halt the conversation around it in the moment before Sarah smiled and said that she and Ella were only cousins.

'What? But you could almost be twins,' the girl blundered on, smiling still.

'We could not be twins,' came the acid reply, just loud enough for Ella to overhear; and by the forced cheerfulness of her conversation it seemed to me that the object of the slight had heard and was consciously ignoring it.

'Oh you could be,' the hapless girl persisted. 'You're almost identical.'

'But our styles are quite different,' came the sweetly damning reply; and Sarah leaned back in her chair, languid and serene, as if inviting comparison between her sleek lines and Ella's painted cheeks. Half smiling, she lit a cigarette with a smooth movement of long fingers and smiled at her cousin; and it was left to Camilla to cover the ensuing silence by redirecting our attention to the splendours of the Chelsea Flower Show.

Lunch finally came to an end with pungent, sweet-smelling coffee in paper-thin china cups shaped to look like rosebuds. There were different colours in the set (mine, for instance, was yellow), and it amused me to see Sarah being handed a pink one. I looked for her eyes, thinking that we might share the joke, but they were set and unseeing. As Camilla exclaimed over the *exquisite* prettiness of the china and asked her hostess where she got it from, I saw Ella's cousin glance at her watch.

We left the lunch table in a troop and moved into the drawing room, an ocean of uncomfortable sofas of ornate wood and sombre pattern. Almost at once the party began to split up, for lunch had lasted longer than anticipated and many of the guests were late for engagements elsewhere. I saw that Sarah was one of the first to say her goodbyes and that instead of kissing Pamela she shook her hand. Alexander she kissed, and Ella, too, although the brushing of the cousins' cheeks which passed for a kiss did not suggest much unspoken affection. Charles, rising, leaned forward to kiss Sarah and was rewarded by the quick outstretching of her fine white hand.

When she had gone, Camilla found a place next to me on a sofa and said, softly enough for only one or two people who would share her opinion to hear, 'Well I *said* she was an odd fish, and you can see that I was right. *Very* strange. Hardly spoke at *all*.' She considered the question gravely for a moment. 'I think she's superior,' she said at last, with an air of finality. 'And frankly I don't see any reason why she should be, do you?'

But her question was merely rhetorical; I was not expected to answer it and when I did not she let the matter drop and spoke of other things. I listened to her vaguely, concentrating most of my attention on the question of how I could possibly get Ella to myself for a moment. A moment was all it would take, I thought. But one by one the guests got up to leave and I felt my time of opportunity dwindling. Ella showed no inclination to talk to me and I had no desire to cross the expanse of carpet and sit with her and Charles. I wanted her alone or not at all.

Again it was Camilla who came to my rescue with her suggestion of seeing the engagement presents. 'Ella darling,' she called from our sofa, 'aren't you *dying* to see what everyone's brought you?'

'Of course she is,' said Pamela, smiling.

Sensing my chance and seeing Ella about to protest, I joined the chorus with a well-timed 'So are we.'

'Well, why don't we open them now, sweetheart?' said Charles on cue.

Ella looked doubtful. 'We could, I suppose,' she said.

'Then let's,' said Pamela decisively, rising. To the few guests who remained, she said, 'You won't mind coming upstairs, will you? It's just that there're too many gifts to bring down.' And with a laugh, taking the arm of her future son-in-law, she left the room and led the way upwards. Alexander followed with Camilla and the girl with the villa in Biarritz. A plump relation, the only other member of the party still present, had gone to sleep in an armchair. Ella and I were left alone.

'So,' I said quickly, my irritation at lunch giving an edge to my voice, 'this is it?'

'What?' She looked at me from under the sweep of her blow-dried fringe and I saw something of the woman I remembered.

'Is this the island?'

There was a pause. The relation in the armchair gave a gentle snore.

'Is this what you meant by events overtaking you?' I persisted, courageous after weeks of pent-up frustration and excitement.

With a sharp nod of the head Ella motioned me out of the room and on to the landing. 'I don't know what you mean,' she said, putting her foot on the first stair.

'No, of course you don't. I forget that in our particular school of fish one should never admit to having said anything real.' There was a note of sarcasm in my voice which I saw made her uncomfortable. 'Particularly if one hasn't said it to someone one's known since childhood.' I was pleasantly surprised by the ease with which my words came.

'Don't talk to me about schools of fish.'

'Why not?'

'Because it's a tired metaphor.'

'All right then, I'll ask you plainly. What on earth are you doing?'

'I am marrying the man I love, James.' But even as she said it, her tone rang false. We both observed this. 'And anyway,' she whispered almost fiercely, angry herself now, 'I don't see what business it is of yours whether I'm happy or not.'

'It's only my business in as far as you've made it my business,' I said quietly.

'Well I'm sorry I mentioned anything.'

'I don't think you are.'

'I beg your pardon?'

'I said that I don't think you are. When you first met me, that day in the park, you were looking for a way out. You were looking for a way out that night at Camilla's party, too, weren't you? I think you wanted me to help you find one.'

It was wise of me at this point not to have come out with any of my wilder theories on the question of Ella's motives; as it was, the gist of what I had said was correct and she did not contradict it.

'And then when your engagement was finally announced,' I continued, warming to my theme, 'and things were truly out of hand, you decided that there was no way out and so you gave in, you accepted what was happening. To use your own phrase, you decided that it was easier to swim with the current than against it.'

'Hush,' she said, 'they'll hear you.'

I lowered my voice but went on. 'Even now, though, you despise yourself for being so weak, don't you?'

'How dare you . . .'

'Tell me that you don't despise yourself. Tell me that you relish wearing that silly pink dress and being made to look like a baby doll that can't think for itself. Tell me that,' I concluded triumphantly, 'and I'll go upstairs and gawp politely at your engagement presents and not bother you again.'

She looked at me, speechless, and I saw to my mingled horror and relief that there were tears in her eyes.

'Tell me,' I insisted, 'and I'll go. Tell me,' for now I was in full stride, 'that you can't imagine ever loving anyone more than you love Charlie Stanhope now and I will go. I won't even say goodbye, if you like. I'll just leave.'

'I will tell you nothing of the sort,' she said, with an attempt at dignity. 'But you had better go all the same.'

'Not until you tell me *why*,' I replied, seizing on a new angle of attack. 'If only to satisfy my curiosity. Tell me *why* you're marrying him.' Confident that I knew the answer, I expected her finally to crumble into the safety of confession. I was disappointed. Instead, she drew herself up to her full height and looked me squarely in the eyes.

'Ella darling!' came a shrill voice from upstairs.

'Go on,' I persisted, 'tell me.'

Ignoring all that I had said up to this point, she made a visible effort to recover herself and when she spoke it was in a tone of quiet command. 'You have no right to expect me to answer you,' she said softly. 'You are a guest in my parents' house. You have certain obligations. Fulfil them and oblige me by doing what I say.'

'What is that?'

'I want you to go upstairs right now and thank my stepmother for a delicious lunch,' she said evenly. 'Then I want you to take Camilla home, to see her safely in at her front door, and to go home yourself. Forget my metaphors; forget everything I said in the park; forget our conversation at the Boardmans'. Put it all down to the confusion of a young girl about to get engaged. Put it down to anything you like, but stop asking me about it.'

'Ella!' came from upstairs, louder this time; a man's voice. I heard the creaking of wood as someone with a tread I recognized came down to find her. 'Ella sweetheart, where have you got to?' The voice was Charlie Stanhope's, cheerful as ever.

'I hope you have understood me,' she said.

Our eyes met. We heard Charlie on the landing above us.

'Please James,' she said, her attitude changing, 'not now.' Seeing the light of hope in my eyes she went on hurriedly. 'Not ever.' She looked at me frankly. 'I've made my bed, I've come this far. Now I intend to lie on it.'

'It's not too late,' I said. 'You've got your whole life still to get through. Spending it washed up on an island with Charles Stanhope can't be a tempting prospect.'

56

'Don't talk to me about *islands*.'

'Why not? It's your word.'

'I've told you. The metaphor is tired.'

'But it's still apt, I think.'

'Think what you will,' she hissed, and I sensed a note of exasperation in her voice.

'Your whole life is ahead of you Ella, don't you see?' I went on more gently.

'That's what you kept on saying that night,' she said, as Charles appeared on the stairs.

'You two been nattering down here all this time?' he said jovially.

'It's still true,' I muttered.

'What is?' asked Charlie.

'Only that trains wait for no man,' said Ella brightly, putting her arm through her fiancé's, 'and that James, no matter how much we beg him, won't miss his.'

'Too bad,' said Charlie as I followed them both upstairs to say my goodbyes.

6

Thus far I had been defeated, crushed by the determination of those steely green eyes. And you may be sure that I took my defeat to heart in the days that followed the party at Chester Square. But you may also be sure that I remained unshaken in my romantic beliefs and that I returned to my thoughts of Ella and her predicament with renewed vigour. I had, I thought, done myself credit on the rainy day of her engagement party; and I felt that the bond between us had strengthened in some indefinable yet concrete way, despite all evidence to the contrary. Youth is optimistic; that is its consolation. And I waited patiently to allow events, if only they would, to follow their natural course.

In so doing I was not arrogant enough to suppose that Ella could not resist the temptation of seeing me again; rather, I suspected that she could not for long resist a temptation of a different kind: she would, I felt sure, want an opportunity to justify herself more effectively than she had done at her engagement lunch. So I settled down to wait and resolved to bide my time.

The Stanhope–Harcourt wedding was set for the following March, seven months away; and as the days since the Harcourts' lunch party stretched into a week, I comforted myself with the thought that time, at least, was on my side. Ella Harcourt, I suspected, was a proud woman; and I held firmly to this suspicion for it served to explain her continuing silence. I told myself, correctly as it turned out, that it would be foolish to badger the house in Chester Square; that I had done all I could. And no more chance encounters with any members of the Harcourt family ensued, though I looked out for them as eagerly as ever. For a week I waited, unencouraged.

On the eighth day I received her letter. I have it with me now, with all the others she wrote me; and looking at its jagged writing, its heavy paper, its brown ink, I think with a sharp sorrow of the girl who wrote it and wish, as so many have wished before me, that the past were more fluid, that it might be possible to return, by a route other than memory, to the day so long ago when Ella's letter found its way on to the mat in my parents' hall.

Talking like this is good for me; it brings me face to face with a past I have spent more than forty years trying to avoid. I see the boy that I was – the romantic, naïve, essentially innocent boy that I was – and I begin to understand him. That is an important step. Realizing his innocence is important; for I know now that he, that I, was not born wicked; that his sin, that my sin, was not original. It came from outside, from an unfortunate collusion of circumstance and chance – and, yes, weakness – which I could not have foreseen and over which I had no control. I know now, in a way I have not known until now, that as I read Ella's letter I was an ordinary young man: an unexceptional, unremarkable, ordinary young man. Essentially innocent. If I was fascinated by Ella Harcourt, my fascination echoed the fascination of countless other young men for countless other young women. If I questioned the structure of the world, so did millions of others also. If I desired to prove my freedom from convention, from the confines of received wisdom, then so did every other moody young man of my or any other generation. I was hardly unique; others might have done what I did.

But they did not; and I must accept that fact.

I must accept, too, that there were many who did worse things than I, that my actions have their place on some sort of scale. History is full of men far more evil than me. Nero; Ivan the Terrible; Hitler. Will they be punished more or I less? Perhaps they, like me, began innocently enough. I would be interested to hear their stories. I would be interested to hear more of Sarah's story. And why? Because extenuating circumstance interests me, and I have little left to live for now save my own intellectual satisfaction. Having seen a sort of justice done, having in fact been its instrument in the case of my wife, unrepentant to the last, I can devote my energies to pleasing myself until the day when my own end comes. Then judgement will be meted out on me, though unlike Sarah I am sorry for what I did and have been so for almost fifty years; perhaps that will count for something.

But before I face my future I feel that I must face my past. If I had one wish it would be to do that. And facing one's past is no easy thing: until yesterday I had no thought for anything but the present, you see. I was afraid to look backwards or forwards: for in one direction lay what I had done, what we had done, Ella and I; and in the other lay the punishment I would receive for it. But I am braver now, I can look more closely.

I have Ella's letter here. I shall read it to you. It is dated *Saturday*; the scrawled address reads *23, Chester Square, s. w. 1.*

Dear James, it begins.

You will be glad to discover that our conversation last week had, if no other effect, at least that of making me see the light about the awful make-up I had plastered over my face. You were right, I looked like a doll. I guess I just needed someone insulting and presumptuous enough to tell me so and I thank you for your rudeness – I thought it had been socialized out of you. Perhaps it has and I got the last drop of it; I hope not. But I didn't look like a doll for long, you'll be relieved to hear. As soon as everybody had gone I went upstairs and scrubbed it all right off; I wet my hair, too, leading Pamela to remark at dinner that I looked 'distinctly bedraggled'. (She likes phrases like that.) She was furious incidentally – we had spent the morning together at her beautician's, you see. My face was the result of a bonding exercise.

How American, I hear you say. Well I guess I am an American and proud of it. But I have an English name and you will remember how we agreed that a name is the least private thing about a person. That, perhaps, will form the beginning of my answer to your question of last week. 'Why?' you asked me. 'Why are you marrying Charles?'

Why indeed. But before you get on your high horse I think you should put yourself in my position, if only for a moment. If your (I don't know how many times great) great-grandmother had also seduced Charles II, you might understand more of what I'm saying. Your name, like mine, might stop describing and begin defining you instead, along strict lines which you don't altogether like. I, heaven knows, am defined by my name. Do you honestly expect that the Hon. Ella, daughter of Lord and Lady Harcourt, niece of the Earl and Countess of Seton, with her very own mention in Who's Who?, *could* possibly *marry anyone other than Charles Stanhope, eldest son of Sir Lachlan and Lady Stanhope, of Barton Manor, Wilts and Windham Road, Fulham, ed. Eton and Oxford? Of course not. This may be the nineties but we are not all as free as we like to think ourselves. (And I say this only half jokingly.)*

Flippancy aside, though, I suppose the time has come to be frank with you. I have got myself, as I said that day in the park, into a mess. And it is a mess, as I also said then, which is entirely of my own making. This I freely admit. That's why I've been considering going ahead with everything over the past few weeks, because I made my bed and I should lie on it. Quite why I insisted on making it, on setting this whole bizarre machinery in motion, I cannot explain to you completely. I have asked myself why a thousand times and if I never get a straight answer why should you? But there is *an answer nevertheless, or rather several little answers which together might explain what I've done. If you'd really like to know why I'm marrying Charles, and think you might have any bright ideas — once you know all the little answers to that very big question — of how I might get myself out of this ludicrously old-fashioned predicament, then meet me under the departure board at Paddington at 2.15 tomorrow afternoon. If I don't see you, I'll know that you have quite wisely decided to steer clear. I would probably do the same in your position.*

Sincerely,

Ella Harcourt.

No endearment, nothing more personal than her name.

But, of course, I went. Who wouldn't have gone in my position? And I went with joy in my heart and music on my lips.

Ella was standing under the departure board at Paddington, small and lost in the crowd. In jeans and an old sweater, her hair tousled from sleep, she could not have looked more different from the woman who had spoken so demurely of engagement gifts and wedding plans a week before.

'Hello James,' she said when she saw me.

'Hello Ella.'

We looked at each other.

'Thank you for coming.'

'There's no need to thank me.'

It was she who bought the tickets and as she did so said to me, half apologetically, 'I'm afraid it's rather a long journey. But I can promise you excellent fare when we reach our destination. There's a sweet pub in the village which I'm sure you'll like. Until then, you'll have to submit to the standard train sandwiches.' And taking my hand, she led me down the platform towards the Cornish Express.

I remember her in that train. I remember the green wool of her sweater against the cream of her skin; the sweep of her newly-washed hair; the scent of her soap. Here was Ella unadorned: not the decadent figure in the park; nor the decorative guest at Camilla Boardman's party; nor still the artificial doll at her stepmother's lunch. Ella Harcourt was a woman of many facets; she possessed a quality of aesthetic malleability that I have known in no one but her, and I have known many women in the course of seventy years. Sitting in the drabness of a second class railway carriage she seemed as lovely to me as she had been on a park bench and in the half-light of a book-lined alcove. And as I stared, trying to explain to myself why this was so, I discovered the truth that beauty is elusive and defies description. Prettiness lends itself to words; but beauty is something finer, a thing apart. Ella was beautiful.

She was also inclined to be communicative. And with only a little encouragement from me she gave me an outline of her life.

'If you really want to know,' she began, smiling, 'I was born in London on a misty day in November almost twenty-four years ago. Exhibited by my proud parents as an example of all that is wondrous in childhood, I was in point of fact an ugly, filthy-tempered

baby with no hair but healthy lungs. I was inclined to scream.'
I laughed and she gave me a wry smile.

Lighting a cigarette, she continued. 'When I was six my mother, a perfectly respectable nice young English girl, took the liberty of dying in a car accident. Most regrettable. For her, of course, and also for my father who happened to be very much in love with her, but chiefly for the family at large. Unable to do anything, they watched as poor Alexander, in his grief, transferred himself bag and baggage to America in the hopes of starting afresh and finding happiness once more. Very poor taste, everyone thought, giving in to your emotions like that. And what was worse, he insisted on taking his little girl with him, who under the influence of some barbarian colonials absorbed, as everyone had feared, some unfortunate habits which have tainted her to this day. It was felt – though such things are never said, of course – that she could only bring disgrace on the family name.'

She paused to tap her ash into a plastic cup. I listened, absorbed.

'When poor Alexander committed the supreme treachery, twelve years on, of returning to London with a new American wife,' Ella continued, her face distorting into an expression of chill disapproval, 'the family despaired. And what was more, his daughter had gone over to the other side. Her vowels were rounded no longer; her manners (never excellent) had deteriorated sharply. Clearly something had to be done. But she was eighteen and very headstrong, altogether unwilling to listen to good advice. An ungrateful child. Yet the fact remained that she was a Harcourt, and showed every sign of remaining one indefinitely. So it was vital that she was taught to behave like one without delay.' She took a meditative drag. 'How to mould her correctly remained a problem; but fortunately she was interested in art history, a relatively proper discipline; and the Courtauld was seized on as a very civilizing place for her to do her degree.' Ella smiled. 'The degree once done, however, and cultured conversation acquired, it wasn't thought seemly for her to have a serious *job*, however much she herself seemed both able and willing to get one;

so she was taken under various wings, introduced to endless people, given a sufficiently smart set of lifelong friends. By the time she was twenty-three she knew people like Camilla Boardman, supreme arbiter of all that is best in young England today, and was engaged to a very nice young man. Even her accent, though it remained far from perfect, had certainly improved. She could at last be married off without shame.'

'And Charles Stanhope was the nice young man?'

'Yes.'

'I see.'

There was a pause.

'So what do you think of my story?' asked Ella. 'Do you like it? Is it as you imagined?'

'Yes,' I said, happily, thinking how correct I had been in my theories all along.

'The unfortunate thing,' she went on, putting the butt of her cigarette into the plastic cup and taking a new one from the packet in her bag, 'is that what I have just told you is not the whole story. By no means is it the whole story.'

'What do you mean?' I asked, surprised by the change in her.

'Well . . . you remember my letter?'

I nodded.

'How I said that there were lots of little reasons which, taken all together, might possibly explain how things have come to turn out as they have?'

I nodded again.

'The explanation I have just given you is one of those little reasons. Perhaps the smallest.'

'What are the others?'

'There aren't many others, in fact. I was exaggerating. There's just one really.' She took a deep breath. 'And it is, on the whole, a little murkier than what I've just told you.' She paused and raised her eyes to mine. 'The two reasons are related, of course, but substantially

64

different. The one you don't know is a little more . . . cold-blooded.'
She looked at me steadily and I felt the challenge in her eyes.

Silently I met it. 'Go on,' I said.

'Are you sure you want me to?' She lit the cigarette and inhaled deeply, blowing the smoke out of her nostrils in a defiant swirl.

I felt the tingling vertigo of one standing on a knife-edge. 'Go on,' I said again.

'Okay then. But you'll have to wait until we get there.' She smiled at me and I saw her shoulders relax. 'There's something I want to show you,' she said. 'Something that will explain things far more eloquently than I could.'

It is from that moment, on that journey (a journey I have since repeated more times than I can count) that I date the beginning of it all. In London I had been fascinated, it is true, but mine had been a fascination based on romantic notions of plight and salvation. Ella had filled my thoughts, but more as a princess in a fairy-tale might have done than as a being of blood and flesh. Her aura was ethereal and I, a mortal, had succumbed to it. But I had been held at arm's length and largely ignored. What intimacy there had been had been haphazard and insubstantial, completely at the mercy of coincidence and whim. But now I had passed a test that I only dimly understood but which I knew enough to value. I had promised myself and had been given in return a right to claim something. What I might claim I hardly knew, but no longer was I peripheral.

This mysterious woman with the changing eyes and smiling lips had plucked me from my life, on a whim, and had taken me on a six-hour journey to be told something I might not even understand. From everyone she knew, of all the people in her life, she had selected me to be her confidant; it was to me that she had chosen to explain the tangle of motive and error that had led to her engagement; it was to me that she looked for help in extricating herself from the depths in which she floundered. From the school of fish which flashed its scales before her eyes, she had selected me to swim with her, to brave currents, tides and oceans by her side.

So slid Ella's metaphors in my mind colliding; joining; mingling with my own romantic dreams of passion and valour. Yes I was a dreamer; to that charge I plead guilty. And as I dreamed I stared at her smooth white neck and felt that there was nothing I would not do to be worthy of her trust.

We passed the remainder of that journey in silence, watching the blur of passing towns from our carriage window; listening to the rattle of the train; allowing its gentle rhythm to lull us to near sleep. We spoke little; Ella smoked a great deal; I watched her fingers as she lit and disposed of her cigarettes.

7

The train followed the coast for the last half-hour of its journey to Penzance. Ella and I sat in complete silence in a carriage which gradually emptied as it passed through Devon. She had stopped smoking. I watched her profile as she gazed at the view, occasionally following the direction of her unblinking eyes, feeling her intent with expectation and wondering what it might be for. She had told me nothing of our destination and I, enjoying the suspense, had not asked. Then I saw it and knew as I did so that I saw what she had been waiting for. Rising tall and many-turreted above the sea, the windows of the Castle of Seton winked at us in the sunset. Behind its bell tower the sun, a scarlet ball, dipped towards the Atlantic, sending rays of gold fanning outwards in a mauve sky, turning the castle's grey granite to a rosy pink, catching the gilt on its weathercocks as they spun in the wind. It was mysterious; distant; thrilling.

'There it is,' said Ella softly. 'Our island.'

I was to hear the same words, with a different emphasis and meaning, as I made the same journey years later as a married man. Seeing Seton for the first time, however, my thoughts turned not to my future but to its past, to the centuries that had come and gone while it, impassive, had commanded the steep cliffs of its small, jagged island, unmoved by the human dramas played out within its walls. It is strange for me now to think that this place was ever new to me, that as I passed it for the first time in the shabbiness of a second-class railway carriage it held no associations, nor much promise of them. Seton is austere and cold; brilliant but aloof; it is cautious of intimacy. Yet its trust, once given, is eternal. It will guard Sarah's body with the untiring watchfulness of a mother for her young; and it will guard my body, too, when the time comes. Yes, it will guard mine too.

Ella and I sat in silence as the train sped on, watching the fairy-tale image recede into the distance.

'It's like Camelot, don't you think?' she whispered.

'Like Camelot,' I echoed.

The station at Penzance was a bustle of people and bags and lines waiting for taxis. 'Come on,' said Ella, tugging my arm. 'Let's walk. It'll only take an hour or so. And the last boat to the island doesn't leave until ten.' So we walked through and out of the town. A light drizzle began to fall. Hot and tired from travelling, we welcomed the rain and the air and the smell of the sea. We walked together, smiling, a little awkward now that we had actually arrived, as two lanes gave way to one and cars grew slower and less frequent. At last we had left the crowds and clustered buildings of the town behind, and Ella led me from the main road and on to a smaller track which led down to the beach. 'Look here,' she said, pointing.

I looked and saw the castle, rising from its cone-shaped island, a natural progression of the granite, ringed by blue sea.

'So this is the view Blanche saw,' I said.

'What do you know about Blanche?' She looked at me sharply.

'Not much. Only that she was your grandmother and that she lived here.'

'Who told you?'

'Sarah.'

'I see.' There was a pause. 'So she's got to you already.'

'I don't know what you mean.'

'No, you couldn't.'

'Tell me then.'

Another pause.

'Not now, James,' said Ella at last. And before I could speak she had moved abruptly on, first walking and then running down the steep incline, thick with binding grass, which led to the beach. 'I think we can make it to the boats from here,' she called as I stood uncertain whether to follow. 'Run!' Her command came to me over the wind. So through the rain I ran, hot from exertion, my clothes sticking to me from the combination of sweaty train hours and the damp of the drizzle. It began to rain heavily now. I ran on. And always Ella was before me, crying out, a long unbroken shout of something lost between joy and rage; a sound I could not explain or understand but which held me in its thrall, even as the sand spilled into my shoes and the rainwater ran down my neck. Running behind her, always nearing, always eluded; it is how I have spent my life. Talking of it now I can taste the salt in the air and feel the pounding of my blood.

We were taken to the island by a bearded fisherman obviously surprised by our lack of luggage. 'This is the larst boat, sir,' he said, 'if you's thinkin' of comin' back tonight.'

'We weren't,' Ella replied for me.

'Very well, miss.'

And in a rickety boat that smelled of mackerel we made the short crossing to the island's harbour as the last of the sun dipped below the horizon. I was half surprised to find a village beneath the castle walls, for in my mind I had already cast Seton as a self-sufficient entity, removed from our world; but I was glad of a beer and a plate of steaming cod, drowned in batter, in the 'sweet pub' of which Ella had told me. It also took guests, and she reserved two rooms before we sat down to dinner, giving her surname as Warrington.

'My mother's name,' she said quietly as she passed the register. 'Only a fool would sign Harcourt on this island; he wouldn't have a moment's sleep for all the attention he'd receive.'

I nodded, understood, and signed my own name.

When we were sitting at a table in the cosy bar, listening to the rain beat steadily on the window-panes, she smiled at me. 'So, here we are.'

'Is this what you wanted to show me?' I asked, feeling the weight of family history even in the worn leather of the pub which bore the Harcourt arms on its sign.

'It is, partly,' said Ella. 'I wanted to show you the island and the castle. But there's something much more specific that I want you to see.' Our fish arrived. She paused. 'But it must wait until tomorrow. Everything's closed to tourists until tomorrow morning.'

'But,' I began, a little surprised, 'I thought this was your castle? Surely you're not a tourist in your own family's home?'

'No,' she replied, smiling at my innocence. 'Of course I *could* take you to lunch with Uncle Cyril and Aunt Elizabeth if I liked. I don't imagine they'd be delighted to see me, particularly, though they wouldn't show that. But I can't, of course, for obvious reasons.'

'Amongst which are?'

'Well for starters, you blind boy, the fact that you aren't Charlie Stanhope. It would never do for them to see me here with anyone but him.'

'At least not until you've extricated yourself?'

'At least not until I have, as you say, extricated myself.'

'I see.'

'But there's another reason too.'

'Which is?'

'I'd much rather show you it in private. The painting, I mean. That's what I've brought you here to see. It might make things clearer; at least I hope it will. One should never underestimate the importance of visual aids.' She smiled. 'And privacy is important. Not that I mind day-trippers; they won't affect us. It's family presence I want to avoid if I can. I want the anonymity of the tourist. And you've been seeing quite enough of my relations as it is.'

Something about the brittle laugh that followed this made me know of whom she was speaking. 'I've only spoken to Sarah properly once,' I said. 'I mistook her for you, in fact.'

'At my own engagement party?' Ella raised an eyebrow.

'No. Before that. In the park, as it happens.'

The eyebrow came to rest again; Ella looked at me steadily. 'Well you must have got very chummy,' she said finally. 'She seems to have told you all the family history you need to know.'

'She told me about your grandmother,' I said. 'I'm sorry.'

Ella paused. 'I never knew her,' she said finally, discarding my sympathy.

'I really wanted Sarah to tell me about you,' I said.

'I bet she was happy to advise in that respect. Did she tell you I was a vulgar little upstart? Or was I just crass?'

'She said that you two didn't see much of each other,' I replied, evasively.

Ella sensed my evasion. 'I'm sure she said much more, which your fine manners couldn't possibly permit you to repeat. I understand, James. I can fill in most of the gaps for myself anyhow.' There was a silence. I felt Ella's eyes on me and busied myself with my cod. Across the table she lit a cigarette, with a murmured, 'You don't mind, do you?'

I shook my head.

'Thanks.'

More silence.

'I wish you'd look at me,' she remarked. I looked up. There was a moment of hesitation on her part, as though things hung in the balance; perhaps, even then, they did. Then she said, in a quiet, low voice, 'Do you know anything about jealousy, James? About what it does to people?'

I shook my head. Feeling as I did so that I was not so naïve, I said, 'Yes. I understand jealousy.'

'Ah, but have you ever felt it?'

'Yes,' I said.

'But only briefly, spasmodically,' Ella went on, speaking quickly. 'Sure, you can think of times when you've wanted someone's car, or someone's money, or something of that sort.'

I nodded.

'But that feeling hasn't lasted long, has it? It hasn't built up into something consuming; it hasn't spread. Has it?'

'No,' I said, truthfully.

'Well, the jealousy you're talking about is only a distant relation of the kind I'm concerned with. You don't mind my boring you with this?' I shook my head. 'The kind I mean is an illness, a disease. It eats away, spreading into everything a person does, into everything a person thinks.' She exhaled, blowing her smoke to the ceiling. 'The jealousy that you experience, and I hope you won't take offence at this, is of the common or garden variety by comparison. Like the common cold it affects everyone at some point, and though it may even affect them badly it seldom leads on to anything more serious. It's not a virulent strain of disease; one shakes it off easily. There may not be a cure for it, but its symptoms can be alleviated, suppressed. Do you follow me?'

I nodded. 'Another of your metaphors.'

'Another of my metaphors,' she said, and laughed. Her laugh did not last long. Her face set again and she looked at me intently. 'The jealousy which I am trying to describe is extreme,' she continued, almost urgent now. 'It is dangerous in a way in which your jealousy is not dangerous. It's out of control, in some ways like a disease. What cures there are for it must be administered in its early stages or all is lost. If allowed to fester, it spreads.'

'Why are you telling me this?'

'So that you will understand what I tell you tomorrow,' she said quietly.

'Tell me whatever it is now,' I said, suddenly decisive, gripping her hand as she rose to leave the table. 'I can't wait another night.'

She looked at me, her eyes narrowing. 'Don't be imperious, James. It doesn't altogether suit you.'

'I don't care.' I was suddenly exasperated. 'You have brought me on a six-hour journey to an island I never knew existed. You have talked to me of oceans and families and . . . and mysterious paintings which might make things "clearer". I don't want paintings. I don't want metaphors. I don't even thrive much on mystery. Just tell me why you've brought me here.'

'Let go of me.'

'I won't.'

'You're making a scene.'

'I don't care.'

I looked up at her in steady earnest and met the command in her pursed lips and blazing eyes unflinchingly. Slowly she sat down again.

'I brought you here because I thought you would help me,' she said after a moment, almost grudgingly.

'And so I will,' I replied, relaxing my grip on her hand. 'But you can't keep me in the dark like this.'

'I haven't.'

'You have. Oh I get odd snippets here and there, I admit. You talk to me about the pressure of convention and the tide of public opinion. You talk to me about your family and a world that I don't understand. And then you talk about jealousy, about your particular kind of jealousy.'

'It's not mine,' she hissed.

'Then whose is it?'

'It's not mine alone, at least. It's . . . Well, if you must know it's mine and Sarah's.'

'*Sarah's?*'

'I know you don't believe me. That's why you must wait until tomorrow. You don't believe because you don't understand. You *can't* understand. I have told you as much as I can . . .'

'About what? About why you got engaged to Charles?'

'About much more than that. But yes, about that too.'

'Then why won't you tell me the rest now?'

'Because you won't believe me. And you might not respect me if you did.' She pulled her hand away from mine. 'I wish that a metaphor about currents and tides explained the mess I've made of things with Charles,' she began. 'And it *does* a bit, you know. It does. But only a bit.' She smiled, calmer now. I listened. 'Of course my family are delighted that I'm marrying. Of *course* they'd be horrified if I married anyone who wasn't as "suitable" as Charlie. That's all true. But there's more to it than that. And I've got myself deep into something I can't quite explain but which frightens me much more than marrying

73

Charlie could possibly frighten me. Something in my past – a habit, a way of behaviour if you like – is out of control. Oh it's not drugs,' she added quickly, seeing the look of comprehension on my face. 'But I am like an addict. I've lost the ability to stop. The fact that I might have married Charlie has made me see that. It – this thing – is taking me over. I can see that because it has made me do something concrete which I despise myself for having done. Have you any idea what it's like to despise yourself? Not only for what you've already done but for what you see you might do. I've been taken there; I've been shown that blackness. But I can't see where it ends. And I'm frightened of it.'

'"It" being jealousy?' I was struggling to see a path through the clouds.

'Oh, no, James. Well, yes . . . But it's more complex than that. All my explanations, even my metaphors, can't do justice to it. It's alive in me, not in a physical way, but it's there nonetheless. My id. It's subtle and elusive; it's not obvious. No one would recognize it, save perhaps one other person; I have difficulty in recognizing it myself. But it frightens me, I tell you that frankly.'

'Why me?'

'What?'

'When you could have shared this with anyone in the world, why did you choose to share it with me?'

My question broke the flow of her tumble of words.

'I don't know,' she said slowly. 'I don't know, but also, in a funny kind of way, I do know. You came when you were asked for, you see. As I sat on that bench, in an empty park, feeling more alone than I had ever felt in my life, you appeared. Oh I don't mean I thought you were an angel, not in those rugby shorts at least.' She chuckled at the recollection. 'And anyway, an angel would have been no use. The help I need is of the most human kind.' She smiled shyly. 'I almost told you everything then. I would have done if you'd only asked. But you didn't; and then something made me hesitate. I knew that before I could explain it to anybody I had to be able to

74

explain it to myself. I knew also that it was no good explaining it to just anyone. So I didn't tell you.' She paused. 'I need another cigarette,' she said, and lit one.

I watched her draw on it, thinking of the cigarette she had smoked in Hyde Park on that warm morning weeks ago. I felt that years had passed since then, that the cardboard figure of Ella which I had taken away with me and made three-dimensional in private hours of day-dream was being dismantled before my eyes. From the wreck of the romantic doll I had created I saw a woman emerge who had no notion of nineteenth-century dilemmas and dashing saviours. Yet she was frightened and alone, as my creation had been, though for reasons other than the ones which I had devised. This new woman was reaching out to me and I took her hand, not knowing where she might lead or pull.

Ella continued. 'But then you appeared again at Camilla Board-man's,' she said, 'just when I was trying to pretend that nothing was really wrong. And you made up that silly excuse about a handbag and endeared yourself instantly.' She smiled. 'Then you listened to me as I talked, and I felt that here was someone who might throw me a rope.' She paused. 'But I didn't want it,' she said at last. 'You need to admit to yourself that you're drowning before you can be rescued and I couldn't do that. It was up to you to tie the rope around my wrists by force if needs be. I couldn't come to you. And perhaps I wouldn't ever have been able to. But as things turned out, you – *you* of all people – appeared at my engagement party, and there you did tie the rope around my wrists, in a manner of speaking.' She put her hand on mine. 'Of course I could see that it terrified you to do it. You've been brought up to believe that one shouldn't speak to a woman as you spoke to me that day.'

Still I listened.

'But you made me see that you might be strong enough to help me, and I know that the hand that pulls the rope must be firm and the arms that hold it powerful. I thought that you might be strong. I wrote to you, not knowing whether you would meet me at the

75

station or not. But you did. And now you're here.' She leaned towards me. 'Thank you,' she said softly. And she kissed me.

Even from a distance of almost fifty years I can feel the touch of those soft lips; can feel the tingling that ran through me as they leaned down to touch mine. Ella's lips: long-observed; long-imagined; finally given. Our kiss: shivering; electric; long; deliberate; gentle. I can taste the cigarette smoke of it.

'Thank you,' I said in my turn.

'And now you know a little more than you did.'

'I do.'

'And the rest you shall know tomorrow.'

'If you say so.'

'I do.'

'Good-night, James.'

'Good-night, Ella.'

She got up slowly and left the bar, deserted now but for a few loyal patrons who had been locked in to continue their drinking uninterrupted. It was long past midnight.

8

The next day was cold. A chilly wind whipped the small streets of the island, sending the tourists scurrying to shelter in tea-shops with Tudor beams and low doors. The islanders themselves paid no attention to the weather, moving with ruddy cheeks through the gusts which ripped the tiles from their roofs and sent sprays of sea into gardens and boats. Above the village, aloof, stood the castle, a disdainful eye on the new army that trooped up its steep hill and paid the uniformed attendants at its gates for admission. The weapons of these invaders were not the halberd, bayonet or musket of bygone ages; they were the camera, guidebook and travelling pouch of the modern era. Their leaders did not exhort their followers fearlessly on snow-white chargers; instead they explained, in as many languages as there are countries, that there was a gift shop selling island memorabilia at attractive prices on the left past the Italian fountain. I listened to snatches of Seton's history from these guides as Ella and I walked behind them. I heard how it had been a monastery since the early twelve hundreds; how in 1536 the monks had been expelled by a vengeful Henry and his cardinal; how the great rooms had lain empty for almost a hundred years. I heard too how the seventeenth century had brought the place fitfully back to life, first as barracks, then as ammunition store and finally as prison. It was Ella who told me how the castle had then been given – by a guilty or grateful king, who is to say? – to Margaret, Countess of Seton in 1670 for 'services rendered', as her descendant put it with a wry smile.

As I listened to all this I felt the castle watching me – and the other invaders who climbed its hill – with cool, untroubled disdain. If cannon-balls and shot had failed to cripple it in the Civil War, it seemed to say, what hope had we with our flashbulbs and chewing gum? Hewn from ancient granite, its walls four feet thick in places, it had the air of grim permanence that only eight centuries' exposure to cold wind and cold sea can impart. Walking with Ella under the delicate swirls of its wrought-iron gates, a Victorian addition, I felt that no alterations, however cosy, could change the primeval nature of the place. Seton would not be moulded; it would not bend to the most persuasive of hands. One might change; add; improve; install hot water and electricity as Blanche had done; heat; furnish as one liked; but the character of the castle was immutable: cast in the very stone of its crenellations; expressed in the thick set of its towers and the defiance of its walls.

Inside we passed heavy rooms of solid furniture cordoned off by silk ropes, the American lilt of Ella's voice making me think of another young American girl, long ago, walking the corridors we walked then. Taking my hand, Ella led me through splendours of library and drawing room; past the dusty brocade and Chinese screens of the King's Bedroom; up stairs and along corridors. At length we emerged in the great hall, a high, cold, magnificent room of flagstones and mullion-panes. The hunting trophies of the Victorian gentleman lined its lengths; at its furthest extreme, set between two huge windows, was a painting, a portrait.

'There it is,' said Ella softly, nodding towards its heavy gilt frame. 'That's what I've brought you all this way to see.' She followed me as I walked towards it, her words joining the echoes of whispered French, German, English and Japanese which composed the secret code of Seton's modern invaders.

The great hall at Seton is a long rectangular room on the first floor, once the monastery refectory, and you enter it in the middle of its west side. The two walls to the north and south hold pairs of great windows that reach almost to the floor. One of these pairs gives on to a narrow balcony with a low balustrade, a quite inexplicable Victorian addition, from which a terrace, far beneath, is visible. The other is exposed to the sea, which pounds on the cliffs a hundred feet below it.

It is a large, dramatic room, not entirely without charm. A magnificent Elizabethan table, of ships' timbers salvaged from the Armada, stands in its centre. Otherwise the hall has no furniture, nothing in fact save the stags' heads on the walls and the painting of Blanche.

Ella's grandmother gazed out at the room, over the heads of the tourists who photographed her picture, towards the windows on the opposite wall and the sea that crashed below them. Her portrait hangs, whether as memorial or cruel joke I do not know, between the windows that give on to the balcony. It is from this balcony that she threw herself, and her death (though not its means) are commemorated by a bronze, Latin plaque set in the flagstones below. The castle guides translate it by rote.

I remember seeing Blanche's picture for the first time; I remember looking up at the features of Ella and Sarah, neither one yet both, distilled in a face of extraordinary charm; I remember the brush strokes of her blonde hair, luxuriant and long, piled high above her face with its small nose and high cheekbones. She is wearing a pale blue dress, and one small hand is visible clasping a closed book. She stares out at the sea, a wistful look in her eyes. Perhaps she is thinking of home.

'Do you see what I'm talking about now?' Ella asked quietly.

I felt the beginnings of understanding stir within me, but they were nebulous and incomplete. I looked at the woman by my side, the living, breathing woman whose hand held mine; and I looked at her again, this time immobile, a thing of canvas and oils in a heavy frame. I started to speak then stopped. 'Explain to me,' I said finally. And quietly Ella led me out of the room and into the long gallery that houses the Seton china. I saw that several corridors opened off it, and that the opening of each was protected by a red silk rope. A guard sat sleepily on a high-backed chair at the far end of the corridor. Looking at him sharply to make sure that he did not see, Ella stepped over the first of the ropes and motioned for me to follow.

'Quickly,' she hissed. And quickly, almost running, I followed her down the corridor, through a door and up the spiral staircase behind it. Up and up we climbed, the darkness relieved on each complete revolution by a small arrow slit of window, through which we could see the blue sea, further and further away as we circled upwards. We passed first one then two doors set into the stone. Outside the third we stopped. 'I'm just hoping this is open,' said Ella as she tried its wrought-iron handle. 'Come on James, push.' So I pushed, and forced the unlocked door open on rusty hinges. We were in a small, oddly-shaped sitting room tucked between the staircase and the tower wall. It was obviously unused; dust-sheets covered the furniture and I saw, as Ella removed one of them, that there was a large doll's house in one corner. 'Kinda spooky, don't you think?' she whispered delightedly as she removed another sheet to reveal a moth-eaten sofa.

'Very,' I said.

'It was my favourite room as a child. My father used to bring me to stay here sometimes, you know. And I colonized this room for myself. There're so many here it was never missed.' She smiled wistfully at the doll's house. 'My mother gave me that,' she said. Then quickly, before I could say anything, she went on, 'You know you're the only person, besides my father, whom I've ever shown this room to? At least while it's been mine.'

'Thank you,' I said quietly. 'It's lovely.'

'Isn't it?' Ella looked slowly about her. 'But I wonder why they've left it just as I did.'

'I don't suppose they need the space. Why should they bother to clear it?'

'You're probably right. Why bother? There're enough rooms to dust as it is.'

'I'm sure.'

'Something like three hundred, as a matter of fact.'

'No.' But I could well believe it.

'It's true.' Settling herself on a window-ledge she motioned me towards the dusty sofa.

'What did you think of that painting?' she began, more serious now.

'Artistically or . . .' I hesitated. 'Or in the context of what you were saying last night?'

'Both,' she replied.

'Well I thought it was beautiful, as a painting.'

'It's by Sargent, you know.'

I nodded. 'Sarah told me about it.'

'*She* told you? What on earth did *she* tell you for?' Ella's eyes were bright with instant fury.

'No idea. She didn't tell me much, anyway.'

'What did she say?'

'Nothing really. Not much more than that Sargent had painted your grandmother.'

'It was a wedding present from my grandfather.'

'I see. I presume, though, that you didn't bring me to see it for its artistic merit alone.'

'No I didn't.'

'Well then . . .'

Ella got up and walked over to another of the low windows by which the room was lit. Sitting on its ledge, her knees pulled up under her chin, she began to speak. I can see her there, framed by the blue of the sea far below her; I can hear her carefully chosen words; I can feel the tension between us, a tension of confidence dared and understanding attempted. I remember the intimacy of that cold afternoon, the way it became almost tangible in that small, strange, awkwardly shaped room. It both tempted and scared me; for much as I wanted it to grow, I felt its power even then.

'I talked to you last night about an id, about my id,' began Ella.

I nodded.

'Well I've been trying to answer for myself the question of how it began, of what it grew from. Do you understand?'

I nodded again.

'And I think that the answer is in that picture.'

'In what way?'

'In lots of ways.' She paused, thinking. 'That picture is about family,' she said at last, 'about my family. It's about unhappiness and brilliance and madness and . . . a million things.' In a few words she told me the story of Blanche's life and death which I had already heard from Sarah. 'When I was six and Sarah was seven,' Ella continued, 'my mother and both Sarah's parents died together in a car crash.'

'How awful. I'm sorry.' Even as I spoke, the words seemed inadequate.

'It was awful.' Ella looked at me; for a long moment neither of us moved.

'And how terrible for Sarah, too,' I said at last. 'Losing both her parents when she was . . . how old did you say?'

'Seven.'

I paused, a faint realization crystallizing slowly in my mind. 'This is to do with Sarah, isn't it?' I hazarded, feeling that I was approaching some sort of truth.

'Yes, James. My life to date has been to do with Sarah.'

'Go on.'

'I suppose I shouldn't jump around like this. First I told you about my grandmother; now I'm telling you about me and Sarah. It might help if I told you about the generation that went between us.'

'All right.'

'Well, Blanche had four children: Cyril, the eldest, who now lives here with his wife; Alexander, my father; Anna, my father's twin; and Cynthia, Sarah's mother. Cyril was ten years old when his mother died; my father and Anna were eight; Cynthia was six. You can imagine what it must have been like for them.' She looked out to sea. 'They each reacted in their different ways, but it scarred them all. Cyril took refuge in eccentricity; my father stopped talking much about how he really felt; so did Cynthia. Anna, on the other hand, was like Blanche: brilliant, very brilliant, but not stable. She became obsessed by her mother's death.' Ella took a cigarette from a packet in her pocket and lit it. 'She devoted her life to being as much like her mother as she could be,' she said, exhaling. 'From the age of eight onwards she was devoted to Blanche's memory, but not in a healthy way; not in a normal way. She wore her mother's dresses; she did her hair in the same way as her mother had done hers; and she hated her father as much as it is possible for one person to hate another.' She paused. 'There's quite a history of insanity in our family, you see,' she said slowly, drawing deeply on her cigarette. 'This house has plenty of dark secrets.'

I sat quietly, waiting for her to continue.

'Anna killed herself eventually, you know. Not here. At Oxford. She also jumped out of a window. Just like her mother. They buried her at Seton, of course, and the car crash in which my mother and Sarah's parents were killed happened as they were driving back from her funeral.'

'Oh my God.'

'So, you see, my father lost his twin and his wife within a week of each other. That was why he took me away to America. I'm afraid I was a bit flippant about it all on the train. I wasn't sure I was going to tell you everything then. Now I see it's all spilling out.' She looked at me and I smiled. 'Anyway, he hates this place. I think he feels Seton is somehow to blame for what happened to his family. Or perhaps it's just too full of memories. I don't know. What I do know is that he's terrified of me turning out like Anna or his mother. That's why he took me to America; first to California and then, when he met Pamela, to Boston. You couldn't get further from Seton than San Francisco, I assure you. He tried to forget he ever knew this place. And although he had to visit it every so often, he kept his visits to a minimum.'

'I can understand that,' I said.

'Can you? I'm glad. Because it's now that my own story starts.' She took a long drag on her cigarette. 'You can see the tremendous influence Blanche had over her whole family, particularly in death. Though no one said it – the Harcourts don't talk, you know – everyone thought about insanity and mental illness. They brooded on violent death. So many of them had died so horribly, you see: their mother; two sisters; my mother; Sarah's father. And Sarah and

I, the only children in the family, could feel that pressure as we grew up: we knew that people worried about us, that they feared for us. And we knew why, too; we knew that our grandmother and our aunt had both killed themselves. It's not a knowledge that's easy to deal with when you're young.' She paused, considering something. 'Of course it might have brought us together, I suppose, if we had seen more of each other at that crucial time. And if we hadn't both grown up looking so like our grandmother. As it was, the way we looked was a constant reminder of how we might turn out. And Sarah felt it even more than I; she saw that picture downstairs every day of her life.'

'You mean she *lived* here?'

'Yes. Uncle Cyril and Aunt Elizabeth took her in after her parents died. They didn't have children of their own, you see.'

'And Sarah grew up here . . .'

'Yes.'

'Poor girl.'

'Yes.'

'And I grew up in America, away from all this. But I knew of it, of course. I came to Seton to visit, I saw that painting, I watched myself turn into its image.'

'And?'

'And I watched Sarah, too. She watched me.'

'And you saw the same person.'

'Precisely.'

'I think I'm beginning to see.'

'We felt like two halves of one whole, so to speak, but it didn't make for closeness. We weren't like twins. We each needed, I think, to conquer the other before we could feel like a complete person. Do you understand that? The feeling that, far away, another possible version of you is living; thinking; growing. If we'd never seen much of each other it might have been all right. But when I was eighteen Daddy married Pamela, who couldn't resist the temptations of London for long, especially with a name like Harcourt to open doors for her. So we came back.'

'And you and Sarah were thrown together again. The two halves were reunited.'

'That was how it felt, sometimes. And such different halves we were.'

'Well, you had had such different lives.'

'Of course. She had lived here, on this island, steeped in tradition, in the cult of our family.'

'I see.'

'No you don't. You've no idea how the Harcourts are treated here. It's positively feudal, a little kingdom cut off from the world. A society of obligation and duty and ritual and ... all the things that I was free from in America. Away from it I could be myself. Growing up within it, Sarah could only be one person: the future chatelaine, the keeper-in-waiting of the castle. And that's who she became.'

I nodded. Ella lit another cigarette.

'The tragedy, though,' she went on, 'is that Sarah never will have Seton. When Cyril dies, if he has no children, which seems increasingly likely, it will be my father's. And then it will be mine. It was given to a woman, you see; an Act of Parliament was passed to make sure that it could be inherited by one too. Oh there are plenty of provisions, of course: no Catholic can inherit; no divorcée; no convicted criminal. That last clause was added by the Victorians, I think. Typical. But since I am neither Catholic nor divorced nor a felon, in the course of time it will all be mine.'

'Which explains Sarah's ...'

'Hatred. Hatred of me,' Ella finished.

'I see.'

'And it's worse because she loves this place, she understands it in a way I never could or will. I'll never be anything more than a tourist here. With my accent and my ideas, how could I ever be anything else?'

'So far I follow you.' I was quiet for a moment, trying to straighten things in my mind. 'But what did you mean yesterday when you talked about a pattern of behaviour you couldn't change? You likened it to an addiction, didn't you?'

She nodded.

'Who were you talking about?' I went on. 'What did you mean?'

'I was talking about me and Sarah, James. You've no idea of the extent to which each of our lives is dictated by the other. No idea. I know that Seton will be mine one day. And I know that I'm not worthy of it. Have you any idea what that feels like?' Seeing me about to reply, she went on quickly, opening the window behind her and letting in a gust of sharp, cold air. 'You couldn't and I'm glad you couldn't. My family has lived here for more than three hundred years. Have you any idea how long that is, how weighty such a history must be? Can you imagine how much responsibility it carries with it?'

I shook my head.

'And to know that you're not equal to it, but that someone else is, that you haven't had the training required but that someone else has. I sometimes think it would be much better for us both if Sarah and I just swapped places. If only I could get rid of my accent and she could acquire it, she could have my name and I hers. Then I could think as I liked, do what I pleased with my life, have the freedom I so badly want and which Sarah's got. And Sarah could fulfil her destiny.' She ran a distracted hand through her hair. 'But the roles are switched, you see. Fate has tricked us. She can never have what I have. And I'm left striving to acquire what she has: that rigid poise; that self-control; that certainty of the world and her place in it. It's so alien to my nature but I want it so badly. I want to prove to her that I deserve her blessed Seton, that I will take care of it. I want to acquit myself honourably, for heaven's sake.'

She paused.

'Can't you understand that?'

'I do understand it, Ella,' I said. 'I understand it completely.'

'Then tell me why I might have married Charlie,' she said sharply, quickly. And I understood the importance of the test.

'You got engaged to Charles,' I said slowly, thinking carefully, choosing my words with caution, 'because he is precisely the sort of man Sarah might have married. Eton, Oxford, just charming enough without being too clever. He would have been the perfect partner for the Countess of Seton. I presume you get the title with the house?'

She nodded.

'But in the end you won't marry Charles. Ultimately your sense of self is too strong.'

'I hope so, James.'

I got up from my sofa and crossed the room to kiss her.

She held up a hand to stop me. 'No. You should know one more thing first.'

'What's that?' I asked, standing over her.

'Charlie Stanhope was not just the kind of person Sarah *might* have married. She would have married him, had I not . . .' Her voice tailed off.

I drew away. 'Had you not . . .'

'Sarah was in love with him, James. Completely in love with him, in that passionate way people who are usually cold fall in love if they ever do. I took Charlie away from Sarah. Partly, I admit, for what he represented; but that was a temptation I could have resisted.' She paused. 'The shameful thing,' she went on slowly, 'the thing that's made me see how out of control all this has really become, is that I took Charlie from Sarah only because she wanted him so badly. Coldly, quite calculatedly, I set about taking him from her; and I got him.' She looked at me. 'Do you see how frightening this thing is? I would have done anything, sacrificed anything – my future, Charlie's future – just to hurt Sarah, just to show her that all her training, all her perfect breeding, counts for nothing.' Ella was crying now. 'I can't believe what I've done.'

It was not a time for words. Not yet. I went over to the cold ledge on which she sat and put my arms around her shaking shoulders. 'Come on,' I said softly. 'It's not too late. At least you understand it, at least you know it was wrong.'

And I thought as I said it that understanding was tantamount to letting go, to a kind of absolution. I omitted the step of confession, which can come before or after understanding but which must come at some point on the path to peace. So too did I ignore the making of amends, which alone makes forgiveness acceptable, even if it remains possible without it. I would not make the same omissions now. When we sin we pay in a multitude of ways. Sometimes acknowledgement and confession can help us towards absolution, but nothing is possible without reparation. Ella was fortunate, even if she did not choose to make use of her good fortune: she could have made her reparations and asked forgiveness from Sarah; she could have confessed; and thus she might have found peace. From a distance of fifty years I envy her that freedom.

I have no one with whom to make amends, at least not in this world. And thus there is no one to forgive me; I remain unabsolved. Sometimes God forgives people. He might forgive me if I could ask Him to; but I cannot, for I have never troubled Him before. I have never considered Him except politely, vaguely, with token prayers at Christmas and Easter and the occasional wedding. And I cannot turn to Him now that my need is greatest and I have nothing to give: no thanks for blessings; no praise for happiness; just bitterness for wasted years. I should add ingratitude to my sins. My guilt is ever with me and I must accept that fact. Eric, who alone might have forgiven me, is dead.

Sin requires confession and absolution: there is a cycle to be observed if one is ever to be cleansed of guilt. I didn't know that this was so as I held Ella on that cold window-ledge, watching the waters of the sea as my neck grew wet from her tears. I thought then that I could save her alone, that my help, my understanding, was all that she would need. I did not tell her to go to Sarah; I did not wish her to share the intimacy of confession with anyone but me. Already I was jealous of her trust. And so I held her as she cried and answered 'No' when she asked 'Do you hate me?' and murmured words of love and forgiveness and hope, only the first of which was mine to give. But they had their effect. Ella stopped crying, believing what I said, and in thus believing she made her grave mistake. She did not know, perhaps did not care to know – and I who suspected did not tell her – that the only person within whose power forgiveness lay was Sarah. I comfort myself with the thought that if she had known, she would probably still have preferred the price of a guilt largely untried as yet to the shame of apology. Ella, as I had thought before and should have known then, was a proud woman. And pride is the undoing of many.

But pride, as it turned out, was not ultimately to be Ella's undoing; it was the lack of trust in the world which comes from betraying yourself that was to be her downfall. Those who give expect much to be given to them; those who take expect much to be taken from them. And by comforting Ella I disguised the dangers of what she had done in the protective gentleness of soothing words. I did not do her a service. Far better that I should have made her – for in that brief moment she would have done anything that I suggested – return to London by the next train and confess all to Sarah and to Charles. Then there would have been a scene; tears and bitterness would have flowed. And something would have been released; the festering wounds in both cousins would have been opened. They might have been made clean again. Injury, like guilt, should not fester; like guilt it often does.

But my soothing of Ella did much to cover over her guilt and so Sarah's injury was allowed to fester undisturbed. I could not have known then that this would be so – on that point at least I am sure – but that did not alter the fact that it was. As I stroked Ella's hair and kissed the soft skin of her neck, I thought only of stopping her tears and of healing her pain. I was too young to know that tears can purify and too unsure to guide Ella rather than comfort her. My soothing made confession, and thus forgiveness – which might have purified in the giving as well as the receiving of it – at first unnecessary and then impossible. How could I have known that it might have saved us all?

9

I had not been long back from Cornwall, perhaps only a day or two, when the telephone rang and I answered it to Camilla Boardman's breathless cadences and elongated vowels. '*Daaarling*. Where have you *been?*' she cooed. It was an accepted fiction between us that after periods of non-communication it was to me that the blame for this lapse should fall. It was ten days since I had taken her to the Harcourts' lunch and ten days since, smiling and deferential, I had deposited her at her door and we had promised to call each other soon.

'I've been here, Camilla,' I lied. 'Just very busy.'

'Musicking again?' Camilla separated artistic endeavour into three broad categories: musicking; artying; and literaturing.

'Yes. Got to practise, you know. The Guildhall starts soon.'

'I *know* darling.'

'What can I do for you?'

'It's more what I can do for *you*. I've just had the most *fantastic* idea.'

'Ye-es.' I was cautious of Camilla's fantastic ideas.

'I can't *think* why it hasn't occurred to me before.'

'Ye-es.'

'There's someone you simply *must* meet. You'd enjoy each other *such* a lot.' Camilla was wholehearted and sincere – though not always completely disinterested – in her social benevolence.

'Who?' I asked, interested; her enthusiasm was infectious.

'My mother,' she said simply.

And so it was that I attended my first Boardman 'morning'.

The house in Cadogan Square appeared to have sustained little damage as a result of Camilla's birthday party: if cigarettes had been dropped or champagne cocktails spilled, the results of such disasters had been artfully concealed or removed. But the feel of expansive emptiness had gone. I sensed this the following day as I was admitted by a Portuguese maid who disappeared with a smile as soon as the door had closed behind me. Furniture and ornament had returned to hall and drawing room, both now a clutter of Victoriana; and through the bibelots, past the open doors to what had been the dancing room, I saw a group of six or seven men and women on uncomfortable chairs pulled in a semicircle around their hostess. Regina Boardman, like her name, was stately and well preserved; and she spoke with the attentive yet authoritative tones of the society patron.

'I think *salon* is such an awful word to use in England,' she was saying as I entered.

Silently I waited for her to notice me, and when she showed no sign of doing so I coughed. She turned slowly, as though careful not to unsettle her hair. 'You must be Mr Farrell,' she said warmly, and offered me her right hand to shake as she indicated a chair with her left. 'My daughter speaks very highly of your talents.'

'Thank you,' I said, as I took my place in the chattering circle.

But sparkling though the conversation of that morning was, its subject matter is not what has remained in my mind; nor can I remember the faces of the people who contributed so eloquently to it. I rack my brain for a memory of Eric and am cheated. It is rather the tableau as a whole which has remained vivid: I see Regina Boardman, fund-raiser *par excellence*, patron saint of struggling artists and other hopeless causes, holding forth to a group of her devoted supplicants. It is a scene which, properly allegorized, might have hung on one of the walls of her heavily Victorian house: 'Charity Throned in Splendour'. Yet Regina's style was not Victorian, though her taste in furniture might have been; and her approach to us, as to all her causes, was thoroughly modern. She was efficient and hard-nosed, you see, with a beady eye for opportunity. And when not dealing with the management of public appeals, she had the leisure and the inclination for private patronage.

That morning I was welcomed under the banner of her protection with a gracious smile and a cup of coffee. I accepted both gladly and joined the discussion with enthusiasm, for I recognized my side of the bargain: Regina, unlike her daughter, had a high respect for culture; and though not a thinker herself she liked to seem one. So she took care to listen to people who thought and to support those who put their thoughts into words for her benefit.

There was a more concrete system of reciprocation in operation, too, though I only learned of it as I was leaving. Regina Boardman was one of the wise who understand that generosity which is not reciprocated is stifling, and by the time we were in the hall, departing *en masse*, she had extracted a promise from each of her guests to contribute to a cause quite distinct from their own professional advancement. There was nothing stated about this arrangement; it simply existed. Regina asked and you said yes. She did not expect you to support her causes with your money but with your expertise and your time. And the cause for which she was marshalling support that morning, as we said our goodbyes, was the restoration of decaying religious buildings. Not for Regina Boardman were the jewels of St Paul's or the Abbey; such national monuments would be no test of her fund-raising prowess. She was interested, instead, in the smaller churches; in the buildings which, as they crumble, are the price a secular age must pay for its indifference to organized religion.

She was organizing a concert at St Peter's, Eaton Square. The success of her appeal depended on it and someone had failed her. 'I had three Beethoven violin sonatas all lined up,' she said to me, her face a picture of pain, 'and the soloist I had in mind has got some sort of recording deal and gone off to Berlin. Very good for him, and I'm quite thrilled, of course, but the timing of it's a nuisance nevertheless.'

It happened that the violin sonatas in question were required pieces for my Guildhall course and I had been working on them for some months. In a flash of clarity I realized that Mrs Boardman probably knew this from her daughter, and that it was not only chance or affection which had brought me to Cadogan Square. But Regina had mastered an art with which Camilla was still struggling: she had a way of presenting her own desires so that they coincided precisely with the interests of the person from whom she was extracting a favour. Inducement was her forte. And as she stood chatting with me on the steps of her house, waving to her other guests as they walked away across the square, she skirted prettily around, and then offered me directly, a sizeable inducement indeed. Michael Fullerton, a reviewer from *The Times*, would be covering the concert at St Peter's.

'He thinks he's coming to hear Donovan,' said Regina lightly. Donovan, I took it, was the protégé, recently discovered, who had promised to play and now could not. 'Michael's writing a piece on rising English talent,' my hostess went on. 'And I see no reason why *you* shouldn't be the rising talent instead of Donovan, who seems to have risen quite nicely without Michael's help.' She smiled benignly upon me. 'Of course we needn't *say* anything about the change of programme,' she added archly, 'until the last moment. You know what these critics are like.' I nodded, though I had no idea. She beamed at me encouragingly. 'If you'd like the chance to play, it's yours.'

I had one reservation. 'Are you sure you wouldn't like to hear me before you put the success of the concert into my hands?'

'Oh darling,' she said, laughing, 'what do *I* know about music? If you're good enough for the Guildhall, you're good enough for me.'

'In that case,' I said, 'I'm yours.'

'But that's *marvellous*. Thank you so much.'

'And when is it?'

'The concert?'

I nodded.

'Next Friday,' she said, breezily.

'So,' I thought, 'I am your last hope.' Aloud I said, 'I see I've not got much time to practise then?'

'But aren't the sonatas on your Guildhall list? Don't you know them already?' She looked up at me in consternation. 'It's just that the programmes and everything have already been printed and . . . Of course there'll be a card insert with your name on it, if that's what's concerning you.'

In a few words I set her mind at rest.

'I am *so* relieved. Thank you so much.'

We shook hands. As I walked down the steps on to the street she called to me. 'Excuse me, James,' her voice rang out, high and clear. We were already on first name terms, for immediate intimacy was the key to Regina's technique. 'I haven't told you who your accompanist is to be.' She smiled at me. 'How silly. His name is Eric de Vaugirard, a really delightful young man. Very French. Very artistic. He was at my "morning", in fact.' Hastily she produced a pen and paper from her voluminous handbag. 'Here is his telephone number,' she said. 'I shall give him yours, too, so that you can contact each other and rehearse over the week.'

'Thank you,' I said, pocketing the paper.

'The thanks are *all* from me,' she replied, kissing me firmly on both cheeks. And waving me down the remaining stairs, she went back into the house, closing its gleaming door briskly behind her.

10

It is cold in this room now; the fire is dying and the radiators are useless. This place resists all heating. But I shall stay here until I have the events of my life in some kind of order that I can understand. For not only must the strands of experience be unravelled and distinct; they must be twisted into place again and understood. It is a laborious process, but a rewarding one, though I am continuously distracted by the poor quality of the tools at my disposal. If you spend fifty years trying not to remember you eventually succeed; if you spend fifty years talking of little that matters you eventually forget how to do so when you want to. Words are powerful weapons and once I was quite adept in my handling of them; but that is a skill so tied up with my guilt – for it allowed me to disguise my naïveté with such success – that I have consciously allowed it to fall into a state of disuse. It has been a struggle to learn how not to remember, how not to think, how not to speak of important things; but it is a challenge to which I have risen with success. With so much success, in fact, that now, when I try to remember, when I try to think and to express those thoughts, my faculties fail me. The frustrating thing about recollection, even once its wheels have been coaxed into motion as the wheels of mine have been, is its sketchiness. About some things, some of them inconsequential, my memory is complete. About others there is hardly anything at all.

Ella was burned into my mind; remembering her has not been difficult. And Sarah lived with me for almost fifty years; I could not forget her. It is Eric who has fallen away. My guilt – my sin – obscures him. It is to him that I would make amends, if only I could. But he is dead; and I hardly remember what he looked like. That is an ugly thought.

I know that I must have met him at some time in the week which followed my attendance at that first Boardman 'morning'. He was, after all, to be my accompanist for the concert at St Peter's. And I know also that as I walked down Sloane Street on that blazing August day, whistling, I had his telephone number on a piece of paper in my pocket. I suppose I must have telephoned him and that our rehearsals together must have gone well, for the concert itself was a success; and as the first quasi-professional performance of my career it will always have a special place in my affections.

I have played at many concerts since, in concert halls far grander than the dank church I played in that night and to audiences far more receptive than the one that gathered to hear me then. But viewed from a distance of fifty years, and at the end of a career which has seen a certain amount of success, I find myself thinking of that evening with nostalgia, for the chill of nerves and the thrill of applause grow more commonplace as the years pass. I see the dark columns of the church; I feel its cool, damp air; I hear the expectant hush as I take my place by the piano on an improvised stage in the nave. And now, looking over to him as I signal that I am ready to begin, I see Eric. In this memory, though I do not know him well – perhaps because I do not know him well – I see him unobscured. He is a dignified figure in evening tails and white tie, his unruly hair tamed for the occasion. Oh yes I see him now, and in seeing I remember. Eric was tall, not so tall as I but tall. He was more thickly built than I, with a strong neck. His skin was almost olive – there was a touch of the Spaniard in him – and his eyes were dark. They and his hands distinguished him from the line of gentleman farmers who had tilled the Vaugirard lands for centuries. Large and dark, almost black, his eyes danced; they flashed; they were joyful.

I remember the applause that night. I remember Ella's face, glowing with pleasure, in the front row beside her father and stepmother. I remember bowing and motioning to Eric to bow also and I remember

. . . But what is the use of all this memory? Remembering that concert will not help my understanding of the events I wish to explain. My career is not a mystery to me. I talk not to chronicle my life but to come to terms with what I have done; I wish to face my crime and to try, if not to explain, at least to understand. But search though I might I can find no sign in the happy pride of that evening, no glimpse of an Oracle who might have whispered silently and told me that in three months – was it four? – Eric would be dead.

No, I find no sign. And as I look for one my mind fills instead with the memory of that first interview with Michael Fullerton. It is his face – so meaningless to me now – which returns to me, not Eric's; it is his bulging belly I see; his whisky-reeking breath I smell.

Regina Boardman was detailed and frank in her instructions. 'Michael Fullerton,' she told me the day before the concert, 'is an old queen. An absolute *dear*,' she hastened to assure me (for Regina Boardman had *nothing*, absolutely *nothing* against homosexuals, as such), 'but let's just say that he doesn't bat for our team. So the fact that you're a good-looking young man isn't going to do your chances of getting written about *any* harm. Make sure you look dashing, and don't mind if he flirts with you. A little judicious smiling – it's all that's required, on top of an *inspired* performance, of course – and you never *know* what he might do for you. He's an influential man, knows lots of people. Lots of the *right* people. He's certainly someone to get on your side. So do *try*. Make sure you do.'

I did. When Michael told me that I really should be photographed for a feature he was writing, I smiled; when he praised my control of my instrument ('very masculine, Mr Farrell, but so sensual; quite erotic') I smiled; when he asked me to tea at the Ritz the following day to talk further, I smiled also and accepted. When he had gone, I told Regina verbatim what he had said.

'But James that's *marvellous*,' she cried. 'You know that means a real interview, not one of these "quick chats" he has with everyone after the concerts he goes to. He's obviously taken a shine to you, my boy. You won't need *my* help any longer. Once Michael Fullerton thinks you're good, things start happening of their own accord. He told me,' she added confidentially, 'that he wasn't a *bit* upset I didn't tell him about the change in soloist. He told me you had raw talent. Those were his precise words.'

And so Regina Boardman went home delighted and I, delighted myself, was free to keep the clandestine appointment in Eaton Square gardens that Ella and I had made the afternoon before. I have no recollection of saying goodbye to Eric or of thanking him, though I must have done both before I left the church. He is as yet a shadowy figure, but as I watch him in memories retained without thought of him I remember more. As others have done with photographs, so have I with memories: I have censored them. But one cannot destroy recollections as one can photographs; one can only bury them in the dust of a lifetime's mental trivia. The details of my friendship with Eric and its conclusion are dusty, for I buried them well; but they grow clearer now; their outlines are filling.

I have no difficulty in remembering my tea with Michael Fullerton, however; or how on expenses I drank tea and ate strawberries and talked to him of music and passion and the uncertainties of youth. A photographer from *The Times* appeared and took photographs of me, windswept in the breeze, in Green Park. That was that. It was not until a week later that any results appeared, and it was not I who saw them first but Camilla Boardman, who came in person to show them to me and who arrived on my doorstep, waving a sheet of newspaper, at half-past nine one warm morning.

'Hello *darling*! You *splendid* boy.'

A little groggy from sleep, for it was I who had opened the door, I looked at her in confusion.

'Morning, Camilla,' I said, wondering what she was doing on my doorstep; then I saw the newspaper in her hand. 'Give me that.' I was awake at once.

'Uh, uh, *uh*. What's the magic word?'

'Don't be coy. Give it to me.' Morning irritability mixed with excitement made me impatient of Camilla's social games.

'I shan't show you at *all* if you insist on being so rude. I think the *least* you could do is ask me in and offer me a cup of tea. I've come half-way across *London* to show you this article.' This was not strictly true, but details of geography had never troubled Camilla. 'Oh all right, then,' she said, giving in with a pout, as I remained impassive in the doorway. She handed me the newspaper. And on seeing the look of pleasure on my face she hugged me, with a sincerity which reminded me why I liked her, and told me that I was *fantastic.*

I certainly felt so. Michael Fullerton's feature on me, entitled 'One to Watch', offered an end to the war with my parents over my future; and the victory was mine. Our struggle had lasted almost two years and had grown bloody in the two months since I had left Oxford. I had explained, cajoled and finally insulted. They had told me, calmly at first and then frostily, that I was an impulsive boy who did not know his own mind. I ran into the breakfast room with Camilla behind me and showed them the article, whooping with schoolboy joy. I have it still today; I have kept it all these years. But there is no need to read it: a few phrases, plucked from memory, will suffice to show that once, at least, I was promising and carefree. 'This passionate young man,' Michael Fullerton had written, 'seems set to take London and the world by storm. At times controlled, at times abandoned, frequently inspired, his playing belies his years.' My mother, to her credit, cried. My father shook my hand. The war was over.

But it was Ella whom I most wanted to see, Ella by whom I most wished to be praised. I was like a dog with a pheasant. So I telephoned the house in Chester Square and asked her to meet me on the steps of the National Gallery in half an hour.

'You've got it, haven't you? He wrote it, didn't he?'

I was silent.

'I'm off to buy *The Times* right this minute. Oh God this is wonderful. What's he said? What's the photograph like?'

But I was enigmatic to the last. 'Meet me in half an hour,' I said again.

'Okay sweetheart. In half an hour.'

Hearing Ella call me sweetheart made up for all my anxieties over our future. She still was not free. We had returned from Cornwall, locked in discussion for six hours on the train, and parted, as decided, with the restrained politeness of virtual strangers. It would not do for us to be seen or for our hands to be forced.

'It's better like this,' she had said. 'I have to ease myself out of this slowly. There are a lot of people I've got to consider before myself. Charlie, Sarah, my parents, my family. No one must see us. No one must suspect about you and me.'

And I had agreed with her.

I number the few weeks of illicit meetings that followed as amongst the happiest of my life. Ella and I snatched our kisses in art galleries; we shared our souls on park benches; we touched in the furtive dark of cinemas. We were living in the calm before the storm; and the difficulty of our meetings only added to their pleasure. There was intrigue, beauty, passion; the stuff of novels. In real life such romance happens rarely; and when it does it is fleeting. That is its nature. For Ella and me, as for all who experience the first rush of illicit love, the enchantment was in the present. It had no future in its first, unaltered state; but it bound us nevertheless with a force that has lasted to this day, despite all that has happened. Oh yes, it has bound us. I might talk of guilt; I might be bowed by sin; but I shall go to my grave with the memory of those few, thoughtless weeks, when we cared for no one but each other and happiness made us selfish. If it was wrong, then it is negligible by comparison with the wrongs that followed it. If it was sinful, then it is a guilt that I can bear. In those weeks I came truly to life, as I had never done before and would not do again. I was not a fish in a school; or if I was, then Ella and I had made a school for ourselves alone, and we swam the ocean together.

It was a time of manifold consummations, for love was a varied catalyst; and it came particularly to be the time of my music's real flourishing. I remember now the hours Ella would spend on the floor of my cramped attic, listening to me play. I remember now how she would sit always in the same position, half curled, half upright, on a cushion in the corner where the eaves came almost to the floor: a delicate crumple of limbs, one hand occasionally brushing the fine golden hair from her eyes. I remember now how she would sit completely still, believing that I played best when hardly conscious of her presence. And although the reverse was true, her quiet exhilaration – all the more felt for her stillness – first calmed me and then dared me beyond the technical shallows in which I might otherwise have lingered. Ella would sit, hardly moving, for two or three hours at a time; she would follow me through my scales and exercises; through the seemingly endless repetition of certain phrases; and then she would open the grimy windows and fill the room with the fresh breeze of summer, smiling and laughing and telling me that I was wonderful, that I made her happy in ways I could not dream. We would drink tea together, perhaps, or wine, as the sinking sun filled the room with dusty warmth; and then she would smoke a cigarette, resume her former position in the corner and listen to me, eyes closed, as I played to her: pieces I had grown up with; the Beethoven sonatas I was preparing for the Guildhall; snatches of the violin lines from orchestral works that she loved.

Her tastes were diverse but she had her favourites, and I spent many hours playing them to her, watching the glow of her cheeks as she leaned her head, unseeing, on one bare, folded knee. Bach's fourth sonata for harpsichord and violin was frequently called for, I remember; so too was the waltz from Act I of *Swan Lake*. And it was at Ella's suggestion, and under her encouragement, that I began to learn the Mendelssohn E Minor, though I had no way of knowing then that it would ultimately prove to be the making of my career. Ella heard me with a delight that taught me the joys of performance. She transformed my natural shyness into a certain delicacy of presence; she taught me to rise to the challenges of my chosen art; and she helped me to rejoice in the power it gave me to move others.

Relationships grow: their pleasures change and their struggles progress. That first rush of joy, as pure as anything human can be, is never repeated: it develops; it grows; it becomes, I suppose, more real. But in doing so it loses some of its power to intoxicate, for magic must fade in the grim reality of a world beyond the control of lovers. Throughout those balmy weeks Ella and I were intoxicated, I see that now; and for many reasons our intoxication did not fade of its own accord, for it had no time to do so before we were overtaken by its consequences. We could not lay foundations; our love could not develop as other loves have developed; it could not grow as other loves have grown. The joys of a later, more stable age were stifled before they could begin.

Ella blew open my notions about life, my preconceptions about how one might live; and I did the same to hers. Together we detonated all history and watched, exhilarated, as worlds of experience and possibility opened in its place and expanded with the frantic energy of romantic fusion. Our nights together – snatched, secretive and few – were eternities. Our days we filled with debate and exploration and music and laughter and . . . But why do I try to relive them?

The shadows were lengthening over us even then; for even as we revelled in the power our union gave us we lost control of its force. Love, though not everything, is many things; its weapons are varied and more powerful than we realize. Ella and I, in love for the first time, were unprepared for the energy of that first intoxicating rush. We were children. We behaved with the abandon of children. But our weapons were adult; they were not toys. We smashed our world with the arrogance of gods: tradition; responsibility; social constriction; all crumbled under the vehemence of our attack. We thought to recreate society in our own image. And in so doing we forgot our place in it and in the heavenly order. Human beings are not gods; they should not play with divine fire. Ella and I committed the sin which the Greeks have taught us is fatal. In our hubris we forgot ourselves. We forgot too that demolition requires rebuilding; that people's hearts are fragile; that to touch them with anything but love returned is evil.

11

My concert at St Peter's was not the last I played under the auspices of one of Regina Boardman's charities; nor was it the only occasion on which Eric accompanied me. That much I know from factual recollection. If it comes to that, I know, too, that we were both regular in our attendance at Regina's 'mornings'. But this I know from what he told me later; I have no memory of him as distinct from the other guests who sat in the library at Cadogan Square and talked with such competitive erudition. I struggle to think now of anything Eric said; any point on which we disagreed; any joke we shared. Nothing returns to me. But we must have been on terms of easy familiarity for I was not surprised to receive his invitation to tea. We had played in two more concerts together since the night of our success at St Peter's, and we had had another good review in Michael Fullerton's column in *The Times*. I remember reading the slip of blue notepaper from Eric as I sat at home one morning, waiting for Ella; and I remember being vaguely pleased to receive it. Certainly it was no cause for surprise, nor even for particular interest.

That fact and my memory of the afternoon I spent with him a few days later prove, I think, how much of my early friendship with Eric I have forgotten. In recollection, he remains a virtual stranger right up to the day of his great Idea; in actual fact, of course, he was by that stage a friend, and someone who thought of me as a good friend. I wish I could unearth the details of our first few conversations, of the gradual stages by which we approached intimacy; but the dust of years, conscientiously heaped upon all thoughts of him, has obscured them from view. They are irretrievable, a fact that frustrates me. Perhaps in them I might find some sign, some clue which might explain what happened later.

But I do see the tiny flat he lived in now, with its grimy view of Battersea power station. I see its narrow hall and poky kitchen; its cramped sitting room and broom-cupboard bathroom. His bedroom I cannot picture, for I probably never saw it, but the rest comes back with increasing clarity. Eric had a theory about houses. He argued, and not always flippantly, that like children they should be taught to overcome their limitations. The limitation of his flat was its size: in any given room it was quite possible for two adults, stretching, to touch the tips of each other's fingers with one hand and a pair of opposing walls with the other. Eric rose above this restriction by ignoring it, and his rooms were filled to their seams with oversized furniture.

'Treat a house as though it will grow,' he said, 'and one day it might.'

Thus the small, rather dark flat in which the budget of a starting-out musician forced him to live was furnished with the opulence of a palace, its treasures looted, I gathered, from disreputable auction houses and estate sales. And although one might not be able to walk with much ease between the Chesterfield and a large potted palm that stood by it, it was impossible to deny that the effect produced by both was anything but impressive. Only Eric's piano stood quite alone, for he believed in showing deference to objects he valued. It was thus that his instrument, unlike his sofa, was not cramped; it stood in an otherwise empty space, aloof from the haphazard indignities to which the other furniture was subjected.

The more I go over that house in my mind, the more I find the character of its occupant returning to me. Eric was not only deferential to things, as so many people are whose intelligence and sensitivity removes them from the world as most understand it. He was not lost in his music, though he lived by it; his mind did not distance him from humanity, though it was superior to most minds. He was someone who engaged with people, whose first thought was more often for the good of his friends than for the satisfaction of his own desires. He had little of the selfishness that city living can inculcate: what he had, he shared. And his roots were in the country, in the fertile fields of Provence. He had something of the gentleman farmer in him, for all his urbanity, which lent a wholesomeness to his erudition while physical strength gave him presence. Regina Boardman – I am remembering now – called him a 'son of the soil'. Unlike Charles Stanhope, education and social training had not robbed Eric of vitality; and although he was softly spoken, he was vigorous.

I remember his vigour, his enthusiasm, his childlike trust.

I remember, too, the afternoon in early September that I spent drinking tea with him. The Anglophile in Eric loved the institution of afternoon tea: its rituals appealed to his Gallic flair, and the delights of his tea table – which I must have sampled more than once, since I know this to be true – were varied and rich. On the afternoon I remember I am sitting on a corner of the Chesterfield, my feet positioned gingerly in the tiny space between sofa and tea table. Eric is busying himself with tea strainers – for he did not hold with tea-bags – and lumps of sugar in an old porcelain bowl. His collection of china was eclectic: invariably of the highest quality, it was nevertheless all second-hand and acquired at random over years. Thus a Spode saucer might go with a Willow Pattern cup – that, in fact, is the combination into which he is pouring my tea as I follow the scene – or a Mason cake plate with a Wedgwood milk jug. Yes, I'm remembering now: the stuffy sitting room; the delicate china; Eric's large hands moving gracefully between teapot and milk jug. I am in the middle of telling him about Camilla Boardman, whom he has not met, when he asks if I take one lump or two, he can't remember. His English is almost without accent or error; only the occasional lapse in idiom betrays him, and he seems to be humorously aware of his mistakes. I reply too quietly that I take one lump and he asks me to repeat myself; so that when I continue my anecdote the thread of my account has been broken, and I grow conscious that it is no longer funny. I finish it nevertheless and when I have done so my friend settles himself opposite me on a large wing-backed armchair, suddenly serious. The chair is ramshackle but comfortable; for comfort, as well as opulence, is what Eric looks for in furniture. In his right hand is a slice of buttered toast; in his left a cup of tea. He turns to face me, smiling, but I sense that he has something important to say.

I was right.

'James,' he began slowly, choosing his words carefully, 'how concrete are your plans for the next two or three months?'

'They're cast in stone,' I replied, with a certain satisfaction that this was indeed the case.

'Stone can always be broken, can it not?'

'Not this stone.'

He smiled at me. 'Any stone can be broken, if only there is the will.'

'Perhaps, but in this case there is no will. Except,' I paused, thinking aloud, 'possibly on my parents' side, although they seem to have given up their objections to the Guildhall. I've got Michael Fullerton to thank for that.'

'Monsieur Fullerton seems to have become an avid champion of yours in these days. Your discovery seems to be starting.'

I was embarrassed by this and said nothing, for Eric had been only briefly mentioned in the review of our last concert and this was not a point I wished to underline. If my companion minded, however, he showed no sign of doing so.

'Which is *précisément* why I think that you should not cast your plans in stone,' he went on, 'at least not until you have listened with the open ear to my suggestion.'

Resolving not to listen, I told him politely to go on.

'Well,' he began, 'my mother's aunt has died. My great-aunt.' As words of sympathy formed on my lips he raised a hand to stop them. 'It does not affect me personally. She was old, you see. And besides, I did not know her well.'

As I remember this remark, myself old now, I am struck by the callousness of youth, which thinks itself immortal. It is closer to age than it realizes.

'She was a painter,' he went on, 'a woman of some reputation.'
I nodded and asked her name.

'Isabelle Mocsáry,' he told me, and I felt a faint twinge of recognition. 'She was a Frenchwoman who married a Czech. A very cosmopolitan person. Very erudite. And as an artist the Communists treated her well.'

I nodded again.

'She has left a large apartment in Prague, completely full of furniture and paintings,' he continued. 'Some of her things may be very valuable; many of them will, in any case, need to be sold. I am going there myself in ten days' time to supervise the arrangements.'

'Why you?'

'My mother was Madame Mocsáry's only relative. I am my mother's only son. It is right that I should go.' He paused. 'And I think that you should go with me.' This was said quietly, almost shyly. Seeing my surprise and sensing the beginnings of a refusal, he went on quickly, 'I have a friend at the Prague Conservatory. You will have heard of him.'

I said nothing. Eric looked at me anxiously and smiled. 'Does the name Eduard Mendl mean anything to you?'

My host leaned back, triumphant now; and I saw – as fully as he could have intended – a wizened head of silver hair; a hooked nose; black pointed eyes. Mendl's was a face I had seen on concert programmes and record covers since my childhood. His was a name I had revered since the day I first touched a violin.

'How do you know him?' I asked, a little awed by such nonchalant mention of greatness.

'He was a friend of my great-aunt,' came the reply. 'When he travelled abroad and came to France, he would stay with us between concerts.'

'But that's amazing.'

'You have not let me finish. I think Eduard Mendl is the man to teach you. He takes pupils, you know, now that he has retired from performing. You are getting a little notice in London, thanks to

Monsieur Fullerton. Think how useful a term with Eduard Mendl would be. Think how it would sound in Monsieur Fullerton's next column.'

I had already thought how it would sound. 'What makes you think he would want to take me?' I asked cautiously.

'He would be willing to hear you purely on my recommendation,' said Eric. 'Although Mendl is a violinist, he has perhaps done more for my piano-playing than any man alive. We have a close relationship; he trusts my judgement.'

'And you think . . .'

'I think that if I asked him to, he would hear you. The rest would be up to you, of course.'

'Of course.'

Eric saw that he had made the impression he desired. Slowly he smiled.

'Do you really think it could be arranged?' I asked.

And it was only after I had spoken that I thought with a pang of how long two months without my love would be; of how great a sacrifice they would represent. The melodrama of youth, I suppose. And I remember that as Eric looked at me I wished almost that he would say no; that he would tell me that things could not be arranged as he would wish them; that the undreamed-of opportunity he seemed to be offering would pass. But then the thought that Ella and I were equal to such a parting made me smile. And then he spoke.

'I am certain that it could,' he said with confidence. 'But you would have to persuade your professor at the Guildhall to defer your entry by a term.'

At this my face fell again; for I foresaw little hope of success with such an unprecedented request. I brightened a little, but only a little, when Eric told me that he had already spoken to Regina Boardman who had promised to use her influence.

'England works in a very funny way,' he said. 'Everything is done behind the scene.' He paused. 'Regina knows the head of strings at the Guildhall. He is a dear friend of hers.'

My heart sank. Anyone in a position to be useful to her was a 'dear friend' of Regina Boardman's. The formula was her own; it did not imply intimacy or affection on either side. Eric's next remark, however, revived my hopes.

'He is also the lover of Monsieur Fullerton,' he said smoothly.

'How do you know?' I was incredulous.

'That is not for you to mind about, James. But I know. With Monsieur Fullerton and Madame Boardman behind us, it might well be possible to arrange something.'

I considered this. Eric was right: if the head of strings at the Guildhall was in a position to be influenced by either Regina Board-man or Michael Fullerton I had a chance of winning him round to my unorthodox plans, for I knew that I could be assured of the complete support of both patron and reviewer. So long as Eric's facts, however obtained, were correct, anything might be possible.

'You're right,' I said, beaming at the realization. 'You're absolutely right. There might just be a chance.'

'And if you came to Prague and it was all arranged,' he went on, grinning now, 'would you like to share Madame Mocsáry's apartment with me?'

'It's very kind, but I couldn't impose.'

There was a pause.

'I should be lonely without your company.'

Another pause followed, as I cursed the polite reserve of twenty-two years' training.

'In that case,' I said, taking the plunge, 'I . . . accept with pleasure.'

'And the only rent,' he continued, 'would be a little help with the organization of the sale. Otherwise it would be completely free. And Prague is, in any case, a very cheap city. We could live like kings, not like,' he gestured about the room, 'the rats we are in London. I do not like to live in holes, James.'

And in high spirits we shook hands on our plan and I got up to leave, glowing with excitement but telling myself not to allow my hopes to rise too high; that there were many hurdles yet to be jumped. But I thanked Eric for his generosity with sincere warmth.

'Not at all,' he said. 'I like you extremely.'

And I, awkward at such direct affection, was irritated by my own awkwardness. I shook his hand again with renewed vigour; for thus does the Englishman express his regard for his friends. And as I did so I thought of Ella's distaste for physical reserve; it was something which we had discussed at length. So I let go of Eric's hand and hugged him, with a certain pride at thus proving my freedom from convention. He returned my hug, pleased but obviously surprised.

'Thank you,' I said again.

'I have told you,' he repeated, looking directly into my eyes, 'it is nothing. To give pleasure to one's friends is to give pleasure to oneself.'

And I left him and walked home through the gathering blue dusk, watching pink turn to gold and then to grey as the sun set over the roofs and smog of a great city. And I thought, as I looked at the heavens above me, enormous in their beauty, that all their splendour could not match the splendour of my own happiness, that all their colour was as grey against the riches of my life. It was a fanciful thought, I see that now; but Ella had made me fanciful. And as the sun set I sat by the river and watched it go, first seeking in its power a metaphor and then resting, quite content, in the pale warmth of its final rays.

I find it strange, now, to think how happy I was that day, to remember how I rejoiced in the opportunities that lay ahead at every turn. Experience has made me cynical; for as innocence was the sin of my youth so cynicism is the sin of my age. I remember sitting by the river in the last warmth of that sinking sun, but the memory seems vicarious, as though synthesized from an account given me by a stranger. The boy who sat there, warm on that summer's evening, is not the man who freezes in this icy room now. The image in my mind is not of me: the boy I see is someone I knew once and whom I know no more. He belongs to my past, an acquaintance from whom I am separated irrevocably, for ever. The gulf between my knowledge and his innocence is too wide to be bridged.

I follow his thoughts as he sits, thinking himself not thinking, and watch them as they fly to foreign cities; to thunderous applause; to praise earned from the wrinkled lips of a great teacher with a wizened face and silver hair. Love for Ella, you see, and the reciprocation of that love, had already made me vainglorious. In the space of a few short weeks my life had been transformed; and I was young enough to think that its transformation had something to do with an innate quality of my own. My father used to say that luck came to those who earned it; and I felt as I sat by that river that I was vindicated by good fortune. Ella's love, Eric's friendship, my own fledgling success, all had been earned and all were mine to enjoy. I had not yet grasped, nor would I grasp for many years, that Fortune with her scales is a capricious force. Sitting by that river I suspected nothing of what I have learned now to be the truth: that she acts independently of her victims, choosing to raise this one up, to cast this one down; to ennoble, to degrade, to protect and to persecute, all on the flimsiest of whims. She ensures her pleasures by devious means, artful in their cruelty. She fans the flames of human pride and extinguishes them without warning; she bestows fleeting immortality and takes it back when it is needed most, leaving wretchedness in its place. Her bounty brings misery and eternal isolation; for it is easier for a camel to pass through the eye of a needle, we are told, than it is for a rich man to enter the kingdom of heaven.

Now that Sarah is dead I am, I suppose, a rich man. Is my wealth to be another obstacle on my path to peace? Is it to join the long succession of barriers I can never hope to cross? I am trapped on a journey I cannot complete; I am alone with no one to turn to. My only companion, the boy who sits, staring dreamily at the golden river, is powerless to help me; he cannot hear my questions and I cannot hear his answers. He knows nothing of me; how could he? He knows no pain; his only pain is irritation, the temporary thwarting of immediate desires. He knows no guilt; his only guilt is the lapse of yesterday, soon forgotten. He knows no remorse; no shame; no despair. I resent him. He, who thinks himself so fine, does not move as I question him. He sits by the river, in an endless idle dream, as I beg for signs I might have seen, for warnings I might have heeded. But still he sits, moving only to toss a pebble into the fast-flowing waters. He pays no attention to the ramblings of an old man; he does not hear them. And I am left helpless, watching.

12

In due course the appropriate authorities were appealed to, the appropriate favours were called in, and a term's sabbatical was granted. A tape of my playing at St Peter's was dispatched to Prague by courier with a long letter from Eric attached; and two days of tense waiting later, a telegram arrived from Mendl saying that he would be delighted to take me on for a term.

Camilla Boardman telephoned as soon as she knew. '*Daaarling!* You're *so* fabulous!'

'I think it's your mother's work rather than mine, Camilla.'

'Didn't I *say* you two would enjoy each other? Didn't I *say* so?'

'You did.'

'And wasn't I *right?*'

'You were. Thank you.'

Camilla required her own portion of recognition.

My only reservation in all the excitement was the thought of leaving Ella.

I had told her immediately, of course, of Eric's offer; together we had endured the tense few days of Regina Boardman's machinations. Neither of us had believed that they would come to anything, though Ella understood my hopes and hoped with me; and when they did it was Ella whom I wanted to be the first to know. But when I called the house in Chester Square I was told that the Harcourts were away; and the deep voice at the other end was not at liberty to tell me when they might be back.

For two days I waited, puzzled, while my mother told her friends of my good fortune and undoubted genius. The atmosphere at home had changed now beyond all recognition; for with the instinct of artful losers – or so I understood it at the time – my parents had come to believe that there had been no struggle between us at all. Of course a little uncertainty on their part was only to have been expected, they told me, but that said they had never sought to stand in my way. Quite the contrary in fact, though they still felt it was important not to forget the value of a safe job, whatever I did. With the indifference of youth I listened to their explanations and thought myself very fine for not judging their hypocrisy.

It was only years later that I was able to see beyond the confines of that struggle with my parents; to understand that, though snobbish, they were not hypocritical; to see the love behind our long-drawn-out conflict. Only years later could I appreciate the graciousness of their happiness for me; and then, as so often in life, it was too late to tell them so.

At the time I gave little thought to anything my parents said but concentrated instead on contacting Ella. For three days I was frustrated: again and again I was rebuffed by the deep voice that answered the telephone at Chester Square; again and again I was told that it was not at liberty to say when the Harcourts might be back. On the third day of fruitless calls a letter arrived from her. Its envelope was heavy; its paper thick; and it was engraved with a blue coronet and an address which I did not expect: SETON CASTLE, CORNWALL.

My dearest, Ella had written.

You would be embarrassed to know how much I miss you; or at least to be told so in a letter. I think my Californian endearments would make you self-conscious. (And being at Seton in weather like this, with sparkling views of a sunlit sea, makes me <u>achingly</u> sentimental sometimes. So I shall be stern with myself and spare you.)

The reason for my presence here is a sad one, I'm afraid. Uncle Cyril has had some sort of seizure; he collapsed four days ago and has been in hospital in Penzance ever since. Things are apparently touch and go and the family has been summoned to squabble by his bedside and awe the villagers. Aunt Elizabeth insists on flaunting unity at times like this 'as an example to the tenants' which of course is a remark guaranteed to make my blood boil. Such is the damage which an American education can do, even to members of the best families; and I have been the cause of much collective disquiet, I'm sure. Aunt Elizabeth and Sarah hum and ha in corners for hours, talking (I bet) of how reprehensible I am and how there is nothing to be done about it. Poor Pamela comes in for most of the reproving looks, however; she doesn't have the protection of blood ties, you see — she's just an interloper whose day will one day come and Elizabeth knows it. My aunt dreads being sent to the Dower House.

The family disapproval of me and Pamela makes Daddy very angry, naturally; and meals are frosty occasions. I hope Cyril is not sent home to recuperate in an atmosphere like this — it would kill him. But we must stay until he is out of danger, and that will mean at least a week, perhaps two. This, I think, is a good separation for us. Much as I love our times together (and I do love them) they distract me from the matter in hand. I am still engaged; nothing has changed; and I cannot go on behaving as though it has. Charlie is beginning to wonder why I'm always ill when he wants to see me, and my stock of excuses is not endless. I feel Sarah watching me, too, and I wonder how much those cool eyes of hers see. She makes me uncomfortable, as well she might. (You see I do have a conscience, after all.)

So I shall spend my time here thinking seriously of what is to be done. And I shall think also of you and your tremendous opportunities in Prague. How I shall miss you if you go (damn Regina Boardman — she'll kill herself to arrange things, I know). But with a feeling as strong as ours there is plenty of time.

I love you and love you,

Ella

I did see Ella once before my departure, for studying permits took longer to arrange than Eric and I had anticipated and we remained in London while the bureaucracies of two governments took their time over us. Uncle Cyril came home, recovered, and sent his family away in irritation at the fuss which it made over him. So Ella returned to London and once again the house in Chester Square became a hive of wedding activities. We met on the day before my departure. Clothes and books had been carefully packed; visas collected; friends telephoned and seen. All was ready. Camilla Boardman had demanded a private interview and, over lunch, had told me that London would be *horribly* dull without me. Michael Fullerton had telephoned to wish me luck. And Regina Boardman, true to form, had organized a last charity concert, and so seen at least an initial return on her investment in my future.

Ella and I met in the triumphant Victorian splendour of the National Portrait Gallery. It was mid-September, one of the last days of that long, warm summer. Outside in Trafalgar Square and Charing Cross Road the crowds were sweaty and loud; inside, in the sepulchral cool of the gallery and its long deserted rooms, there was silence. I can see her as she walked up the stairs towards me; can see the expectant haste of her quick, light step; the smile on her lips; the glow of her cheeks. She was wearing a short, flimsy dress of pale blue cotton; her knees were bare; her hair looked wet and was brushed back from her face.

I don't remember all we talked of, though she must have told me about her visit to Seton; about her uncle's recovery; about the suppression of family bitterness in the invalid's presence at least, if not elsewhere. I remember telling her of Regina Boardman's supremely focused efforts on my behalf; of the fraught days before Mendl's acceptance of me as a pupil; of the fact that Eric's great-aunt had been Isabelle Mocsáry. I remember going next door with her to the National Gallery to see its small collection of Mocsárys and our disappointment on being told that they were on loan to the Musée d'Orsay in Paris. Above all I remember the intimacy of those few hours, the ease with which we talked and laughed and, over tea in a Covent Garden café, kissed. It was only as evening drew on that our talk grew serious, with the seriousness of lovers about to be parted.

'I can't say how glad I am for you,' Ella told me quietly. 'And how sad I am for me. But I think this separation will be good for us.' She paused to light a cigarette and I watched the elegant arch of her fingers as she clasped it and put it to her lips. She lit it and took two meditative puffs, slowly. 'And I think that it should be a complete separation, at least for the moment.'

'In what way?'

'I don't think we should communicate at all, Jamie.'

'What?'

She smiled at me. 'We know what we have. It won't go away. But I want us only to write or speak when I've done what I have to do and not before. This . . . hide-and-seek isn't good for either of us, and I'm sick of running around like a guilty child.'

I nodded, though I did not wholeheartedly share her distaste.

'It's time to get things sorted out, once and for all,' Ella continued. 'I haven't thought of Charlie as I ought to have done; I haven't thought of Sarah, either. And I know she's watching, watching everything I do. She knows something's up. That's why we mustn't write to each other.'

'I don't understand.'

'Don't you see? When I'm with you I'm too happy to be tragic. And it would be the same if we wrote to each other every day while you were in Prague. You need to be my reward, Jamie, not my distraction. I must extricate myself from this tangle so that I can enjoy you . . . unfettered, as it were.'

'But Ella . . .'

'Please Jamie.'

'But . . .'

'Don't you see how a clean break, even for such a short time, will help me? How it will help me to arrange things?' She took my hand. 'I want this to be permanent; I want us to be permanent. Open; above board; acknowledgeable. I don't want us to sneak around like this any more. And I need an absence of distractions if ever I'm going to sort out this mess. I owe that much at least to Charlie, don't you think?'

I nodded sullenly, beginning to understand.

'Now don't get like that. We have time. You'll only be away for two months. And when you get back we won't have to skulk around like criminals. You can meet Daddy and Pamela properly; I can meet your parents. We can go down to Seton and not have to stay in the village pub and avoid the guards. Don't you see how different it will be then? How lovely?'

I nodded again, less sullenly this time, slightly mollified.

'So go to Prague and don't write. Your letters – anything from you – make me too happy, as I've said, to be tragic. And tragedy is the least I can do for Charlie; I owe him that much at least, don't you think? I'm going to have to take my time over this. You can't break off an engagement overnight, you know; particularly when the circumstances are as they are.'

I nodded again.

'Do you understand what I'm saying?' She looked at me anxiously from across the table.

'I think I do,' I said. 'I don't like it, but I understand.'

'Good.' She squeezed my hand.

'But you've only got until Christmas,' I said. 'Once Christmas comes you won't be able to get rid of me.'

'I won't want to, stupid.' She squeezed my hand. 'I don't want to now. But for both our sakes I must.'

'I know.'

And we kissed each other lingeringly.

13

Prague spread below me: a city of arched bridges; sharp steeples; gracious domes. Bathed in a morning light sharper and colder than the light of London, the mist rising from the Vltava was a brilliant, dreamy ribbon in the grey blanket of the city. 'Close your eyes,' said Eric beside me, as the wing dipped. 'We are about to pass over the suburbs.' So I closed my eyes and was allowed to open them only as we landed at an airport with a name full of consonants, a concrete carbuncle designed – so far as I could make out – to deter visitors and thus secure and protect undisturbed the splendours of the city it served. My memories of Eric are clearer now. I see him sitting in that aeroplane, his large frame cramped by an encroaching pair of armrests, his eyes bright with the excitement of travel, his voice softly pointing out the landmarks of a city neither of us had ever seen but which he at least had read about.

Prague and I were yet to be introduced. But even as I saw her for the first time I knew, as sometimes one knows instinctively, that I would not find her as I found London; that she was not reserved, not distant, not cold. Proud, yes. But Prague's pride was alluring, enticing, and shrouded in romantic mystery. Not for her, as I was to discover, were the triumphant boulevards of Paris or the sneering skyscrapers of New York. She was a city of cobbled streets and hidden staircases; of courtyards hung with flowers and filled with whispers; a city where palace and tenement lived side by side, together, and crumbled uncomplainingly with picturesque dignity. Brutal investment and unthinking, unquestioned improvement were foreign to her as yet. Developers and housing ministers might corrupt her suburbs; *paneláky* and office blocks might rise steadily on her perimeter; she might be under siege from all sides. But the centre of the city, the few square miles that held her essence, had kept themselves pure. Prague is at heart a town of romantic guile; it knows how to charm and to seduce all who would conquer, change and improve. Governments might come and go, regimes might rise and fall; but the Hrad would remain impassive, standing guard over the city it has protected for centuries.

All this I sensed dimly, as a taxi took Eric and me on to the highway and then through leafy suburbs with strange, *art nouveau* houses set in overgrown gardens. Decay was almost tangible here; but the once magnificent buildings faced the change in their fortunes with dignity and a certain impressive acceptance. Not so the newer, uglier achievements of the Communist housing initiatives. These towers, the *paneláky* which ringed the city's approaches, turned sullen faces to the world and stared malevolently out over ill-lit streets.

'Where did your aunt live?' I asked Eric. 'Somewhere out here?'

'Oh no. She was a woman who had to be in the thick of things. Without the smell of traffic fumes she was unhappy. Her house – her apartment, I should say – is in the centre and just as she left it *apparemment*. We will live in the real Prague. These prisons are not for us.'

And with a secret relief I watched as we left them behind and descended the steep cobbled avenue that cuts down from the Strahov Monastery to the Malá Strana, the baroque 'little quarter' of winding streets crushed together beneath the castle which was to be my first contact with the city proper. Before us was the Vltava; in the distance the twin towers of the Charles Bridge and its line of statues, sinister and black with age and soot. It startles me how vividly I see this all, how completely the view forms in my mind. I have never gone back to Prague since Eric and I left it, for its associations are painful; but I have never forgotten it. It strikes me that the city I know and the city it is today are probably different, must almost certainly be different. Perhaps all Prague's streets are tarred now; perhaps its corners boast the fast-food outlets of other cities; perhaps its monasteries and palaces are hotels. I do not wish to return. I am content with a mental revisiting of the city that awed a young, impressionable man, quick with life. I wish to dwell again on her mysteries, to laugh at her mannerisms, to sample her tastes and smile at her eccentricities. I wish to experience again the tingling of those first few moments, the rush of that first spectacular view.

As I stared out of the window Eric was asking our taxi driver, in German, how he felt about the fall of Communism. I listened idly, my attention fixed on the great sweep of the city fanned out below us.

'He says his countrymen have become like Americans,' Eric translated for me. 'Money, money, money. It has become the new obsession.'

Our driver nodded. 'I speak English. A little. Too,' he said shyly. Eric nodded encouragingly. 'This is Georg,' he said to me.

Georg and I nodded at each other in the rear-view mirror and I said my name.

'Before the Fall,' Georg went on, 'people used to talk, to discuss. There was much . . . going to the theatre. But now,' he looked at us sadly in his mirror, 'there is only work. Work to make money. That is all there is. Since the Fall it is the foreigners who fill our theatres.'

Georg was a dignified old man; and the tranquillity with which he described the infiltration of his culture belied the strength of his resistance to it. He faced the new army of invading imperialists defiantly. 'They,' he said – meaning me and capitalists like me – 'try to conquer our minds. They want to make us slaves. All we think of now is money and sex, sex and money. That is all that matters.' As he tackled the increasing traffic he warmed to his theme. 'Not even Havel has written a play since the revolution,' he told us. 'He sits in his palace up there on the hill' – a wave of a wrinkled hand indicated the Hrad behind us, its mullion-panes glinting serenely in the morning light – 'and is cut off from us. He leaves us to be exploited by the West and by each other. It must not go on.'

There was nothing for us to say; and the drive continued in silence until, with a shake of his head, Georg deposited Eric and me on the corner of a street of grand old houses. Motioning us towards number twenty-one, the address Eric had given him, he accepted his money as though it were he, not us, who was giving something up.

Left on the pavement in the chilly air I waited while Eric fumbled for keys.

'This,' he told me, 'was once the Sherkansky Palace. Now it is flats.'

'Quite grand flats,' I said, looking at the marble steps and heavy doors.

'My great-aunt was a flower of the regime,' he replied, smiling. 'She was an artist admired by the world. She was at the top of the housing lists.'

He had found the keys and opened the door, leading the way forward under the arch. In the interior gloom the mouldings on the walls and ceiling loomed ghostly: cherubs smiling when the wind changed, trapped for ever in delirious wantonness. Light streamed, muted by dirt, through large windows on both walls; and before us there was a staircase, relic of an age more elegant than our own, which led upwards graciously into darkness. As my eyes grew accustomed to the dim light cast by a weak and solitary bulb I saw the true state of the building: the chipped paint; the broken tiles; the cracked plaster. Then all was dark. With a muttered curse Eric groped for a light switch, found one, and another ineffective light, far away, flickered to life. Thus began our ascent. For intervals of ten seconds at a time it was possible to move up the staircase with something approaching adequate illumination; but the weight and number of our bags meant that we inevitably trod the last few steps of each flight in darkness. On the third and final floor Eric produced another key before another set of heavy doors.

'The apartment has not been opened since the funeral,' he said.

'I wonder what we'll find.' My heart was quick with excitement as he put the key in the lock.

'I wonder myself.'

With a grind of rusty bolts the door opened and, on cue, the light in the passage went out. We pushed on in darkness and Eric fumbled once more for a light switch and once more found one and flicked it on. This time, however, we were bathed in a tremendous wave of electric light. The chandelier above our heads – as I later had leisure to count – had thirty bulbs; and it illuminated every corner of the Aladdin's cave in which we stood.

I remember that first glow of light, the physical shock of that brightness, and I remember that my life has not been wholly without adventure.

Eric and I were standing in a long, narrow room, the stone of its floor carpeted haphazardly with Turkish rugs, its walls completely bare and painted a deep, rich red. A film of dust covered everything, hushing the colours of the carpets and the drapes, an imperial yellow, which hung tent-like from the ceilings. I sneezed and the sound broke the tension and made us laugh.

'My God,' I said, 'I've never seen anything like it.'

Eric's eyes danced. 'Let's explore.'

So together we explored the apartment; and, excitedly, like awed schoolboys in a museum, we went through its rooms, occasionally picking up and showing each other some of the more eccentric examples of Madame Mocsáry's taste: a small golden elephant with sparkling red stones for eyes that sat on the piano; a cheap plastic fan of lime green and pink which lay, for decoration, on an occasional table; an ashtray of old blue crystal, heavily cut. The room we were in served as a kind of entrance-hall-cum-sitting-room – what purpose it had served in the Sherkanskys' days I could not tell – and from it opened two doors, each set back in pillared alcoves. The first opened on to a dank little passage which led to a poky kitchen and a bathroom with a large porcelain bath and no taps. The second – which we explored only after a hopeful but disappointing examination of the kitchen equipment – was more rewarding.

'*Mon Dieu*,' said Eric as he opened it. 'Come and see this, James.'

So I came and together we entered the Picture Room for the first time. It was a perfectly-proportioned square, its walls twelve feet apart and set at right angles to each other, a false ceiling setting their height at twelve feet, too. Every inch of the four walls, saving only the door through which we had entered and two long casement windows overlooking the street, was covered with canvases. Some framed, some not, they clustered together as if for comfort in the chilly room, hiding the wall – which was a deep red like the hall – in a riot of colour: fantastic, half-realistic shapes painted over many years in a progression which – as I later discovered – could be traced.

'So this is it,' Eric said quietly.

'What?'

'My great-aunt used to write to my mother about her Picture Room. She was convinced that she would not finish it before she died.' He paused and looked about him. 'It has something of the grand effect, has it not?'

I nodded.

I can see that room now: the single most cohesive creation of a brilliant mind. It housed an explosive outpouring of artistic inspiration, from the first ink sketches of a young girl to the assured, experimental works an older, more mature artist. The images were varied: some were small, some huge; some in oils, some in ink or acrylics; most were on canvas, some were on board. They coagulate in my mind though I once knew them so well. I cannot make out their individual subjects, for the passing of the years has cast a film over them which blurs their outline and their detail. It is strange that I should not remember, for I came to love those paintings and the room which housed them; they came to mean a great deal to me. Perhaps that is why I have forgotten. Who can say?

The spirit of Madame Mocsáry was everywhere in that eccentric apartment: from the faded yellow drapes which hid the cracked ceiling of its hall to the collection of bric-à-brac that covered every available ledge, surface and shelf. For an hour Eric and I wandered about, fascinated; only then did the practicalities of our situation occur to us. Madame Mocsáry, it seemed, had had no use for a bed.

'She must have had one at least,' said Eric. 'We must find it.'

But search though we did we could unearth nothing that even resembled a mattress, let alone anything more sophisticated or comfortable than that. It was I who discovered the key to the secret of where Madame Mocsáry had slept, and by the time I had done so Eric and I had been searching fruitlessly for almost an hour. The dust in the apartment had been making me sneeze, so I decided to air the drapes that covered the furniture. It was when I removed the blue velvet square from the sofa that I discovered that it was not a sofa at all but a single bed pushed against the wall with cushions on its three sides. How we laughed to have been outwitted for so long by a ghost.

I remember Eric's laughs. He abandoned himself to them. They were throaty guffaws of white teeth and dishevelled hair and streaming eyes. And they will return to my nightmares with the smile that preceded them and the clap of his hand on my back. It has taken fifty years to banish all thoughts of Eric, to close my dreams to the sight and sound of him. Now I have undone the work of decades; I have remembered. And Eric will return to haunt me; tonight he will revisit me, no longer happy but tortured, no longer carefree but hunted. Who is he? What is he? An image. A sound. A touch. A young man who had a happy life but an unhappy death. He is nothing more than that, surely? He is dead. But he lives on within me; my conscience will not lay him to rest for it no longer stomachs deceit. And so his laugh shrieks at me, accusingly, across the years.

That afternoon, though, I heard his laugh with pleasure and laughed, too. We laughed and laughingly wrestled each other for the privilege of the bed. Eric, though broader than I, was the loser; and it was decided that after an adequate cleaning and airing, the velvet drapes with which the apartment was full should be piled on top of each other to provide him with a makeshift mattress. That important issue resolved, we turned our attention to the prospective difficulties of the job at hand, opening cupboards; examining shelves; exploring the nooks and crannies of an eccentric old lady's private world. And we discovered that the cleaning of the house, unlived in since Madame Mocsáry's removal to a nursing home almost a year before, would be no easy task. Whatever skills a boarding-school education had equipped me with, the handling of dusters, detergents and the like had not been amongst them; and Eric was hardly more skilled than I was. Our enthusiasm gave us confidence, however. And we went to DUM at once and armed ourselves with mops and buckets – for my friend insisted on viewing the process as a military operation – and returned exhilarated by our expedition to face the immediate task of airing the fabric.

Thus it was that a rather bemused Czech audience was able to observe us, over the course of that afternoon and early evening, dancing wildly in the street below our balcony and tugging huge squares of velvet – red, yellow, blue, purple, green – with all our force. We beat them with tremendous vigour and a great deal of noise on anything that presented itself: lamp posts; building walls; railings. Nothing was safe from our furious efforts. But by nightfall we had finished and were ready to hang the velvet to air on the balustrade of the central staircase – giving it, incidentally, something of the splendour it must have assumed on feast days in the past – and to climb to our apartment, naked without its fine fabrics. There the furniture stared at us, grimy, bare and uninviting; and we left it in search of dinner and wine, drinking and laughing together until we could barely walk, returning unsteady at dawn to the glorious decay of the Sherkansky Palace and the desolate grandeur of Sokolska 21.

It was those public fabric-beatings which first brought Blanca into our lives: Blanca, the wrinkled old woman with the carefully dyed blonde hair who had been Madame Mocsáry's cleaner and confidante. She lived in a much shabbier building further down Sokolska Street, on the opposite side; and we learned from her later that she had watched, horrified, as two unknown men had gone about destroying her old mistress's possessions in the street below her very own apartment. Our impertinence, she told us afterwards, had required immediate action on her, Blanca's, part; and although not a large woman, she, Blanca, was both fierce and unafraid, not frightened of young upstarts, and not about to let their impudence go unavenged. So she had gone to meet us, bent on violence, and she had found us as we were carrying the last of the drapes down the palace staircase. An unexpected, neatly aimed kick at Eric's shins had been enough to incapacitate him, while a loud barrage of enraged Czech had awed me into silence.

We calmed her eventually, but only with great difficulty, repeating our explanations first in English and then in broken German, Eric nursing his ankle all the while, I doing my best to placate our unexpected aggressor with soothing phrases from a half-remembered Czech phrase book. When at length the situation was clarified, Blanca's apologies were scarcely less alarming than her previous fury had been. On no account were we to clean the apartment by ourselves, she told us; she must make amends for her insult. And in any case, men were notoriously unreliable. What did we think we were doing without a woman's guidance? There was no knowing what damage we might cause if left to our own devices.

Faced with such an implacable opponent, there was little for Eric or me to do but to submit, so submit we did; and from thenceforth Blanca assumed control of the project in hand and worked with expert energy, talking nineteen to the dozen all the while and delegating enthusiastically as she did so. Under her guidance the days which followed our arrival at Sokolska 21 saw a whirlwind of activity on a par with anything the building could have experienced in the course of two long centuries. Arriving promptly at nine o'clock, Blanca worked her 'troops' (as she came affectionately to call us) from the moment she crossed the threshold until late into the night, setting us to scrub, clean and sort with tireless authority.

It was understood that any furniture which the Vaugirard family did not want for itself was to be sold with the paintings; and the six days of our house-cleaning were devoted to salvaging the odd treasures from the amorphous heap of junk which Madame Mocsáry had accumulated in the course of nearly eighty years. We found things in curious places. One of the floorboards – suspiciously creakier than the rest – lifted to reveal a bundle of neatly tied letters; the lid of the piano concealed, below the strings of the instrument, a tiny black box with an old amber brooch in it; and taped to the top of a kitchen drawer was a gentleman's pocket watch made of a metal which looked to me like gold.

All these items – and many more – I showed to Eric on discovery, and it was he who decided their fate. Of the letters he said slowly, 'Love letters. Let us burn them.' And so, itching with a curiosity I could not satisfy, I placed them in the corner of the balcony we called the bonfire site. There were about fifty in all, written on the same paper and now cracking with age, in a spidery handwriting and a language I did not recognize. Eric cast an eye over them. 'Not my great-uncle's writing,' he said sternly; then he softened. 'But let us preserve an old lady's secret.' And holding them in his left hand he lit his lighter under them and we watched as they burned brightly and turned to ash.

Isabelle Mocsáry and her unusual style intrigued me; and if I could not read her letters I could at least follow Blanca's unceasing reminiscences with great interest. 'Madame was a very fine lady,' her former cleaner would tell us in reverential tones as she scrubbed. 'A very fine lady. I was her servant but she treated me like her friend.' And as Blanca dusted she would tell us a brief history of each object she touched. Eric and I listened, fascinated, as she reeled off the names of the people who had drunk from Madame Mocsáry's teacups; the works of the intellectuals who had frequented her card table; the genius of the musicians, Eduard Mendl foremost amongst them, who had sat at her piano. 'Oh yes, she was a very fine lady,' Blanca would finish. 'Even in the hard times she was generous and kind. A very fine lady. And she never held with the Communists, never. Not once did she hide it, either. She said things to strangers that one didn't say to friends in those days. Oh yes she did. And what is more: they never dared to touch her. She was a woman who could make a noise and they knew that.'

With a little prompting from Eric she would expound for hours, too, on the state of the country and its new regime. 'Life was not so bad under the Communists,' she said once, as she cleaned the windows. 'There was safety at least. Now there is no safety. Only the young can gain; we who are old are left to die. To die,' she repeated, almost savagely, eyes narrowing in a cracked face lined with work. There was an awkward pause. 'But one must not complain,' Blanca continued, sensing our discomfort, 'one must go on. That is what Madame used to say. "While there is food on the table and love in the heart you cannot be unhappy for long." It is an old Bohemian saying which she liked to use. I think she liked this country, Madame. And Mr Mocsáry too, though I did not know him so well. He died many years ago.' She paused meditatively, looking sadly around the room we were dismantling. 'Yes, Madame liked this country despite everything,' she finished at last. 'It seems a pity, somehow. Her pictures should not be sold and separated. She would not have liked that. They should be put in a museum for people to see.'

I agreed with her. I had spent many hours in the Picture Room amongst the vibrant colours and flowing lines of Madame Mocsáry's personal collection; and I came to know her paintings intimately; to appreciate the richness of their texture; the provocation of their subject matter; the hidden technique of their execution. I came also to trace in them a steady progression from the passions of youth to the tranquillity of age; and I saw by their dates that she had painted one a year, quite incidentally to the rest of her output, for almost sixty years.

'There was always a painting. Always she would be painting,' Blanca told us one day. 'She began this room the year that she married; and she used to say that when she had covered the Picture Room her life's work would be complete. She didn't care what happened to the paintings people bought from her. She cared only about the ones she kept for this room.'

Hearing this, I thought with amusement of the crowds queuing outside the Musée d'Orsay to see the Mocsáry retrospective there; and I chuckled as I did so, wondering what they would think if only they could hear Blanca's words now, as I did. Eric smiled too; and our eyes met, sharing the joke, before a stern word from our self-appointed supervisor sent us back to our work. I returned to my scrubbing, pleased to think that the Picture Room had been finished before its creator's death, that Madame Mocsáry's grand plan, adhered to for so long, had finally borne fruit.

'She lived very alone when she grew older,' continued Blanca, following the train of her own thoughts. 'And her family did not visit her. They came only to the funeral and what good is that I ask you?' A pair of gimlet eyes met us both in a moment of beady interrogation. 'A person needs other people in life, not in death. Once they are dead they have the angels for company.' Blanca paused. 'The good ones, at least,' she added after a moment's consideration.

Eric looked down at the painting in his hands.

'I think, maybe,' the old lady continued, with uncharacteristic gentleness, 'that the best ones have the angels with them on earth too. I think, maybe, that Madame had the angels with her on earth.'

And with that she went on with her work and we returned to ours. No one spoke; and it was only when Blanca sniffed that I saw she was crying.

14

I know – and this is a knowledge I cannot escape, however hard I try – that we are responsible for what we do; and that I am responsible for what I have done. I acknowledge that. I am no longer concerned with masking my guilt. But when you're twenty-two and footloose in a foreign city you give no thought to the future. Certainly I did not. I devoted myself instead to adventure and enjoyment and music; and from this last at least I gained something whole, something good.

Our days passed happily, mine divided between the conservatory and Madame Mocsáry's apartment, where Eric spent his time sorting his great-aunt's papers, arranging the sale of her things, playing her newly-tuned piano. Not long into our stay we both bought bicycles and on these it was possible to dodge through the crowds of traffic on Sokolska Street and the forest of tourists who spent long hours on the Charles Bridge, anxiously consulting out-of-date maps, marvelling at the view, touching the bronze base of St John of Nepomuk's statue with superstitious delight. I remember how we loved that bridge with its looming statues and sinister towers, its street musicians and pavement artists; I remember the hours we spent lounging in the cafés beside and beneath it, talking of everything and nothing.

The machinery of permits and exemptions and death duties necessary to begin the sale of Madame Mocsáry's effects was slow to grind into motion; and Eric and I delighted in its inefficiency, for it left us longer undisturbed in the now gleaming splendour of her apartment. Our days were carefree; and as I search my memory of them I find no sign that the coils had yet begun to twist. My life was light, then, and I rejoiced in its lightness; I had not learned to look for creeping shadows.

Eduard Mendl extolled the virtues of simplicity and clear thinking in the baroque elegance of his rooms at the conservatory. He was a small, precise man with a sharp tongue and a mischievous flair for the debasement of Communist ideology. Thus it was that every instruction became an initiative and my practice was divided into weekly Five-Day Plans. He told me that he was not there to teach me technique – that was my own concern – but to teach me to understand beauty and to express it in a way that was uniquely mine. 'I shall teach you to think,' he told me in his clipped tones. 'To see things in your own way, to hear them in your own way. And I shall teach you also the beauty of expression. But the ease with which you express yourself' (by which he meant the facility of my playing) 'must be your own affair. You must work at it alone.' And I was a conscientious student as worlds of musical possibility opened before me, illuminated by the genius of that fine old man whose silver hair and creased face, lit occasionally by a smile of praise, are as clear to me now as they were, then, when I saw him every day.

I have never forgotten Mendl; he was never buried in my mind; there is no dust to clear from his image. His lessons, though I did not know this as he gave them, later saved me from myself. And I have always been grateful for that.

I played from early morning until late afternoon every day and devoted the remaining hours of daylight to endless walks in the cobbled maze of streets beneath the Hrad or to lazy boating on the Vltava with Eric. We spent our evenings in cafés or clubs or in the splendours of the Rudolfinum or the State Opera. Sometimes we stayed at home, experimenting with cooking and praising the results of each other's efforts, however dubious. It was a time of near tangible freedom, I remember that now; and we lived as we pleased, revelling in the lives we created for ourselves and for each other.

One's twenties are a time of reinvention, of regrouping and rethinking after the battles and fiery uncertainties of adolescence. And Eric and I learned that reinvention is easier and more pleasurable when the expectations of those you know are removed. Social ties can stifle growth, or at least alter it, and we relished their absence; we lived serenely in the present, content, with little care for the future or the past.

Slowly we settled into life in Prague and made Sokolska 21 our home, filling its kitchen cupboards; fitting bulbs into unused sockets; even organizing the delivery of daily newspapers. Needing somewhere to work, we turned the sitting room into an impromptu rehearsal space, moving the piano from its corner and setting it instead between the two long windows that gave on to the street. Restored once more to its former glory, hung again with the yellow drapes of Madame Mocsáry's day, that room became the focus of our Prague lives; and we spent many happy hours under its haphazard canopy, working hard – together and alone – but talking also. And as the days passed and familiarity (far from breeding contempt) bred intimacy instead, we found in each other and in the bond between us something which sustained us both; which gave us both a sense of excitement and adventure which neither of us, I think, had found in friendship before.

Artistically Eric and I challenged each other, you see; personally, we supported and upheld; and in retrospect the easy companionship of those nights seems strange, for by nature I am a solitary worker and find the company of others a distraction from my music. Remembering Eric, and my friendship with him, I remember most that curious admixture of frivolity and commitment which characterized all he did; which became the basis of our joint artistic endeavours; which sustained us on the hard days and rewarded us on the good.

Once a week we played together in the benignly august presence of Mendl himself; and in his quiet, measured way he took our youthful efforts and made something of them, or pointed the way for us to do so. Praising rarely but warmly, he was no easy master; certainly he put me through my technical paces at the conservatory, whatever he said about the facility of my playing being my own affair. But in Eric's presence he unbent a little, rewarding our efforts with a dreamy, glazed look of absorption which was thrilling from one such as he.

And sometimes, when I was practising alone, Eric would assume the role of audience which Ella had made her own in London; and on the mattress of velvet squares, his head in his hands, he would sit while I played to him; while I thought with pleasure of how Ella's hair fell into her eyes when she listened to me; of how her lips curled sometimes into half-smiles at the passages she loved most.

Of course I missed her; but Ella did not write, as she had warned me that she would not; and I was sure enough of her not to mind, though I still thought of her constantly: seeing her supple form in every passing beauty; hoarding my anecdotes for her amusement; remembering my adventures so that one day she might share them. Once or twice I almost wrote or telephoned, but Eric argued against my doing so with a forcefulness I did not understand but which was strong enough to persuade me. So I waited, as Ella herself had told me to wait; and by and large I was content to do so, for there is a certain thrill in the anticipation of intimacy; and Prague, I felt, was a fitting setting for a star-cross'd lover.

As time passed we settled down, separated ourselves from the tourist crowd and lived with the discernment of permanent Praguers. We became regular and recognized patrons at a few establishments, patronizing for preference the Café Florian, a bar run by two Czechs who spoke English with American accents and sold marijuana covertly after midnight. Florian's was the haunt of the expat community of artists and their hangers-on who came to Prague in search of the inspiration which Paris had offered the generation of their grandparents and great-grandparents. They were a motley crowd, a cosmopolitan collection of hopeful geniuses who sat in huddles on the sofas – the café was furnished with faded red and gold Chesterfields and armchairs grouped about low tables – and talked in low whispers of coming masterpieces. Occasionally one of the groups would explode in passionate argument, and the opinions of the other patrons would be volubly sought by the participants. Jean, a French-speaking waiter of Yugoslav extraction who had grown up in Warsaw – how he managed this curious combination he never divulged – was the supreme arbiter of such discussions, and when not waiting tables he spent his time writing poetry which appeared occasionally in some of the less underground magazines. He seemed to be the only published writer in the place, and as such his opinions carried appropriate weight.

'Hey Jean,' an ageing American who spent his life at Florian's would call, 'come and play backgammon and tell me about this new play everyone's mad about.' But Jean would shake his head and leave the American to grumble sorrowfully into his gin. 'Never *did* understand modern theatre; never *will* unless someone gets off his ass and explains it to me.' It was one of Jean's rules never to talk to customers unless their arguments threatened the peace and required arbitration. He wisely cultivated his aloofness, and thus his mystique amongst the patrons who provided his tips.

Another American, this time a gangly woman with red hair and a severe nose, took a shine to me and would lecture me frequently, and at great length, on the subject of women poets. 'In a patriarchal world,' she would say, 'a woman can't get her poetry talked about unless she commits suicide. It's the only way. Look at them all,' and she would reel off a list of female poets of whom I'd never heard. 'You've never heard of them, have you?' she'd crow triumphantly, her point proven to herself at least. 'But I tell you, if one of these girls plucked up the courage to top herself for her art, your grand-children would say she was the flower of her generation. Look at Plath.' Eric, who found the confidence of her pronouncements infuriating, would sometimes take her on; more often he didn't, and we would both sit and listen to her, proving point after point to her mute audience, in cadences which reminded me of Ella and him of I know not what or whom.

After a time, since we rarely participated in their arguments and seldom joined any of the groups on the larger sofas, the other regulars began to ignore us. We didn't mind; in fact we rather enjoyed being left alone, free to talk to each other and to form our own judgements on the issues debated with such passion around us. I enjoyed talking to Eric, and over many nights ensconced in two armchairs of purple velvet in one of the quieter corners of the café I learned a great deal about his opinions, for there was much to learn. Of mine he must have learned less, for there was less to know; but Eric possessed the gentle art of making his friends interesting, even to themselves, and he drew me out of my shell as few had done before.

He talked to me of Oxford, of my parents, of my music. And he listened with an air of affectionate understanding as I explained my confused but sincere attempts to break free from the path my family had laid out for me to follow; to define and to achieve my own place in the world, independent of their influence and prejudice.

'You are a very true person, James,' he told me one evening in the smoky half-light of Florian's. 'I admire you for that. And for the way you want to strike out for yourself. It is not a universal quality.'

And I thought as he said this of how Ella and I would strike out for ourselves; of what the future held for us both. And I smiled at the friend who had provoked these happy thoughts.

'Are you not glad you came here?' he asked me, quietly.

'To Prague?'

'To Prague.'

I nodded. 'Very glad.'

'I think we will remember this as the finest time of our lives, James.'

'I'm sure we will.' And seeing that Eric's glass was empty, I ordered two more gins from Jean, who brought them with the smiling alacrity with which he honoured his most deserving regulars. This pleased me. And after some minutes of silent contemplation, I asked Eric what his own family was like, for it struck me suddenly that he had not spoken much of them. All I knew, in fact, was that he was the elder of two children, and that he came from a line of gentleman farmers who had tilled the lands around Vaugirard and its small château for centuries.

'What are my family like?' He repeated the question, more to himself than to me. 'What are they like?' He paused. 'I will tell you, James, what they are like. And one day, maybe, you will meet them yourself and form judgements of your own.'

Eric's English, excellent since I had first known him, had improved still further. He had developed a style of his own, a curious, considered way of speaking which lent his conversation an appealing gravity and inspired the trust of his audience.

'My sister,' he began at last, choosing his words with care, 'is two years younger than I. She is called Sylvie, and she is very pretty but not so clever . . .'

'. . . As you are,' I finished for him, humorously chiding.

'No. Not so clever as she might be.'

'And why is that?'

'She does not question things, James. She does not question things as any intelligent person must do. As you do, for example. She accepts. All the time she accepts what she is told.'

'Such as?'

'I don't know. Everything. She lives her life according to a plan someone else has designed for her. She is happily married. She lives near my parents at Vaugirard' – his family still lived in the village and farmed the fields around it, though the château had long since passed out of their hands – 'and knits socks for the foreign legionnaires. A very safe, very narrow little life.' The disdain in his tone was unusual and real. It surprised me.

'Sylvie is a devout Catholic,' Eric continued. 'She spends her early mornings in prayer, her days in family duties and her nights in the duties of the wife.' He paused. 'She will have many children,' he added wryly.

'And how do you get on?' I asked, though I suspected I knew the answer already.

'Well enough. But it is for the benefit of my parents. We do not discuss the things we disagree on.'

'Things like?'

'You must know me well enough by now, James, to suspect.'

There was an awkward pause, during which I tried to silence the promptings of a social reserve which told me that to ask further would be to pry. But life habits are difficult to break; and rather than pursuing my friend's overture I smiled and signalled to Jean for another gin, nodding to the woman with the severe nose and saying something funny about her to cover the momentary tension between us. Unlike Eric I did not actively seek out confidences from others. Ella had whetted my appetite for them but I was still cautious. I had a vague fear still – explained, I imagine, by the repression inherent in any privileged English education – of emotional intimacy which might go too far; and I did not enjoy prolonged contact with the deeper, more secret sides of people's natures. I still don't. I might listen but I seldom pursue.

With Ella, love and desire made me fearless and I relished her confidence; but with Eric there were no such powers to drive me and I remained wary. I liked people to be what they appeared to be. I shrank from the private fears and insecurities of others because, perhaps, by admitting theirs I had to move closer to admitting my own. I don't know. But what I do know is that there are certain doors in one's mind which are better left closed. And when they are opened by another, as the doors of Ella's mind were opened by me and the doors of mine by her, their opening carries with it a great responsibility. I had no wish for the responsibility that Eric's secrets might bring; despite my affection for him I desired no glimpse of what lay behind the secret doors of his mind. I wanted the easy understanding of friends; nothing more.

And Eric, taking his cue from me, seemed to understand: for he turned the conversation, with characteristic deftness, from the intimate to the general, and from then on he offered me no more secrets. Instead he talked of his family history, and spoke with amusing erudition of the long line of knights in war and farmers in peace who had served their kings and emperors over centuries. 'We have lived at Vaugirard, with brief absences for understandable reasons around the time of 1789,' he told me, smiling, 'since the conquest of England.' And as he talked I thought of another ancient family and another smile and another voice telling me a similar story. And I thought that life was fine.

15

When Eric and I had no taste for the spirit-induced artistic confrontations of Florian's we used to go to see English and French films at the Lucerna cinema, one of the few places in Prague where one could talk, in English, unhindered by sociable Americans. It had been left in a state of splendid decay: unbombed by invaders; untouched by restorers; unloved by developers. Its only concession to modernity was its selection of films and its prominent display of their posters, and Eric and I were amongst a core of loyal patrons who were not distracted by the flashing lights and glitz of the newer establishments which had sprung up since the revolution.

It was on our return from one screening at the Lucerna that we discovered Mr Kierczinsky's note and learned to our disappointment that the clogged wheels of bureaucracy – for so long our unlikely protectors – had finally ground into motion and produced all the documents required for the Mocsáry sale to begin. Under the smart letterhead of the estate's lawyers we read that Mr Kierczinsky himself, the head of the firm, would call the following day at eleven if that was convenient; and as the following day was a Friday and I had no classes, it was. He arrived promptly an hour before noon, an urbane little man with a small moustache and high cheekbones; and he explained the situation to us very patiently in correct but hesitant English.

'You will see that there is much of . . . value here,' he said to us as we sat over tea in the sitting room. 'Your family has taken what is of . . . sentimental merit, has it not?'

Eric said that it had.

He and I had dispatched a small parcel to Vaugirard the week before filled with letters from Eric's grandmother to Madame Mocsáry and with one or two pieces of old jewellery, amber and jade mostly. The gold pocket watch had been sent, too. The rest we had left in place, and our cleaning and care had done much to restore it to something of its former condition.

'We cannot delay the sale of furniture and paintings . . . any longer,' Mr Kierczinsky continued. 'Your grand-aunt,' he was addressing me now, and seemed to take it for granted that I, too, was a Vaugirard relation, 'was a great lady and she lived . . . beyond her means. Especially after the revolution. Before that,' he chuckled to himself, 'it was difficult to find anything to buy to push you beyond your means. No one . . . had any means. Nor was there anything to buy, for the matter of that.'

Eric and I nodded, unsure whether to laugh or sympathize. At once Mr Kierczinsky's face straightened again.

'I shall begin the . . . process of the sale,' he continued. 'I shall have everything here valued at once. If your family would like any of the pieces I suggest that they inform me with the least possible of delays.'

When he had gone we wandered sadly through the rooms which we had come to consider our own. They had grown to symbolize something, something of the freedom that we had found together in Prague; and they were filled with memories of the work we had done there; the things we had talked about and laughed over. Our time in the city, like the apartment which had housed us during it, had been rich; unusual, full of diversity and beauty and . . . a thousand times and talks and views that I shall carry with me to the grave. But this is no time to speak of them; this is no time to pause.

The process of the Mocsáry sale moved forward at a brisk pace. A valuer, in a shiny suit he did not seem at all accustomed to wearing, came and made detailed notes a week after the lawyer's visit and returned two days after that with a colleague. They held long discussions in hushed tones and Eric and I stood awkwardly, uncertain whether or not it would be polite to listen. At length they went away, but their visits became longer and more frequent and as the last leaves fell from the trees – for it was late autumn now – talk of auction houses and catalogues began with the lawyer.

Mr Kierczinsky took Eric and me out to lunch, at the estate's expense, to discuss the situation and be introduced to the head of the best of the establishments to have sprung up since the revolution. 'It is like Christie's or Sotheby's,' he said in his introduction to Mr Tomin, of First Auctioneers Ltd. 'It caters to a very ... discerning clientele who think nothing of paying Western prices.' He was speaking of the new Czech rich, of the developers and speculators who had made a killing out of the political uncertainties surrounding the fall of Communism. They were a class despised by the majority of their countrymen for usurping the first fruits of freedom; but for men like Mr Tomin they were the lords of the new market and thus clients to be favoured and fawned over.

Pavel Tomin was a tall man with sunken Slavic cheekbones and black oiled hair. He bowed very low when introduced to Eric and me and spoke English to us with an aggressive American twang. I did not warm to him. 'There would be nothing that would honour me more,' he told us, 'than to be able to assist with the disposal of your collection. I speak, specifically, of the paintings.' There was a pause. 'The furniture is very good, too,' he went on quickly, anxious not to seem indifferent to any of our concerns, 'and some of the pieces, particularly the piano, for instance, will fetch high prices.'

'There are many new ... enthusiastic musicians in the new republic,' said the lawyer blandly. He was a master of neatly timed irrelevance.

I made a tentative suggestion about the desirability of interesting a museum in the sale. The two Czechs looked at each other awkwardly.

'I think that will be ... difficult,' Mr Kierczinsky said at last.

'Of course,' said Mr Tomin hurriedly, 'we will do our best to ensure that as many of the pictures remain together as possible. But the Czech museums are really not in a position to buy them for anything like their market value. And foreign museums might be interested in one or two, but not all. There are many enlightened private individuals who would appreciate them, I am sure, in a manner which Madame Mocsáry would have liked.'

And that was the best we could do, for as Eric explained to me his father was not a rich man who could afford to keep and look after the paintings, even if he had been interested in art, which he was not. So lunch ended awkwardly, with Eric and me disgruntled but impotent and Mr Tomin suspicious of our philanthropy and concerned for his commission. There was nothing more to be said or done; the day after our lunch the valuer made his final visit, this time unaccompanied; and the day after that, in impressive full-page advertisements, the sale of Madame Mocsáry's private collection and personal effects was announced in the national and international press.

It was on the day of this announcement that I received a letter from Camilla Boardman. I recognized her handwriting – large, rounded and confident – as soon as I saw it; and by the thickness of the overfilled envelope I knew that life in London had not been dull for her whatever she might say; for it was one of Camilla's endearing affectations to dismiss all pleasure as drudgery.

She had written on several sheets of lined file paper, which surprised me, for I had expected Regina's embossed stationery at the very least; and she had written her address by hand on the top right corner of the first sheet. In bold round letters I read *16 Cadogan Square (the underline unfashionable side)* and the date of a week before.

Dearest James, Camilla had written.

It's no use my fanning your ego and telling you how utterly utterly Utterly boring London has been since you left it so I won't but believe you me it has. Mummy's been in a frightful temper about her churches appeal – now that you've gone she's got no more tame stars on hand you see – and everyone's been having far too many parties full of girls who are far too pretty for their own good and really quite unfair competition for someone as dowdy as me!

Camilla, you see, wrote as she spoke; and her indifference to the comma was legendary.

But I have been soldiering on bravely through it all because one simply <u>has</u> to as you <u>know</u> but it's been hell really it has and I'd've liked nothing better than to leave this bloody city and go somewhere <u>wildly</u> romantic like Prague. Speaking of which how are you liking it? Is Mendlevitch or whatever his name is treating you well? Tell him from me that he's got me to deal with if he's anything but lovely to you and see if that scares him. I know what these famous musicking types are like – bloody-minded more than likely and far too impressed by their own genius to even consider the <u>possibility</u> that another person on the planet like you for instance might be talented or even gifted or even perish the thought potentially better than them! They've got to be kept under control so don't you let him get away with anything!

Is Prague very beautiful Jamie? Someone at lunch yesterday was saying that it's just like Paris was in the 1930s and full of struggling writers and painters and everything and <u>so</u> beautiful and so <u>cheap</u> too it sounds like heaven. London's far too expensive and dirty and full of people one knows and the weather's lousy on top of that. I'm sure it's cold in Prague as well but at least you'll have snow when winter comes and the northern lights and things of that sort . . .

Camilla's interest in natural phenomena had always been vague.

. . . and it'll all look just like the set of <u>Anna Karenina</u> and there will be beautiful women wearing furs and those big cuddly bear-like men so much better than the crummy variety we have in England. All the ones here keep getting colds and Ed Saunders is the only one who's even <u>vaguely</u> interesting (though I shan't marry him of course no matter what Mummy has to say on the subject) but taken as a job lot they really are very cold fish indeed and so <u>tiresome</u> at parties just standing there gawping and looking awkward or else getting drunk and throwing up. Why can't English men <u>talk</u> properly? It's something I've always wondered and a question which concerns me increasingly the more I come into contact with them present correspondent excepted naturally of course.

Life has been very dull indeed and I've not got much gossip to report except oh yes! you might be interested to know that Ella Harcourt's broken off her engagement to Charlie Stanhope. You remember Ella don't you? She was at my birthday party and you were a darling and took me to her engagement lunch at that fabulous house in Chester Square — so sweet of you — but anyway there's more to that particular story than meets the eye. You remember her cousin Sarah? The pretty but superior one who hardly said a single thing at lunch but just sneered and was quite unnecessarily frosty to Sophie Scott-Chivers . . .

Who was, I remember now, the girl with the villa in Biarritz.

. . . who really is a sweetie even if she's not all that gifted intellectually but one shouldn't hold that against her should one? Anyhow you remember Sarah. Well a few weeks after you left she published this monograph in a historical journal called Living History all about how American money supported English feudalism or something of the sort and she used her own family as material and included everything right up to the suicide of her grandmother — who jumped out of a window quite tragically you know — and the interesting thing was that this was the first public mention of it. The suicide was all hushed up at the time you see. And the tabloid press being the thing it is questions were soon being asked and then it emerged that Sarah's grandmother wasn't the only member of the Harcourt family to die in tragic circumstances and you won't believe this but Lord Harcourt's sister (Ella's aunt) also killed herself and driving back from her funeral Ella's mother and both Sarah's parents died in the most terrible car crash. Awful isn't it? And of course the newspapers have got hold of all this and trumped it up into a big story about a family curse and unearthed all this silliness about insanity running in families and of course as Ella's the one who'll inherit when her father dies — and is just the kind of person the tabloids like writing about being rich, pretty, etc. etc. — they've started saying that she's living under some sort of ghastly curse. All the most ridiculous nonsense but papers must pump up their circulation somehow I suppose and the result of it all is that they've been besieging Chester Square and taking photographs and asking all sorts of questions and generally being a complete nuisance. And in the middle of this all — silly timing if you ask me — Ella quite unexpectedly announces that her engagement to Charlie is off and the very next day there's a

headline in the Sun about 'Cracking under the Strain' and a whole lot of awful rot.

So that's been interesting I suppose and to tell the truth Ella has been behaving quite strangely lately but I don't even begin to dream that it's at all as serious as the papers say. Can you imagine how Sarah's feeling being the one who sparked the whole thing off in the first place? So stupid. I bet she's kicking herself. But I'm sure it'll all die down these things always do.

And when it does London will be even more deathly dull than it is already (even unfounded scandal about one's friends is quite fun you know) and then I don't know what I shall do. So hurry up and come home and entertain me and for heaven's sakes please play in some of mother's concerts because her anxiety is driving me quite mad (no pun intended because Ella Harcourt is a friend as you know) and that would never do would it?

Anyhow I must be ending now because I've been writing this in a history of art lecture – Mummy's making me do some frightful course – and the class is just ending so take care Jamie darling and write soon and be good and don't let any of those Czech beauties tempt you from the virtuous path and all that.

 Much much Much love,
   Camilla

    xx

I was standing in the Picture Room when I read Camilla's letter, looking at the pictures complete in all their glory for the last time. I remember reading the line about the breaking of Ella's engagement; remember smiling to myself over the fact that Camilla felt it necessary to remind me who Ella was; remember my rush of pure joy on hearing the news of my love's freedom; remember thinking that it would mean mine, too. I gave no thought to Camilla's gossip about curses and publicity; I suspected, rather, that much of what she had written was coloured by the taste for drama which was as much a part of her as her incredible curls and breathless emphases. As a personality Camilla chafed against the limitations of the common-place: if excitement did not exist she invented it to tell; and I thought then that her letter was another example of a little news being made to go a long way, and dismissed it as such with a smile.

As you pass through life the future shrinks and the past expands. I could not have known then that the future is seldom as it appears; that the present passes with the blinking of an eye; that the past is an Atlantis, a sunken island in the sea which we can never hope to reach again. I know it now. I know that Eric is buried on it, amongst the sharp spires and gracious glinting domes of a city we loved, of Prague as my memory has preserved it. For me he died there and not in France; for me he never floated in that icy pool of water far below; I never watched his body as it . . . But still I cannot speak of it; I have not yet found the courage to face what I did, what I have done. I will. But not now. Not yet.

Now I sit toying with the idea that maybe life is a game after all, a game we play just once. I am coming round to Sarah's view, perhaps. But if life is a game then it has no practices; no training; no preliminary rounds. It is a game played on the principle of sudden death. And to play it properly, to play it fairly and well, we need all the strength that self-knowledge, courage, will and discipline can impart. At twenty-two I had none of these things, or if I had them I could not use them then. I had not yet learned to take life seriously; to know that it is not like other games; that it matters who wins and who loses; and that how they win and lose matters also. I had no idea either that victory could be Pyrrhic; nor did I know that the end seldom justifies the means. I could not have known any of this without experience, and of that I had none. I was innocent; and innocent of my innocence.

16

The following day chaos reigned on the top floor of the Sherkansky Palace. A large burly Czech with hair cut short at the front and sides and left long at the back was directing operations. He nodded to us on arrival, but was soon too busy barking orders at his minions to pay us much attention. Men were running up and down the palace stairs, rolling back carpets, screwing doors off hinges; folding; packing; lifting. The grand piano, dismantled, was the first piece of furniture to go, and it was carried down the stairs like a sedated elephant. The other pieces in the apartment followed it: a large dresser that had stood in the kitchen, its china carefully wrapped and packed into boxes; the heavy bed on which I had slept; a prettily-carved bookcase; two occasional tables; an armoire; lamps; Madame Mocsáry's dilapidated collection of French novels.

The paintings were moved last, when everything else had been carried down to the waiting removals van; and with agonizing, painstaking slowness they were taken from the walls they had graced together and wrapped in great sheets of thick plastic that dimmed their colours and hid their outlines. As each was lifted off its hook a square of wall, garish and red, unbleached by the sun, was exposed where the painting had preserved it; and ranged together these gashes looked to me like wounds, like flesh that has been stripped of its skin; but I did not say so. Eric and I watched the removals men in dejected silence, as if they were dismantling the house we had been born in – and in some respects that apartment had witnessed something of a rebirth – but our reserve passed unnoticed by the voluble Mr Tomin.

'There are several foreign collectors who are showing an interest

147

in this sale,' he told us proudly. 'A friend of mine at Christie's in New York has spread the word. And I myself was in London last week and told some people. I think you are selling at a very good time.' And he trotted excitedly around the apartment, talking to the chief of the removals men, supervising the packing and transportation of the paintings, poking and peering and prodding, meddling delightedly in everything and all the time keeping up a patter of conversation with us in English, punctuated by the odd hoarse order in Czech.

Surrounded by dust and activity and sharply-barked orders Eric and I stood, ignored, by the Picture Room windows. He tugged at my sleeve.

'This is no place for us any more,' he said; and he led the way abruptly out of the apartment, past the line of workers on the staircase and the removals van blocking the street outside. He did not stop walking until we had reached Florian's, where we spent the rest of the day morosely drinking hot chocolate and talking occasionally to two American poets, the sole other occupants of the café, who sat surrounded by torn sheets of densely-covered notepaper, smoking joints fixedly and staring into space. They were not enlivening company.

'There is not even our friend with the nose here to amuse us,' whispered Eric as we ordered second cups of chocolate from Jean.

'No, not even her.'

And because the café was unusually quiet and we needed diversion, we longed for the crowd of debaters with their long words and lank hair; we missed the sound of their passionate, short-lived conflicts; we listened vainly for their championship of ideas which we – and I dare say they – only dimly understood. In the smoky gloom of their habitual haunt their voices rang out to us, ghostly in the silence.

'The most important thing about Kafka was that he was a Jew . . .'

'Was that he was a Nationalist at heart . . .'

'Was that he lived in inspirational times . . .'

'In beautiful surroundings . . .'

'In a changing world . . .'

'The most important thing about Havel is that he is a thinker . . .'

'A philosopher . . .'

'A playwright . . .'

'Who's written nothing since the revolution, incidentally . . .'

'A president.'

'Marginalized.'

'A focal point.'

'Obscured by Klaus.'

We missed the rhythm of their arguments, the regularity of their disputes, the violence of their reconciliations. And we realized how much we would always miss them.

But regardless of our despondency, the day of the sale moved inexorably nearer. Originally set for a fortnight after the removal of the paintings and furniture, it was brought forward – on the advice of a member of the Musée d'Orsay's purchasing committee – so that it should fall before the passing of an imminent bill expected to restrict French spending on foreign artworks. 'It is not something one usually does, of course,' said Mr Tomin, 'but in this case I think it would be wise to make an exception. The French museums are highly interested in Madame Mocsáry's work. And their involvement might spur on the Czech museums. This country is in need of a cultural icon.'

He was right. Madame Mocsáry's death had come at the best possible moment for the preservation of her reputation for posterity, and national interest in the sale of her work ran high. After the first flush of revolutionary fervour, Czech cultural officialdom was casting its eye about for evidence of a new Golden Age, a suitable parallel to the flowering of arts and letters which the First Republic had witnessed. And the fact that Madame Mocsáry had been French by birth and had done most of her work under the Communist regime did not deter it, or the wider nation, from honouring her as one of the most significant artists of her generation. 'Mocsáry,' said the *Prague Post*, an English-language daily that Eric and I read, 'revivifies the long tradition of Czech cultural excellence, and lights the flame of national creativity in our time. Her work is a moving testament to the power of the human spirit in adversity, and her later paintings are full of the frantic optimism of our new age.' When we were asked for comment Eric and I forbore to say that her later paintings were probably less frantically optimistic than rushed. We were not about to tell the world what we had discovered from Blanca, namely that Madame Mocsáry had only finished the Picture Room in the final weeks before her removal to a nursing home. It seemed somehow disloyal to her memory to do anything to endanger the formulation or the acceptance of her myth; and we were grateful for all she had done for us, even in death.

Mr Tomin, who scanned the papers, too, and whose self-satisfaction and excitement increased with each passing day, talked frequently to us of the preparations. 'We have had an expert from Vienna to hang the paintings,' he told us, 'and the lighting at the auction house has been especially redesigned. I also have great hopes for the furniture now. With all this excitement it may develop an historical value which outweighs its intrinsic one.'

Mr Kierczinsky, whom we occasionally saw too, also grew notice-ably more dapper as press interest in the sale increased; and one morning he showed us a newspaper photograph of him standing on the steps of his law firm's office. 'I said that I could not comment . . . of course. But it is a good likeness, is it not? Do you think you can see the name of the firm clearly? I am not sure you can see it clearly.'

We told him you could see it clearly.

'Ah that is good. Very good.' And he went off chuckling to himself to draw up the last of the requisite papers. Madame Mocsáry's will had been highly specific in the assignation of trinkets; but, written years before her fame and never updated, it had largely ignored the possibility of her having any money to bequeath after her death. She had left her paintings to her sister Laure, little suspecting the international attention which she and they would later receive. And as Laure in the event had predeceased her sister by three years, the paintings had gone to Eric's mother. Though this seemed quite simple to us, the probable success of the sale seemed to cause a variety of 'urgent . . . paperwork matters' to spring up which required Mr Kierczinsky's detailed and expensive attention.

The showrooms of First Auctioneers Ltd, which occupied a good half-block of Wenceslas Square, were done over especially for the sale just as Mr Tomin had promised. Teams of painters and polishers brought to their walls a pristine shine unknown in Czech auction houses and hired crates of Bohemian crystal – vodka and champagne glasses mostly – were delivered daily. The details of the sale and the run up to it were complicated and extravagant. There was to be a reception for important potential buyers on the night before the Mocsáry effects went under the gavel, and the sale itself was to take place a week after the paintings went on show for the first time.

That week was perhaps the only time that the collection was ever seen in its entirety by the public. And each day, for the price of the catalogue, a long line of people – Czech and foreign alike – trooped over the pale wooden floors of the viewing rooms, pointing, admiring, discussing. Each day, too, Mr Tomin came to show us another illustrious name in the auction house's visitors' book.

In the busy days that succeeded the arrival of Camilla Boardman's letter I had no time to reply to it and I was unwilling to write to Ella. I waited instead to hear from her, for I was mindful of my promise not to write until she had told me that her freedom was secured; and having kept my word for so long I had no intention of breaking it now. Each day I scanned my letter box and each day I was disappointed as no envelope from her arrived, something that might have worried me had I been less certain of her. As it was, I felt secure enough to wait and I managed to avoid the temptation to write myself. If Ella did not think the time yet ripe for contact then I would trust to her judgement.

It was on the Wednesday of 'Showing Week', as Mr Tomin liked to call it, that I discovered that the Harcourts were in Prague; and I discovered it completely by chance. My attention was being drawn to the fact that Princess Amelia von Thurn und Taxis had come the previous afternoon when, two lines below her flowery signature, I saw another entry in the book and read 'Lord and Lady Alexander Harcourt, Grand Hotel Europa', written in confident ballpoint in a hand I did not recognize. Ignoring Mr Tomin's excited description of the princess's kind words to him I asked him if he remembered anything about an English milord and his wife.

He paused, thinking slowly, but his eyes were trained to miss nothing. 'Yes. Good-looking. Lady Harcourt spoke with the accent of Boston,' he said as my blood began to race. 'They were quiet, though; they seemed worried. They talked so that I could not hear them.'

I could barely contain my excitement as it occurred to me that Ella, even now, might be in the city; that Ella, even now, might be asking for my whereabouts at the conservatory or at Sokolska 21. After weeks without her I saw suddenly how self-controlled I had been; how successfully I had devoted myself to the delights of Prague and to the challenges of my violin; how conscientiously I had not written. Now I could be self-controlled no longer.

'The princess said she would come in person to the sale.' Mr Tomin looked at me, glowing with pride.

'That's wonderful. But I wonder if you could tell me anything more about the Harcourts.'

He looked at me, surprised by my evident curiosity, and began to shake his head.

'I ask only because they're very important British collectors,' I said; and I waited for my bait to be taken. Occasionally Mr Tomin had to be galvanized into recollection.

'You know them?' he asked shrewdly.

'Yes.'

'And you think they have the . . . resources to make an impact on the sale?'

'I know they do.'

My confidence revived Mr Tomin's powers of recollection at once. He went on to describe to me a couple who could only be Ella's father and stepmother.

'He has blond hair, thinning on top, and walks very straight. Her hair is red and very . . . big.'

'Did they have anyone with them? A daughter perhaps?' I endured a knowing look from the auctioneer.

'I don't know,' he said slowly, teasing me. 'No, I don't think so.' But seeing my disappointment he took pity. 'Wait, though. Let me see. Now that I come to think of it, they *did* have someone with them.'

'A woman with short blonde hair?'

'I think so. Yes. But she left before them.'

I snatched up the visitors' book and looked again at the Harcourts' Prague address. The hotel which they had listed was perhaps a minute's walk from where I stood; and I made an effort to control my excitement as it occurred to me that Ella might, at that very moment, be in one of the rooms under the gables which I could see from the large windows of the auction house. Excusing myself hurriedly from Mr Tomin, I dodged through the lines of people staring at the paintings and vaulted down the gallery steps into the crush of the square, crossing four lanes of traffic without a sidewards glance, arriving breathless but quickly in the foyer of their hotel.

Youth demands such instant gratification of its desires. It has not learned patience.

Certainly I found it difficult to be patient as a polite receptionist informed me that the Harcourts were out and I settled down to an hour's long and fruitless wait. Gradually my excitement gave way to frustration. But I waited. And finally I was rewarded by the sight of Pamela's severe form and sculpted hair entering on Alexander's arm. Husband and wife were talking anxiously together.

'Excuse me,' I said, planting myself on the carpet in front of them. 'I wonder if you remember me. James Farrell. I'm a friend of your daughter's.'

Their minds had so obviously been elsewhere that it took a moment for them to register the unexpected presence of a former guest and for the machinery of polite greeting to slide into motion. Alexander took my proffered hand.

'Hello,' he said, shaking it. 'Whatever are you doing here?'

The words were jovial enough but their lightness was forced. Without knowing why this was I explained briefly the reasons for my presence in Prague and accepted their congratulations on the showing of the Mocsáry collection with a smile.

'I don't deserve any of the credit,' I said, 'but I'm glad you like the way it's been done. Will you be coming to the sale?'

They nodded politely – perhaps Pamela said 'Of course' – and made as if to move on. I detained them a moment.

'Do you know where Ella is?' I asked, smiling, keeping my voice steady.

Her father and stepmother turned and looked at me. Their faces, I saw now, were drawn; and there was a note of dulled resignation in Alexander's voice as he said slowly, 'Unfortunately, no. She disappeared yesterday. Went off by herself. We haven't heard a thing from her since then.' He looked at me as though still struggling to believe that this could be so. 'We don't know what has happened to her.'

'I'm sorry,' I said; and the evident worry in my own face and voice was something of a bond between us. There was a pause.

'We last saw Ella at the viewing,' said Pamela eventually. 'But she left us there. There was something of an argument. We thought she'd be back at the hotel but there was no sign of her last night nor all this morning. We're half sick with worry.'

'You must be.'

'And if you hear anything from her, *anything*, you will let us know, won't you?' This from Alexander.

'Of course,' I said.

'That's very kind of you.' We shook hands. 'Well we mustn't take up any more of your time, Mr Farrell. It was good of you to have come to see us.'

'If there's anything I can do . . .'

'Of course. Thank you. I'm sure she'll turn up any moment now.'

'Yes.'

They turned from me and began walking towards the lift. 'Have you told the police?' I asked after them.

'A person must be missing for a week before they'll do anything about it,' Alexander replied, turning. 'And stray foreign nationals aren't high on their list of priorities.'

'You will call and tell me when she comes back?'

'Of course. Pamela darling, take his number.' And while they waited on the stairs I scribbled it on a piece of paper which Lady Harcourt put in her purse. Then we said our goodbyes again, a little awkwardly, and they went up to their room.

Outside, the square was full of people laughing and talking, but I moved through them unseeing. In the grip of something between suspicion and hope, I walked quickly home; and as I let myself into Madame Mocsáry's apartment I found that I had been correct in my assumption. Eric and Ella were sitting on the music-room floor, drinking tea.

The sight of the two of them together comes back clearly to me now, though I thought I had banished it for ever. I see them sitting side by side on the stone of that floor; I see the shining gold of Ella's hair beside the gleaming black of Eric's; the pallor of her creamy skin beside the olive tones of his. It must have been the first time they had met, though they had known of each other for some time. I see the look in Ella's eyes as I open the door. I watch her put down her cigarette and rise to her feet in one graceful movement; I hear the tap of her shoes on the stone as she moves towards me; I see that she is wearing black trousers which cling to her thin legs and a black jacket with a wide collar of black fur. In such dark clothes her pallor is almost ghostly; but the green of her eyes could not be more alive. She is smiling, hugging me, holding me; and then we are kissing, and her taste fills me as I run my hand over the fine bones of her spine and pull her closer, holding her tight. It is only as I bury my nose in the fine skin of her lemon-scented neck that I see Eric watching us from the floor with something in his eyes which I dismiss because I don't understand; and it is only then that I remember myself and pull away from Ella, happily, all the frustration of my waiting and my worry gone, and introduce her properly to my friend.

'We have met already,' Eric says with a certain curtness.

'Yes we have.' Ella pulls me to the floor to sit beside her at an improvised tea table of packing crates and short discarded planks. 'Eric's been telling me all about the wonderful time you two've been having.'

I hardly remember the rest of that conversation. What I do remember is that my eyes met Eric's as Ella said this and that I smiled. I remember also that he did not respond at once, but that as I went on smiling his face softened and he grinned at me and I felt relief at the passing of an awkward moment. I remember that tea was poured. I remember also that as I took my first sip I thought of Pamela and Alexander, alone on their hotel staircase.

'I've been talking to your parents, Ella,' I said quietly.

'Have you really?' She made an attempt at nonchalance. It was not convincing. 'How are they?'

'Worried sick.'

There was a pause. I watched, excited despite myself, as she opened her bag, found a packet, took a cigarette from it, put it to her lips, lit it. Slowly, deeply, she inhaled. 'I know you must think me awful for running off and leaving them like that,' Ella said.

I did not reply.

'But I can't tell you how badly I needed to see you. And they don't let me out of their sight for a minute.'

I began a question but she raised a hand to stop me.

'There's plenty of time for all that later. A lot has happened since I last saw you, James. A lot.' She looked at Eric and then at me. There was silence. 'I suppose I'd better go and find Daddy and Pamela and let them know I'm all right,' said Ella at length. 'Oh

God, this is awful.' She got up to go. 'If you'll walk with me I'll tell you all about it.'

'All right.'

My lover extended a hand to my friend. 'It was lovely to meet you,' she said, smiling. 'I do hope we'll see much more of each other now that we've finally met.'

Eric took her hand and murmured something. 'I'll see you later,' he said to me.

I nodded.

And together Ella and I left the apartment and made our way down the great shadowy staircase bathed in short bursts of inadequate light. In the dark on the second landing I felt her hand in mine and smelled her scent and kissed her. And as we kissed I knew the sheer joy of reunion; the complete and overwhelming power of our passion; the force of its fusion. And I did not have the sense to be frightened by it.

17

I struggle now for the precise words Ella used. I can catch her tone; can follow her expression; can watch her face and trace the changing patterns on it. But her words come back to me only slowly, for when I first listened to them I was distracted by the flick of her hair; the tap of her light quick step; the neatness of her waist; the outline of her breasts; the ring of her voice. I don't remember being mystified by her presence in Prague or by the sudden way in which she had deserted her parents; for the arrogance of youthful love provided all the explanation I required. But as I listened to her I remembered Camilla Boardman's breathless letter and Ella's own words in the empty sitting room of Madame Mocsáry's apartment; and they pierced the haze of my euphoria as we threaded our way through the crowds on Sokolska Street and turned left into Wenceslas Square.

'I can't face Daddy and Pamela just yet,' Ella was saying, almost pleadingly. 'I need to talk properly to you, Jamie. I need your help. Isn't there anywhere we could go just for a moment? Somewhere where nobody would know us?'

'You forget that this is not London,' I replied. 'There's no need for secrecy.' And smilingly I guided her into a small coffee shop I knew on the corner. Being so centrally placed it lacked the back-street charm of other establishments but it would serve our purpose. And soon we were sitting at a back table and ordering espressos from a waitress with badly dyed blonde hair and alarming eyebrows.

'Now,' I began when the coffee had been placed before us, 'what do you need to talk to me about?'

'I don't suppose you know anything about it at all, do you?' she said slowly.

'I know some things, I think,' I ventured, unsure precisely what 'it' was but guessing that it had something to do with the breaking of her engagement to Charlie.

'What do you know, Jamie? What can you know?'

Briefly I told her the outline of my letter from Camilla Boardman. She paused, taking it in. Then, sighing, she said wryly, 'No one steals a person's thunder quite like Camilla, do they?'

I shook my head and smiled. Ella was not smiling.

'Well, she's given you the outsider's version, and it's interesting to know what my friends think of me, certainly. But the truth is a little more complex than what she's told you. A little more complex and a little less pretty.'

'Go on.'

'Well the fact of the matter is that my family – and from what you say at least some of my friends – are beginning to consider the possibility that I may be a crackpot. Off my rocker, you know.' Ella paused as I took this in. 'And the worst of it is that it's my own wretched fault.' She took another drag on her cigarette. 'I suppose I had better begin at the beginning, hadn't I?' she said, taking my hand.

I nodded.

Silence.

'I thought it was all some silly mistake on the newspapers' part,' I began at last.

'If it were only that I wouldn't mind. But unfortunately it's more serious than gossip. Oh I'm not *really* mad,' she went on hastily. 'It's a complete . . . But I should begin at the beginning. Forgive me if I repeat some of the things I said at Seton. It's just important for me to keep some kind of grip over where reality ends and fiction begins in all of this.'

'All right.'

There was another pause. Ella took a deep breath.

'You know about my grandmother and my aunt and the generally shaky mental history of my family,' she said quietly.

I nodded.

'Well my father's obsessed by it. Understandably, I think. If your mother and your twin sister had killed themselves you'd worry about your own children, wouldn't you? Particularly if your only daughter happened to be the living image of her grandmother. It would be a constant reminder. Do you follow?'

I nodded again.

'Well Daddy's always on the lookout for danger signs; signs that I might be unhappy, that I might not be coping. He doesn't want to take any risks with me, which puts a certain amount of pressure on a person, as you can imagine.'

'I can.'

She bit her lip. 'Oh, God, I've been so *stupid*.' She stubbed out her cigarette, half-smoked, with exasperated violence.

'In what way?'

'I've played *right* into Sarah's hands.'

'How?'

'Well, when she published her monograph and the papers caught on to the suicides, I thought I saw my chance of getting rid of Charlie. I thought he wouldn't want a madwoman as the mother of his children. Not even if she *did* stand in line to inherit a castle.' She paused. 'So I staged a confession.'

'You did what?'

Ella fumbled in her bag for another cigarette and lit it. 'I cried and I told him how unstable my family was, how there was something wrong with our genes. I even said I had a duty never to have children, for fear of passing it on.' She stopped. 'Mental illness is probably genetic, you know. I thought it would scare him off.'

'When in fact it did quite the opposite.' The mist was slowly clearing.

'Not exactly,' she said quietly. 'At first Charlie wouldn't budge. He was going to stick by me loyally and all that. He kept on saying it was only my family, it wasn't me, I had to rise above it.'

I thought of Charles Stanhope's earnest, uncomprehending eyes and a sudden fear gripped my throat. 'What did you tell him?' I asked quietly.

Ella took a deep drag on her cigarette. For a long moment there was silence. Finally she spoke. 'What did you expect me to tell him?'

'Don't tell me you . . .'

'All right, I won't. But I did.' Her voice was small and thin, like a child's.

'You told him you were . . .'

There was a pause.

'Yes. All right,' she said at last. 'I told him I was worried about *myself*. There, I've said it. I told him it wouldn't be fair to marry him.'

'Oh God.'

'And do you know what *he* did?'

I saw with complete clarity how things stood. 'He told your father, didn't he?' I said grimly.

She nodded.

'Oh Ella you stupid . . .' I could not find the words. Love and anger welled inside me; then pity too as I saw she was crying.

'I thought Sarah was giving me a way out,' she said through her tears. 'For the first time in her life, in her own twisted way, I thought she was being magnanimous. By stirring everyone up and making everything so public, I thought she was offering me a way to escape and so I took it. I had no idea things would turn out like this.'

'Oh no.'

'It seems strange to say it now, I know, but you have no idea how perfect it all seemed at the time. I thought it would be the least painful way of breaking with Charlie. He'd noticed I'd changed towards him, you see; he's not stupid. He needed an explanation. And I could hardly have told him the *truth*.' She paused. 'I didn't think he'd tell anyone.'

'I don't believe you could have been so . . .'

'Don't judge me James.' Her voice rang suddenly sharp. 'Don't judge me.'

Mutely we stared at each other. I took her hand.

'If you knew what these past two months have been like you would be kinder,' she said more quietly at last, drying her eyes. 'I've been paying for my freedom I can tell you.'

I sat silently, groping for words.

'If you knew what it's been like seeing my father so worried, so worried and with so little reason, knowing it's my own fault . . . If only you *knew*. Seeing him suffer like this has been punishment enough.' She looked down at the floor, away from me. 'But what could I have done?' Her eyes met mine, searchingly. 'Short of telling everybody everything, right down to why I got engaged to Charlie in the first place, there was nothing to do but pretend. I was trapped, Jamie; I couldn't go back then. So I pretended.'

I put my hand on her arm.

'And God it was awful,' she went on. 'I can't tell you how awful. The situation got completely out of hand. I couldn't control it any more.' She paused. 'And that was when it got frightening. I tried to be myself again and found that I wasn't allowed to be normal any more. The whole system had already swung into gear, you see.' She drew breath deeply. 'And then the talking started. And the newspaper articles. And the photographers. You've no idea what that does to you. Knowing that people are always watching: your family; your friends; the goddamn newspapers. I've been living in a goldfish bowl these past two months.'

I nodded, still lost for words.

'And the worst thing is that I know it's all my own fault. I don't know *how* I could have let it happen.'

'Neither do I.'

Ella gripped my hand. 'Don't say that to me. You've got to help me. You've got to help me get through this.'

There was a pause. Her eyes met mine unflinchingly.

'I will,' I said. 'Of course I will.'

'Oh Jamie. Thank you.'

She leaned across the table and kissed me. Our lips met and I knew in that brief sweet touch that I would do anything for her. I knew and like a fool was pleased by that knowledge.

'If you only knew what it was like,' she went on, sitting back, calmer now, 'how *draining* it is having to be happy all the time. And I've got to be happy to convince them I'm sane. I'm not allowed one morose minute to myself before Daddy suggests I see a new therapist or Pamela wants to take me away for a "change of scene". That's how I come to be in Prague, you know. This is a "change of scene".' She paused. 'And you've no *idea* how many frauds I've been taken to see; I've sat in consulting rooms from one end of Harley Street to the other.' She made an attempt at a smile. 'You can't imagine what it's like. These people ask you to *remember* things, to tell them about traumas you've never had and insecurities you've never dreamed of. And the frightening thing is that things *do* start occurring to you; that all this attention *does* make you think that maybe there's a reason for it after all. You start to doubt yourself and those around you. You begin to remember childhood nightmares.' She lit another cigarette and drew on it deeply. 'And because I thought I should try to seem open with the doctors – they're the ones you have to convince, after all – I told them all about my childhood, all about everything. Except Sarah of course. I could hardly tell them about her, about her and me.'

I watched her shaking fingers as she put her coffee cup to her lips. 'So what did you tell them?' I asked.

'All sorts of things.'

'Give me an example.'

'All right.' She paused, thinking. 'Well, when I was nine or ten I used to have a nightmare about a witch who lived in the closet in my bedroom. A wicked witch, like the one in *The Lion, the Witch and the Wardrobe* who turned Mr Tumnus to stone. Remember her?'

I nodded.

'Well in this dream she was always just about to turn me to stone and I was always running away from her, running and running through woods and fields and . . . you get the picture.' She smiled.

'I was always looking for my father to rescue me. And I always woke up just as the witch caught me. Daddy never appeared.'

'You told the doctors about that?'

She nodded.

'And what did they say?'

'Well you must remember that shrinks aren't paid to tell you you're *sane*.'

'What did they make of that dream?'

'Oh all the usual stuff: lost mother; fear of stepmother; need for father. They told me that I was angry with Daddy for marrying Pamela – which couldn't be further from the truth, incidentally – and started talking about Electra complexes and the dangers of repressed grieving for a parent turning to self-mutilation or violence as a sort of attention-seeking measure. It was quite ridiculous.'

'Go on,' I said.

'So I told Daddy I didn't want any more doctors, that they were filling my mind with all sorts of evil things. You've no idea, as a matter of fact, quite how stable you have to be to emerge unscathed from a session with a really respected psychiatrist. And Daddy went and told *them* that. He got very angry, actually, and stormed into Dr Jefferson's rooms and demanded an explanation, which was of course precisely what the bastard wanted. I was in *denial* now, you see. If I had a pound for every time some nut-case quack who doesn't know me from a bar of soap has told me I need to "face my problems" I'd be richer than my father.'

She stopped and there were tears in her eyes again. 'Oh God Jamie. What have I *done*? What have I done?' Silently she took my hand.

'Hush,' I whispered, getting up and taking her in my arms, holding her tightly. 'It'll be all right.'

'Will it?'

'Yes.'

'I can't tell you how badly I need to hear that. Or how much I've missed you.' She clung to me. I held her until her tears had stopped.

'And now tell me why you ran away from your parents yesterday,' I began when we were sitting opposite each other again.

'That's the final part of the story,' she said, fumbling in her bag for yet another cigarette. A pile of half-smoked butts filled the ashtray between us and the packet she pulled out was empty. Ella seemed surprised by this and screwed it up into a tight ball in her hand. 'After the big blow-up with Dr Jefferson, Pamela suggested one of her "changes of scene",' she said at last. 'Basically London was no place for the invalid. The papers were having a field day as you can imagine. Which reminds me. Look at this.' She took a page from a tabloid newspaper out of her bag and handed it to me. In the centre was a large photograph of her at a party. She was standing on a staircase alone, very pale. 'Heaven only knows where they got this from,' she said. 'Read what it says.'

I took the newspaper from her and read the column quickly, scanning its melodrama with disgust.

> She looked as though she had everything, but Ella Harcourt, 24, heir to one of the country's most stately stately homes, has a dark family history looming over her. Young, beautiful, intelligent, she is the toast of London . . . but how many years remain before the tragic curse of the Harcourts claims a new victim?
>
> *Family Tree.* . . Page 2 *Psychological Report.* . . Pages 15 – 17

'*That's* why they thought a change of scene would do me good,' said Ella drily. 'But they wouldn't let me go alone – I've not been allowed to be alone at all since this thing started – so they came with me. I chose Prague because you were here.'

I thrilled with gladness as she said this. 'But why did you run away?'

She paused. 'I guess I figured it wouldn't make much difference. We had an argument, at the Mocsáry viewing actually, and Daddy said something . . . about my "condition". And I thought: "Well if they're convinced I'm loopy, and will be whatever I do, I might as well take a night's freedom." Have you any *idea* how wonderful it is to be alone when you've spent two months being watched constantly, day and night?' She looked at me. 'Oh, I know it was wrong. But I was angry and fed up to the *teeth* with the kid-glove treatment. Can you understand that?'

I nodded.

There was a pause.

'But now you've got to face the music,' I said firmly.

There was silence. 'You don't mean you think I should *tell* them, do you? All about Sarah and Charles and . . . what I did. They'd think I was really mad if they knew the truth.'

I saw her point. 'No, I don't,' I said slowly, trying to think. 'But when I left them a few hours ago they were sick with worry. You've got to go home and let them know you're all right. And I think you've got some heartfelt apologies to make.'

She bowed her head. 'I know,' she said.

'Then let's go and get them over and done with.'

So we got up, paid, and left the café. As we emerged into the crowds of Wenceslas Square, Ella slipped her hand into mine. 'Thank you, Jamie.'

And she kissed me.

Sin is a strong word to use; an ugly one. But I am no longer afraid of it. I know that Ella sinned by taking Charles from Sarah. I think perhaps that I sinned too by wanting her confession for myself alone. I was jealous of her confidence. When I might have advised her to tell the truth, to admit what she had done, I did not. I didn't show her the dangers of deceit; I didn't know them myself then. I see now, though – and this is the first of the lessons I have set out to learn – that lies are like the bars of a cage; that they solidify with time; that once you have built and left them about you, all is lost.

The original sin of Ella taking Charles from Sarah shaped the events of her life – of all our lives – from then onwards. And in her

166

weakness, which was partly my weakness also, she protected her sin with lies: lies to Charlie; to her parents; to herself, perhaps. She did not admit what she had done nor seek forgiveness for it; at least she did not until made to do so by forces by then far from her control. And the truth, when it came, came too late; too late to save any of us, perhaps. At least that is how I understand it now; and I know that it is such resignation which I must seek. It is no use doing battle with events long past; my only hope is to understand, not to change them. If only I could do that I would be grateful; more grateful even than I was to Sarah. That gratitude, like its predecessor, might give me peace; it might grant me rest. And that, I think, is all I have left to wish for.

18

The Mocsáry sale was set for the following Monday; and over the weekend the galleries of First Auctioneers were filled to overflowing with buyers and the kind of people who dress to look like them. The casual crowds which had come to see the collection at first were thinning, their jeans and T-shirts giving way to the elegant suits and power ties of more serious money. Each day brought scores of telephone bids; and lengthy articles on the importance of preserving the art for the nation appeared in the serious newspapers. The less serious newspapers also chronicled the viewing – or more accurately, the clothes and love lives of the celebrity viewers – and Mr Tomin had to have a press stand constructed at very short notice at the back of the bidding room.

This and the fact that Princess Amelia remembered his name on her second visit made his swagger insufferable. In increasingly garish jackets he appeared smiling each day, telling favoured clients in stage whispers that the catalogue estimates were really very conservative. Eric and I followed him at a discreet distance, listening fascinated to his patter; and loath though we were to admit it we had to acknowledge that he was impressive. Sharp-nosed collectors from Western Europe and the United States unbent in his flattering presence; prominent members of the European aristocracy – taking their lead from the pink-cheeked and pearl-hung Princess Amelia – outdid each other to be charming; the gallery's visitors' book was eagerly passed from hand to hand by buyers anxious to record their presence at this self-styled historic event.

Yes, Mr Tomin did a good job. Even now I can marvel at the way he took a reputation and turned it into something legendary; at how he convinced the moneyed of Europe that Madame Mocsáry's was a name to invest in and the nationals at home that it was one to glorify. By such men are great artists made.

Eric's mother arrived on the day before the sale, a tall, stately woman with fine bones and beautiful hands. I remember meeting her for the first time; remember the easy elegance of her conversation and dress; the silver of her long hair; the sparkle of her dark, grave eyes. She must have been as old as my own parents or older, but her movements had the easy suppleness of youth; and her face appeared lined only when she smiled. I can see that smile now, and as I see it I remember that it was Eric's smile too; that when mother and son smiled their faces lit up; that when they laughed their mirth echoed and rang together. I hear them laughing sometimes, even now, in my dreams. But I heard their laughter later, when I knew the Vaugirards better. In Prague I saw Louise only twice: on the afternoon of the sale itself; and on the night before it, her first in the city, when she took me and Eric out to dinner at Czardas, one of the chic new restaurants to have sprung up since the revolution. It occupied the first two floors of an old palace block in the Malá Strana, was within easy walking distance of both the French and the American embassies and was patronized almost exclusively by foreigners. As a result its prices were extortionate, its service impeccable and its atmosphere negligible. I thought it an odd choice until I learned that it had come with Mr Tomin's strong recommendation.

Louise de Vaugirard was sitting on an uncomfortable modern chair when we arrived, an elegant figure in a long black jersey dress which hugged her thin hips. She wore no jewellery but a silver crucifix on a thin silver chain; and as she stood up I knew who she was, even before Eric had kissed her on both cheeks.

'*Maman, je te présente mon ami* James Farrell,' he said.

'But we must not speak in French,' she said in barely accented English. 'The English do not care for languages not their own. Yes?'

I blushed and said awkwardly that I thought French a beautiful language.

Louise turned to Eric. 'But he is every bit as charming as you said he was.' Turning to me again she gave me her hand. 'I am delighted to meet you at last, Monsieur Farrell. My son has nothing but praise for you. And my husband and I are deeply grateful for all you have done for the family here in Prague. I only wish that Eric's father were here himself to thank you but unfortunately his affairs keep him in France.'

We sat down; dinner was ordered and arrived, steaming, on gilt-edged dishes. In his mother's company Eric was affectionate and deferential and slightly on edge. Though there was undoubtedly a closeness between them it seemed to me an uneasy one, based on a certain sympathy of spirit rather than emotional confidence or intimacy. Certainly Eric was not as easy with his mother as he was with me; nor, in her company, did he behave with me as he usually did. He watched more and spoke less; and his eagerness for us to like each other, expressed in many ways, touched me then. So Louise and I talked – of my childhood, my music, my time in Prague with her son – and Eric did not speak much unless appealed to.

I liked Louise; I enjoyed her easy, uncalculated charm, the precision of her sentences, the irony of her observations. And I talked easily enough, distracted only by the crucifix she wore. It was unusual: small; delicately-made; beautiful. But the face of its Christ caught so truly a note of human anguish that I was uncomfortable looking at it, and I was fascinated by my own discomfort. Again and again my eyes returned to it; and my hostess, seeing where I looked, asked me whether I would like to touch it.

I nodded, smiling.

'There is an interesting story attached to this,' she said as she undid the clasp of its silver chain and put the cross in my hand.

'Oh really?'

'Yes. It was the reward given to an ancestress of my husband.'

I saw Eric frown slightly and make an effort to hide his irritation. 'What had she done to deserve it?' I asked.

'She was a spy at the Congress of Vienna,' Louise replied, smiling.

'She took the secrets of the foreign negotiators with her feminine wiles and her reward was this cross, among other things. She was a great lady. Another Louise like me.'

'She was a whore, *Maman*,' said Eric quietly, 'as you should know.'

There was an unearthly silence.

Louise gave no outward sign of having heard her son. Calmly, deliberately, she took the crucifix back from me, threaded it through its chain, and hung it once more around her neck. Then quietly, she said, 'I want you never to speak to me again like that Eric. Am I understood?' and began once more to eat. The clash of her cutlery was, for a moment, unnaturally loud on the china of her plate; then she controlled it. And turning to me once more she began to speak again, laughing and smiling as though nothing had happened.

For the rest of the meal Eric did not say a word; and an hour of strained conversation with Louise, who paid no attention to her son's silence, passed very slowly for me. When our dessert plates and coffee cups had been cleared and the waiter had brought the bill, Eric still showed no signs of movement or of speech. So I thanked Madame de Vaugirard, a little awkwardly, for a lovely dinner and she rose.

'It was a pleasure to meet you at last, James.' During the course of the evening she had elegantly appropriated the use of my Christian name. 'I look forward to seeing you tomorrow afternoon at the sale.'

'Likewise,' I said, meaning it.

Eric got up now from the table and kissed his mother on both cheeks. Then, without another word, he turned and walked out. I shook hands with Louise, who smiled again as though nothing had happened, and followed him. Outside the restaurant we walked together in silence, my friend setting a furious pace, for ten minutes or more. We were walking along the river, heading for the Charles Bridge and the tram that would take us home; our breath turned to smoke in the icy air of approaching winter. Block after block of cobbled streets and darkened buildings passed; the floodlights illuminating the castle on the hill above us went out; I registered that it must be midnight. Still Eric did not speak; and as it became increasingly obvious that he had no intention of doing so I turned to him and asked him what was wrong.

'Do not bother yourself about it, James,' he said, an ominous note in his voice which I had never heard before.

We walked on in silence.

'I think you might tell me,' I said at last, doing my best to stem a rising tide of irritation. 'Don't you think I'm entitled to some sort of explanation?' More silence followed, broken only by the quick regular tap of Eric's step on the hard pavement and the flow of the river. 'Have you any idea how awkward it was for me in there?' I asked finally, exasperated.

My friend turned to me, eyes flashing. 'So it is I who am at fault is it?' he exploded. 'My mother's hypocrisy earns her nothing but praise. It is I who try to puncture it, I who try to be honest, who gets the blame. Even from you.'

I was lost. 'I don't see how the manner in which your ancestors obtained state secrets is a test of how honest you are. And what do you mean by your mother's hypocrisy? You're not making any sense.'

'My mother pretends to be a good Catholic,' he replied tersely. 'She talks endlessly of the sacrament of marriage, about what sex is good and what is wicked. But she praises prostitution, so long as it is done for the glory of France.'

I heard to my alarm that his voice was shaking. Uncomfortable now, my irritation evaporating, I said nothing. Eric sensed my discomfort.

'Do not bother yourself, James,' he said. 'You will not understand.' His pace increased. The silence was tense and I waited for it to snap as I knew that it must. When he spoke again his words were quick, almost hoarse. 'You will never understand, James. You will never understand what I mean because you will never leave the safety of your nice, civilized shell. You will never risk yourself or let others risk themselves with you.'

Lost and bewildered by his vehemence I considered defence and justification; for a moment even, I was angry again. And I might have spoken had we not seen our tram rattling down the street towards our stop and run to meet it; but we did. And in silence we went home and to our respective beds without exchanging a further word.

The next day, the day of the sale, dawned cloudy and patchy rain fell in short bursts on the crowds which thronged the entrance to First Auctioneers Ltd. Eric and I arrived together at five in the afternoon, an hour before the gavel went up, still not speaking. We found Louise, already in the care of a gleaming Mr Tomin, sitting in the middle of the first row. Her chair, and the two on either side of her which she indicated to us, had large cards on them on which someone, in painstaking copperplate, had written '*Réservé*'. She betrayed no signs of unease with her son; and it was as if the tension of the evening before had never existed.

'Dear James,' she said to me after she and Eric had exchanged their customary twin kisses, 'Monsieur Tomin seems to think that the sale will be a great success. My family feels indebted to you.'

'Really, there is no need.'

'And before it begins and everything gets too – how to say? – frantic,' she smiled at me, 'I wish to make you a little present.' She took the crucifix from her neck and put it in the palm of my hand, which she closed over it. 'You were admiring this last night. I wish that you would keep it. Christ has watched over the many generations who have worn it.'

I, conscious of Eric's eyes on me, did not know what to say and began to mumble something about not possibly being able . . .

'But I insist,' she said. 'You are my son's friend and therefore mine. If Eric does not think it fit that I should wear this, then I should like you to have it.' And with the air of giving a benediction she clasped my left hand and Eric's right and squeezed them tightly in hers. 'And now,' she said to Mr Tomin, who was awaiting her signal, 'we are ready.'

And he in his turn signalled to a flunkey who went ceremoniously to the double doors of the bidding room and threw them open with a flourish. In streamed a long line of people, Princess Amelia amongst them, who made their way with much excited chatter to the rows of gilt and velvet chairs. Gradually they filled them; and the auctioneer was just mounting to the podium and beginning his opening address, the crowd was just hushing itself and the doors closing, when in slipped a figure with short, shining blonde hair and excited green eyes. Ella slipped into a seat in the last row; Eric saw me look at her; his mother smiled approvingly as I put the crucifix into my pocket; and the sale began.

The bidding started cautiously, the crowd at first unmoved by the shrieks of the auctioneer. A few of the less prestigious lots went for just under their catalogue estimates: a table; some porcelain; a writing desk which had stood in Madame Mocsáry's hall. Seeing the furniture we had come to know so well go under the gavel, lot by lot, made me nostalgic for lost times in that eclectic apartment; and my resentment gave way to tenderness for the person I had shared them with. I looked past Louise at Eric and smiled at him. His eyes met mine; and after a moment's hesitation he smiled back.

Ella came up to me as the crowds were dispersing and took my hand. 'You were too lovely the other day,' she said. 'I don't know what I'd've done without you.'

'How are things with your parents now?' I asked.

'Better. But this must be the last of my little escapades. From now on it's sanity all the way.' She looked up at me and smiled.

'Are they here now?' I was anxious to meet Alexander and Pamela properly, on the new terms of my intimacy with their daughter.

'No,' she whispered. 'Can you believe it? I told them I'd run away because I was never allowed a moment alone. So they've let me come by myself.'

I can see her shining eyes looking up at mine, can feel her small hand and the tightness of its grip. 'That's brave of them,' I said, grinning.

She kicked me playfully. 'Don't be rude or I shan't say what I've come to ask you.'

'And what is that?'

'Well . . .' She smiled. 'Daddy and Pamela have to go home to London the day after tomorrow, but they don't want to take me for obvious reasons. The fuss still hasn't died down, you see.' She paused. 'The world must have its pound of flesh, I suppose. What was it Oscar Wilde said? Something about there being only one thing worse than being talked about and that's *not* being talked about.'

'Something like that,' I said smiling, pleased by her good humour.

'Well that's how I've decided to view it all.' She reached into her bag for a cigarette. 'But that's not what I wanted to speak to you about.'

'Oh?'

'Don't look at me archly like that, Jamie.'

'But you're a free woman now,' I leaned down and whispered into her ear. 'I want to claim you.'

She put her arms around my waist. 'Then why don't you come and stay with me for a few weeks until Christmas? Daddy and Pamela don't want me to be alone. And we've got a lovely place in France I want you to see – I'm going tomorrow.'

'I'd love to,' I said simply; then I thought of Eric and our argument. I didn't want to leave him without clearing the air and I suspected that his temper would take a few days to settle. 'But I'm not sure I can leave Eric at such short notice.'

At that moment he joined us. 'Ella,' he said stiffly, 'what a delight.' And he kissed her on both cheeks.

'Just the person I wanted to see,' she said. 'My father and step-mother are going back to London soon and giving me the use of a place we have in France. I want you and James to come and stay, just for a few weeks until Christmas.' She smiled at me as she said this, and I warmed to her for thus including my friend.

'That would be wonderful,' Eric replied, in a tone so polite I could not judge the sincerity of what he said. 'But I am afraid that I cannot.'

'But you must,' she went on. 'James has said he won't go if you don't, and I can't be left all on my lonesome in some God-forsaken house in the middle of nowhere.'

Eric looked at me; I looked at Ella; then I looked at him. His dark eyes met mine steadily, almost questioningly. I thought him still angry about the previous night. And anxious to let him see that I had forgotten and forgiven I put my arm around his shoulders. 'I've got used to having you around,' I said, smiling. 'You've got to come.' His eyes held mine a moment longer.

'Go on Eric,' Ella said.

'Yes, do.' This from me.

There was a pause while – had we but known it – all our fates hung in the balance.

'Very well,' he said finally, 'I'll come.'

19

Eric and I travelled to France alone, Ella having left Prague with her parents some days before us; and we said sad goodbyes to people and to places that neither of us would ever forget. At Café Florian we listened sadly to the drunken reminiscences and loud debates which would continue, we knew, whether or not we stayed to hear them; alone for the last time at Sokolska 21 we had Blanca to tea and thanked her for all she had done; on our last afternoon we drank coffee with Mr Kierczinsky in his elaborately-appointed office as we handed over the keys to Madame Mocsáry's now empty apartment.

In my last few hours in the city I took my leave of Eduard Mendl, who sent me on my way with a piece of 'lucky resin' which I have to this day.

'I have enjoyed teaching you,' he told me gravely as we parted. 'And I do not say that to all my pupils. With dedication you may go far.' As I put my violin in its case he told me that he had enjoyed my concerts with Eric, also. 'They give me hope for you both,' he said. 'And it pleases an old musician like me to see the rapport that you two have together.'

I thanked him warmly.

'God bless you James,' he said as we shook hands.

And I left his splendid rooms with words of praise ringing in my ears, thinking with pleasure of the excitement of travel, of bags packed and couchettes booked, of Ella waiting for me in France. I remember leaving the conservatory; remember bounding down its steps in the cold sunlight of that early winter day. I was happy and carefree, brimming with ambition, full of vain hope and wild plans, of . . . But what use is all this now? What point am I trying to prove? Does it matter so much that I have at last learned humility?

Our last days in Prague were good ones. Neither Eric nor I referred again to the dinner with Louise or to the argument which had followed it; and he, it seemed to me, made as conscious an effort to forget both as I did. Easy relations were re-established between us and our journey to France was light-hearted and happy, full of laughter and jokes and the telling of our first Czech anecdotes. We arrived at the border in the early morning of a misty, cloud-covered day; and bleary-eyed with sleep we endured an hour of waiting on a freezing railway platform – inevitably extended to three by an unexplained delay – and then caught two slow, connecting trains in haphazard succession. Eric had been responsible for choosing our route, and he had not chosen well; but his company was too amusing for me to be long irritated by his incompetence with timetables ('Only dull people are good with trains,' he told me) and we arrived at our destination in the late afternoon, grubby but high-spirited.

Ella did not come to meet us at the station; instead she sent the housekeeper's son with a note addressed to me in the jagged brown letters which I had come to know so well.

Darling James, it began,

As you will have noticed the day is very cold and I have been instructed not to brave the drive or the weather. (Daddy and Pamela have put the village doctor in attendance, you see, just in case I should do something silly. He's very over-protective.) So I've sent Jacques to collect you and I hope you don't mind. Be sure to give him a tip – it's important to get people on your side in this country.

Can't wait to see you.

E

I read this in the car as we drove from the station; and I listened absently as Eric and Jacques spoke to each other at intervals in polite French. As the countryside rattled past and we slowed, approached

178

and passed through a pair of dilapidated stone gateposts I thought excitedly that Ella would soon be in my arms. I remember my excitement then, the impatience with which I waited as we rattled down a long uneven drive towards the house, an ancient block of faded stone dotted by cracked blue shutters. It surprised me that such a house should belong to the Harcourts and that it should be left in such an obvious state of disrepair; certainly the splendours of 23 Chester Square had led me to expect something grander than this, something less desolate.

I saw Ella as we rounded the final curve in the drive. She was waiting for us on the narrow flight of cracked stairs which led to the front door, a fragile figure in pale blue cashmere with ruffled hair and glowing cheeks. I flushed with pleasure as I saw her and looked at Eric to smile too, but he was staring ahead and did not see me. I remember that now. But as the car came to a halt I gave no thought to the firm set of his mouth or to the tension in his shoulders, supposing – if I supposed anything at all – that our long journey had tired him. It had not tired me. As soon as Jacques had braked I was out of the car and Ella was in my arms and I was holding her and swinging her off the steps and she was laughing and pressing herself against me and pulling my shoulders tight to hers. I remember the bones of her neck, the delicate arch of her nose, the strands of hair flying about her face as we moved together. Even now the sweet thrill of our reunion on that cold day makes my heart race. And I know with a certainty which will sustain me that our love was not evil, that its end was not inevitable, that Eric's death and even Sarah's could have been avoided had either of us been older or stronger or wiser than we were. But we were not; and I ache now for that lovely smiling girl and for the lost passion of the time before my guilt.

It's ironic, you know: that my tears tonight and all this week will not be for my dead wife but for the lost love of her cousin; that Sarah's bloodied body has less power to move me than Ella's sweetly acrid smell of soap and cigarettes, forgotten for so long but now remembered. As I held her in the icy wind I filled my lungs with it.

She was laughing wildly when I let her go and she pushed me playfully away as she offered a rosy cheek to Eric.

'Leave your bags here,' Ella said to us, smiling, as she led the way into a low, dark hall, cheerless despite the vase of flowers on its central table. 'You should see the house before you unpack.'

And so we saw the house; and as she led us through it I thought that her vitality was out of place in its sombre corridors and draughty rooms; that the click of her heels on its flagstones should be heard in lighter, younger air than that to be found between the unloved walls of that decaying house. Recollection is curious. I never went back to it after Eric's death, and that was almost fifty years ago; but every detail of Les Varrèges – for that is what the house was called – is etched in my mind still. I can trace the patterns of its thick walls, the sequence of its few large rooms; I can recall the number of doors in its low-ceilinged hall, the musty odour of woodsmoke and dusty rugs which hung heavy in its air. I remember its fireplaces, large enough for a small person to stand upright in; its pock-marked wooden beams made from the timber of sixteenth-century warships and blackened by centuries of soot; the layout of its guest wing, a nineteenth-century addition; the plan of its gardens.

'I'm afraid we haven't opened all the bedrooms,' Ella told us as she led us down a vaulted passage. 'There are only us three in the house. And Doctor Pétin, of course, who's in there.' She pointed to a door. 'Jacques and Madame Clancy live in the village and we didn't think it worth while opening and airing everything for so few.'

I followed her, delighting in the lilting cadences of her voice.

'You'll meet the good doctor later,' she went on. 'I expect he's gone for one of his rambles.' As she spoke she paused outside a panelled oak door. 'This is your room,' she said to us. 'I thought I'd put you two in one without any leaks.' And she turned a handle and motioned Eric and me inside a large, airy room, more homely than the others, which gave on to the garden. A strong smell of lavender mingled with the odour of wood and fire met us and Ella, sniffing, pretended to choke. 'Madame Clancy is a great devotee of scented bedrooms, you know,' she explained as she went to one of the sash windows and opened it. 'But we'll clear the stench soon, don't you worry.'

Outside, a fog was creeping over the thick screen of yews at the garden's end. It was a garden past its prime, a once formal grid of gravel walks and hedges and pruned trees in long lines which had thrown over the yoke of human control and run wild once more. It was ghostly, that garden; romantic and appealing as all ruins are.

'We don't use the house any more,' Ella said quietly. 'It was my mother's favourite, you know. She and my father bought it just after they married and I don't think Pamela likes it much.' She paused and looked about the room. 'But Daddy would never sell it. He lets it moulder instead and thinks that a weekly visit from Madame Clancy is enough to keep it in working order.'

'Do you like it?' I asked.

'I do.' Her eyes met mine. 'But I don't like it falling down like this. And it's terribly gloomy this time of year.'

I nodded.

Ella smiled at me and Eric. 'That's why I'm delighted you're both here,' she said lightly. 'You can relax after all your hard work in Prague and we can keep each other company.'

I nodded and looked towards my friend but he was facing away from me, looking out of the window at the long expanse of garden. I could not see his face and as Ella talked easily of towels and bathrooms I noticed a tension in his shoulders which I dismissed as weariness, remembering how little we had slept in the past twenty-four hours. So when Ella asked whether we were tired, I said that I, for one, was exhausted.

'Well that's hardly surprising after your journey.' Her small hand squeezed mine. 'Why don't you both have a rest? Shall I see you for a drink at sevenish?'

'That would be perfect,' I replied, thinking with pleasure of all the time that lay ahead of us to be filled as we wished. Eric, still by the window, said nothing.

'Well then, till seven.' And Ella was gone, closing the door gently behind her as she left.

Slowly I unpacked, dreamily examining the room about me as I did so, catching lingering traces of Ella's smell. By the bed were old French novels, nicely-bound; an armoire held a large china wash-bowl and a jug with blue flowers painted on it: forget-me-nots, I think. By the fire was a screen embroidered with courtly figures in a stylized rose garden. The house, I could see now, showed traces of once careful attention only half-forgotten; and I wondered what Ella's mother had been like, the woman who had chosen the furniture for this room, who had placed the novels by the bed for the amusement and edification of her guests. I went to where Eric stood, quite still, and looked at the view with him. What flowers there were, and they were few now, ran amok; and I saw row upon row of gravel paths lined with yew hedge stretching to a tall boundary line of trees. In the middle was a fountain; and as I watched it sputtered into life and water poured from the open mouths of its frogs.

'What do you think of it?' I asked, but Eric's only response was a non-committal grunt. There was a pause while I wondered if anything more serious than tiredness had caused the change in his mood, for even I could not pretend that the taciturn figure at the window bore any relation to the laughing companion I had travelled with; and I thought that maybe the strange atmosphere of that lonely house had depressed him. Certainly it could not have been further in mood from the eclectic splendours of Sokolska 21 and the deep rich colours of Madame Mocsáry's apartment.

Abruptly he moved away from the glass. 'I think I shall have a walk,' he said, and left me.

'Do you want some company?' I called after him as he shut the door. For a moment he paused, opened the door again and looked back at me through black, unbrushed curls.

'It is not me who you want to keep you company now, James,' he said quietly; and before I could speak again he had closed the door and I could hear the measured tread of his feet on the stone as he went away down the passage.

Alone in the house with Ella I conquered my impulse to go to her, telling myself that there was plenty of time; and instead I had a hot bath and a shave, for a lover's vanity could not be satisfied by my dirty travel-stained reflection. I wanted to be fresh for the evening. And as I was dressing Eric returned from his walk more cheerful than he had been when he left for it and full of talk of a deserted quarry beyond the trees at the end of the garden. Pleased at the improvement in his mood I spent a pleasant half-hour talking to him before dinner, which we ate with Ella in a small dining room that led off the kitchen. I remember that meal; I remember the old-fashioned china on which it was served, the cosy fire which crackled as an accompaniment to our conversation. We were alone, just us three, for Dr Pétin had been called out to deliver a baby in the village and was not expected back until very late. We ate a selection of cold meats, left that afternoon by Madame Clancy. We talked of Prague, of the Mocsáry sale, of the quarry which Eric had seen on his walk.

'It's where they mined the stones for the house,' Ella told us. 'It's very deep; my mother had it flooded for her guests to swim in.' She took a sip of wine. 'Now most of the water has drained away and I'm not sure how deep the pool still is. But you're welcome to a dip, of course, though as December is beginning I wouldn't advise it very strongly.'

It was Eric who said he wanted to see the quarry by moonlight, and when dinner was over and Dr Pétin had still not returned we decided that there was no time like the present. So armed with torches the three of us made our way across the gravel paths and through the yew trees, laughing at first – for the atmosphere between us had eased – but gradually falling silent as the spell of the garden took its hold over us. Ella's small hand found mine in the darkness and held it tightly. Eric, out in front with the torch, shone it back for us and then forwards. Beyond the screen of yews there was nothing to see but a field with rows of neatly planted apple trees that loomed sinister in the darkness.

'We're heading up there, past the orchard,' Ella whispered to me and pressed me on over the hard ground.

We passed through another line of trees and as we emerged from their cover Eric flicked off his torch and plunged us into darkness. For a moment all was black. Then the moon appeared from behind a bank of cloud and from far off schooldays a line of poetry recurred to me, sole survivor of many, and I thought of Tennyson's *Idylls of the King* and of the line about The barren lake/And the long glories of the winter moon. Here was a barren lake; here was a winter moon luminous in pale gold. Before us was the steep cliff of the quarry, dropping away to black water many feet below. From a cloudless heaven the moon cast an eerie light over the scene and turned bushes into hobgoblins and trees into scrawny giants. We were all silent. In the moonlight I saw Eric's profile: the prominent arch of his Gallic nose; the line of his jaw; the curls of his black gypsy locks. Beside him was Ella, fragile as china, her skin glowing ghost-like, her fingers interlocked. I stood between them, watching her play with her rings.

I remember telling myself as I stood there that here was beauty. But there was something uncomfortable about the beauty of that scene nonetheless, something disturbing about the quarry's isolation and its vast unplumbed depths. I thought of huge beasts moving at its murky bottom, waiting. And when my eyes left Ella's and their glinting rings I looked up and saw Eric watching me with something like pain in his eyes. I saw that Ella was watching him, but it was too dark to see the look on her face. My eyes met my friend's and he switched on the torch once more; the spell, cast so delicately, was broken abruptly. 'Come on,' he said, 'I'm cold.' And he led the way back to the house with quick, defiant steps. Ella and I followed without a murmur.

During that walk a change came over us. Nothing was said; none of us spoke at all, in fact. But when we reached the house things were not as they had been when we left it. There was no comfort in our silence. And as we passed the guest wing on our way to the front door I saw with relief that Dr Pétin's light was on.

Ella walked past his windows without acknowledging them. 'I can't face him now,' she said as we climbed the steps; and she looked at me and began to say more but thought better of it. She had not taken my hand or offered me hers on the walk back and as I touched her shoulder now she moved away. 'I have to be bubbly and vivacious at all times,' she said eventually with a weak attempt at a smile, 'or I don't get a good report sent to Daddy and Pamela. I'll introduce you tomorrow.' And she let Eric and me into the darkened hall and bolted the great oak door behind us. 'This place gives me the creeps,' she said suddenly, looking about the dim room.

'Me too,' I answered feelingly, wishing that Eric were not with us and that I could be alone with Ella. My friend's presence and the strange mood which had overtaken him on the walk back made me uncomfortable.

'I think it's beautiful.' Eric's tone rang out, unnaturally loud, from the half-darkness. He was standing by the fireplace at the other end of the room, hardly visible in the dying glow of the embers.

'Don't drift off like that,' I said, startled, surprised by my own edginess.

'Are you two frightened of ghosts?' His tone was derisive, and I saw Ella trying to decide whether the mockery in it was friendly.

At length she spoke. 'You're right, this is silly. Good-night to you both. May you sleep dreamlessly.' And with a kiss on my cheek she slipped out of the room.

I began to follow her but at the door she turned, looked back, and shook her head. I stood hesitating in the middle of the room. She disappeared. Irritated suddenly, I turned to Eric. 'Come on, bedtime,' I said.

'Are you sure I'm the person you want to be sharing with?' His tone was coolly level.

'Shut up.'

Silently I led the way to our cosy room, lit now by a coal fire burning in a recently polished grate. The scent of lavender was once again everywhere and I detected the conscientious presence of Madame Clancy. In the warm half-light Eric and I undressed without much conversation and got into our respective beds. The sheets were crisp and cold.

'Sleep well,' I said.

'You too.'

And he turned out the lights and left me with my thoughts of Ella. But I did not sleep for many hours. I lay awake instead, struggling with my disappointment that on this, the first night of my reunion with her, I should be sleeping alone.

And thus ended that first day.

20

The next was brighter than its predecessor, a cold day of clear winter skies and sparkling light. Frost covered the ground. Eric and I woke early and were the first to take our places at the breakfast table, where a garrulous Frenchwoman (Madame Clancy, we supposed) handed us croissants and made dire predictions about the weather. Her speech was so fast and her accent so new to my ears that when she had gone I looked to Eric for a full translation.

'She says it will get very cold now,' he said. 'Very cold. And she says also that Ella has gone out for a walk. She will be back shortly.'

As he finished speaking Ella walked in, cheeks apple-red. 'Mornin' boys.' Her tone was cheerful but she avoided my eyes.

'Good morning.' I was sullen in her presence, a little sulky after the dismissal of the night before. She ignored this.

'The good doctor Pétin usually comes down at about nine for a cup of coffee and a croissant,' she said. 'I imagine that's him now.' And as she spoke a rather apologetic middle-aged man walked in, slightly rotund, more than slightly balding, with wispy grey hair grown long at the sides and brushed over his head to hide this.

'Good morning, Ella,' he said in a gentle, ingratiating voice, the tone of one humouring a child. 'I trust that you slept well.' His English was perfect.

'Very well, thank you,' she replied, smiling with a brightness I thought studied as she poured the coffee and introduced us.

The doctor nodded his greeting.

'I'm glad,' he said to Ella. 'It is important for you to get as much sleep as possible before you return to London.' Turning to Eric and me he went on, underlining his points with leisurely jabs of his fat fingers. 'Sleep, rest, warmth; and moderation above all,' he said. 'These are what I believe in, gentlemen; these are my principles.' And with this he took his place at the table and proceeded to eat four croissants in quick succession.

It was not until the middle of the morning that I was able to get Ella to myself, for she disappeared soon after breakfast and I was left politely observing a game of chess between Dr Pétin and Eric. They played in the *salon*, a large square room in the middle of the house with long windows which gave on to the gravel paths of the garden. Sitting on one of its sofas, smiling occasionally to the doctor and my friend to assure them of my continuing interest in their game, thinking continuously of Ella, I saw her emerge quite suddenly from the yew trees and hastily excused myself to the two men. When I reached her she was by the fountain, walking quickly towards the house, tightly muffled in a man's greatcoat, with a pale blue school scarf which must have been her father's wound around her neck. She stopped when she saw me. There was a moment's pause.

'Hello,' she said finally.

'Hello.'

She made as if to move on but I caught her arm. 'Why are you treating me like a stranger?' The wakeful hours of a frustrated night gave an edge to my voice which I could not disguise. 'What's wrong?'

She looked at me steadily for a moment. At last she said, slowly, 'Don't you know?' and looked away from me.

I shook my head. She raised her eyes to mine and studied my face for a moment. The confusion she found there seemed to satisfy her, and she felt in her pockets for a cigarette. I watched as she put it to her lips and lit it. She inhaled slowly, deeply, and blew the smoke upwards, tilting her head. I followed it until it was lost in the bright, cold blue above us.

'Talk to me,' I said simply.

Abruptly she turned away. There was a tangible moment of hesitation which made my heart beat. 'Very well,' she said finally, seeming to resolve on something. 'But follow me. This way.' And she walked quickly down the gravel path and through the line of trees. I followed her, seeing to my relief that the orchard by day was picturesque and unthreatening, its giants apple trees once more. The frost on the grass glinted in the sunlight and crunched under our feet as we crossed the field. I realized then that I was being taken to the quarry; and as Ella led me through the trees that separated it from the orchard I felt a residual shiver from the night before. But like the orchard the quarry had been robbed of its terror by the daylight; and it stretched, a pool of dirty water, nothing more, beneath us. On its edge was a bench I had not seen the night before. Ella sat down on it and motioned for me to join her.

She lit another cigarette and took two meditative drags on it. There was silence.

Feeling her distance from me and not understanding it, I spoke. 'Why?' I asked, more gentle now than I had been before.

'Why what?' She looked at me sharply.

I blushed but steeled myself. 'Why did you send me to my room last night when I could have been with you?' I took her hand. She let me keep it, but grudgingly. 'I've wanted you so badly for so long. We've been separated for so long. I didn't write from Prague because you asked me not to. Now I . . .'

She took her hand from mine and raised it to stop me. 'You really don't know why, do you?' she said again, ignoring everything but my question, her voice quivering.

I looked at her and saw the tenderness in her face tinged with something I took to be derision. Again I shook my head. Then I looked away and when my eyes returned to hers I saw with a shock that she was on the verge of tears; and she saw that I saw and set her thin lips together. When she spoke again her voice was even and firm.

'I don't know how anybody could be so naïve,' she said at last.

'What?'

'I think you heard me.' The tenderness had gone from her face now.

'What am I being so naïve about?' I asked humbly.

She looked at me steadily. 'Do you really want me to tell you?'

'Of course.'

'And you really don't know?'

'I really do not know.'

'All right.' She took a deep breath. 'Eric is wildly in love with you,' she said slowly, framing each syllable with deliberate precision.

I can hear her saying it now; can see the way her eyes looked into and held mine; can feel the wave of my own surprise and her almost tangible astonishment as I started to laugh. I, who had thought something seriously wrong between us, laughed partly with relief and partly with humour at her error. 'Rubbish,' I said. And it was only as I said this that I remembered odd moments of my time with Eric in Prague: truths half offered and refused; looks observed but not understood; secret smiles. 'Rubbish,' I said again, more weakly this time.

'It's not rubbish,' she said evenly, still holding my eyes with hers. 'He can't bear the sight of us together; he hates me because you love me; he looks at you when he thinks I don't see.'

'Nonsense,' I said.

'You know it's not, James.'

I sat still, fighting the dawning realization that maybe she was right.

'How can you possibly know?' I asked at last.

She flicked her cigarette, half-smoked, into the quarry. 'Women can sense these things,' she said quietly at last. 'It crossed my mind in Prague, but I dismissed it then. I thought he might resent my presence for other reasons. But last night I knew; standing by this bench I knew. That's why I didn't sleep with you.' And as she said this something in her seemed to crack. 'You know it too, Jamie,' she said, her voice wavering again and the suggestion of tears reappearing. 'You know he's in love with you. You may not admit it to yourself but you know.'

There was a pause. 'Since I'm not in love with him, what bearing can Eric's feelings have on us?' I asked hoarsely.

Ella straightened herself. 'How do you *know* you're not in love with him?' Her eyes met mine coolly now; her tone was more level.

'What?'

'How do you know you're not in love with him?'

'Because I *know.*'

She looked at me steadily. 'No, you don't. The way you've buried your knowledge of his feelings only proves how frightened of them you are.' She breathed deeply. 'You won't admit to yourself that Eric loves you or that you might love him back because you've always been told that one man can't love another.'

'I . . .'

But she held up a hand to stop me. 'You're frightened, that's all,' she said, and there was decision in her voice again. Turning to face me squarely she continued, every word measured and even. 'Before we can go on as before I want to know that it's me you really want.'

'It is you I want.' I took her hand but she pulled it away.

'You can't know that.'

'Oh, yes, I can.'

'No, you can't. You can't make an informed decision unless you . . .'

But I cut her off. 'I'm not . . . like that, Ella.'

'How do you know you're not unless you face the possibility that you might be?'

'I . . .'

'I don't want to be your safe option, James.'

I looked at her helplessly, incredulous. 'Are you trying to say that you want me to sample the alternatives?'

'In a manner of speaking.'

I tried to look into her eyes but she turned from me towards the quarry and wouldn't shift her gaze to meet mine. 'You're crazy,' I said. 'You're completely crazy.'

From the twitch of her shoulders I saw that I had touched a chord. 'Don't ever say that to me again,' Ella hissed.

'But . . .'

'But nothing. Don't *ever* say it again.'

I nodded, humbled by her anger. Mutely I looked at her, searching for an explanation for her words; none was given me. Instead she rose to her feet.

'I cannot love emotional cowards,' she said with slow deliberation.

Fighting a spreading sensation of numbness I asked her what she meant.

'Precisely what I say.'

There was a pause; my pulse beat a steady tattoo in my head. 'Are you trying to test me?' I ventured at last, lost.

There was silence. 'I suppose so,' she said finally.

She turned away. 'I want you to prove to me that it's me you want, that I am not a safe option, that you know yourself and your desires.'

'And how can I do that? How can I prove anything to you if you won't believe what I say?'

There was silence.

'A simple kiss would probably suffice,' she said softly, still not looking at me. 'Once you've kissed him I imagine you'll know how you feel. You'll have forced yourself to face something. Then you'll know whether or not it's me you really want.' And with that she walked quickly away and I heard the crunch of her shoes on the gravel as she disappeared into the trees. I sat numbly, staring after her retreating form.

The boy on that bench long ago is a stranger to me now. He does not hear as I call. He sits numbly as wave after conflicting wave crashes over him; he cares nothing for my warnings. I tell him not to be distracted by the letter of what Ella has said, but to look for the meaning hidden in her words. He does not hear me; he cannot. He feels sick and lost and dizzy with the effort of thinking. He is falling, falling into swirling waters he does not understand; and as he falls he reaches out and clutches on to a small shard of unthinking, unexamined resolution. It is to this he clings, for in it he sees his salvation; he clings to it in the mistaken belief that it will help him to float. He does not know treachery yet; nor what it does.

From a distance of fifty years I call to him, for I understand now what Ella said in a way he could never have hoped to do. I see her again in that café in Prague. I hear her as she tells me that you've no idea how sane you have to be to survive a session with a really respected psychiatrist; that doctors with their endless questions could make anyone doubt themselves and those around them. But he will not hear me; and he sits impassive as I tell him that when we sin we must accept the possibility of those we love sinning, too; that when she took a man she did not love from her cousin Ella dealt herself a blow just as damaging as anything she did to Sarah.

I tell him that his love betrayed herself; and that from the moment she had done so she had to live with the terrible fear that others she loved would betray her in their turn. It was that fear which made Ella push me away; that fear which made her need me to prove – by whatever means – my devotion to her. I know now that betraying her own trust made Ella lose her trust in the world; and my heart aches for the fragile girl who wanted only the safety of the knowledge that I loved her completely.

I curse the cruelty of a Fate which did not grant me the perception to see that there are some things which even love does not sanction.

I had neither wisdom nor experience, you see; I was a child playing an adult's game. In my youth and weakness I succumbed to the logic of her insecurity. I came to believe as I sat on that lonely bench that I had been set a challenge, that to prove my worth to Ella I had to pass the test she had set me. And I knew as I sat there that I could not bear the derision of her cool green eyes. I did not know that what I took for derision was in fact fear; that my love was also a child playing an adult's game; that other proofs might have done in place of the one I finally offered her. As my world spun before me and all ideals of friendship and faith crumbled under the weight of her challenge, I did not know that the test Ella set me was in fact the reaction of a proud mind to the fear of grave loss, however unfounded that fear might be; I did not know that what she needed so desperately was a proof of my devotion to her and not of my courage with others.

It is true, you know: those who give much expect much to be given to them; those who take much expect much to be taken from them. Ella took the person Sarah valued most from her and after that she could never be sure of anyone completely. As Charles had been taken from Sarah so might I be taken from Ella; that was her fear, and fear is the undoing of many. That is how I understand it now. The only way Ella could be sure of me was to drive me away and have me back on her terms; and because she was young and Eric – sweet, trusting Eric – was on hand, he and his love for me were the means she chose. And I, tormented by love for her, driven by the coolness of those haunting eyes – a coolness in which I saw no fear, no weakness – set my mind to the task ahead; I resolved to accept Ella's challenge, to prove myself to her on her terms.

That was my undoing; that was my crime. And like Ella's crime it shaped my life from that moment onwards. Sitting on that rusty bench above the quarry I decided that I would give up the riches of friendship and self-respect for Ella's love; I decided – and here I was weakest – that I could not imagine life without her love, that it was worthy of any sacrifice I had it in my power to make.

I was wrong. No love is worth that. No human being is worth the total abdication of self. But I did not know that then; and though I dimly suspected the damage I might do by accepting Ella's challenge I ignored all scruple. My only thought was the selfish gratification of my own desire, my only prize the restoration of our mutual trust. I was not old enough to know that this trust might be restored in other ways; that it was not emotional cowardice which Ella feared but betrayal; that as I sat by the quarry then, trying to think, I was being presented with my last chance to save us both.

I knew none of these things; and because this was so I got up slowly from the bench and went in search of Eric. I found him alone in the *salon*, reading; and with a first shiver of treachery I put my hand on his and said that we should leave. I remember his surprise, remember his wide brown eyes and his mouth opened to protest. I remember too how his protest died on his lips, how his look changed from one of mystification to comprehension, how he bounded from his chair and went to pack, spurred on by sudden joy and undreamed of hope. I saw Ella for a moment before I left and I kissed her goodbye with a fury that was new to me. It scared her and I was glad that it scared her; I wished her to know the strengths in me which she had stirred; and I wished her to doubt, perhaps, whether I would return: I wished her to doubt the outcome of her test so that when I passed it her confidence in me would be all the greater. Sitting in this icy room now I can hardly speak.

21

It is cold outside; the sun is setting over a roaring sea; the light is fading. For the first time I do not want to go on. For the first time the telling of what I have done sticks in my throat and I cannot speak. The boy my story has concerned so far has been innocent; wilful perhaps and undoubtedly weak, but innocent, naïve. Now he is no longer so. He can no longer claim to have no knowledge of what he does; he cannot escape judgement for what he will do; and I must live with the consequences of what he did again. I have spent my life living with them, living with them and trying to forget. Now I must remember. I must seek out the images that Sarah taught me so well to bury; must trace thoughts and motives I had thought obliterated for ever; must steel myself to the sound of Eric's laugh ringing back at me in my dreams. I think that that laugh will be the hardest memory to bear, for it is so trusting, so fearless. Eric's love for me was pure and warm and freely given. I abused it coldly and calculatingly. And I have spent a lifetime trying to forget that, trying to bury what I did. Now I owe it to Eric to follow this story to its end in all its wealth of shameful detail. I owe it to him to spare myself nothing, to remember; for frankness is the only reparation I can make and I must make it freely. That much I know.

My first memory of the days we spent together is of the train journey we took after leaving Ella's house. We were going to Vaugirard to stay with Eric's family – though what possessed me to go there I do not know – and I remember our journey because it contrasted so completely with the one we had so recently taken together from Prague. I mean, of course, that I contrasted so completely with the excited boy who only the day before had gone to see his lover full of hope and joy and thoughts of future happiness. I was different on the second journey because I understood Eric's smiles now and returned them; because I knew with absolute clarity that Ella was right and also, though this sickens me to say, that I would pass her test. I try to remember precisely what I felt beyond this, whether I gave any attention to the possible consequences of my actions, whether I would have cared if I had done so. Behind each and every thought of mine were my love's eyes, distant and derisive, the eyes I had seen by the quarry that morning. I wanted to make myself worthy of their approval, to make them shine for me again. I wished to prove, once and for all, that I had the qualities which Ella sought. I thought that by passing her test I would cement our love and for that prize I would have risked anything.

The ease with which my ties of friendship with Eric dissolved under Ella's influence shames me now. Then I'm almost certain that it didn't. And as I talk I remember why it didn't. I remember the tricks I used to bypass all considerations that might have weakened my resolution, the cunning by which my possessed mind protected itself and its intentions from all complicating scruple, from all distracting thought. I remember now how I taught myself to separate the Eric I knew from the Eric I had been challenged to explore. And I remember that I was so successful in this separation that the two sides of his nature – the passionate and the platonic – grew in my mind until they had formed two complete personas, linked of course but ultimately distinct.

Eric the lover I did not know and did not care to know; him I transformed, with deft precision, from a person who might have feelings into a trophy whose sole purpose was to be won. Questions of loyalty and even of gender dissolved in the harsh face of my determination to conquer. Eric the friend could not, of course, be so dealt with. He was the Eric I knew, the Eric I would have turned to for advice in any situation but this, the Eric I had laughed with, drunk with, fought with and worked with for three heady months in Prague. He could not be made into a trophy and had instead to be separated so completely from the prize I wished to win that no concern for friendship or history would stand in the way of my desire for victory. I separated Eric the lover from Eric the friend with cold deliberation; and with the treachery of a Judas I saw the first fruits of my work even as our train pulled into the small station at Vaugirard. I found myself able to smile without affection; to put meaning into looks that held none; to make action and thought discrete. I had worked fast, that I knew; and I knew also that my work could not last long. I had anaesthetized my mind, nothing more; but I thought, correctly as it turned out, that this would be adequate for my purposes. When my conscience stirred I had the duplicity to tell it that Eric himself had encouraged the separation which I so artfully executed. He, I whispered to it, had never said anything to me of his feelings for me. He had never been open or honest about them, had not attempted to widen our relationship to include or at least to acknowledge them. This I told myself so frequently and with such assurance that I almost believed it. I tried not to think of the signs he had given me, of the overtures he had made; for I knew that no betrayal of friendship can resist the light of examination for long.

We arrived at Vaugirard in the late afternoon and were met at the station by Eric's sister Sylvie, a large woman, prematurely middle-aged, in whose face the Vaugirard nose and jaw sat incongruously with a weak mouth and tranquil eyes. She kissed her brother and offered me her cheek, pointing as she did so to an old red Citroën parked nearby. As we pulled out of the car park she asked me, in correct but hesitant English, whether I had enjoyed my time in Prague.

'Very much,' I replied.

'I would have liked to go too,' she said. 'It would have been wonderful.' She paused. 'But I have my duties here.' And as she spoke she looked with a certain smugness at her brother, who ignored her.

After this we drove on in silence, past the modern flats of a growing town and into the cobbled streets of its medieval past. On a hill which commanded the entire district was a château, fortress-like in construction and bearing, which was proudly pointed out to me as the family's own.

'Of course we do not own it any longer,' said Sylvie as we waited at traffic lights, 'but the family stays on here nevertheless. There will always be a Vaugirard in Vaugirard.'

And I thought of another castle, far finer than this one, and of another voice talking of ownership and duty. Eric said nothing.

Louise de Vaugirard welcomed me with open arms and a hearty dinner. The family lived in one of the old houses in the centre of the town, a high narrow building which from the street looked cramped but which was in fact cavernous, with low-ceilinged rooms leading into and out of one another in haphazard profusion. It was longer than it was wide and had been extended at various times into the garden behind it, so that only a small square patch of lawn now remained.

'We play croquet there in the summer,' said Louise, pointing it out to me. 'What a pity you have come in the winter, for I fear the weather will be very harsh.'

I had no desire for lazy summer afternoons with Eric's family and looked at the cloud outside with gratitude. In the comfort of his own home, under the strain of his family's kindness, I felt that my ingenious separation of him into friend and trophy would be difficult to prolong; and as I replied that the weather could be no worse than it would be in England, I wondered why I had come at all and thought with relief that I had only promised to stay five days. For five days the anaesthetic might endure; beyond that I could not be sure and I had no wish for its effects to wear off in the bosom of Eric's family itself.

After Sylvie had left us, to cook for her husband and child, Eric's father arrived and shook hands with his son and then with me with heavy dignity. He was a great squat man with huge hands and a powerful, vice-like grip. It was possible to see, as Eric stood beside him, that although my friend resembled his father his features had been softened by his mother's genes, for a prominent nose and strong jaw gave the elder man an air of terrifying caricature which the younger had escaped. Eric *père* was a friendly giant who sat quietly through dinner while his wife's conversation warmed the room; occasionally he bestowed a hospitable smile on me, but more he did not do or say. When we had moved upstairs for coffee, however, he pulled me to one side.

'I would like to thank you for what you have done for my family,' he said in a deep, gruff voice. 'Eric speaks very well of you as do all who met you in Prague.' I thought of Mr Kierczinsky and Pavel Tomin, remembering with a start that they existed, they who only a few days before had played so large a part in my life. Eric's father spoke English slowly with a heavy accent.

'It was a great pleasure to be able to help,' I said. 'An honour.'

'And the paintings were interesting also, no?'

'Fascinating.'

'Yes. It is a pity we could not have kept some of them. But what use do I have for pictures?' He smiled at me and shook his head while I, trying sincerely not to like him, smiled back.

I don't know why even the polite trivia of that time seems worthy of retelling. I retell it, I suppose, to delay the recounting of what I did. Though it shames me to do so I linger on the Vaugirards, on the ease with which they accepted me into their home and their lives, an ease which makes my treachery all the worse. I, who intended their son nothing but harm – or who at least was prepared to sacrifice him on the altar of my love for another – was welcomed into their lives; and I accepted their hospitality as Judas might have accepted Christ's at the Last Supper: duplicitously; deviously; deceitfully. I was accepted because I was their son's friend; on that recommendation alone I was welcomed as a member of the family. I stayed in their house; I shared their food, their wine, their conversation; and all the time they harboured a traitor in their midst and they did not know it. Though outwardly friendly I never allowed myself to warm to Louise's charm or to Eric *père*'s clumsy kindness, and there also I was deceptive: for I behaved as though I was their friend when I was not; as though I deserved their trust when I did not. And I distanced myself from them because I knew enough to be wary of any closeness with Eric's family.

In deceiving the Vaugirards, in disregarding their humanity because I knew that recognition of it would sway me from my purpose, I behaved as shamefully as I had ever done and steeled myself to behave more so. It makes me sick to remember it now, to see their smiling faces, to think of Louise's cooking or Eric *père*'s wine. Those dinners in Vaugirard return to me in my dreams with the sound of that family laughing. The memory of them makes my own laugh hollow, joyless and insincere. And I know that it is all these things.

The actual taking of my prize was easy, and I say that without vanity. On the evening of my second day with the Vaugirards I decided to act, for I feared their kindness and was uncertain how much longer I could endure it. I knew enough to know that treachery had its limits, you see, and I was fearful of testing them. So I sat through a second dinner, which like the first was long and very good, drinking little and watching, waiting for my opportunity. It came as the last plates were cleared and Eric excused himself and got up to go to bed; and I, sensing that it had come, excused myself too and left the room with him, smiling my good-nights to his family.

We ascended the narrow flight of steep stairs that led to our bedrooms in a silence which for me was grimly purposeful. On the landing outside my room, high up in the gods of the house, Eric said good-night to me and turned to open his own door.

'Good-night,' I replied. And there was an awkward pause as I steeled myself to take the plunge. Thinking of Ella's eyes, of the smooth hollow beneath her collarbone, I twisted my lips into a smile. 'I'm not very tired,' I said, keeping it fixed.

My friend turned to me, surprised.

Unseeing, I looked through him. 'Come and keep me company for a while,' I went on, walking quickly into my bedroom. As he followed I took a sip from the glass of water by my bed, for my mouth was dry. When I looked up I saw Eric framed in the darkness of the doorway, hesitant, uncertain.

'It is so wonderful to have you here,' he said, at last.

'It's good to be here.'

'And my family likes you so much.'

'I like them.'

'You are an old charmer, James.' Bolder now, he moved towards me and sat on the foot of my bed. Awkwardly I stood next to him.

'We are very easy around you,' he said, and I knew that this was true: there had been no further signs of the tension between Eric and his mother which I had seen in Prague, for the family had drawn together to show its best side to its guest.

Slowly, trying not to shake, I sat down on the bed next to him. Our knees touched, as if by accident, but Eric didn't move his away and I forced myself to keep mine where it was. There was silence between us, though inside my head I could not think for sound; above the quick, hard beat of my blood I heard Ella's voice, cool and even, telling me that she could not love emotional cowards.

'You are a mystery to me, James,' Eric was saying.

I looked down, not trusting myself to speak.

'I never know what you mean or what you want. You seem so different since we left Ella's. What happened there? What happened between you two?'

With a supreme effort of will I forced myself to raise my head. I looked steadily into Eric's eyes, found my voice, and said, hoarsely, that I didn't want to speak of Ella. With a deep breath I put my hand on his.

'Now I really do not understand you.'

'I think you do.' My voice was measured; I was determined to keep it steady. I took his other hand in mine.

The uncertainty on Eric's face resolved slowly into a smile. 'This I cannot believe,' he said, looking at me shyly.

'Why not?'

'Because I . . . *Mon Dieu*, how does one say this?' He hesitated and then decided to trust me. 'Because I love you and thought you wanted me only for a friend. I thought *she* had taken you for ever.' He spoke quickly, his words falling over themselves in his eagerness to get them out.

I let them glide past me, leaving no mark on my mind. Silently, adrenaline making me light-headed, blood pounding in my brain, I leaned forward to kiss him.

I remember that kiss. Oh God, I remember it. I see Eric's broad, unbelieving face with its frame of dark curls moving towards mine even now; I smell his foreign, unknown scent of sweat and shaving foam; I feel his hands on my shoulders and the violence of his quick embrace. His kiss itself was rough and harsh, as unlike a woman's kiss as anything could be, and suddenly I felt him on top of me pulling at my buttons and I was pushing him away and saying 'No' with all the force in me. Ella's voice rang in my brain, saying over and over that a simple kiss would suffice, that once I had kissed him I would know; and as I pushed Eric away from me and sat upright, breathing heavily, shaking from what I had done, I knew that I did know, that I had come as far as I could safely go, that I had passed my lover's test, that I deserved the sparkling praise of her shining eyes, that I could claim it now as my own.

It was only then that I saw Eric smiling delightedly at me, his face glowing with a passion I had never seen in it, his body taut with excitement. It was only then that I had the first inklings of what I have since come to know with such certainty: that human beings cannot be divided; that their constituent parts cannot stand alone; that they cannot be separated into distinct halves for the moral convenience of others. Breathing heavily, eyes dancing, Eric took my hands and leaned towards me; and as he did so I knew with sudden certainty that I had lost my friend for ever. I said nothing, sickened by that thought; but as his lips moved towards mine again I pushed him away and stood up, reeling with what I had done.

There was silence.

'I . . . I'm not ready for this,' I said at last.

Slowly, respectfully, he released my hands. I could see the effort it cost him to restrain himself, to leash once again the unleashed desire of so many months, and I admired him for it. Sitting upright on the bed once more, however, he leaned over to where I stood and took my right hand in his again, raising a questioning eyebrow as he did so. I didn't have the heart to refuse it him.

'I love you, James,' Eric said quietly.

I said nothing.

'I have loved you since the day I first saw you, since the minute you walked into Regina Boardman's drawing room.'

My brain was spinning; Eric tried to pull me closer but I pushed him away and went to the window. I could not bear his touch any longer. Far below us the street lights twinkled and cars drove back and forth over the cobbles.

Strange as it may seem I had given no thought to how I would deal with my prize once it was won. I hadn't thought beyond the passing of Ella's test, beyond the proving of my own emotional courage to her. And I discovered that I could no longer bear even to look at my friend; I knew that I had no reserves to deal with his words of love. All my energies had been focused on rising to Ella's challenge. And now that I had done so, now that victory was mine and Eric was sitting on my bed telling me that he loved me completely, I had no idea what to do. I knew then as I stared into the street beneath me that he had never been two distinct personas, that I could never have taken one half as a trophy and left the other intact. I knew then, I think, that whatever I did now I would break him.

He left me that night puzzled by my silence but thinking that he understood it.

'Tonight has been enough for me,' he said as I stood by the window, unable to meet his eyes. 'I will leave you now. The rest will come later, in our own time.' And he came up behind me and laid a hand on my shoulder. Feeling me stiffen he removed it. 'Good-night,' he said. And at the door he turned and some last vestige of dignity made me turn and face him. 'I am happier now than I have ever been in my life,' he said softly as he left me.

I am trying to remember what I felt as I undressed and got into bed. I know that I turned out the light and tried to think of Ella but that I could no longer see her eyes or feel her lips on my lips. I felt only the harsh energy of Eric's kiss, the fury of his passion. And it was then that I had my first bitter taste of treachery. I knew then that I could not stay another night in that trusting house, that the next day I must leave, that any lie would be worth my freedom. And sweating, cold with what I had done, I lay awake and tried not to think.

I didn't sleep until the sun was turning the black sky to a misty grey, but when sleep came it was so deep that I didn't hear Eric opening my door the next morning; I slept on as he crossed my room and was woken only by him stroking the hair out of my eyes. Then I knew that the night before had not been a dream, that its nightmare logic was part of the real world, that its effects would not fade with sleep. I knew this all; and in my desperation further deceit came smoothly and easily. After a hasty breakfast, during which I forced myself to meet Eric's shining eyes without embarrassment, I telephoned Camilla Boardman. She answered on the third ring, her speech as shrill and her emphases as frequent as ever.

'*Daaarling!*' she squealed. 'I thought you were *never* coming back! Where are you? What are you doing for lunch?'

I explained that I was in France staying with friends and that lunch would thus be impossible, a fact I sorely regretted.

'But how *tiresome*. London's been just *too* deadly without you and I want to know when you're coming back to liven things up for me.'

'Soon, Camilla. Soon. In fact, I'll be home all the sooner if you'll do me a favour.' Rapidly I invented a story about staying with dull people from whose hospitality I needed a polite excuse to escape. Camilla drank it in greedily, for social intrigue was her forte. 'I want you to help me,' I finished, 'by calling in an hour and leaving a message saying that I must come back to England immediately.'

'But, darling, how *exciting*! What reason shall I give?'

'I don't know. I'm sure that you of all people don't need inspiration from me.'

'Of *course* not, darling. You can trust me.'

'I know. That's why I called.'

And with many kisses blown and endearments exchanged, the conversation ended and I hung up.

Calmer now, but eager for my abrupt departure from the Vaugirards to be thought unavoidable, I asked Eric if he would like to go for a walk. I wished Louise to receive Camilla's call, for then I would be beyond suspicion.

He took me over the grounds and buildings of the castle, a picturesque ruin, and told me the history of the town which it commanded. Thankful for so neutral a topic I nodded and smiled and in my uneasiness heard nothing and counted the minutes. I was at my most relaxed when there was silence between us, for with each word I spoke I felt myself more false. But even the silences were untrue: for Eric they were times of quiet communion; for me they were a brief respite from the pressure to be tender. When an hour had passed I suggested that we go home and out of the cold.

Louise, when we arrived, was in a state of great distress. She met us at the front door and led me into the sitting room, taking my hands in hers and asking me to sit down. 'I have some bad news for you, my dear James,' she said gravely.

I looked suitably anxious.

'Leopold is dying,' she said gently. 'He may not have long to live.' And with infinite tenderness she looked into my eyes and stroked my hand. 'Your mother has just telephoned. She thinks you should go back to England at once. She sounded very upset.'

Leopold, it dawned on me, was Camilla's King Charles spaniel. Struggling to overcome the absurdity of the situation, I looked away from Louise.

'Now, now,' said Eric's mother, putting a hand on my shoulder. 'You must be brave.'

206

'I had better get my things at once,' I said hoarsely.

'Perhaps you had. Eric will drive you to the station.'

And so, light-headed with relief, I went upstairs to pack.

22

I am guilty, I know that. But if only . . . If only great events didn't hinge on trivial ones. If only I had been more thorough, less frantic when I left Eric's house. If only I hadn't left my violin in Vaugirard. If only . . . I don't know. With time perhaps Eric's passion might have cooled. Ella's trust might have grown. We might, all of us, have had space to breathe. I don't know.

But I did leave my violin in Vaugirard. And because I left it Eric was told, when he telephoned my parents that afternoon to ask whether or not to send it on, that my family knew no one by the name of Leopold and that I had not said anything about coming home before Christmas.

With no idea of how soon events were to overtake me I made the short train-journey between Eric's house and Ella's slumped in the corner of a deserted carriage, letting the awful memory of the past two days drain from me, thinking with relief that I had escaped. And as the hard fields sped past I began to think with pleasure that in a matter of hours I would have my beloved to myself once more, that soon her hair would be in my eyes and her fragile body in my arms. As Ella filled my mind the events of recent days took on an air of increasing unreality, and Eric became unreal with them. This calmed me, for it obscured my motives and made it easier for me to forget what I had done to him. I was glad of that; I wanted to forget. I tried hard to put away all thoughts of my friend. And because I knew that I would see Ella soon and that it would be weeks before I saw Eric, I was able to tell myself that time and space would be my teachers; that somehow they would show me how to make amends; that they would light for me a way to reclaiming his trust.

Youth is famous for its optimism and I had supplies in plenty. It's strange to think that now, knowing myself as I do; but it was true of me then.

I telephoned Ella from the station when I arrived and her delight touched me and made me feel that all would be well, that all was almost well already. She collected me in Jacques' dusty Renault and for the first time since I had left her in London there was something of the old magic between us, undimmed by worry, uncomplicated by the company of others. The old house no longer seemed so gloomy with her by my side as we rounded the last curve in its drive; its desolation was a refuge, a protection from all thoughts of the outside world. And even then I needed protection.

I did not give Ella any but the barest details of what had taken place between me and Eric. I had passed her test, that was all I cared for her to know; and she, perhaps already guilty for setting it, did not probe me. After my brief account of the past two days we talked together as if nothing had happened; as if Eric and Sarah and Charles did not exist; as if we were alone in our love and fed solely by it. We touched that afternoon with a passion that was new, even to us; and I basked in the caresses of her warm white body with something approaching perfect joy. Thinking of her now, I miss her supple limbs; her soft breasts; the arch of her nose; the warmth of her silvery laugh. Even now I miss her, though I am an old man and I sit alone in a darkening room. Despite all that has happened, I want her. And I shall take my longing to the grave.

I have reached now the most painful part of this long story. I have reached the first of the dreadful consequences of my sin and Ella's, the first of the many that were to follow. I cannot speak of the sweet dinner we shared that night, or of the way our delighted laughter and warm words lit up that cold old house. I had no idea then how near the end we were, how little untainted love was left to us, how soon the strands would turn. We ate alone together in the small dining room which led off the hall. Dr Pétin was away again in the village and we were left in delicious peace. I remember the cosy crackle of our fire; its warm light on Ella's face; the smell of woodsmoke and cigarettes and sweat and perfume which hung about us. We had not dressed but sat side by side at the small table in dressing gowns, hair dishevelled, touching sometimes as we ate, watching the movement of each other's forks, listening to the muted clash of silver on china, drinking sweet wine. Remembering that night I see my love's tousled hair; the glow of her cheeks; the line of her cheekbones in the candlelight. I hear our lazy candid words; her light laugh; my deeper chuckle sounding with hers. I watch her eyebrows furrow as the doorbell rings and hear her say that it must be Dr Pétin back unexpectedly from the village, that it's just like him to come home at a time like this. I hear her giggle and say how compromising our near nakedness is and I see her tie her dressing gown tighter round her slim waist and run a hand quickly through her hair, to little effect. I watch her as she moves past me through the dining-room door and into the hall and I listen for the deferential greeting of the doctor. There is silence for a moment. Then the scraping of a heavy bolt and the turning of a key in an unoiled lock. Then a short sharp cry and the sound of a man's step on the flagstones and I hear Eric's voice, wild and high, asking for me and Ella's reply that I am not here, that he must go at once. And I hear his hurried forceful steps in the hall and his raised voice calling my name, and I stand up, sick, and go to the dining-room door and open it and see him standing there, in the same clothes I left him in that morning, his hair wild, my violin case in one strong hand. And then I remember where I left my violin and know with awful clarity what has happened, how he has found me. And I go to him but he looks at me in horror and throws the faded leather case on the floor with all his might and there is a twanging of strings and I watch him bound through the doorway and down the steps of the house into the cold black night.

What could I have done but follow him?

With a word of caution to Ella standing silent in the hall I went down the steps after him in my dressing gown, the wind of that chill night whipping my ears, its frost freezing my feet. I called my friend's name once, twice, but there was no reply but the steady beat of shoes on gravel as he ran away from me. In the dark I followed him, guided by my ears and by the lines of yew hedge which scratched my hands but kept my path straight. At first I called, but when I knew that my voice only made him run faster I was quiet and listened instead, following the crash of his footsteps and trying to make out his flying form in the dark. As the moon appeared from a bank of clouds, full and luminous, I saw him in the line of trees at the end of the garden and ran towards it; and as I emerged I saw him across the orchard, calling to me to leave him alone, a sharp, wild note in his voice like the cry of a hunted animal. On I ran, on and on until I had left the orchard behind and was standing by the edge of the quarry, panting, calling softly to Eric, telling him that I could explain. He appeared quite suddenly as the moon shone once more through a crack in the clouds and I saw that he was standing by the bench. As I called his name he sat down on its rusted seat, his head in his hands, his shoulders shaking. Muffled, breathless sobs came to me through the damp air and I, appalled, moved towards him and put my hand on his shoulder.

'Do not touch me.' His voice was small and unsteady, almost reedy; I had never heard it like that before.

'Eric . . .' I began, and fell silent. No words would come.

Slowly he turned and looked at me; and as my eyes grew accustomed to the dark I saw that his face was wet. 'Why are you here?' he asked; and there was something pathetic in his helpless look and streaming eyes. 'Why are you here, with her?'

I looked at him and said nothing. What was there to say?

'I love you, James.' The man by my side now took my hands in his and held them as I tried to pull away. 'I have loved you since the first moment I saw you.'

'Eric, no . . .'

'And I know that you love me.' He was talking quickly now. 'I know that you do. I did not think you did at first. I tried to be content with your friendship, with what we had in Prague.' I got my hands away from his and waited awkwardly, willing him to end. He sensed my unease. 'But . . . last night,' he went on eventually. 'Last night I knew that you loved me, too. No, do not say anything. I knew.'

Mutely I shook my head, my brain reeling.

'What is the use in pretending, James? A love like ours is a fine thing. There is nothing shameful about it.'

'But Eric . . .'

'Do not say "But Eric" to me like that. You know that you love me. Say that you do.'

And as he took my hands once more and pressed them to his lips I knew that I had to speak, that I had to make him see. 'Eric,' I began, shaking my hands free from his grasp again, 'I . . .'

'What James?'

'I . . .' I searched vainly for a form of words, for a formula which might mask the truth, which might conceal my betrayal of his trust. After a moment's thought I found it. 'You are my friend,' I said, 'one of the people I like most in the world.' I paused, seeing the hope in his eyes. 'I confused my affection for you with something else.'

'No.'

'I did, Eric, and I'm sorry. I do love you, but not in that way. I can never love you in that way.'

'But last night?' He looked up at me in helpless misery.

'Last night was madness. I was confused. I had no idea what I was doing.'

'I do not believe that.'

'It's the truth, I swear it.'

'But you kissed me.'

'It was a mistake,' I said quietly, numb with self-loathing.

'A mistake?'

'Yes. A mistake. I cannot love you like that.'

'Why not?'

'I'm not made that way.'

There was a brief, awful silence.

'Do you love her?' he said at last.

'Who? Ella?'

'Who else?'

'Yes, I love her.'

Eric looked at me helpless, uncomprehending. 'And you do not love me?'

I sat down on the bench and put my arm around him. 'I like you as much as I have ever liked anyone,' I said.

'But you do not love me.'

'No I don't.'

He started crying at this point, first slowly and quietly, then fast and loud; and I did not move as he leaned against my shoulder and cried large hot tears which wet my neck and the collar of my dressing gown. Slowly I put my hand on his shaking back and as I did so I realized I was freezing.

'Come on,' I said gently. And as I opened my mouth to say more I saw the sharp beam of a torch in the darkness and heard Ella's voice calling for me. Eric heard it too and clung to me with all his might, burying his face in my neck, his tears still hot and wet on my chest. 'Come on,' I said again; and as I spoke I blinked in the harsh beam of the torch which caught and then held us. Ella stood beyond it, her face ghostly and white above the high collar of her coat; and dazzled though I was by the brightness of the light I saw that there was fear in her eyes.

'What are you doing?' Her voice was sharp and brittle.

'It's not what you think,' I said, and began to push Eric away. But as I did so I knew suddenly that I had done proving myself to Ella. She could take me on trust now; I had sacrificed enough to earn her confidence. So I continued to hold my friend as his huge frame shook. Quietly, firmly, I asked Ella to leave us for a moment.

'What are you trying to say?' she replied, her voice quivering now.

'Nothing but what I have said. I'll come back to the house in a moment. Please. Eric and I need to talk in private.'

There was a tense silence, broken only by Eric's whimpering.

'Before I go tell him that it's me you love.'

The sound of Ella's voice seemed to rouse Eric from his misery for he raised his head and looked at her.

'Tell him,' she said again, her face hard and set.

'Go away.' The man by my side had stopped crying. Slowly he stood up, and his great bulk loomed terrible in the moonlight. 'You have done your harm,' he said thickly. 'You have done your damage. You can go now. It is me who James loves. Nothing you can say will change that.'

I watched as they faced each other. 'Please, you two . . .' I began.

'Tell him, James.'

'Please Ella. I'll be in in a minute.'

'Tell him now, before I go.'

'Please.'

'Tell him why you kissed him.'

There was silence. Eric looked at me.

'What is it she wishes you to tell me, James?' he said at last.

'Nothing. Nothing, Eric. Now please . . .'

The beam of the torch swung into my eyes again. Behind it Ella's face was pinched and drawn. 'Tell him,' she said again. 'There's no use pretending now. We're past that, we three.' And as she spoke she walked over to me – I had risen from the bench now, too – and deliberately put her arm through mine.

'What is this, James? What does she mean?' Eric's voice was quieter now, but I could see the veins on his temples throbbing.

'It's nothing,' I said.

'Oh, yes, it is.' Ella's voice was high and defiant.

'Please Ella.' I looked at her, trying to show with my eyes that she had nothing to fear. She looked away from me.

'I won't leave until you've told Eric the truth,' she continued, her voice set. 'I want you to tell him that you love me, that you kissed him to prove yourself to me.'

'It is me he loves.' Eric's voice was angry now. 'You have done your best to cause us harm and you have failed.' He moved towards me. 'Come James. Come with me.' And he looked at Ella with fury in his eyes.

'Eric . . .' I began, searching for words. 'Eric, I . . . I love Ella.' I stopped.

'Tell him, Jamie.'

'I . . .'

'But what about last night?' Eric's eyes met mine and I forced myself to face them.

'I . . . I didn't mean it.'

'Tell him, Jamie.'

'It was a test,' I said finally, sick at heart.

'A test?' There was a frightened note in his voice now.

'I had to prove myself.'

'What did you have to prove?'

And I knew then, too late, that I had proved nothing but my own weakness.

'He proved that he would do anything for me.' Ella's eyes were shining now. She put her hand in mine.

Her touch and her smiling lips revolted me; I shook my hand free of hers. 'Don't,' I said; and I felt a rising tide of nausea wash over me. 'I had no idea what I was doing,' I murmured hoarsely to Eric. 'You must believe that.'

'You had every idea.'

And all three of us knew that he was right.

23

I don't remember how I got away from them that night, how I made my way back to the house and to the warm shelter of its dusty rooms. I do remember running through the orchard and slipping on its icy grass. I remember also Eric's eyes and Ella's smile, surreal in the moonlight, and the ghostly pallor of their skin. In my need to get away from them both I ran without thought of direction, past stark trees and ill-pruned hedges and a silent fountain sinister in the darkness. I ran until the lights of the house loomed before me, a beacon in the night; and I did not stop running until I was in its bright hall, dripping with sweat, my knees bloody from where I had fallen, my hands red and frozen. I was still in my dressing gown.

I could not face either of them again that night, that much I knew; and I stripped a bed in the bedroom which had been mine and Eric's and put sheets and blankets on the floor of a disused little room off the pantry. I worked quickly, worried that one or the other might return, and breathing hard and nearly in tears I locked myself into cramped darkness like a child hiding from punishment. Alone at last I still had no peace, for the room filled with sights and sounds; with the rough scratch of Eric's lips on mine; with the acrid sweetness of Ella's smell; with wild laughter and streaming eyes and the sight of Eric's face by the quarry, frightened like a wounded animal's. From far off I heard the front door open and close and thought with relief that neither of them would find me until the morning. Sick at heart I tried to sleep.

Sleep came as the sun was rising and when it did it was deep and dreamless. I slept so soundly that I didn't hear the shouting; and I had hidden myself so well that Ella had to search the house for me when they found him the next morning. I remember waking to the ache of a night spent on a hard stone floor; to the deep chill of that dank, airless room; to the frantic note in her voice as she pounded on the door.

Eric was lying face down in the water, floating in the depths of the quarry like a piece of timber. It took four men from the village with ropes tied round their chests to abseil down and pull his body to the side and drag it up the steep incline to the little group by the bench. Ella and I stood watching as they tied their ropes to the yew trees and began to lower themselves downwards. We heard the splash of their rubber dinghy as it was lowered into the murky water. We watched two of them get into it and heard their paddling; their heaving as they pulled the body into their boat; their slow return to the others suspended on the quarry sides. Then winches and harnesses appeared and Eric began his jerky solitary journey upwards, back to us, back to dry ground. I remember the ghastly stare of the eyes in his waxy face; the way his mouth hung open; the immense weight of his dripping body as it was laid out on the cold earth.

Dr Pétin signed the death certificate, his rosy face pale and sombre, his hair dishevelled. For the probable cause of death he put drowning; and I watched the doctor fill out the forms in silence and saw him kneel over my friend's bloated face, examining his body. It was when I saw the tears in his eyes that I realized I was not crying. I was numb; impervious to the bustle that follows a death. And calmly, almost mechanically, I greeted the village gendarme; saw them put Eric into an ambulance and drive him away for further examination; listened to the condolences of Madame Clancy and Jacques; thanked the men who had hoisted Eric's body from the quarry. As one in a dream I stood by Ella as she explained to the detective that Eric had followed me from Vaugirard to return my violin; that he had arrived towards the end of dinner and that she and I had offered him coffee and a bed; that he had decided to go for a walk before turning in for the night; that he had seemed perfectly happy, quite his usual self in fact. And I, when asked, said that I was one of his greatest friends; that Eric had said nothing to me about any unhappiness; that the night had been dark; that I could only think he had fallen; that he was not the kind of man to take his own life.

It was only when the policeman asked if I knew the address of the deceased's next-of-kin that reality penetrated the cloud. I saw the Vaugirards at once: Louise at the market, examining ingredients for the evening; Eric *père* sitting gravely in his study, looking forward to lunch; Sylvie with her son, collecting him from nursery school, asking him what he had done that day.

'I know them,' I said to the gendarme.

'Then perhaps it would be better if you informed them,' he said. He was a small, anxious man with kind eyes. It was, he told me, the first time he had seen a death.

So it was I who telephoned Louise; I who endured her anxious questioning after Leopold; I who told her that his illness had been exaggerated and that he was now out of danger; I who endured her joy at this news. It was I who told her that something awful had happened; I who told her that Eric was dead; I who listened to the first sharp cry of a mother who has lost her son; I who answered the rush of her questions and explained how Eric had gone walking at night without a torch and had fallen into a quarry. And still I did not cry; I could not. Numb and as calm as the dead I took my place at the dining-room table with Ella and the gendarme and Dr Pétin and waited for Louise and Eric *père* to arrive, thinking nothing, conscious only of a dull ache and of the steady throbbing beat of the blood in my head. I looked at Ella but did not see her; I watched her smoke cigarette after cigarette but did not register that she moved; I could not smell her. I knew then that I would never tell anyone of the reason for Eric's death and that she would not either. I told myself that it was better for Eric's parents to curse Fate and to rail against the tragedy of an accident than to know that their son had ended his own life. But I no longer had the energy for self-deceit. I knew quite clearly why I had lied, why I would always lie; I knew that I was a coward, that I had neither the will nor the courage to stand to public account for what I had done. And by lying then, by passing up my only opportunity for honest confession,

I gave up my only chance of expiation. I condemned myself to my own judgement and made myself a criminal. And as I sat with that silent group at the table I knew that however much I tried to pretend, however hard I tried to forget, the certain knowledge that I was worthless would always be with me.

The Vaugirards arrived in the late afternoon and I submitted to their tearful embraces. Madame Clancy disappeared to make up two bedrooms: one for them and one for me, for I could not bear to re-enter the room that had been Eric's and mine. And while we waited for her to return I sat with Eric's parents and told them how Eric had followed me to return my violin; how he had gone off for a walk in high spirits; how he had not taken a torch; how Ella and I had gone to bed, little thinking that he would not return; how he had been found that morning, face down in the water. Louise, like me, was calm. She sat, stately, in a high-backed chair beside mine, her arm on her husband's, the bones of her shoulders clearly visible, her back rigid. Eric *père* cried like Eric *fils* had cried the night before: the loud ugly sobs of a man unused to tears. His crying, alone of all the sounds I heard that day, penetrated my numbness; and I heard Eric crying and felt the warm flood of his tears on my neck. Then I heard his laugh. Distant and quiet at first, then louder, fuller, heartier, nearer. And then I saw his eyes streaming with mirth and the flash of his white teeth and his wide smile and I thought that I would cry but I didn't.

I cried later, when I went into the bedroom which Eric and I had shared to return the blankets and sheets I had taken from it the night before. Numb as I was I could think clearly enough to know that it would not do for them to be discovered in a dark room off the pantry; so I left Louise and Eric *père* talking to Dr Pétin and crept down the vaulted passage that Ella had led Eric and me down such a short time ago. Everything in the room was precisely as I remembered it: the armoire; the novels; the fire screen. And as I opened the door I smelled the familiar smell of lavender and wood smoke and another smell which for a moment I could not place, a smell of sweat and aftershave. And then it hit me and slowly I sank to my knees, burying my face in my arms, my nose in the thick wool of my sweater. I could not bear Eric's smell. And while I was crouching on the floor I heard the door open and felt Louise kneel next to me and hug my heaving back with the long slender arms and bony hands she had given Eric. We rocked together in silence and with horror I felt her tears on my shoulder, mingling perhaps with the salt from her son's.

'You must not blame yourself for letting Eric go out alone last night,' she said. 'He was foolhardy. It was what we loved about him. It was what you loved about him.'

And as she spoke I thought that I would have preferred the clean thrust of a knife.

The coroner delivered a verdict of accidental death and Eric was buried in hallowed ground in the tiny cemetery adjacent to the château at Vaugirard. I was a pallbearer at his funeral, my eyes the only dry pair in that overcrowded chapel of hard pews and Norman arches, my shoulder the steadiest of the six which lifted his heavy coffin and carried it down the narrow aisle. I lived through that day with the grim determination of a man beginning a life sentence; and I watched the movements of my body with detached interest from a recess in my mind, the only refuge I could find. I watched myself dress that morning; watched my fingers knot the black tie which I had bought for the occasion; watched them run a comb through my hair; registered that I looked older, more haggard than I had done a week before; saw without concern that I was presentable nonetheless. I had hardly slept for seven consecutive nights; my cheeks were sunken; there were dark purple circles under my eyes. Exhaustion calmed me; it separated and distanced me from the world, from the acting-out of my role in the last act of Eric's tragedy. It insulated me from the tears and grief of those around me; it protected me from the knowledge of what I had done; it numbed my pain to a dull ache.

I remember that small chapel high above the town; I remember the rustle of its black-clad congregation as they took their seats on small pews of dark wood; I remember the stately calm of Louise and the wild red eyes of Eric *père*. I remember the coffin; remember Eric lying in it; remember the calm, pale dignity of his face; the unnatural neatness of his black curls, brushed for the last time. Standing before him in the line of people paying their last respects I found that I had nothing to say, for the suited body before me was not my friend, was not the Eric I had played my first concert with; was not the Eric I had laughed with at Café Florian; was not even the Eric I had sacrificed so deliberately to prove my love for Ella. His soul was gone from his body, that much I knew; and all I could do was hope that it had found peace. In a state of eerie calm I looked at him and tried to say goodbye, but no words would come. The face of Eric's dead body held no meaning for me any more; and it was not until I saw his shoes that the tears came. They tied the body before me to a living reality, a reality which I missed suddenly with a wrenching, crippling pain; and I remembered the scene at Florian's when Eric had bought them and heard his laughing voice telling me gravely that he did not like new things. He had bought them from a friend of the woman with the severe nose, an Englishman who had fallen on hard times. They were brogues, old-fashioned and scuffed in, and had been circulated amongst the regulars of Café Florian with an old tweed suit and some ties which had gone to others. Eric had bought the shoes without haggling over their price as the buyers of other articles had done, for he did not exploit those in need. He had paid their owner the sum requested for them and had put them on at once. It was this that made me cry.

Ella came up to me as the mourners were beginning to stream away from the grave, a line of black figures under a grey sky, shivering in the wind. I had been only dimly aware of her during the past week; I had seen her red eyes and pinched cheeks without noticing them; her pale face and the dark circles under her green eyes without caring for them. I had made sure that I was never alone with her, for that I could not have borne. And as she slipped her cold hand into mine in that churchyard the smoothness of her touch sickened me, for it reminded me of what I had done to win it, of what I had done to be worthy of her. I could not meet her eyes.

'Jamie . . .' she said at last. 'Please don't do this. Don't pretend I don't exist.'

I walked on faster.

'Please. I can't go on.'

'It was Eric who couldn't go on,' I said quietly. 'Not you. Not me. Eric.'

Her hand tightened its grasp on mine. I shook it away.

'He killed himself because of what we did,' I said, 'because . . .' I stifled the accusation on my lips.

'Say it.'

'Because of what you made me do.'

There was silence.

'Jamie,' she said at last. 'Jamie please don't do this.' And there was real pleading in her tone. Still I could not meet her eyes.

'You honestly think we can go on blithely as before?'

'No, not as before perhaps, but . . . Can't you see how much we need each other? We need each other now more than ever. You're my only hope. I'm yours.'

We were nearing the other mourners now; and I heard the shutting of car doors and the tap of high heels on cobbles.

'What did you tell him?' I asked suddenly, quietly. 'What did you say to him after I left you?'

There was silence.

'What did you say?'

'Please, Jamie . . .' She was crying now.

'What did you *say* to him?'

'I . . .' Ella looked at me. I met her eyes stonily and for the first time their beauty did not move me. 'Please don't,' she said again.

'Tell me.'

'I . . .' She hesitated and opened her bag for a cigarette.

I pulled her hand. 'I don't want you to smoke. I want you to tell me what you said to Eric after I left you.'

'I told Eric the truth,' she said quietly. 'He was very angry after you left. He said that you loved him, that you had kissed him, that I was trying to do you harm. So I told him why you had kissed him. I made him understand that you did it for me.'

'And then?'

'And then I left him.'

We walked on in silence, through the churchyard gate and into the street. I heard the tap of Ella's shoes on the stones, the desultory conversation of the other mourners, the growl of car engines. I cannot describe how I felt; I have no words for the numbness which ran through me. I tried to speak but no sound would come. And as Ella and I walked on together I felt as though I were floating, as though the world around me was no more real than a dream. For an instant I clung to this hope. Then I told myself that the world was real, that I was not a shadow but a person who lived and breathed like other people. In a moment of clarity the future stretched before me: a life lived in the shallows of my mind, from whence it would be dangerous to stray.

I am straying now and I know the dangers I face; but I am past caring for such things.

As the street began to steepen, for we were walking from the castle down the hill to the town, I looked at Ella once more and drank my fill of her fine, delicate face; of the indentation made by her collarbone above the line of her black dress; of the green of her eyes and the symmetry of her cheekbones. She looked at me, too, and pressed closer towards me; for the last time I smelled her subtle, complex scent. 'I don't ever want to see you again,' I said slowly.

And then I left her and broke into a run, frightened of the sound of her voice, of its power to sway me; and I did not stop running until I was lost in the crowds of the town and she was far behind, an isolated figure in a black dress, face whipped by the wind, eyes expressionless, hands shaking.

24

It is difficult for me to talk of the days and months that followed my home-coming. Eric's friendship and Ella's love had gone from my life at a single stroke and I mourned them both, with a pain I could not share. I did not mourn the loss of my innocence, for I hardly knew that I had had it to lose; but I felt that things had changed, that I was not the boy who had gone to Prague three months before; and in that I was correct. I remember my journey to England on a grey day of choppy waves and circling gulls. I remember the lurching of the boat, the salt of the wind on my face, the crowds of people meeting the ferry. I passed through them all, oblivious, and when I reached home I slept, resolving to rely no longer on the opiate of exhaustion.

Sleep shielded me for a day or two as the Christmas cards mounted on the mat and my mother started to talk of trees and tinsel and mince pies and of how difficult it was to buy presents for my father. Delighted to have me home earlier than expected – and wishing, I suspect, to smooth away all traces of past struggles between us – she included me resolutely in her plans for the festivities; and finding me sombre and inclined to solitude, she thought me resentful of her attentions and pressed them on me all the harder. Day after day my opinion was sought on the pressing issues of the hour. Should we or should we not give a dinner party on Christmas Eve? Should we or should we not ask Aunt Julia to spend the holiday with us as usual? Should we or should we not invite the vicar to lunch on Boxing Day? (My mother, you see, was strict in her social observance of religious principle; and the annual entertainment of such minor clergy as were known to her was a sacred rite.)

Through all this flurry of seasonal enthusiasm I moved numbly, as one in a dream, adding my name to the greetings on the Christmas cards; murmuring my approval of the mince pies that appeared, fragrant and warm, at regular intervals; suggesting presents for my father. But I felt removed from the jolly bustle around me; and my parents, relentlessly cheerful in my presence, said privately to each other that my music was doing me no good and that I was in need of more fresh air. Exercise, you see, was always the solution in my family; and so I was encouraged, when Aunt Julia came to stay, to adopt her dog and to take it on its daily walks: a solitary task in which I rejoiced, for in it lay my only respite from the forced conviviality of home life.

Aunt Julia was a tall, straight woman with intense brown eyes and pugnacious eyebrows. Traces of *risqué* chic lingered about her still, though she was approaching seventy; and they manifested themselves in her tastes for smoking and swearing, both of which she indulged with military gusto in the manner of her long-dead brigadier husband. Splendidly indifferent to my mother's disapproval, she took a maternal interest in my father (whose mother's best friend she had been) and she rather enjoyed her courtesy title of aunt, I suspect, for she used it to assume the endless licence of a family intimate. Advice for my parents flowed freely from Aunt Julia; and on me she lavished a sort of barking kindliness which she supposed, not having children of her own, to be the correct way of conducting oneself towards members of the younger generation.

An iron will and unchanging habits were two of her most obvious qualities; and it was these that made me look forward to her visit more than usual in the bleak weeks which followed my return from France. I needed old assurances then: I needed to feel that life would go on; to believe that the passing of time would help me to live with what I had done. And there was nothing so reassuring as a visit from this time-honoured Christmas *habituée*, in whose presence life assumed a kind of military efficiency, an efficiency relieved and made charming by the incongruous irreverence of the old lady herself.

Her movements were exact. She arrived without fail three days before Christmas and left, without variation, on the day after Boxing Day. And the method of her arrival was consistent too: she came in two taxis from Waterloo ('One for bags, one for owner and dog'); and descended, accompanied by the lazy barks of a sleek basset-hound, to present one wrinkled cheek to my mother before paying the taxi drivers and sending them away with loud wishes for a 'bloody good Christmas'. Inside, safely ensconced by the fire, her bags upstairs and unpacked ('I can't abide people who live out of suitcases'), she would light a small cigar, accept a glass of water – for Aunt Julia didn't drink – and question her audience with a ruthless directness which offended my mother and occasioned the first of the icy silences which inevitably punctuated the five days of her visit.

I remember the day she came. I remember standing in the hall, waiting to submit to her inspection and to her two, efficient Christmas kisses; and I remember thinking that Julia's visit might divert me from myself; that she might take the attention of the household from me and allow me some of the space I needed, without resorting to the emotional intrusion I so dreaded from my parents. It was by Julia, you see, that I hoped to be removed from the immediacy of Eric's death. I looked forward to the unquestioned authority of her conversation and to the way in which she assumed control of my Christmas entertainment. I wanted her to protect me from myself in a way in which my parents, who knew me better, were powerless to do; and I felt that her protection, like mine in the beginning for Ella, would come at a time when it was sorely needed.

It was my mother who suggested I take Jep on his daily walks; and the privilege was graciously bestowed on me by Julia, who thought no honour higher than that which came with the entrustment of his care. He was a happy, self-important little dog, with the shiny coat and benevolent eyes of the well-loved basset-hound; and his impatience for his daily exercise gave me the opportunity and excuse for solitude, for I pretended to be jealous of Jep's affection and would allow no one to accompany us on our excursions together.

It's strange, you know: strange that those few walks through the windy drizzle of an English December should have been so important to me; strange that now, from a distance of fifty years, they should recur to me with such vividness. I wonder why they do. Perhaps already I was tired of drama; perhaps already my hopes and dreams were shrinking, or had shrunk, and my desires were tilting towards the secure mediocrity of a warm bed and a quiet life. I don't know. I know only that I found something reassuring in the uncalculating, uncomplicated affection of Jep; something endearing in his long ears and waddling gait. The trust of animals is easy to keep, easier than that of humans: for it carries with it no real burdens; no real temptations. It is a bond that ties us to reality, to the limitations of the everyday; and that was precisely the sort of bond I most needed then. Even through my grief I was human enough to be grateful for Jep's companionship, and I showed my gratitude in an endless affection which he accepted complacently as his right.

The solitude of those walks was a welcome release for me too, for at home I had no time to myself. The house was filled with a constant stream of guests whose coats I had to take, whose glasses I had to fill; and whose conversation, smooth with the practised fluency of countless Christmas drinks parties, I had to listen to and smile at. In only one room could I be sure of privacy, and that was the tiny one at the top of the house in which I'd spent long summer afternoons playing to Ella. But it, of all places, held no peace for me. Her laugh rang there continually; I could not go near its door.

And so, with an irony I didn't appreciate then, I sought solitude amongst the pavement crowds of a large city; and amongst faces I did not know, faces which held no memories for me, I found some release from memory and some, very fleeting, peace. With Jep the basset-hound by my side, I walked through the stream of shoppers making hasty purchases on Christmas Eve and the days immediately before it; I listened to frenzied discussions about food and gifts and clothes and lovers and holidays; saw friends laughing loudly at bus stops and couples arguing quietly about nothing, their faces pinched from cold and irritation. I walked through these vignettes of other people's lives and listened with the frightened enthusiasm of one who is no longer interested in his own life. I tried to care about the nameless faces I saw; about the passions and desires which fuelled their smiles and gave an edge to their angers. I tried to wonder about the resolution of their conflicts; about the continuance of their friendships and the futures of their loves. I tried even to envy them. For I felt then that I had lost such things for ever; that my own life had lost the power to move me; and I dreaded the cold blandness of a spiritual divorce from oneself.

I was not yet ready to face what I had done; to return even mentally to the scene of Eric's death or to the events that had preceded it. I lived in constant terror of my own memory, for I knew what pain it could inflict; and so I tried to interest myself in the lives of people I did not know, hoping thus to escape from myself and to re-establish some kind of emotional reality in my own life, vicarious though it might be.

Christmas came and went and I ate and drank and tried to laugh as I was meant to, watching my mother's concealed irritation as Julia lit cigars at the dinner table and fed Jep bits of turkey and called my father an old dog. The vicar's wife came alone to lunch on Boxing Day – her husband being 'terribly run down with 'flu' – and held forth on the subject of the Church Bazaar while Julia asked whatever anyone saw in antimacassars. I took Jep out twice a day: hour-long oases of time alone to which I looked forward with an eagerness I could not quite hide and from which I returned, cheeks flushed, to face the social obligations of life in my mother's house with renewed energy.

It was from one of these expeditions, made on the eve of Julia's departure, that I returned, at six o'clock, to find no guests present and Julia in full flow on the subject of the vicar's wife.

'Bloody awful dress, I thought,' she was saying as I came in. 'I for one see no reason why ugliness should be next to godliness, do you?'

'None whatever,' replied my father, handing her a glass of water.

Julia was sitting bolt upright in her favourite chair by the fire, a cigar in one hand, her iron-grey hair scraped back from her face. Helping myself to a gin and tonic from the drinks table, I sat down in a dark corner by the window, a corner from which I could watch my father laughing and listen to the conversation without necessarily having to contribute to it myself.

'Damned cheek, dressing so badly,' Aunt Julia continued. 'It must be an awful embarrassment to her husband.'

And I thought with pity of the vicar's dowdy wife and of what she must have suffered at Julia's hands over lunch, a pity which did not prevent me from laughing at her misfortunes and at the good-humoured malice with which her character and tastes were systematically assassinated before me. Sitting with Jep on my lap I felt with relief that the cold flagstones and peeling shutters of Ella's house in France were very far away; that the events which had taken place under its blackened beams and in the unloved decay of its gardens had taken on the quality of a nightmare; that they belonged to a different world from the one to which I had returned, and in which I was safe once again.

Surely the cosy domesticity of the scene before me was my reality now, I thought. Surely I could come to accept it, in any case, as the only reality that mattered; and perhaps if I did so I might find in its warmth a refuge from the pain of recollection. Surely . . . But what is the use of my remembering my early hopes of self-delusion? I might have seen safety in self-deception even then, but I was powerless really to overcome my guilt or to forget what I had done. Only years of expert training could show me how to sever myself from my past and to forget even the most rudimentary tools of emotional analysis; and I had had no such training. I was a child, trying in a child's way to deal with the consequences of actions committed with an adult's strength. My instincts were to regress: to seek the safety of my earliest world, the world I looked at from my dark corner on that cold evening. I wanted a world of family and familiar faces, of warm conversation beside blazing fires in rooms I had known all my life.

I derived comfort from the very presence of childhood figures like Aunt Julia. I needed security and stability and affection, the last of these so badly that even the unthinking devotion of a basset-hound could move me.

I tried not to think of the details of Eric's death, not to ask myself why I had not confessed to my part in it when I had had the chance. I tried not to think of the Vaugirards' Christmas: of Eric *père* and Louise and Sylvie; of the forlorn group which they would make beside the Christmas tree in their narrow, rambling house with its croquet lawn behind. I tried not to think of Eric's shoes; of the way he had laughed at our long search for a bed in Madame Mocsáry's apartment; of the woman with the severe nose at Florian's with whom he had argued. I tried not to think of him playing the piano in the impromptu music room at Sokolska 21; of the way his eyes used to flash when we played together well; of the smell of aftershave and sweat which had lingered in his bedroom at Ella's. I tried to focus on the group before me, to listen to Aunt Julia's acerbic wit, to smile at my mother's irritation when a stray piece of cigar ash found its way on to the carpet. But the room swam before my eyes and all I could hear, listen though I might, was Eric's voice telling me that he loved me completely; all I could see was his swollen body laid out on the hard ground by the quarry with Dr Pétin bending over it in tears.

'My God, the boy's crying.' It was Julia's voice that spoke; and it was her thin arms that circled my shoulders; her cracked voice that told me, with a soft sympathy far from her usual tone, that I should get a grip at once and stop being so silly.

25

I did recover. One does. And the recovery I made, though never more than partial, was remarkable; I see that now. I see what Sarah did for me; and I appreciate the skill with which she taught her chill lessons of self-delusion and deceit. But as I stood with Julia's arms around me on that cold December night, trying to avoid my parents' worried eyes, I had no idea what lay before me; no real suspicion of how difficult the path ahead would prove to be. The worries of children never endure; their fleetingness is one of the compensations of childhood. And child that I was, I did not suspect then, as I told my family that I was tired and that they should take no notice of me, that I had been initiated into a harsher world. I did not realize that those few weeks in Prague and France had taken me for ever from the cheerful confines of previous feeling; that Ella's love and Eric's death had raised me to a colder, more adult plane of experience; that suffering in this new world could be lasting and real. I did not suspect because I had not yet tasted the bitterness of unresolved grief; and my lesson, soon to come, was protracted and painful in a way it has taken me years to forget.

But the pain of those first weeks could not prolong itself indefinitely; and the fires burned themselves out in the end, as all fires do, though they left smouldering coals which destroyed my hopes of peace. At last the Guildhall term began and I was thrown into a busy round of classes and private practice which took some of the immediacy from my misery, for routine is a great palliative. And in devoted industry I found some relief. I found it too in the comforting presence of people and of places I knew; and so I learned, little by little, to live with what I had done.

People who think they understand say that life goes on; that time heals. And bland though they are, there is some truth in such platitudes. My life *did* go on after Eric's death; without my actively ending it, I suppose, it could not have done otherwise. And slowly I learned to laugh at people's jokes again; to listen to their troubles; to hear of their loves and their plans with something approaching enthusiasm. I learned to get through the days; and gradually, with time, they became bearable. No more than bearable, I know that now; perhaps I suspected it even then. But I was grateful for the smallest mercies.

My practice room at the Guildhall, a tatty little space that held no memories, became the centre of my life; and as I talk I see again its cheaply varnished upright piano; the lime linoleum of its small square floor; the steel music stand that stood beside its dirty windows of frosted glass. I remember the mustiness of its smell; the cigarette burns on its small table; the faded prints of original scores and Viennese waltzers which were all that enlivened its four brown walls. Nothing could have been further from the splendours of Madame Mocsáry's apartment, that is certain; but I rejoiced in the anonymity of its ugliness. In Room 32 I was safe, you see; and I spent many hours playing in it, undisturbed and alone.

My violin was my chief comfort in those dark days. And sometimes, when I played, Eric faded from my mind as the music filled it; sometimes, for an hour or two, seldom longer, I was free from the memory of what I had done to him. But I could never be so for long. My guilt always returned; and with it came the sound of my friend's laugh and the sightless gaze of his open eyes as his body was laid out by the quarry. For weeks such sights never left my mind, whichever way I looked for distraction. But it was when I did not play that Eric was with me most frequently: a haunting presence with wild hair and dull eyes; a silent apparition with words of love on his lips. He lived in my dreams and sleep ceased to be a refuge; instead it became a frightening cacophony of sight and sound and smell, of tears and yells and long, steep falls into darkness. I began to lie awake in bed, willing the morning to come; telling myself that nothing is ever so awful by daylight; that even Eric's laugh would not outlast the coming of morning and the chasing of the shadows. With no one to confide in I was alone. And I learned the hard truth that isolation has little to do with the number of people who fill your days; that solitude follows you everywhere; that the mind itself is our keenest gaoler.

I did not see Ella, though I read of her in the newspapers and magazines which chronicled her return to England a week after my own; and with disgust I saw the lurid headlines which screamed stories of insanity above close-up photographs of her white face, pale with exhaustion, as she walked out of Customs at Heathrow. I read the florid stories of the Harcourt curse; read also how it had claimed a new victim, a young and promising French pianist, one of the family's guests at their 'picturesque villa in north-western France'.

On such nonsense does the popular imagination feed.

On such nonsense did my imagination feed, too, in a way; for such drivel was the only contact I allowed myself with Ella over the three years of my study at the Guildhall, a time I filled with the intense work that is, for some, one of the by-products of loneliness. She wrote to me, of course: long, frightened letters that grew more frightened as the weeks turned to months and I left each one unanswered, some unopened even. I missed her; of course I missed her; and with a kind of wrenching sorrow. More than once I nearly wrote. But my conscience would not allow me to see Ella; and the greater my desire for her, the more important it became for me to deny myself the comfort of her presence in my life. I had not been punished for my role in Eric's death, you see. Punishment was impossible without the confession I dared not make. And I yearned for punishment; for in its absence my guilt could only increase. I longed for some way to expiate my crime; to purge myself through suffering; and Ella was my chief privation.

Gradually her letters stopped; and my life, devoted more and more to music and to the playing of my violin, continued without any concrete reminders of our love. The days merged into one another and I passed through them all, trying not to think, working hard to resist a secret voice which told me that my silence was cruel, that the fragile woman whose photograph I saw in the papers did not deserve to be severed so completely from my life, a life in which she had shared so briefly but so fully. Thinking of it now I can see that my treatment of Ella *was* cruel, that without adding to my own guilt – or to hers – I might have written, at least. And though perhaps it would have been wrong for me to tell her that her image haunted my dreams still, that no day went past without me thinking of her ringing laugh or of the softness of her touch, I might have said that I grieved for her, that I mourned for her, too.

But it is easy to wish that one had acted differently once the time for action is past; it is easy to wonder and to hope for what might have been. Hindsight is notorious for its clarity, I know that; but I have no use for it. The fact is that I did not write. And my silence grew also from the fact that secretly I blamed Ella for Eric's death more than I blamed my own naïveté, which was the true culprit. It was easier and more comfortable for me to see the root of my sin in another; to think that I had been corrupted; that I was a victim, though even I could not pretend to be a guiltless one. Lacking the insight to see the insecurity behind Ella's cruelty, distracted by my struggles to understand my own, I oscillated in my judgement of her, unable to condemn or to forgive completely, eager only (and sometimes despite myself) for a reunion which my conscience would not grant. I wanted to see her too badly, you see; I needed her too much. And the absence of such comfort, I thought, was the least I owed to Eric.

Perhaps death will give me knowledge as well as judgement; perhaps it will reunite me with those I have loved in a way in which I never can be on earth. Perhaps . . . But I am rambling again. I must go on, for it is evening now. I must not be distracted by the metaphor of this darkening room and the frail old man who sits in it, alone.

My sun has set; it set years ago. I have grown to be comfortable with that fact. Now I must press on. I must not move until everything has been said. One night has passed since Sarah's death; another must not be allowed to do so or I shall lose all resolve. This is no time to stop.

I was alone in those years after Eric's death; and without the support which only Ella could have given, the knowledge of what I had done made me secretive. Over my years at the Guildhall I learned to disguise how I felt, to shield my unhappiness from the concerned enquiries of my friends and my family; and as I learned to do this better I became more adept at deceiving myself. True, I did not become as proficient as I would years later, when Sarah's example had shown me the means to self-deception with such unspoken clarity; but I made a valiant effort, and with that I had to be content. Try as I might, though, I could not escape one frightening truth: that human nature needs a punishment to fit its crimes. And I came to writhe under the very absence of hardship in my life; to see in every kind word and happy coincidence a reproach which could not be silenced. Separation from Ella would not suffice as my only punishment; and with no recriminating words to hurt me, deprived of the catharsis of confession, there was nowhere for my guilt to turn but in on itself. So I devised other self-inflicted privations – food I liked; certain pieces of music; access to my violin – all the while knowing that they were not enough, that they never could be enough.

Frenzied in my guilt, I came increasingly to think that any joy, any satisfaction I might derive from my life or my art, was tainted by what I had done to Eric; that I owed it to him to turn my back on all which might please me, to renounce my chance of happiness since it was I who had made him renounce his. I thought that I was worthless; and I could not enjoy any feeling higher than that of earnest drudgery without thinking that I was cheating Eric further of what might have been his. I had already taken too much of what belonged by rights to another, you see; I had taken, or helped to take, that most vital and short-lived possession: life. And I dared not allow myself any pleasures save those my playing gave me, worried as I was that weakness then would lose me the last vestiges of my once prized self-respect. Frightened to confess and thus to obtain punishment from others, frightened too of remaining unpunished for ever, I sought to punish myself; and in the private paying of my penance I was careful to allow myself no slack. I was a hard task-master, and therein lay my only relief.

But nature was too strong for me in the end; and the harder I tried the more I learned that the human spirit cannot quite be silenced, even by the sternest, most implacable foe; that I was not equal, at the last, to ridding myself entirely of my own humanity. Ella had forced me to live, you see; more than that, she had made me alive to the possibilities of life; and such knowledge is impossible to forget, however good one's intentions may be. Mine were very good, you may be sure of that; but they failed because I tried to drive all passion from me with an ardour which was passionate in its determination: passionate and thus self-defeating even at the peak of its power. Again and again I tried; again and again I did not succeed. And slowly I came to realize, with the certainty of repeated demonstration, that what I had done to Eric had made a numb and senseless life impossible for me; that my crime and subsequent grief had given me resources of experience and sensation which most people never accumulate in a lifetime of sober contentment.

It was with this knowledge, and its consequences for my guilt, that I grappled as I worked with the furious energy of frenzied confinement. My soul – which is what I will call it until someone proposes a better word – was resisting its imprisonment, I see that now; I understand that it was struggling for release. And as my playing was its only avenue of escape, its only way to the lighter air of a world beyond my sorrow, it came out in my work with a focused intensity which is denied to happier minds. Slowly I came to realize that the extremes of joy and pain to which I had been exposed, first by Ella and then by Eric, had informed my art and had taken my talent to the threshold of genius; and such knowledge sickened me.

I do not use words like 'genius' lightly; that last phrase, for example, is not my own but Michael Fullerton's; and it is from the headline of a review he wrote of the first concert I played after leaving the Guildhall. I have it somewhere in here, part of a neat bundle of reviews tied years ago by Sarah's tireless fingers. But there is no point in finding it or the others with it; they all say much the same thing. I need no reminding of my career; or of how much I came to dislike adulation when I received it, how much I fought against the knowledge that my music had a power that I alone could not have given it. I came to be scared of the origins of that power. Now I am less so. Time has calmed me; and it is right that I should acknowledge the debt I owe my dead friend; right that I should admit to myself that art, though not always born of suffering, can be; and that mine was.

It requires the peace of age to admit certain things; to state them out loud. And it is only now, now that I have nothing left to prove (to myself or to anyone else) that I can give Ella's love and Eric's death the credit for my musical success. It was love that first tempted me from the shallows and which taught me to swim alone, I can see that now; and it was the part I played in my best friend's death which so nearly made me drown. It is to these two experiences that I owe the riches of my later musicality. Left to myself I would have been technically impressive, nothing more; for I would not willingly have exchanged the shallows of my own mind for the waves in which I later floundered. It was Ella who threw me into the sea of life; it was she with whom I might have swum, out of my depth though I was. But I did not swim; and when Sarah offered me her hand I was only too willing to be pulled back to safety; only too relieved to regain once more the sight, if not the touch, of dry land. But my security was won at a price; and from that moment on my inspiration grew less urgent, less compelling; and I myself became less of a musician. My talent, as one of the reviews in the bundle will tell you, lay in the public translation of private passion. My only personal contribution to my art was the craft that allowed its expression; and beyond that the feeling was not mine, or at least it was not mine alone. It is something of a release to be able to say that at last.

26

I graduated from the Guildhall in the summer I turned twenty-five; and my next concert, as I have said, was reviewed by Michael Fullerton with much enthusiasm in *The Times*. I keep his review in my desk drawer, for sentimental reasons, I suppose; and I cannot help but look at the photograph that accompanies it, a severe but dramatic shot of me standing on the stage of the Albert Hall, tiers of empty boxes rising above me and beyond the frame. I am simply dressed, for I have been rehearsing; and although I am holding my violin as if about to play, my face is tense and slightly stern.

It is a face much more recognizably my own than the one which belongs to the boy who first met Ella, who first saw her youthful form as she sat alone on that sunny bench in the park. Only three years separate the faces, it's true; but people can change, even in so short a time, and I had changed. Staring at my image now, the face seems older than its twenty-five years: there are lines where there used to be none; the eyes are narrower; the lips thinner; the cheek-bones more pronounced. My hair was still long, of course, for my agent thought that long hair increased my stage presence and enhanced what she called my 'romantic appeal'. But save the severity of my haircut now – for flowing locks do not survive middle age with dignity – I am little changed from the man who stares at me from the newspaper on my lap. Of course the passing of the years has heightened the signs of age, which is a difference between us; and naturally his lines have become my wrinkles. But I share a look with my twenty-five-year-old self which was unknown to me at twenty-two. It is a sad look; hard and reserved: a look which softens now, as then, only when I play. I was resigned at twenty-five, resigned to the sorrows of life; and I can see the resignation in my eyes.

Perhaps Ella saw it, too, for by that stage I was in the newspapers almost as frequently as she had been, though for different reasons. Perhaps she looked at my image as I looked at hers, and read in my eyes the signs of a suffering which mirrored her own. Perhaps . . . But what is the use of wondering now? In my craze for punishment I had pushed Ella from my life; and though I cherished her memory still, though I thought still with frightening pleasure of the way she smiled, or of how she lit her cigarettes, I was separated from her by three years of painful guilt, a barrier which I, unaided, could and would not cross. Perhaps she followed the progress of my career with excitement; perhaps she bought my recordings and tried to relive the afternoons we had spent together, in my tiny attic, over the course of that golden summer we shared. All this is possible.

What is certain is that I read of her with interest in the intervals between my practice and recording commitments; but interested though I was, I could not be excited (as I hoped that she might be for me), for the news of the Harcourts was not good. Press interest in them had died down since Ella's return from France; but it picked up again and reached new heights after the publication of Sarah's book – a life of her grandmother – which received much public attention and a certain amount of critical acclaim. *The Times Literary Supplement* pronounced it 'eloquent in its portrayal of the unstable brilliance of a remarkable woman', according to the jacket of my copy at least; and after its launch photographers once again trained their lenses on the house in Chester Square in the hopes of capturing the fragile beauty of Seton Castle's youngest heir.

For a week or more the journalists were disappointed; but then a lucky reporter in Harley Street caught Ella in tears, emerging from her psychiatrist's, and the newspapers leaped with glee on both photograph and story. So great, in fact, was the public interest which greeted the ensuing articles that even the broadsheets ran small columns on the Harcourts and their history, while tabloid fantasy on the subject of curses and castles knew no bounds. Throughout the summer that followed my graduation, Ella and her family assumed an importance in national gossip second only to that enjoyed by the royal family; and the various characters in their drama were discussed everywhere with an unthinking, good-natured intrusion which it made my blood boil to hear.

Even Camilla Boardman, so indiscreet about her friends in private, felt bound in public to talk loudly about what *nonsense* it all was; thus subtly underlining her intimacy with celebrity to anyone who cared to hear, while maintaining at the same time a strict loyalty towards her friends. The years had not changed Camilla, whatever they had done to me; and as her twenties progressed she remained as perfectly curled, as flawlessly turned-out, as effortlessly confident as she had ever been. Her emphases did not decrease in frequency or in strength; her enthusiasms did not dim; her lack of punctuation remained legendary. She remained true to her promise and did not marry Ed Saunders. Instead, with a rare show of mettle, she left home and took out a bank loan; and when I graduated from the Guildhall, Camilla & Co. had already been open – in smart premises of elaborate design on the Fulham Road – for some time. Originally a dress shop, it had gradually become an outlet for Camilla's own creative flair; and soon she had four seamstresses under her and her clothes were being worn by a wider clientele than that provided by her mother's friends and her own.

I, less in awe of her as I grew older, saw her often during those dark times: for Camilla demanded an absolute attention which distracted me from the pressures of my own mind; and I was grateful for the unfailing diversion from my own thoughts which she offered. Never having known a moment's guilt herself; never, indeed, having experienced any mortification stronger than that of being asked to wait unduly long at her dentist's, Camilla was unvaryingly cheerful in a way that was balm to my depressed spirits. And though she must have itched to know the details of my time in France (for she knew, I think, that I had been there with Ella), she forbore from asking for them with a tact which surprised and pleased me; which made me, in fact, reconsider my view of her and decide that I liked her wholeheartedly. Over the Boardman dinner table I heard, of course, occasional snippets of the news about Ella; but as I did not encourage them, the daughter of the house derived no satisfaction from their retelling and they soon dried up.

I did not encourage them because, easy though her company was, I could enjoy Camilla's conversation on certain subjects only; and her telling me, in hushed tones, that Ella Harcourt was utterly *miserable*, and secretive in her misery, too, was more than I could bear to hear. Reliable, uncomplicated friendship was what I needed at that time; and by a happy chance it was what Camilla did best. Her warmth endeared her to me (as my willingness to listen endeared me to her, I suspect); and over the years our superficial friendship blossomed into a closer one, into an amicable bond which came to be important to us both, a bond which lasted well into the early years of my marriage.

I do not digress when I speak of Camilla. It is important for me to place her in some kind of context once again; it is vital that I remember the precise sequence of events that led up to and beyond Ella's trial. Detail is important to me now, for so much happened so quickly, you see; and I must make one last effort to remember. I must penetrate the haze of concerts and competitions, of radio interviews and relentless rehearsals which obscure my view of those few weeks before I won the Hibberdson. I must retrace the progression of my friendship with Camilla and remember my partnership with Regina Boardman, in whose charity concerts I regularly played.

Impervious as ever to all obstacles, the fund-raising efforts of this redoubtable lady went from strength to strength as my degree proceeded; and although memories of Eric prevented me from frequenting her 'mornings', I was always grateful for her kindness and for the expertise which she had once shown in her management of the Guildhall authorities. I owed Mendl's teaching, after all, partly to Regina's influence; and I did not forget this or the fact that she had given me my first break. So I played, when asked, in a series of her benefit concerts, my growing fame drawing ever larger audiences; and although I declined to play again at St Peter's, Eaton Square, I came to know the interiors of a good many other London churches in this way, churches which I might otherwise never have seen.

But my architectural opportunities are not what concern me here; I have no time to dwell on afternoons long past spent rehearsing in icy naves and crumbling side chapels. I must remember Regina's words after the annual meeting of her Society for the Preservation of Ancient Buildings. I must see her again, legs neatly crossed, at her desk in the drawing room at Cadogan Square. I must remember the purposeful tones of her commanding voice; the massive immobility of her sculpted hair.

She has returned from her meeting bright with enthusiasm at a new idea; an idea that involves a new series of concerts, held this time in private houses and preceded by champagne receptions; an idea which, she assures me, can't *fail* to double the efficacy of her fund-raising. 'After *all*, darling,' she says with an arch smile, 'what *is* the use of having friends with large houses if one doesn't *use* them?'

There is a brief silence while I, to whom the point has never occurred before, can do nothing but ask, 'What indeed?' And inevitably I fill the expectant pause by volunteering my services for the first of these concerts, an event which I am told is set for the day after the Hibberdson semi-finals.

'It will be at Cheverel House,' says Regina with pardonable pride; and she goes on to reward the prompt offer of my time with some mild flattery which I try not to hear. 'Just *think* what fun it will be to play to a *friendly* audience for a change,' she finishes, smiling. 'You do *far* too many competitions, James.'

I am tempted to say that the Hibberdson is my first; but before I can speak Regina is saying that I'll have carried off the prize before I *know* it and that then I really *will* be too grand for the likes of her.

Thinking that nothing and no one could be too grand for the likes of Regina Boardman, I smile politely at the compliment and promise to come back in a week to finalize the programme.

'That would be *splendid*,' Regina says, rising from her seat to kiss me. 'I don't know *where* my appeal would be without you. I'm so grateful, James, for the way you share your genius with us.'

And I, uncomfortable with such gratitude from others, make my excuses and leave; and I go home and take out my violin, which I play all afternoon and well into the evening, frightened of sitting alone with my thoughts, Regina's praise burning my ears with its well-intentioned kindness.

It was a busy summer for me, that first one after graduation; but because I continued to find my best escape in music, I did not resent the hours of intense practice which recording commitments (and my progress through the rounds of the Hibberdson prize) demanded. I found freedom in the endless hours of hard work which my life required of me; and in the concentrations of performance I found a release from myself, a release which sustained me through the dark times.

I did not see Ella, though I read and thought of her frequently; and I might never have tried to see her had not Fortune, with characteristic cruelty, devised otherwise and tempted me into undoing the work of years; into unleashing the pent-up desires of so many lonely months. But Fortune did; and she chose the night of Regina Boardman's concert at Cheverel House to do so, a night that found me at my weakest, trying guiltily to suppress my delight at having secured a place in the finals of the Hibberdson. I still had not resolved my attitude to success, you see; I still had not learned how to accept it with anything approaching ease. And as I played on an improvised stage at the end of a long room filled with respectful faces, I tried not to think of Eric's face, of his glassy stare as his body swung slowly up the sides of that quarry in the chill wind.

I did not see my audience as I played to them; I did not distinguish more than the blur of their heads and the enthusiastic clatter of their applause as I bowed my thanks for their attention. I played well to them, but cautiously; and after my performance I allowed myself to be led meekly, numbly, to a small dark room where a glass of champagne waited for me. And there, telling the attendant that I needed to be alone for a moment, I remember sitting with my head in my hands, unwilling to face the congratulations of those who had spent their evening listening to me, steeling myself for the smiling and the hand-shaking which I knew would be necessary before I could leave.

'Darling, you were *marvellous.*'

The creaking of the door told me that I had been found, and I knew that Regina Boardman's embraces could not be far behind her daughter's.

'Come out and enjoy your success,' Camilla said to me, eyes shining. 'Everyone's *mad* about you. Mummy's told them *all* that you're going to win the Hibberdson and I shouldn't be a *bit* surprised if you did, after the way you've played tonight.' She waited, smiling, as I put my violin into its case. 'Come on, James, don't be bashful,' she whispered as she slipped her arm through mine and opened the door on to the landing. 'You've got to get used to all this if you're going to be famous, you know.'

'I'm not going to be famous,' I said, irritated for once by her cheeriness.

'But you are already,' she said simply, leading the way out of the room. 'And there's not much you can do about it now.'

Certainly I could not politely avoid the crowd which waited for me on the stairs; and so I smiled grimly as the men shook my hand and introduced me to their wives: deftly made-up women who told me, according to personality, that I was either as dashing or as good as they had been led to believe. The audience that night was an invited one, you see: a selection of Regina's richest and most influential friends; and her guests seemed to take an introduction to the per-former as one of the unspoken rights of their expensive admission. So I was duly introduced, for Mrs Boardman never disappointed her public; and as I was led slowly down the overcrowded stairs, smiling awkwardly, trying not to hear the words of adulation, I looked forward to my departure and to solitude as a man in a desert dreams of water.

It was only as I neared the last of the couples waiting to meet me, only as I turned to complete the last flight of the staircase, that I saw Alexander and Pamela Harcourt standing near the end of the line; and I saw as I did so that three years had changed them sadly. Though Pamela's *coiffure* was as complicated as ever, though her fingers still wore their large rings, she had an air of weariness that elaborate grooming and expensive clothes could not disguise. And I saw white where the knuckles of her bony hand gripped her husband's arm, an arm that showed thin and almost frail through the sleeve of his dinner jacket. Alexander had lost his vigour also, I saw that at once; I saw too that his eyes no longer shone with the confidence of one used to the admiring glances of others. He looked gaunt and old; and his hand, as it stretched to shake mine, shook slightly.

'Hello,' I said, thinking of the last time we had met, in the lobby of the Grand Hotel Europa, when Ella's troubles were just beginning.

'Hello, Mr Farrell. How good to see you again.' It was Alexander who spoke, and his voice was older than I remembered it too; older and sadder, I thought.

'We did enjoy hearing you play.' Pamela smiled at me: a formal movement of made-up lips.

There was a moment's silence between us. Then I thanked them both for coming and made as if to move down the staircase; but Alexander's fingers caught at the sleeve of my coat.

'Could I . . . see you for a moment? In private?' His blue eyes met mine steadily.

I said nothing.

'Please.'

I felt Regina coming down the stairs behind me, ready to move me on.

'I've almost written to you before now,' said Alexander quickly,

246

seeing her also. 'Please. I can't tell you how much I'd appreciate a few moments alone.'

The quiet dignity of Ella's father touched me, for Alexander's ageing face had a look about it which caught his daughter's exactly; and I nodded. 'Of course,' I said, as I moved away down the last of the stairs.

He was waiting for me by the steps of the house as I left it; and I saw Pamela's face in a disappearing taxi as her husband quickened his stride to match mine and walked with me down the road towards the Tube station. There was a moment of awkward silence; then Alexander spoke, and as he did so I heard that his voice was trembling.

'Something is very wrong with my daughter,' he said slowly.

More silence.

'What do you mean?' I asked at last, though I knew.

'I mean that she hasn't been the same since she went to France with you and that poor boy who died.'

We walked on a few yards, neither of us speaking.

'You mustn't think that I blame you,' her father continued. 'I was worried about Ella before she went away. Even then she wasn't behaving like the person I knew. But when she came back she was much worse. She wouldn't talk to Pamela or to me; she wanted to be alone as much as possible. She seemed to have lost her interest in life.' He paused. 'We thought at first that that Frenchman's death . . . What was his name?'

'Eric,' I said quietly.

'Quite so. We thought that Eric's death had upset her, as well it might.'

Another pause.

'So we gave her time; we didn't press things. But she got worse and worse. She stopped seeing anyone; she seemed to lose the ability to enjoy herself. And that was hard, because Ella had always taken such a delight in life before that. She seemed so happy around the time of her engagement.'

Alexander looked down; and as he did so I thought of the days and nights of that passionate summer when Ella and I had thought ourselves immortal.

'We all tried to help her,' he went on. 'Her cousin Sarah, in particular, was a great source of strength. But now Ella won't see anyone. And all this newspaper attention doesn't help, of course. She spends all day alone now, in her room. She won't talk to me any more. She . . .'

But he could not speak.

'Please James.' His eyes turned to meet mine, and I saw that they were wet with tears. 'I'm worried about my little girl. I've no idea what to do. I feel like I'm losing her. And the only person she talks of, the only person she says she wants to see, is you.'

We were at Notting Hill Gate now and it had started to rain.

'I've almost written so many times . . . And then tonight, seeing you, I felt I had to tell you. She says you don't answer her letters and I've been anxious not to interfere. But now I'm worried. If only you would see her, it might make a difference.'

There was silence again.

'It's worth a try at least, isn't it?' he said; and there was something tragic about the pleading of this middle-aged man.

'What is there that I can do?' I said slowly, more to myself than to Alexander.

Eagerly he grabbed my arm. 'Write to her, James. Telephone her. Come to see her.' He paused. 'My brother is giving a party at Seton next month. Bring her to that.'

I shook my head.

His eyes fell. 'Please James, do something. Don't abandon her like this.'

There was a long silence as I stood, my head reeling. 'All right,' I said at last. 'I'll write to her. Tell her that I'll write to her.'

'I can't thank you enough.' Alexander held out his hand to me. I shook it and our eyes met.

'Goodbye,' I said, trying to smile. And turning quickly, without another word, I went down the steps and into the Underground.

27

I cannot tell you how I felt that night. I can only say that I didn't sleep; that I went instead to the attic, where I knew my light would not be seen; and that I sat in the corner where Ella had once sat, trying to think, searching for some raft of resolution to guide me through the storm.

I found one eventually. But the search was hard and success required the confession of my own weakness. I had to admit to myself, in a way I had not done before, that I could not spend the rest of my life as I had spent the last three years; that whatever I had done to Eric, however much I deserved to be punished, I could not resist the pull of my old love any longer. Separation from Ella, for so long the mainstay of my self-denial, was no longer possible for me; however little I deserved happiness, I could no longer resist it. And that was a hard admission. Hard because it involved accepting the fact that I was not strong enough to mete out or to endure the punishment which I knew I deserved; hard because it entailed the surrendering of a last shard of cracked self-respect; hard because I, who had thought myself numbed for ever, came suddenly to life once more in a way which was as painful as it was wonderful.

Alexander's pleading had its effect that night. I sat awake, unable to resist the force of memory any longer; and the darkness of the room filled with sights and sounds and shapes which I had thought lost to me.

Oh yes, Alexander's words had their effect. Until I saw her tearful father I had thought myself able to sacrifice Ella's love, to sacrifice it towards the payment of an unpayable debt. Blindly, numbed by pain and guilt, I had determined to renounce the joys of our union in the hopes that thus I might find punishment; that thus, somehow, I might atone for what I – what we, together – had done. Before Alexander's anxious words I had resolved to live in a world beyond the reach of feeling; to confine myself to a dim space lit meagrely, and only occasionally, by the far-off light of my music. In so doing I had looked to find rest, I had hoped to find peace; and from a distance of fifty years I can see that I had wished, almost, to share spiritually in Eric's physical death.

That night I gave up the effort. For the first time since returning from France I tasted the wildness of real hope; the sweetness of love returned again. For the first time in three years I rejoiced – with almost adolescent wonder – in the mysteries of the night, in the beauties of a star-filled sky; and I did so because the darkness no longer shrieked at me, because it no longer filled with dreams of Eric, but with thoughts of Ella. It was not my friend's lifeless form that I saw that night, but my love's fragile body; not Eric's eyes, glazed with death, but Ella's, sparkling with life. Shaking, hardly daring to breathe, I saw her beside me. I watched her as she lit her cigarettes; as she brushed the hair from her eyes. I heard once more the silvery chuckle of her laugh; the gentle accents of her voice. I kissed again the velvet space beneath her collarbone.

Alone in the dark I thought that nothing would keep Ella from me; that our love had earned us a second chance; that it had saved us from oblivion. I swallowed my pride. I admitted my weakness. I accepted that I could resist Ella's pull no longer; that if she needed me I would go to her; that if she called I would run.

I see now what a step that was; I see and understand. For in retelling the story of my life I have come to know myself in ways I did not dream of then. And fifty years on, from the vantage point of knowledge, I know that the bonds from which I broke free so briefly were mighty indeed; that they could only have been broken by the force of a love like Ella's and mine. Our passion *did* give us power, I know that now beyond all doubt; and we might at the last have used it for good. We might have seen some light come out of tragedy. We might have been happy.

But I am dreaming again of what might have been; and I know how useless such musing is. What matters is my narrative; what really happened. And what really happened is this, I suppose: that the floodgates of my love for Ella opened once more. And my longing for her flowed with a force I could no longer control as I sat in the attic that night, writing by the light of a small bright lamp; scribbling a letter which covered six sheets of large notepaper with the small dense characters of my cramped hand.

I cannot recall the words I used, for they were chosen long ago and at great speed; I cannot remember the phrases which came to me as I sat, hunched over the paper on my knees. I know only the gist of what I said and the fervour with which I said it. I wrote to Ella of love, you see; of my love for her and of hers for me. I told her of my sorrow for times past and of my hope for times to come. I told her what I should have told her before: that I had never stopped thinking of her; that I had never stopped dreaming of her; that she was right: that we needed each other more than ever now.

I signed my name as day was breaking with a new splendour; and it was only then, exhausted by words, that I went to bed and had my first hours of dreamless sleep in three long years. I woke late, when the sun was high in the sky; and for the first time since Eric's death I took pleasure in the simple luxury of quiet observation. I heard sounds hitherto lost; saw things not usually seen. I rejoiced in the pattern of the sunshine on my wall; in the colour of the book spines on my shelf; in the glistening puddles of the previous night's rain. My life was changed; I felt sure of that, sure that things would be well once more.

Slowly, easily, I got up and dressed.

Outside in the sunshine I posted Ella's letter. Then I went to the Guildhall, thinking with wonder how different this morning was from those which had gone before it; how all mornings in the future would be different too; how I had changed. I took delight again in the freshness of the world; in the thought that Ella and I, united, would make things right; that we would face the demons of our guilt together and conquer them as we could not hope to do alone. I remember my slow deliberation that day; the quiet, distinct pleasure I got from the subtlest taste, the dullest view. I was alive once more, alive to the possibilities of life. And years later, as I sit in the dark, watching the moon rise on the lashing waves of a rolling sea, I remember what that was like; I remember the return of hope as a thirsty man might remember his first sight of water. I had not drunk yet, but I could see the oasis ahead; and in my desire I thought that nothing could stand in my way now; that my thirst, for so long endured as the only punishment I could inflict on myself, was about to be quenched. Slowly, with almost childish delight, I savoured that day and the ones which followed it; and I enjoyed the fleeting thought that life might be a fine thing after all.

Such feeling was expressed in my playing with a force that was as exhilarating as it was irresistible; and throughout the week that followed I worked with unquenchable enthusiasm. I had decided long before, in unconscious homage to Ella, to play the Mendelssohn E Minor if ever I got as far as the Hibberdson finals; and now, remembering my inspiration, I worked with untiring passion. In hours of practice I relived the sunny afternoons in which I had played its first movement to her; and I remembered how she had sat, silent with pleasure, on her cushion in the corner of my dingy attic.

Days passed in this way; more than I knew, I think. But I worked on in excited contemplation of the future, giving little thought to the limitations of the present. To be sure, there was no immediate reply to my letter; but I could not be disheartened by a delay of a few days after so many months' unconscious waiting. My suffering had taught me patience, if nothing else. And I told myself – quite rightly as it turned out – that a thousand things might have prevented Ella from writing at once; that she would reply as soon as she could. And I felt sure enough of her once more to face an empty letter-box with cheery equanimity.

Other things happened in that time too; meetings and conversations to which I gave little thought then, but which I must remember now if I am to grasp the facts in anything like their precise order. Precision is important now; I can see that. So I try to remember. And as I try I hear the emphatic tones of Camilla Boardman's voice, higher than usual; and I feel her hand as she leads me across a crowded room full of loud people and brittle laughter and the hard clink of stainless steel on china. We are in a restaurant in a small street off the King's Road; we have met for lunch; my friend is brimming with excitement. We have barely taken our seats at the window table which my name now secures before she is squeezing my arm and telling me that she has *fantastic* news, that her great opportunity has come, that she is about to make her mark.

I remember her that day. I remember her animation, her infectious enthusiasm as she asked me if I had ever been to Seton. 'Because it's *the* most incredible house. An absolutely *vast* castle on an island off the Cornish coast,' she told me excitedly. 'Full of *amazing* history and *fabulous* furniture and . . .' There was a pause, for Camilla's stock of adjectives was not inexhaustible.

I waited and said nothing, trying to control my excitement as I heard my friend speak of Ella's island, of the house which one day she and I might share.

'It's the Harcourt family seat, you know,' Camilla continued. 'And they're giving a *huge* party to raise money for some charity or other. Mummy's involved. I can't think what it's called now. The Society for the Preservation of Ancient Buildings, probably. But that doesn't matter much in any case. What *does* matter is that it's going to be *the* big party this summer. And between us Mummy and I know practically *everyone* who's going and you can bet on it that *I'm* going to design *all* their dresses.' Camilla paused, out of breath. 'They don't *know* this yet, of course,' she added with unconscious irony. 'But I'm already doing Ella Harcourt. And everyone else is sure to follow her lead, just you wait and see.' So saying she smiled brightly and ordered champagne; and I laughed inwardly, thinking that I had heard of this party from Alexander several days before; that I, for once, was better informed than the omniscient Miss Boardman.

Ten days or so passed without my hearing from Ella; and by the end of this time I *was* worried, worried that perhaps she had left my letter unopened as I had left so many of hers. But in spite of creeping misgivings I worked as hard as ever, for the final of the Hibberdson was almost upon me; and my days were filled with rehearsals and conductors and the thousand tiny details of competition preparation. It was on my return from one especially long rehearsal that I saw her letter: peeping from a pile of others on the entrance-hall mat; a blue envelope this time, though the jagged letters of its address were in the brown ink I knew so well.

I remember the excitement of that moment: the way my throat went dry as I picked up Ella's letter and took it to the tiny room at the top of the house, the room which she had made her own three summers before. I remember the touch of the heavy paper as I tore open the envelope; the thickness of the sheet which fell from it; the raised print of the address which told me that she had written it at Seton. She did not use my name, I remember; and her note was not long. But she said:

Darling, my darling,

I can't believe you've written at last. I can't believe you've come back to me. I thought you were lost for good.

You cannot know how much I've missed you; how badly I've wanted to see you. These have been hard years — though you don't need me to tell you that, I imagine. And I'm sorry for not replying to your letter sooner. I've not been in London, you see — I'm down here helping Uncle Cyril with his plans for a party. The house is in chaos and the younger generation has been drafted in to help out. So I've not been at home, and Pamela is very bad about forwarding mail. I only read your words this morning — and since then I've not been able to sit still. I can't wait to see you; to touch you again, my love. I have missed you.

But I can't leave here until next week, when the party's over and the caterers have been and gone. Of course you could come to the ball — though on second thoughts I can think of nothing worse than seeing you again in front of thousands of people. It's a Regina Boardman sort of party anyway and I want you alone. . . So will you wait for me a little longer? And while you're about it, will you take care to win the Hibberdson? I've been following you to the finals and I wonder what you will play. You've no idea how much I want to hear you again.

There is so much to say; so much to tell. A letter is not the way.

I long for our reunion.

Ella

Those were her words; and as I say them I can hear her saying them. Alone in the dark I can hear Ella's voice, calling to me from long ago; I can see her eyes, looking for mine.

Events followed thick and fast on each other after that.

And it is the night of the Hibberdson final which fills my mind now, a night of judges and lights and television cameras, of sweat and nerves and anxious friends. A night of glory for me: for I played with a passion I had not known before. A night when Ella's love gave my playing a lightness it had never yet enjoyed, a delicacy it was not to have again. I remember it all. I remember how it felt to win. I remember the rush of relief as I set down my violin and took my bow; I remember smiling; remember thanking the judges and telling the interviewers how delighted I was. And I *was* delighted, for nothing can quite dim the pleasure of playing really well, of pushing one's art beyond oneself. And though I felt still that the victory was not mine alone, that the daring with which I had played would have been impossible without the shrieking memory of Eric's laugh and the sight of his sightless eyes, I felt too that Eric would have wanted me to win; and I thought that Ella's love would protect me henceforth from such demons.

Standing on the podium, the bronze laurels in my hand, my eyes flicked over row upon row of cheering faces and a blur of clapping hands; and as I bowed again I saw a slender, tilting neck and a smile that made the breath catch in my throat. I looked again; and surer now, reeling a little, smiling still, I moved along the stage, shaking hands with the other finalists, accepting their words of congratulation, thinking only of how to leave the concert hall, of how to escape into the night with the only person I wanted to see. Backstage there were television cameras and newspaper reporters and my agent telling me to go back on for another bow, to milk the applause; and as I did so the blood beat furiously in my head and my hands were wet with sweat from the fear that Ella might get lost in the crowd, that I might not find her after all.

I did not go on for a third bow but went straight to the finalists' dressing room, where my fellow competitors were putting away their instruments and taking off their ties. In a frenzy, almost, I said my goodbyes and put my violin into its case; and then I raced through cavernous corridors to the players' entrance, hoping to slip out before the crowds arrived. But as I opened the door I heard with quick exasperation the high-pitched shriek, 'There he is!', and I found myself in the centre of a group of excited well-wishers and reporters, questions and autograph books flying.

Telling myself that Ella would find me, that in fact it was best for me to stay in one, obvious place, I breathed deeply and faced the barrage of words and notebooks. My pulse racing, I took out my pen and began to sign my name, telling myself to be calm.

'May I join your devoted supplicants, James?'

I had seen her before she spoke; and the rounded vowels of an English accent made me pale with disappointment.

'My God . . . Sarah.'

She smiled up at me as I recovered myself. And as I took another programme and automatically signed my name, I recovered sufficiently to ask her what she was doing there.

'Watching you, of course,' she replied, smiling still; and I noticed that she seemed less forbidding than I remembered her. 'I thought I should demonstrate my acquaintance with the winner if I possibly could.'

'What?'

The din of the crowd drowned out her quiet voice.

'Congratulations,' she called, louder this time. And she leaned forward and kissed my cheek.

Someone took our photograph and a reporter asked who the lovely lady was. 'Come on, give us your name!'

Sarah blushed and I thought with longing how beautiful her cousin was.

'It's been such a long time,' she said as I began to push my way towards my car.

'Yes.'

'And how have you been since I saw you last?'

'Oh . . . well. Working hard.'

'Winning prizes.'

'Only one.'

'But what a prize.' She looked up at me and her blue eyes met mine as though we had known each other always.

'It was kind of you to come and seek me out,' I said finally. 'I thought your family had a three-line whip on their presence at Seton.'

'I've been in London today, collecting a dress.'

'I see.'

She smiled at me again. There was a slight pause.

'Well, goodbye,' she said at last. 'Congratulations on tonight. I'm sure it will be the first of many.'

'Thank you.'

'And now that we've bumped into each other so unexpectedly, we mustn't lose touch again.'

'Of course not.' My key was in my door now.

'Goodbye again, James.'

'Goodbye, Sarah.'

And I leaned down and kissed her cheek. As I did so I smelled her scent, a scent of different cigarettes, of unknown soap, of strange perfume: the smell I smelled yesterday afternoon, made richer then by the thick sweetness of warm blood, as I bent over her bleeding body.

28

The days between the Hibberdson final and the Harcourts' party were busy ones for me; and between the giving of interviews and the receiving of congratulations I had little time to myself. What time I did have I spent with my family, whose praise was reserved but wholehearted, or with Camilla Boardman, whose predictions of future glory knew no bounds. But the person I really wanted, of course, was Ella; and I chafed at the days that still separated us, though I understood why they must do so. I, like her, had no wish to be reunited under the watchful eyes of her family and our friends; and having waited so long, a week was nothing.

In any case my days passed in a haze of euphoria the like of which I had not thought to feel again.

For the first time in three years – and from a distance of fifty years I know this to be true – I had a sense of participating in life in some real way; a sense that in its details, in which I had feigned interest for so long, there was some meaning for me again. By writing to Ella I had admitted defeat; I acknowledged that. I accepted, in my own mind at least, that I had been unable to continue indefinitely in self-inflicted imprisonment for the part I had played in Eric's death. And this acceptance freed me; Ella's love, or rather the knowledge that she loved me still, liberated me from the past in a way which I was helpless to resist. Try though I might I could not silence a quiet, insistent voice which told me that life might be a fine thing after all; that perhaps there were better ways of making amends to Eric than the spiritual mutilation which had been my only recourse until then. And for six nights he disappeared from my dreams, his sightless eyes replaced by the sound of Ella's laugh, the image of his soaking body by the warmth of her cheek against mine.

I almost told Camilla everything in my desire to share my happiness; but she was full of her own news and plans and no opportunity arose for me to speak. For too long I had assumed the role of appreciative listener; and the run-up to her night of glory was no time to choose to alter things.

'It's *so* much work, darling,' she told me one evening on the telephone. 'Even now people are coming for last-minute alterations. And you've never *heard* so much conversation about shoes. It's enough to send the puritan in one insane.'

Camilla's facility for martyrdom, be it social or commercial, had only increased with the passing of the years.

'You've no *idea* how draining it is.'

'None at all, I'm afraid.'

'Lucky old musicker. I'm sure playing old ditties on a fiddle can't be *half* as difficult as advising Lady Markham on handbags.'

'Not half as difficult.'

'Don't be *cheeky*, young man. We can't all have just won the Hibberdson, you know.'

'Hmmm.' But I was thinking of Ella and of how she would congratulate me.

'Speaking of which,' my friend continued, 'I'm taking you to dinner to celebrate next Wednesday. Eight-thirty sharp. I'll pick you up.'

And with that she rang off.

So three nights before the ball, over a dinner broken by frenzied interruptions from Camilla's mobile phone ('It's *so* tiresome, I know. But clients *must* feel that one is contactable.'), she told me several things: some important, some less so. Details, at any rate, which I must chase now and recapture if ever I am to do the planning of it all any justice.

I remember Camilla describing her clients to me ('*Terribly* indiscreet, I know, but *such* fun – and you're quite trustworthy'). I remember the hushed tones in which she told me that Ella would not be wearing a dress at *all* but a suit of men's evening clothes, especially cut. I remember her saying that Sarah Harcourt ('You remember her, don't you, Jamie?') had come to her for initial fittings but had finally chosen some *hideously* obvious red concoction from a rival designer. '*Such* a pity, darling, since she's *actually* rather pretty and could have looked quite good,' whispered Camilla with more than a hint of pique. 'But there's no accounting for taste, *is* there?'

From her mother, my friend had learned details of the party's arrangements; and she related these eagerly too as our food arrived. Over steamed asparagus I learned that there was going to be a bonfire (because Atlantic winds can be *freezing*, even in September) and fireworks and hothouse roses and a huge marquee. 'They're not letting the guests into much of the house itself,' said Camilla confidentially. '*Perfectly* understandable, of course, because there're *so* many valuable things. And I think a marquee will do *fabulously* in any case.'

I nodded; and asked whether reports that an American film star was flying her hairdresser over for the night were true.

'*Probably*, darling. That's just the kind of stunt Mummy would dream up. You know how she is.'

I did know; and together we laughed.

I remember Camilla's undisguised excitement; the eagerness with which she related her titbits of pre-party scandal; the professional pride which lent a weight to her pronouncements which they had lacked in the early days of our friendship.

'You can count on it that everyone dressed by me will look *fabulous*,' she promised as she signed her receipt – for *she* was taking *me*; it was *her* celebratory treat – and kissed me goodbye. 'I'll show you the pictures when I get back. And I'll tell you all then.'

Wishing that I had written to Ella sooner, for then we could have enjoyed the festivities together, thinking wistfully of how lovely she would look, I left the restaurant with my arm around Camilla's shoulders and saw my friend into a taxi.

'*Bye*,' she called from the back window. 'See you soon with *lots* of news.'

'Goodbye,' I called after her, waving.

But it was not Camilla who told me of that party, though she filled in the details for me later, days later, when most of the events were a matter of public knowledge. It was not from her lips that I learned of what had happened; Fate permitted me no such civilities. I read it all on the front page of a fellow commuter's newspaper in the heat of a crowded Underground train four days after our dinner. PEER MURDERED AT SOCIETY FUND-RAISER bellowed the headline; and my mouth dry, fear catching at my throat, I saw Ella's father staring at me from the centre of the page, his eyes smiling, his arm around his daughter's dinner-jacketed shoulders.

In disbelief I left the train at the next station, moving slowly at first through the crush on the platform; then quickly, impatiently, brushing past the queues on the escalator, swearing at the broken barrier-machine, running at last with the blood beating on my brain to the newspaper stall at the station's entrance.

I was sitting at home, numb with disbelief, when Camilla called that afternoon, almost in tears. 'Oh God, James,' she said. 'Oh God. Have you heard?'

I had heard; of course I had. It would have been impossible for me not to have done. The story was in every paper; on every channel; by now it seemed the subject of every overheard conversation. In front of electrical-shop windows people in their lunch hours watched the banks of television screens for news of it.

'Everyone *saw*, you see,' she said. 'Hundreds of people watched her do it.'

And as I listened I thought inconsequentially, as one does think at times like that, that Camilla's voice as she spoke was oddly expressionless for one with such a talent for colourful delivery; that she sounded distant, distracted, unlike her usual self. I listened to her story as though its characters were unknown to me, as though they formed no part of my life and never had done. I followed their fortunes as one might follow those of famous figures whose experience is far removed from one's own. Only later, alone, did the delayed realization dawn that Ella was a murderer: that the girl I had loved, the girl for whom I had twice sacrificed my self-respect, the girl with the lilting voice and the bitten fingernails, was the person at the centre of the story Camilla told; was the child who had killed her father in cold blood in front of more than two hundred witnesses.

'I couldn't believe it, Jamie,' Camilla told me tearfully. 'And I wouldn't have believed it.' She paused. 'But I saw her. I *saw* her do it. And in front of so many people. There was no way she could possibly have got away with it.'

I was silent.

'And she must have known that.'

'Tell me what you saw,' I said slowly.

And Camilla did. It is from her account and the fuller one given later at the trial that I learned the facts of that night; and recalling them now, even from a distance of fifty years, part of me can only marvel at how daringly it was executed; at how arrogantly it was done. Yes, it is her arrogance which shocks me now; her arrogance, more even than her callousness, which leaves the bitter taste.

But memory is rusty and its work slow. It is difficult for me to remember precisely what Camilla told me; to call to mind the whole wealth of ugly detail which emerged in the weeks which followed Alexander's murder. Over fifty years I have taken care to bury the details of Ella's trial with those of Eric's death: far from the intrusive scrutiny of easy recall. I have not wished to remember; and I have had remarkable success in forgetting. I see that more than ever now. More than ever I understand my debt to Sarah; for it was she who was my teacher. It was she who showed me how self-deception might be achieved; she who taught me to insulate myself against anything that might ruffle the smooth calm of a placid inner life. My wife was so untroubled herself, you see; and her calmness was exemplary in its control.

Now I must remember. As I have done with Eric, so must I with Ella and her father's death: I must open locked doors, exhume old ghosts. It is hard for a man of my age; hard because disillusion is the saddest of life's scars. And there is self-pity in my anger now;

for life, so recently offered to me again, was snatched from my grasp before I could sample it once more. And I cry for that man – he was a boy no longer – who sat, stupefied, as Camilla Boardman told him what Ella had done, what she had watched her do. I long to comfort him. But I cannot; and if I could, what would I say? There was nothing he could have done; no steps he might have taken. He was lost already; lost in ways he could neither have imagined nor understood.

Ella as murderer changed everything. It made a lie of all we had had; a lie of which I could tell no one.

And I went up to the attic that evening and sat in the moonlight where she had sat, hearing her voice, watching her smoke her endless cigarettes. I remembered our meeting in the park; the announcement of her engagement to Charlie at Camilla's birthday party; the way she had taken me to Seton. I saw her flick the hair out of her eyes and curl up on that window-ledge above the sea. I heard her tell me of Blanche, of the history of her family, of Sarah. 'This house has plenty of dark secrets,' she had said. I remembered her frightened eyes by the quarry with Eric; the clipped intensity of her voice as she told me to tell him the truth. I saw it all; heard it all. And I felt that some kind of spell had been broken; that the person I had loved had ceased to exist, if ever she had existed at all.

Reading of Alexander's murder in the papers, in the hot and crowded ticket hall of an Underground station, I had clung still to some sort of crazy hope; to the blind faith that had made me draw short of condemning Ella in the years since Eric's death. But listening to Camilla describe what she had seen, in a quiet voice I had not heard before, I came to see that I had been wrong. And later, alone in the room where I had played to her, where so recently I had written of love and of longing in the passionate language of naïve adoration, I felt a wave of disgust sweep over me. Eric's body, heavy with water, returned in the darkness; I saw it swing jerkily up the sides of the quarry, to be laid out before me. I remembered the tears in Dr Pétin's eyes. And I thought with something like hatred that I had twice sacrificed myself for a girl who had killed her father. To earn her trust I had betrayed all notions of friendship; to see her again I had undermined three hard years of self-punishment. And as I cried I wept not for Ella, nor even for Eric, but for myself.

29

Even the horrors of the past deserve some recognition, I suppose; and the obstacles to her success were great. I can see that more than ever now. For a start, the access of guests to the house was strictly limited; and the great hall itself was locked (for all the most valuable objects in the open rooms were stored there for the night). It is only from the great hall that access on to the balcony is possible; and Cyril Harcourt had the only key to this room, a key later found secure and untouched in his desk by the police. When it happened there must have been more than two hundred people on the terrace: standing by the bonfire; talking and laughing; apparently preferring the fresh air, cold though it was, to the heat of the reception rooms. So more than two hundred people watched her do it; more than two hundred people, some of whom knew her well.

It is sad for me to trace the events of that night, sad because I know the house in which they happened so well now. Everything is so real. When Camilla told me the story I could only imagine how everything must have been; I had none of the feeling for the place which fifty years' kinship has given me. Now I know precisely the layout of the terrace; precisely the angle at which one must tilt one's head if one is to see the balcony which overlooks it far above. I know the smell of the sea in September; the colour of the stone in bonfirelight. I can feel the chill of an Atlantic breeze on my neck. Recounting it now I can see it all; feel it all; and I watch for a sign which someone might have seen, a detail which someone must have overlooked. But all I can sense is the happy anticipation of the crowd; all I can hear are its sporadic cheers as Alexander and Ella appear.

But I am anticipating myself; losing the thread of events. And just once, however painfully, I must trace them precisely once again. Having come so far I can hardly turn back now. Slowly, dispassionately, I must remember all that Camilla told me; and to her account I must add the details established later by the police. With so many witnesses their investigation was hardly a challenging one, hardly a test of any great detective powers. But they were thorough. Uninspired, perhaps, but thorough. And one can hardly blame them; for they, like me, were out of their depth. So it is a clear, balanced narrative which I must attempt; and attempt it I will. It is the least she deserves.

The Setons' guests arrived between seven and seven-thirty. They were given champagne cocktails in the ballroom and many, as I have said already, strayed out on to the terrace. Between half and three-quarters of an hour later, immediately before dinner was announced, Ella and her father appeared on the balcony above them, from which access is only possible through the windows of the great hall. According to the testimony of most present they seemed relaxed, though it was noticeable that the years had taken their toll on Alexander and he seemed older than many remembered him. An expectant hush fell and cries of 'Speech!' were heard. Some people cheered. Ella in her dinner jacket moved behind her father and put her hands on his shoulders, a gesture which seemed sweetly affectionate. Standing behind the taller man, little of her was visible but the stylish cut of her sharply-parted blonde hair, and Lord Markham called, 'Show yourself, Ella. Don't be shy.' Someone laughed.

Alexander began to shuffle his notes.

And as he did so, with unhurried grace, Ella lifted her arms and brought them down with a crack on his neck. Her father cried out, startled, and dropped his papers. Some fluttered down into the crush below. People scrambled to catch them; one or two went into the bonfire. Some guests on the edges of the crowd, who could not see, began to laugh. But those in its centre watched, increasingly confused, as Alexander turned in surprise towards his daughter; and as they watched they saw her bend down and lift his feet from under him in a quick and practised movement, pushing him over the rail. Clutching wildly as he fell, he caught at the balustrade with one hand and for a sickening moment he hung there. Everyone stopped laughing. In the silence Ella bent over him, and it looked to some as though she were holding his arm, pulling him back to safety. A woman screamed. Then he fell. Alexander fell to his death with a long shout which ended sickeningly on the flagstones of the terrace below. Ella disappeared from the balcony.

When they found her she was in her father's bedroom, calling for him, apparently quite unperturbed by what she had done. At first she seemed shocked to see the policemen; and when they made it clear that they had come to arrest her, she went 'quite crazy', as one of the officers described it at her trial: 'quite crazy, like a mad thing'. Screaming, hysterical, she refused to be handcuffed. Calling for her father, for Pamela, screaming abuse at Sarah – who was in tears in the entrance hall – she was forcibly taken down the staircase and led out through the front door, watched by silent lines of shocked guests.

'You can't *imagine* how awful it was,' Camilla said the next night. 'That look in her eyes. The way she screamed. And when Sarah tried to get the policemen to treat her gently, she lashed out like you've never seen.'

On the other end of the telephone I heard my friend begin to cry.

'I've known Ella for seven years,' she said through her sobs. 'Ever since she came back from America. And I can't *tell* you how ghastly it was seeing her like that. Screaming abuse; calling Sarah a lot of unrepeatable things. Even saying that Sarah must have done it.' She blew her nose. 'That was when I felt sorry for her, you know; if you *can* feel sorry for someone who's done such an awful thing. It was when she tried to point the finger at someone else, in front of people who had watched her do it herself. There was something pathetic about the way she did that, Jamie. Something truly pathetic.'

I listened, sick at heart.

'Perhaps the papers were right after all,' Camilla went on. 'You know about the madness in her family, don't you?'

I said nothing.

'Don't you, Jamie?'

There was silence.

'Yes,' I said at last. 'Yes, I know all about it.'

And I listened as Camilla, whose mother had heard it from Pamela, told me how Ella had had to be sedated at Penzance station: 'Kicking and screaming like a wild thing,' my friend said.

In the ensuing search the police found a key in the pocket of Ella's dinner jacket, a key later shown to be a replica of the one to the great hall, the original of which was found safe in her uncle's desk. A London locksmith came forward and testified at the trial that she had had two copies made a fortnight before the party; and because the other copy was never found it was assumed that she had hidden it or thrown it into the sea.

'You've no idea how awful it was,' said Camilla. 'Listening to Alexander scream. Watching her push him.'

And I went to bed that night with those dreadful words echoing endlessly in my head. *Watchingherpushhim Watchingherpushhim.*

The next morning news of Ella's arrest was all over the papers; and she did not leave the front page more than three times in two months. A trial like hers, I suppose, was not likely to go unnoticed. And the press, swooping like vultures on the story's principals, scented in the details of Ella's crime all the most beloved staples of popular journalism: celebrity; beauty; violence; death. No paper could resist such ingredients; and no one missed the fact either that the story added a spectacular new chapter to Sarah's recently published family history. Insanity, in all its tragedy, became a national obsession; a glamorous accessory, almost. And for several weeks Ella's fragile image stared out at me from billboards and magazine covers and I learned to harden my heart to her eyes and to her small face with its delicate bones and ivory skin.

Sick with bitterness, I was helpless as old demons returned. And through nights of wide-eyed wakefulness I heard again the shriek of Eric's laugh, come back to haunt me with renewed force, to punish me for presuming ever to escape the consequences of what I had done to him. Impatient for daylight, for the fading of such sounds, I found when it came that in fact it brought no release: only newspapers bearing fresh news of Ella and her trial beneath courtroom sketches of her gaunt face and pursed lips. Sitting at breakfast, hunched over my coffee, I read of her case with a sort of morbid fascination; with horror and sadness also for a family I might once have claimed as my own. And alone once more, in new and doubly lonely isolation, I felt that I was being punished for my hubris; that nothing would save me now.

It was a strange, disjointed, lonely time; lonely because I had nowhere to turn, no one to tell. The irony was that only Ella or Eric might have shared my grief with me; and both were lost to me for ever. I had no one. And in my anger – for I was angry with Ella; mad with rage at the thought that she had tricked me, that she had never been true – I felt the first tremors of disillusion. Reading of my old love in the papers, seeing her trial progress and her guilt appear ever more conclusive, I grew to be disgusted with myself. And that disgust has lasted all my life. What self-belief I ever had, already so badly battered by Eric's death, died that autumn and winter as Ella's trial progressed. I lost it for ever. And I was only twenty-five.

She denied all charges, of course.

In recognition of the horror of the offence bail was denied and the defendant, I read in the papers, did not leave her cell except to appear in court. Ella saw no one but her barrister. No visitors came: no family; no friends. She wrote to me once: a long, rambling note of desperate defence and counter-accusation; but I hardly read it and I did not reply. I would be tempted by her no more, I decided; and when I didn't answer she did not write again. On the witness stand she was unshakeable; and the increasing hysteria with which she denied the charge, despite the insurmountable evidence of her guilt, did nothing to endear her to judge or to jury. In her statement she said that she had not known of her father's death until told of it by the police. And although the prosecution produced witness after witness who had seen her on the balcony, she defiantly refused to change her unlikely story; refused even to make the plea of temporary insanity which commentators predicted with increasing confidence as each day passed.

From Camilla, who had it from her mother, I learned that Ella had broken down completely in prison, that she had descended into semi-articulate ravings about Sarah, about how Sarah must have done it. But Sarah, in her red dress, had been seen everywhere at that party; she had talked to everyone. And when not on the terrace she had been in the ballroom or the entrance hall or the kitchen; supervising the caterer's staff, welcoming her uncle's guests. Her alibi, though peripatetic, was unshakeable. And so the police dropped their enquiries into her movements after a few hours of polite questioning and tearful co-operation.

In court Ella claimed to have received a note while she was dressing which had asked her to meet her father secretly in his room at eight o'clock and to wait for him if he was late. Under cross-examination she said that she had thought he wished to go over the notes for his speech; but she was unable to produce the note as evidence in her defence and was left saying weakly that someone must have taken it from her bedroom. The evidence of the court psychiatrists came next; evidence which sealed the matter. And I discovered, to my half-surprise, that Ella had told a court-appointed doctor all about her obsession with Sarah; had told him, in fact, all that she had told me in that circular tower room at Seton long ago. But her openness, if that is what she thought it was, only prejudiced her case. And her wild accusations against her cousin, made at the time of her arrest and once – disastrously – in open court, were cited as evidence of an ungovernable paranoia; the tragic but unsurprising consequence of earlier instability. Confronted by endless reports from endless expert witnesses, Ella's explanation of her earlier breakdown as a feigned and foolish attempt to break an awkward engagement – the explanation she had given me also in Prague – sounded hollow and insincere. And I loathed myself for ever having believed it; for ever having been seduced by the disarming compliment of her crazy confidences.

Certainly the jury showed no signs of repeating my mistake.

Ella's stubbornness alienated her from its sympathy; and her barrister – who advised her again in mid-trial to change her plea to one of temporary insanity – fought the last few days with only half-hearted enthusiasm. By the end of a fortnight it was clear that the maximum sentence was almost unavoidable. And in his summation the judge said that Ella's was one of the most terrible cases he had encountered in all his years on the bench.

I went to the final day of Ella's trial. I could not have stayed away. And I heard the verdict delivered and watched her being led from the court, back down to the cells from which she had come. In the crowded, overheated courtroom her face was pale, her eyes bloodshot; she was very thin. And I realized, almost to my surprise, that she had aged in the years since I had seen her last; that she was no longer the girl of my memory, or even of recent photographs, but a woman with a prematurely lined face and a broken walk. Moving unsteadily between the hulking policemen who escorted her, she didn't look at anyone, didn't seem even to be aware of the long line of Harcourts in the front row of the visitors' gallery. Her friends, if she still had any, had not come; all London, save the media, was eager to wash its hands of her, to rid itself of her taint. And I thought, as I watched her being led away, that Ella as a murderer made things easier: sadder, but easier. In dread of my guilt once more, I tried to believe that Ella's conviction removed my responsibility for Eric's death; that it made me a victim, too. I told myself that I had been an innocent, led astray by this mad young woman; that Ella's insanity cleansed me of my wrong; that my share of our joint guilt could be transferred to her. But I lacked the requisite tools of self-deceit then, you see. And try though I might I saw the future: sleepless and dark;

relieved only by hard work. And I told myself it was all that I deserved.

As she reached the door to the cells Ella stopped and looked at the courtroom. Her eyes were dulled and red but they had something of their old essence nonetheless, something of their old magnetism. I watched them travel slowly over her family, as if locking their images in her brain for the last time; I saw Pamela look away from her. She took in the reporters, the public, Sarah sitting in the centre of her family, her brown hair falling over the lapels of her coat. Finally her eyes met mine; and I knew that it was me she had looked for. For a moment we connected. And I didn't look away; I couldn't. But I didn't move either; I didn't smile or mouth any words of endearment or pity. I looked at her and she looked at me.

Abruptly she turned and allowed herself to be led away.

30

In the stream of people leaving the court that day I saw Charles Stanhope, his face taut and unmoving. Standing still, lost in the crowd, he seemed to have no idea of what to do or where to go; and I felt for him as journalists brushed past to swoop on Pamela. I felt for him; but he was beyond my help, just as I was beyond his. I could not even meet his eyes. So, pushing past the microphones and cameras, past the clusters of tourists shivering under their umbrellas, I walked quickly down the steps. And as the rain began in earnest I hurried down the street, eager for my violin, for the escape which only my practice and my playing could offer me now. And as I walked I told myself that I was alone in the world; and that the sooner I accepted this fact the better it would be for me. In the cold wind I pulled my scarf tighter round my neck and moved briskly, trying not to cry.

She caught me at the steps to the Underground, I think. Yes, I can see her by the rail now: long hair streaming over her shoulders; her face white; her shoulders shaking. She was shivering. Perhaps I returned her greeting. Perhaps I shook her hand or even kissed her. Perhaps . . . But I can't remember. That first meeting is hazy for me still in some respects, for it happened in the midst of so much else; and Sarah never encouraged me to remember. Even later, years later, we did not speak much of our early days together; and I came to take her silence as a tacit acknowledgement of my love for another, as a sign of the tactful understanding for which I came to value her so much. It was that reticence which first drew me to Sarah; that quiet sense she had that things were known and understood but not spoken. It was what I had once, mad with love for Ella, taken for awkwardness; but three hard years had taught me the shallowness of that judgement. And I sensed, even that first afternoon, that I might safely rely on that reserve; that it was a better insulator than any I had yet devised myself.

My wife, as I was to learn, preserved a comforting silence on all painful things, a silence that at first relieved and then seduced me. And gradually she taught me to preserve that silence in my own mind, also; to preserve and to maintain it with diligence and care.

But I am wandering; moving beyond myself again. I keep wanting to explain before I have told; and I should have learned by now that truth comes only in the telling. Sarah's silence must be broken at last; I know that and am resolved to my task. I am remembering. And it is the oddest things that recur first: the fact, for example, that her hair smelled clean as she hugged me in the rain; and that we ate frogs' legs and steak at the lunch which she insisted we have together.

'I don't want to be alone today,' she told me as she put her arms around me; and her look, so like Ella's that I almost cried, was too much for me to resist.

So I let myself be led through the crowd to a small French restaurant where obsequious waiters whispered in corners and Sarah told me of the trauma of the past two months, her large pale eyes seeking and holding mine, her hands mutely asking to be held as they shakily lit her cigarettes. I noticed with surprise that she was no longer the severe figure she had been in the park, nor the chill young woman I had seen at Ella's engagement lunch. In some way Ella's trial seemed to have liberated her; and I thought, as I watched, that through her tears she seemed warmer.

She was a woman of many wiles, my wife; a sophisticate whose affects were as calculated as they were concealed. And I, a man, was no match for her; I admit that freely now. Perhaps I knew it even then. Perhaps even on that first day I found security in Sarah's mastery: the kind of security which my life had lacked for so long. Certainly I succumbed to her with ease. Sitting at that corner table, as the rain streamed down on either side and the wine warmed us both, listening to her tell me of Pamela's grief and her own, I was lulled by her smooth, round voice; moved by the tears which she could not hold back; thrilled, perhaps – as only now I can admit – by the way in which Ella seemed to have been returned to me. Human attraction is a complex thing; complex and powerful in ways even a lifetime cannot teach. At seventy, when I might be expected to have gained wisdom, I can only begin to understand its force, to make sense of its caprices; or at least to acknowledge them in a way I was too young to do at twenty-five. I begin to see that we are drawn to physical beauty in ways we cannot always know, and by subtle steps we cannot always trace. Recounting the events of my life I have come to see the truth in the idea that romantic love is bound intimately with its physical expression; and to know that my love for Ella was inseparable from my fascination with her body and her face.

It was that fascination that drew me to Sarah and she knew it. She knew it and she did not hesitate to use her knowledge. It was her body, more than her words, which sought out and offered itself to all that was most vulnerable in me that day; and remembering it now, from the distance of endless years, I find something fascinating in her calculation, something awe-inspiring in the way she bent my will to hers with the seeming gentleness of shared memory and sorrow.

We made love that afternoon, as Sarah had known that we would.

And as though drawn by an irresistible yet invisible force, we left the restaurant and hailed a taxi in the pouring rain and went to my house and thence to the attic room which Ella had made her own years before. It seemed an appropriate place to banish old ghosts. And though it was Sarah who guided me, Sarah who leaned to kiss me as we stood on the steps in the wet and I fumbled for my keys, I was willing to be led; and our love-making, so different from mine and Ella's, comforted me in its curious mixture of the familiar and the unknown. It comforted me and excited me and it made me think that perhaps I had been rescued; that perhaps all was not lost.

In the weeks that followed, missing her cousin in ways I could not admit, I came to rejoice in the sight of Sarah's slender form; in the touch of her smooth, pale skin; in the feel of her lips on mine. I learned to watch as Sarah, rather than Ella, lit cigarettes with unconscious grace and looked at me from large blue eyes. I learned to find charm in her quiet, diffident humour; affection in the tranquil way she assumed control of my life. I found that her presence offered me security, as I had sensed that first afternoon that it would; and I was grateful to her for her willingness to rescue me from myself. Our times together were simple and calm: all that my life had not been for so long. And I sank into Sarah's serenity with unthinking relief, hoping that in it I might find peace, knowing that in her strength I would find shelter. Though it is hard to remember now, and even harder to admit since illusion has succumbed to truth, I know that Sarah's poise balanced me; that her control, and the first lessons in self-deception which she so unconsciously gave, protected me. It was she who lit the way to my forgetting; she who tempted me back to the safety of the shallows; and I was grateful.

In bed that first night she talked to me of Ella; and I can see her now, a sheet pulled over her breasts, leaning against the wall, smoking, speaking softly in the rounded tones I would come to know so well.

'You must have known how much she hated me,' was how she began. And her voice was quiet, soft, unassuming. 'I think I told you once myself, in the park.'

And we both remembered a summer's afternoon when I had bought her ice-cream.

'Yes,' I replied, wondering how much Sarah knew of what had happened between Ella and me. 'Yes, I knew.'

'And she told you I hated her, too, no doubt.'

Watching her against the wall, absorbed by the curve of her breasts and the delicate bones of her wrist as she held her cigarette, I said nothing. Perhaps I hesitated, for almost the last time, before betraying so old a confidence of Ella's.

'It's all right,' said Sarah, sensing my reluctance and taking my

276

hand. 'You don't need to tell me. She's accused me of murder to my face. She can't have said much worse than that to you.'

'No.'

There was silence. And I looked at her: at the outline of her nose in profile; at the curve of her nostrils as she blew out the smoke. Her skin was very pale against the white wall.

'Poor Ella.'

'Yes,' I said.

And my head burns as I think of it; I tremble with rage at the thought of Sarah's sympathy that night. Remembering her face and the way her eyes looked sadly into mine has laid all uncertainties to rest; for I know suddenly, and beyond all doubt, that she deserved to die. My killing her was right; in some way it served a deeper, truer justice than the petty bureaucracy of earthly warders and gaols would have done. God will judge her; only He is capable of it. And I, sitting here alone and old and unable to go back, can only wait for His judgement, too; can only wait and remember.

In bed with Sarah that night I was beyond saving.

Let that calm me now; for I was trapped already by then. As surely as Ella herself was trapped, though not as cruelly. I could have done nothing, for Sarah was not fighting her equal; she never did. And we were playing on ground that she knew all too well and I not at all; that she had made it her business to know. Would it have helped me to have been warier of her calculated intimacy than I was? Would it have helped Ella? What chance did either of us ever really have against her? By that stage none, if truth be told. And though it shames me to say so I must. My wife was an instinctive manipulator, you see. With her dead and nearly buried, released from her influence, I can see that. I can see also that she had honed her powers with care; that she acted against her cousin only when she was ready, and that she brought to her campaign three tense years of stealthy observation. Sarah knew how people worked, you know; by then they seldom surprised her. And she had long been expert in her handling of them.

I know that now. The truth, though it has come late in life, has helped me to see. I understand what Sarah did to me now in a way I could not have done until yesterday.

It is strange: how in twenty-four short hours my whole life should have disintegrated; how the foundations of forty-five years of married life should have given way in such a little time. Learning the truth has been destructive. In remembering I have undone Sarah's work; I have removed the cornerstones of her edifice. And although I have hardly rebuilt – for there is nothing and no one left to do so with – I have come to understand, at least; to understand the power she had. My wife's was a personality which never forgot an injury, which seldom forgave a foe, but which rewarded loyalty with a generosity that bound its recipient to her for ever. Those were Sarah's methods; and as I listened to her words that night I was unaware – and I swear that this is true – by what gentle, subtle stages I was being brought under her influence.

'I tried so hard to help Ella,' her cousin said with shy frankness. 'I knew she needed help. You've no idea how much I wanted to prevent . . . what happened at Seton. I . . . I feel in some ways responsible.' And I think her eyes even filled with tears.

I remember how Sarah cried; how prettily she did it; how her tears made you want to touch the velvety skin beneath her eyes. I remember wiping them gently away that night as she kissed my fingers.

'Thank you,' she said, and stroked my hair.

'I tried so hard to warn people,' she went on, slowly. 'But no one would listen. No one but Uncle Alex. He was the only one, apart from me perhaps, who recognized Ella's condition. He had seen it in his mother and sister before, you see.'

I nodded, sick at heart.

'He tried to help Ella; he was the one who sent her to all those doctors. I suppose that's why she . . .' Sarah's voice tailed off. 'But Ella wouldn't accept his help, or anybody else's for that matter. She was always stubborn. And when I tried she . . . But I can't tell you what she did; it was too awful.'

'Tell me,' I murmured; and some part of me really did want to know the worst.

'I couldn't.'

'Do.'

She looked at me, her blue eyes filling with tears again. 'Well, if you must know . . .'

'Tell me,' I said gently.

'She threatened to kill me also.'

There was a pause as Sarah waited for her words to take their full effect.

'Of course I never thought she'd do anything,' she went on when she saw that they had done so. 'If only I'd known she was serious . . . I might have been able to do something. I might have been able to . . .'

'It's not your fault,' I said softly, right on cue.

'But I feel responsible.'

'Well you shouldn't.'

For a long while, in horrible sympathy, I held her close.

'No, you're right,' she said eventually. 'I shouldn't.' With delicate grace Sarah dried her eyes. 'It was Ella, after all, who would never admit her problems. And doctor after doctor told her the same thing: that you have to acknowledge your illness before you can deal with it. That was what Ella refused to do. And she was so stubborn. Short of having her committed, what could Alexander or Pamela or I or anyone else have done?'

'Nothing,' I murmured. And I tried not to hear Ella's voice in a crowded Prague café years before; I tried to drown the sound of her asking me, with wry humour, if I knew how stable you had to be to survive a session with a really respected psychiatrist. 'You did your best,' I said to Sarah; and as I did so I resolved to let go of the past. I wanted no part of it.

'Yes I know,' she said slowly. 'I know I shouldn't blame myself.' She leaned her head against my chest. 'She was so jealous of me, James; so terribly jealous.'

'I know.'

'Did she tell you?'

'Yes.'

'And what did she say?'

'She talked about your grandmother mainly.'

'And about Seton?'

'Yes.'

'She never could bear the fact that I was better suited to it than she was. She used to hate me for being English, you know; English in a way she never could be, I mean, despite being born here.'

I said nothing.

'She hated me for understanding the island in a way she never could. She spent her whole life trying to prove that she could care for it better than me. And the sad thing is she hardly knew it.'

'Really?'

'She only went there for birthdays and the occasional Christmas.'

I looked at Sarah and the tears had gone from her eyes.

'It was a terrible responsibility for her,' she went on, changing tone slightly. 'A real weight around her neck. She was terrified of not rising to the task, you see.'

'Poor Ella.' And I remembered the warmth of her tears on my neck as she had cried in that tower room above the sea years ago.

'Yes, I was sorry for her also.' Sarah paused. 'Perhaps that's why she killed Uncle Alex so publicly. Perhaps, on some level, she wanted to get caught. That's how I understand it, at least.'

'Why should she do that?'

'Well, she's saved herself from Seton.'

'What do you mean?'

But even as I spoke I heard from distant memory Ella's voice telling me that no Catholic could inherit; no divorcée; no convicted criminal.

'She can never have it now,' my love's cousin said softly.

'So what will happen when your uncle dies? Now that Alexander's dead.'

Sarah's face looked up at mine, suitably grave; but there was something faintly uncomfortable about the intensity of its large blue eyes. 'It'll be mine,' she said slowly; and remembering it now she seemed almost to caress her words as she spoke them. 'The island, the house, the title,' she said. 'All mine.'

'And Ella?'

'Ella will get nothing.'

We lay in silence as Sarah stroked my back.

'I can't believe I'm here,' she said at last.

'Neither can I.'

'But you're glad I am?'

'Glad you're here?'

She nodded.

'Very.'

'And you mean that, don't you?'

There was a pause.

'More than you can know,' I said at last.

For a while we lay together, not speaking; and I felt Sarah's long hair tickling my chin. As I moved my head she rolled over, away from me; and when she looked at me it was with sudden seriousness.

'May I ask you a question?'

'Of course.'

She said nothing for a moment, as though considering her words. And her voice, when it came, was all disarming gentleness.

'Does it frighten you to think that Ella was mad?'

'What makes you say that?'

'It does, doesn't it?' she went on slowly, ignoring my question.

I did not reply. But in the silence I could feel the tears coming; and blushing, embarrassed for some reason, I nodded as I blinked them away.

'Then we won't ever think of her again,' said Sarah quietly; and her tone, though gentle, was final. 'We won't ever think of her again.'

Gazing into Ella's face, though it had blue eyes now instead of green and a forehead higher than I remembered, I leaned down to kiss a mouth I hardly knew but which I had fallen in love with years ago.

'Never again,' I said.

And six months later we were married.

31

It is curious, you know; I find it curious to think that the story of my life seems so nearly told, so nearly done, though I have left more than forty years of it untouched. Forty-five years, in fact; for that was the length of my marriage to Sarah. And talking of it now it seems a long time; certainly it sounds like one. Forty-five years. The bulk of my life; the time so many call the best days of it all. And it's strange to think that a week, a year, ten years ago, I would have called it that, too. Unthinkingly, and yet feelingly, I would have credited my wife for what happiness I had. And in some sense I would have been right to have done so. Even now I think that; even now that I know what she did.

My gratitude persists, you see; for old habits are hard to break. And ours, by any standards, was a contented marriage. Sarah was, in many ways, an excellent and loving wife. I will not find it hard to cry at her funeral. On the contrary, my tears will come easily. Standing at my place in the chapel next week, on the Harcourt daïs above and at right angles to the congregation, under decaying banners and cobwebbed arches, I will cry. Publicly, appropriately, I will weep for my dead wife; for the mother of my child. Privately I will cry for us all: for Ella and for Eric as well as for Sarah; for myself also. Perhaps particularly for myself, if now – at this late stage – I can admit to such selfishness. I am the last of us, you see; it is I who must continue unjudged and alone. The truth, which might have been expected to free me, to have given me at the least a new lease of life, has in fact done neither. The telling of all this, the remembering, the undoing of all that Sarah taught me, has left me . . . tired, more than anything else. I have had a long day. And part of me is unwilling still to see through all Sarah did, to destroy the edifice she built so carefully over so long. Part of me hankers even now for the security of her deception. But the foundations have been rocked; the walls are tumbling. Old waters rise again. Having come so far I cannot turn back now; I cannot seek once more the safety of the shallows in which she kept me with such quiet, gentle authority. I must remember our marriage; I know I must. I must see it with the harsh clarity of new knowledge. I cannot comfort myself any longer as Sarah once taught me so well to do.

But what is there to remember? The years, though long, seem curiously free of incident; at least now they do, by comparison with what came before. Sarah had a way of glossing over life, you see; a way of reducing its impact. Emotion frightened her, I think; and she taught me to be frightened of it also. She worked to eliminate feeling in both our lives, to reduce the power sensation has to unsettle and provoke. And she was masterful in ways I am only now beginning to suspect.

I remember my first journey here as possessor; I remember the way the sun glinted on the weathercocks as we passed it on the train; I remember Sarah's whispered words of victory: 'There it is, our island.' And remembering that moment I remember also how she loved this place; and I know that she was not frightened of all feeling.

On the contrary, my wife was capable of an intense, possessive love. And what she felt for this house she later transferred to our child; for she was always feudal at heart. Sarah needed her heir. And when Maggie was born I was in some way secretly relieved that she was so obviously a Farrell. Blanche's features, so truly preserved in both Sarah and Ella, found no expression in her great-granddaughter. And I was pleased by that; pleased by this symbol of another break with the past.

We called her Margaret, at Sarah's suggestion, after the first Countess of Seton; and she is grown-up now with children of her own. She will be here in the morning; and her family will come with her,

I suppose. The house will be full of life again; life in the midst of death. And I will have to tell her how her mother killed herself; how she shot herself, cleanly through the temple, in her private sitting room. I wonder what the children will be told; but I will leave that to their mother. It is she who must decide. And perhaps Sarah's death will bring us closer, for Maggie – and her husband, I suppose, whom I do not like – is all I have left in the world; and we were distanced more by Sarah's obsessive love for us both than by anything else. My wife's love was selfish; I see that now. She wished to be everything to Maggie and to me, and as a result we were not allowed to be much to each other. Certainly I, encouraged to be an approving yet distant father, became just that; for Sarah had trained me well by then and I did not think to question her.

It is odd to think how subject I was to my wife; certainly now I find it odd, for though by no means a natural leader I am hardly subservient. It is not in my nature. But subservience was not the keynote of my relationship with her. That was Sarah's trick. She had a way of masking her authority, you see; of making one's quiescence to her wishes seem a case of voluntary self-will. She was similar – in that respect, if in no other – to Regina Boardman; and as Regina had done for the early part of my career, so Sarah did for my later emotional life. She assumed responsibility for it; and I was more than happy to grant it her.

Under Sarah's expert guidance I learned to forget; to block the avenues of recollection and recall. It was what I had tried, unsuccessfully, to do in the years which followed Eric's death; but it was only under my wife's unspoken tutelage, and by her silent example, that I learned to bury my past with anything like success. Uncertain of how much she knew, I was wary of discussing her cousin with her; in fact I said almost nothing about Ella over forty-five years and Sarah did not broach the topic. She had meant what she said in bed with me that first night; and I took her lack of intrusion as illustration, were it needed, of her endless tact. I never analysed her calm beyond my admiration for it. I never thought – and this is where her genius lay – that Sarah's sovereign poise concealed any darker truth; or that there might be secrets beneath her serenity.

I was thirty when Cyril died; Sarah and I had been married for five years. And I came to Seton with her, to the house which might have been Ella's and mine, with a curious feeling of appropriate progression. My wife had woven her spell on me by then; I had been properly prepared. And I was not troubled by memories of my first visit here or of the girl who brought me on it; for by then I had come to see my love for Sarah as a saner expression of an earlier, misguided feeling for her cousin. Sarah, by artful stages, had assumed all but a tiny portion of Ella's former place in my life. And though I never went to the tower room again, I did not often think of it either.

Married life changed me; Sarah's strength reshaped me in ways that only now – having remembered the boy who married her; having called him fitfully back to life – I can begin to understand. It is only now, now that I have looked honestly for the first time at what really drove my music, that I see how Sarah disliked and worked against it. And I understand her dislike now, and the subtle ways in which it manifested itself. My music was something apart from her; an outlet of feeling beyond her control. And she would not have that. For Sarah my violin was a rival; and its competition for my devotion was keener than any that another human being might have offered. It was for that reason she hated it; and she worked against it with determination and a cold deliberation which I realized, perhaps, but did not wish to admit; and to which I succumbed in the end.

Sarah and I did not fight; her methods were not violent ones. She was no obvious autocrat. The storms that rock most marriages had no place in ours. Instead, by gradual stages, she drew me into the world of this place: subtly, slowly, she saw to it that Seton's rhythms became mine; that I adopted its code of ancient duty and privileged ritual as my own. The world outside – which Camilla once, in a moment of frustration on a visit, called the *real* world – became less real as a result; the pressures of recording schedules and concert commitments seemed distracting, inconsequential details. And gradually I gave them up.

But I gave up performance for another reason also; a reason which more clearly illustrates all that Sarah did, all the power which she held. Under her influence I lost respect for my playing, you see; and with respect went all desire to perform. You cannot play without feeling; and feeling is precisely what Sarah denied me. My belief in my music, for so long so central to my survival, evaporated with my marriage. And it was proper that it should have done so; for having played as I once did, having played as I did the night of the Hibberdson, for example, when it seemed that Ella's love and all it meant were about to be returned, mediocrity was no destiny for me.

Alone tonight, with nothing for company but a yellowed bundle of ageing reviews, such arrogance jars sharply. Who am I to make such pronouncements? Who am I to say what I might have been? I am no one, it's true; and hard though that is to make, it is an admission I cannot avoid. Pretence is no use now. But I know at least what I once was. And in remembering my life I have shared the credit for my playing; I have shared it in ways I could never have dreamed of doing – or of attempting to do – before today. And so I can say this without arrogance: that my recording of the Mendelssohn E Minor ranks with the best; and that such an achievement carries with it a certain responsibility. I could only have moved forwards after that, not backwards; I could not have permitted myself the dubious luxury of poor but continued performance. And I am lucky that I have always, deep down, been a good judge of my own efforts. Such knowledge saved me years ago from spoiling the one unsullied achievement of my life.

It is a blessing that my music – even later, when Sarah had taught me so well – was immune to self-deception. I knew when my playing died; I knew and I mourned it but I did not fight. When technical prowess was all I had to offer, when I was reduced to the status of master technician merely, I stopped. And I am glad that I did. Technical accomplishment can be learned and it must be practised;

but real playing – like real living, I suppose – requires feeling. And that is what I ceased to have.

I did not resent my loss then; and though I mourned it, I did not realize, as I have done now, that it was Sarah who deprived me of it. Perhaps dimly I suspected; perhaps dimly I knew that the bond between my wife and me could not have hoped to fuel my playing as either Ella or Eric, in their different ways, had done. But I did not know consciously; and if I had I would not have minded: for Sarah offered me a peace for which I would have sacrificed anything. And it was a peace, I think now, which stemmed from her capacity for stability. That – and the deception on which it relied – was central to Sarah's creed; that and an hypnotic calm which encouraged the years to fade into one another; which blurred the greatest events with the smallest; which made emotional differentiation at once impossible and undesirable.

My violin was not the only sacrifice I made for a place in Sarah's sanctuary. My friends, few but loyal in the years before my marriage, were given up also; and that I minded more. My wife did not share; certainly she would not share me. And one by one my friends – and even my family – gave way to the icy chill of her smile in welcome and accepted my invitations with less enthusiasm, inviting me instead to parties in London; parties which the duties of Seton life increasingly prevented me from attending.

Camilla Boardman, less enthusiastic at the news of my engagement than I had thought she would be, persevered the longest; she tried, I think, to make friends with Sarah in a way I might have told her was impossible. A frequent guest in our early years here, she was Margaret's godmother, for my wife acquiesced easily in small things. And there was something comforting about Camilla's consistency; about the way in which her curls stayed as tight, her breasts as prominent (though not perhaps quite as pert), her emphases as wonderfully pronounced in middle age and after as they had ever been in youth. At her last dinner here – I see it so clearly now – she talked loudly of her clients, for success had made her more indiscreet than ever, and she tried to make Sarah accept tickets for one of her charity shows.

'Now Mummy's gone, *someone's* got to take on the mantle, I suppose,' she said, pressing the envelope into Sarah's hands. 'And it's *so* tiring having to endure the after-party on one's own. You *must* help me.'

But such effusion only made my wife more severe; and under her cold stare even the energy of as lively a butterfly as Camilla found it difficult to endure. Gradually my friend found that the pressures of business kept her in London far more than she would like, though she continued to invite Sarah and me – and later Margaret – to anything she had or did with the social perseverance which was her hallmark.

'I *know* Sarah doesn't like me,' she told me once, in her cups, perhaps, at one of the few parties – I think it was again her birthday – to which I had been able to go. 'And truth to tell I don't like *her* much either.' And she took my hand with an affectionate squeeze. 'But that's *no* reason to see so much less of you, Jamie darling. Besides, there's my *divine* god-daughter to think of. And who could *possibly* teach her to survive in London but me?'

'Who indeed?'

But even as I spoke I knew – and Camilla did also, I think – that the days of friendship we had known before my marriage were over and irreclaimable. Sarah's price was loyalty: unquestioning and unbroken. And I needed her too much to break our unspoken compact.

Remembering all this brings my marriage back as it really was; in ways which I can understand only now, now that my bond with Sarah has finally been broken. Killing her has broken a spell; it has freed me. I see that now. And I see in what deep seclusion I have spent the last forty-five years: isolated not only from my music and my friends, but from myself. It is that self which the truth has allowed me to reclaim; and I see that painful though they have been to learn, the facts of yesterday have given me my freedom, a freedom I did not know I had lost.

My wife was subtle in her mastery; subtle and instinctive. And it is a tribute to her power that I heard of Ella's death unflinchingly, unmoved almost.

I was in the garden; it was winter, I think. There were workmen to supervise. On a day of grey skies and squabbling gulls I stood by the cliffs, smelling the salt on the breeze, giving instructions, in the sting of the wind. I remember it all. And I remember Sarah, her hair in a bun, her face drawn – for maybe, at the last, her conscience pricked her; who is to say? – walking down the steep path from the castle: a quiet, sombre figure; dark against the cloud.

'I need to speak to my husband,' she said; and the workmen, mindful of their manners, raised their caps and disappeared, leaving us.

'Yes, darling?'

She told me quickly; and in even tones she said that Ella was dead, that she had hanged herself in her cell the night before. 'I had word from the warden this morning.'

It was almost lunchtime then.

'And he sent her personal things.'

There was silence. Perhaps I nodded.

Sarah stood, as though hesitating. 'And two letters,' she said at last. 'I've looked into mine. The same ravings as at her trial.'

'I see.'

'It would only upset you to read yours, darling.'

Again I did not speak. My wife walked towards me; towards the cliff. And I saw in her hand an envelope with my name on it in jagged brown letters.

'But of course the choice rests with you. Would you like to see it?'

And I know now that that was her supreme moment. That was the apex of her daring.

I was silent.

'I don't think you should,' Sarah went on gently. 'Believe me, I know. She was raving when she died. It's no way to remember her.' She looked at me; and the request on my lips dissolved.

'In fact, there's only one thing to do with it,' she said.

And in front of me, a yard or two away, she tore the letter, with slow deliberation, into little pieces. We watched them scatter downwards, into the sea.

'Let's go in,' she said, linking her arm with mine.

32

There's little more to be said now. All that remains are the loose ends; and those Sarah tied for me yesterday with chilling egotism. I am glad this telling is done; I want the end to come. And when my wife has been buried and I have watched her coffin slide slowly into the vault in the presence of a weeping family all will be over. There is something poignant in that, I think; something poignant in the fact that when I, too, have died we three will all lie together, united at last. Ella, Sarah and I, side by side in lead-lined coffins, decaying in harmony.

At my age such symmetries are pleasing.

By then there will be no outward signs of our tragedy; no hint – bar the reports of ageing, inaccurate newspapers – of the bonds that really bind us. And that is as it should be. Margaret must never know what her mother did and she never will. Better far for her to think, however sadly, that Sarah ended her own life; that she was not, perhaps, as stable as she seemed. For the truth would destroy her; and thus our tragedy – mine and Ella's and Sarah's – would spill into generations in which it has no place.

Pretence, for so long the key to Sarah's methods, must now become the key to mine.

And I was expert yesterday. Certainly the police will not suspect; and I say that without smugness. The coroner will be helped towards his verdict of suicide by an array of evidence that quite exonerates me: for my wife's fingerprints are on the weapon that killed her; the gun itself was found in her hand, her grip already vice-like in rigor mortis. Earthly justice and its petty officers will have no hold over me; having failed to find the truth so long ago, they will have no chance now. And I shall go alone, unhindered, to the greater justice that is death.

But I anticipate myself again.

A day's events are all I have left to tell; a week's at most. And as I go over them now I am struck by the curious irony of it; by the fact that I might never have found her out, might never have stumbled on the truth, had Sarah been less considerate about the arrangements for my birthday party. It was her thoughtfulness that exposed her in the end; her thoughtfulness and the little signs by which she intended me to know that she was thoughtful. She liked her wifely duty acknowledged, you see; acknowledged and appreciated. And I have known for weeks that something was up. But I'm particular about parties. I don't like the tenants invited; and I don't like some of my wife's more fawningly agreeable friends. Sarah did not collect equals about her but sycophants; and I had no wish to entertain them on my birthday. So it was only natural that I should have tried to consult a guest list, so that by hinting at least I could have made my wishes known. My wife was always receptive in that way; it was a part of her genius to acquiesce easily over trifles.

I chose last Monday afternoon to search her desk because she was out, supervising the extension to the ticket office. And quite by chance I found the drawer she has kept it in all these years: a tiny drawer, hidden in the scrollwork, opened by a secret spring.

It was an odd key: heavy, large, but made of shining steel that seemed too modern for its design; cut for an old lock. And for a minute or two I turned it over in my hand, wondering why it was there and for which room it was intended. It seemed strange that my wife should have put it in so secret a drawer; strange also that though ancient in design the key itself could have been no more than forty or fifty years old. And it bore the stamp of a London shop, though all the house keys are cut – as they have been for generations – by a firm in Penzance. Curious, though not very, I put the key in my jacket pocket, resolving to ask Sarah about it once my party was over and I could confess – in a moment of lightness – to having searched her desk for a guest list. For the best part of a week it remained there; for though the jacket is a favourite one of mine and I wear it frequently, I give little thought to what its pockets hold. They are always cluttered with things.

It was pure coincidence, really, which showed me the truth. But then life owes more to Chance than we often admit; and it has played too great a part in my story to go unacknowledged now. It was Chance which introduced me to Ella; Chance which brought Eric from Vaugirard on that dreadful night with my forgotten violin; Chance which made me choose this jacket as I changed yesterday for an afternoon of interviews and castle tours. Sarah and I are both particular about guides, you see; and before someone is taken on to the permanent staff we ask them to give a tour which one of us joins: a kind of final evaluation, if you like.

It was a young Miss Reid yesterday afternoon, I think; and I joined her tour, preoccupied a little by other estate business but pleasant, as I always am, to the group of tourists which joined it too. Pleasant but detached; for that is the way to be with them. And through the house we went: down the china gallery; past the staircase door, now locked, which leads to Ella's tower room; through the King's Bedroom with its nineteenth-century four-poster and Chinese screens; finally to the great hall. My mind elsewhere, for I had heard and overheard the tour a thousand times before, I paid little attention to the monologue being given; and it was only outside the great hall, where the group had gathered to examine the door, that I remembered my duties as observer and listened. The guide, correctly and confidently, was explaining the provenance of the lock, thought to be the oldest still in use in the county; and it was only as she finished and we moved again that I felt the key in my pocket. It was clanging against some change.

Remembering it, and remembering also – as Miss Reid was reminding me – that the lock of the great hall is the largest in the house, I took the key out and tried it in the door. Unthinking, unaware, completely unconscious of the significance of what I was doing, I took the key and tried it and was pleased when it fitted so easily. Yes, I was pleased; for I used to think it pleasant to have things neatly explained. And with a heavy effort – for yearly oilings were due but had not yet been done – I ground the bolts slowly back.

It was only as I did so that something stirred; and even then it was only the faintest creaking of memory. Ella's trial, like Eric's death, belonged to the years before my marriage; and I had avoided thinking of them both with careful diligence. Not wanting to remember I had tried to forget; and by and large I had succeeded. But I have always had an eye for detail. And something stirred in me as I took that key from the lock yesterday: something deep within me shifted; shifted and refused to settle. As the tour proceeded I gradually fell back from it, troubled by something, grasping for a memory I could not quite define but which I knew was there. And slowly, obscurely, lines from a far-off court report recurred to me; and as I tried to make them out I heard a prosecution witness state his name and place of work and explain how most keys are the same but he had remembered this one. And it was then that I knew.

It is difficult to describe the first impact of that knowing; the way things fell so suddenly, so alarmingly, into place. The quickness of it frightened me, I think; the speed with which so much disintegrated: my past; my marriage; my unthinking, unquestioned trust in my wife. I was not immediately angry; no, anger was not my first response. I was numb at first, I think; numb and disbelieving. I could not understand. And for the first few awful minutes that numbness shielded me; it allowed me to smile encouragingly at Miss Reid; to wait calmly until the tourists had left the room; to compose myself before returning to the corridor and nodding good-day to the guards at its far end. The rage came later, as I walked back to my study, through the long corridors of the house which should have been Ella's and mine. And alone in the sanctuary of my book-lined room the tears came; and I sobbed with the ugly retchings of a man no longer used to them.

Sitting here now the events of yesterday afternoon seem an age away: further than Ella's trial or Eric's death. It seems years ago, though it was only yesterday; only yesterday that I sat crying at my desk amongst the scattered, silver-framed records of my and Sarah's joint past; only yesterday that the realization came of what I had to do.

It was much later that I went to her sitting room.

And I was calmer by then; the hours had soothed me. I was soothed also by the thought that everything was in place; that I was properly equipped. I did not trust my nerve, you see; even then, knowing the truth as I did, I knew also my wife's power to move me. And I knew that I could not hope to endure a night of tearful explanation without losing all resolve. If I was to act, I had to act soon; and I steeled myself with the memory of Sarah's quiet voice telling me that Ella had hanged herself in her cell and that it would only upset me to read her letter.

Waiting in her room, surrounded by her clutter, I looked at Sarah's things: at her books and her papers and the pictures scattered about; at the photograph of Margaret's christening which stood on her desk; at the one of me, so conscientiously kept, taking my final bow on the night of the Hibberdson final. And I could not believe that the woman to whom all these innocent things belonged, the woman with whom I had shared so many years of my life, for whose security I had sacrificed so much, could possibly have done such a thing. Even then I hoped I was wrong; even then I was willing to be persuaded. The consequences of Sarah's guilt were looming already, you see; and already I was afraid of them. I had no wish to hear what she had done; to know for certain what had happened. And with more self-possession she might have fooled me still; for we were not equals yet. With more self-possession she might still have convinced me – in the face even of such damning evidence – that I had made a terrible mistake; that it was I, and not she, who deserved punishment.

Waiting in her sitting room I heard the crash of the waves far below: relentless; eternal; relieved, at last, by the tap of her heels on the stone of the corridor; by the creaking of the hinges as she opened the door. And seeing me she smiled, surprised perhaps by my promptness. I am not usually the first at meals.

33

It was the look on Sarah's face that betrayed her; the way the colour drained from her cheeks and her hands shook. Not greatly, and she stopped them quickly; but enough for me to know. And remembering it now, now that all else is clear – was, indeed, made clear by my wife herself – I find, beyond the knowledge of what she did, beyond the revulsion of it, a kind of . . . Incredulity? A fascination rather, I suppose; for there was daring in her horror. A distorted courage, even; the courage of which she was so proud. I haven't the words to describe how I feel. At the end of this long day too much has been disturbed for me to find the rest I had looked for; hoped for. And I know now that understanding does not always bring peace; that knowledge does not always bring clarity.

She was raving by the end, you see: moving restlessly about the room; talking quickly, almost eagerly; excitedly. And there was something mesmerizing in her intensity; in her lucidity even then. She was relieved to have found an audience at last, I think; relieved and resolved to claim the recognition she had never thought to have. It was that resolve which shocked me most; the pride with which she told me – hoping for what? for praise? – of what she had done. I had expected denial, perhaps; or at least a show of remorse. I had hoped for both; I see that now. But she was unrepentant to the end; and it never occurred to her that I would have the strength to punish her for what she had done.

But I am rambling again; trying to find some sense in all of this; some sign – and any would do – of a grander plan. For surely there is some purpose in our suffering: in mine and Ella's; even in Sarah's. There must be; I know there must be. But what it is I could not say.

*

My wife began on the offensive, but her attack did not last long. 'Is it customary for a husband to rifle through his wife's desk?' was all she said.

And when I did not reply she shrugged slightly, as if to admit that indignation was a clumsy defence, unworthy of one such as she; and patting her hair, which was straying from its bun, she came to the sofa and sat down – with every semblance of normality, her composure quite regained – at the tea table. Sarah had a gift for smoothing things over, you see; a gift she had used many times in forty-five years of married life. And perhaps she thought that she could work her magic again yesterday, for she began to pour, quite in her usual manner; and all that betrayed her agitation was the unusual clatter of the cups and saucers as she arranged them.

'What is this?' I said quietly: said, not asked; for I knew.

'I beg your pardon, darling?'

My wife did not look up, pretending to busy herself with the tea things. And I can see her now, her dark hair streaked with grey, her body as slender and as graceful as it had ever been, bending over the teapot, uncertain. It was that uncertainty which betrayed her; that sudden vulnerability which was not calculated and which exposed the pretty, manipulating tears of the past. Her façade, so long maintained, was cracking. I had pierced it; I knew that even then. And her strength, once seemingly so endless, drained through the puncture before me.

Silently she poured the tea.

And as it splashed into the cups I thought, inconsequentially, distractedly almost, that she had grown more beautiful with the years; that the fragile, misleading beauty which she had shared with her cousin suited the lines and straight-backed deliberation of age. She was wearing a long, old-fashioned dress of teal blue, a shade darker than her eyes. And her arms seemed thin as they lifted the heavy pot.

'Tell me what this is,' I said again, but less insistently this time; for now that power was mine I found – as I had known I would –

that I had no idea how to wield it. Having deferred to her for so long; having in so many ways allowed my wife's wishes to lead and to direct my own, I was uneasy with this upsetting of the balance between us; uneasy and confused. And some part of me – a part which feared that at the last I would succumb; that at the last I would lack the resolve to punish her as she deserved – was relieved that I had made my plans already. Even in my anger I pitied her, you see; and Sarah sensed from my voice that I did so and lifted her eyes to meet mine and looked at me silently with great art. She was expert in her affects even then; I realize that now. And it took all my strength to resist her mute appeal.

But I said nothing; and in the silence she handed me my tea.

'It's the key to the great hall,' she said unexpectedly, a few moments later. And when she spoke she did so calmly, with quiet consideration; for Sarah knew my weaknesses. She knew that I was helpless in the face of her vulnerability. And so she sat, the bones of her neck showing taut and delicate above the neck of her dress, her hands in her lap, her head tilted a little.

'Tell me how you got it,' I said at last: almost willing her not to; dreading what she might say.

'I have nothing to hide, James,' she said slowly, a picture of bruised innocence. And it was only then that her fragility – so artfully maintained until then – gave way for a moment to a brief flicker of pride. For a moment, no longer, she looked proud and unafraid. And although she looked away again, and wiped her eyes as though a tear had trickled from them, it was too late. And Sarah knew it. When she spoke again it was in quite a different tone.

'Have we really come to this?'

'Yes,' I said evenly, drawing strength from my repulsion; allowing her ill-concealed pride and all it provoked to feed my fury; struggling to conquer the sensation of a rising nausea. From the sofa my wife continued to look at me; but her spell was broken and she knew it. For the first time in our married life I was immune to the power of her pale blue eyes; they had lost their hold over me. And from that moment I was free.

'In that case ask me any questions you like,' she said almost haughtily, sensing this perhaps. 'I see that you have rifled through my desk; that you have found something you should not have found.' She rose and walked across the room to the windows; and looking out to sea, or perhaps at the rocks below, she turned her back on me with splendid indifference. All efforts at placation were over now, I saw, for Sarah did not waste her energies in vain or throw her tender glances to the swine. The lines were drawn; and her last effort at concealment was delivered with the air of a grave warning.

'You would do well to think carefully before asking me anything,' she said, 'because I will tell you the truth. And that is not always as palatable as one might wish it. If you take my advice you will return what you have taken from me and think no more about this.'

But I knew as I listened that I had done with Sarah's forgetting. There was no way back now; we had come too far. Her illusion was shattered. And so I asked the first of many questions; and perhaps I knew, even then, that we were nearing the end.

'Did you kill Alexander?' I asked quietly.

And in the silence that followed I thought that Sarah had probably not expected anything so direct as this; that she would break now into confusion. But her answer, when it came, showed only irritation; annoyance at my rebellion. She was not accustomed to losing the upper hand, you see; and my new-found daring seemed to infuriate her.

'I see you have decided to ignore my warning,' was all she said; icily.

'Yes.' And as I spoke I felt something close to exhilaration in my defiance.

'Then you must have my answer.'

'Yes.'

'And my answer, also, is "yes".' For the first time since she had gone to the window my wife turned to face me. In silhouette against the setting sun I could hardly see her face; but her hair seemed ringed in fire. 'I killed him,' she said slowly; then, after a pause: 'And to anticipate your next question . . . another "yes". It was no coincidence that Ella went to gaol for her father's murder.'

So it was done; it had been said. I knew the truth now; knew it more certainly than I had known it hours before, when I had stood in the great hall watching the backs of retreating tourists in disbelief, thinking only of being alone. I knew; I had knowledge. But truth to tell, at that moment – at that precise moment – I hardly felt at all. I was drowning already, perhaps; drowning though I did not know it. And it was Sarah and her quiet calm – for so long my only lifeline – that was dragging me under. I see that now.

Then I could see nothing; and conscious only of a room beginning to blur as quick, hot, childish tears filled my eyes, I could only ask her why; why she had done it.

There was silence; my wife seemed to be considering the question; and she chose her words with chilling succinctness.

'Ella had everything,' she said at last; slowly. 'And from me who had no one and nothing, she took the person I valued most.'

She had moved from the window as she spoke and walked now across the room: very upright in her blue dress; her hair falling in wisps from its neatly-pinned bun. And as she sat beside me on the sofa I smelled her clean, warm smell: of powder and rose water. She no longer smoked. But it was her eyes, not her smell, which will stay with me; her eyes and her words. And remembering it now I cannot bear to think of the hardness in them as she spoke; of the way she underlined, by her physical proximity, the vastness which separated us. For I learned then – as I am beginning to accept only now, I think – how little I had ever meant to her; how little she had ever cared for me in any but the most material of terms. I tell myself now that my wife's calculation made connection with others impossible; that she could not share herself openly, however hard she tried, because of what had been taken from her. And I think as I do so that I am probably right; that by the time she married me Sarah was incapable of feeling, though she simulated it with such ease. I was no more than the crowning glory of her success; I see that now. And part of me knows that it could not have been otherwise.

It was the knowledge of my wife's dissimulation that hurt me most, I think; the dawning suspicion as she spoke that she had never been true. It was that which destroyed our past; that knowledge, as certain as it was unspoken, which made a mockery of all our years. And I realized, as I listened to her speak, that the Sarah I had known – the Sarah I had loved, even – had never been anything more than an artful façade, designed to preserve my allegiance and prolong my subjection; for Ella's cousin never lost her fear of betrayal. In the glow of the setting sun she came alive; alive with triumphant radiance. And there was something terrible in the contrast between her beauty and her words; something chilling in the way she spoke to me of loss and jealousy and grief and revenge with such barely containable pride.

'You hardly need me to enumerate Ella's blessings,' Sarah said; stiff still, almost childlike in her stiffness. She sounded like a little girl. 'She had a father who doted on her; freedom; friends; this house. The best of all worlds. And still she took him from me, from me who had no one.'

'Took whom from you?' Even through the blur I had to ask; I had to know.

'Charlie Stanhope,' said Sarah quietly.

And I thought, for the first time in years, of Charlie Stanhope: tall; awkward; loyal.

'Charlie?'

'Yes.' My wife looked at me. And she stood up again and crossed once more to the window, restless as she spoke. The sun was slipping over the horizon; the room was hazy now. 'Ella took him away. She took him away and she showed me she could take him and then she discarded him. That was what hurt most; the fact that she didn't even want him.'

And from far-off years I saw Ella by another window looking out on to the same sea and I heard her tell me, in tears, what she had done.

'And the day she broke her engagement to him I made myself a promise,' Sarah continued. 'A promise to take all that she loved most from her. To show her what loss was really like.'

I said nothing; I could not.

'And I think I have kept it,' my wife finished with quiet triumph. Still I could not speak.

'It was no easy task, I assure you. Even as you judge me understand that.'

'I do.' And I understood also, I think, that this was Sarah's moment; that now she could not help but claim her glory.

She had told no one, you see; over long years of enforced secrecy she had remained silent. But the urge to tell had always been there, I suspect; the urge of a proud nature which seeks acknowledgement. And I think that yesterday afternoon, her guilt exposed, she was fearless and past caring. That is how I understand it now, at any rate. Even then Sarah thought herself invulnerable, you see; and she spoke with a readiness made compelling by its lack of shame if nothing else. Standing at the window, the sun behind her, she glowed with victory; and I see her now, though it is dark in here and cold, and she is dead and nearly buried, with a clarity which will never fade. I see her and I hear her and I listen to her still.

She began boastfully, exulting coolly in the challenge of it.

'You have no idea how difficult it was,' she said. 'Depriving Ella of all she had: of her father; her friends; this house and all that went with it. No easy task. And it required daring, believe me. Courage.' She paused, looking out to sea. 'But also a great deal of meticulous planning,' she went on at last. 'That was where success lay and I realized it. I knew that attention to detail was everything; and I think you will agree that although a risk was involved – and, frankly, that was unavoidable – I did all that I could to eliminate it, to reduce it to manageable levels.'

'But . . .'

'Don't interrupt. It was all such a long time ago. I haven't thought of it for years; my train of thought mustn't be broken.' And she continued with splendid indifference, talking as much to herself as to me; relishing all the intricacies of her daring. 'Of course Uncle Cyril's party was a blessing,' she said quietly, introspectively almost. 'And the fact that Ella and I looked so alike. That had to be the foundation of my plan, I knew; and curiously enough, it was you who proved to me how things might work.' She turned from the window.

'Me?' I asked hoarsely.

'Long ago. In Hyde Park. A summer's afternoon. Don't you remember? You thought I was Ella. And the way you behaved at the Hibberdson prize-giving just confirmed things. It was so obvious from your disappointment when we spoke that you'd made the same mistake. That gave me confidence.' She smiled. 'And it made me sure that if you could be convinced, from a distance, others might be convinced also; particularly if all the details were right. Hair; clothes; posture. You know.'

I did know.

'So without asking Ella, which might have given everything away, I had to find out what she was wearing. That was the first step. And that was where that ridiculous friend of yours came in so handy.'

'Who?'

'Camilla Boardman her name was, wasn't it?'

I nodded, my throat dry.

'I went to her for fittings, you see, counting on her notorious indiscretion. And predictably, without my asking, she told me on my second appointment, in the *greatest* confidence' – Sarah's eyes sparkled as she imitated my friend – 'that Ella would be wearing a man's dinner jacket. Admirable for my purposes, of course, because at once distinctive, unusual for a woman to wear, and easily obtained.'

'I see.'

'And Camilla was hardly happy when I stopped going to her and wore a dress by someone else. But that couldn't be avoided. I needed to be brashly noticeable in the crowd, you understand. Brashly noticeable so that enough people would see me to cover my disappearance for five or six minutes. That, I thought, was all it would take if I planned properly; and in the event I was only away for seven. Not a long time in the middle of a party, particularly when you have made certain of speaking to enough people.'

'Which you did . . .'

'Of course.'

'And everything else was planned in advance.' Sarah was talking quickly now; almost tripping over herself in her eagerness. 'I had the right clothes; a blonde wig of real hair, cut and parted like Ella's; two keys to the great hall, one of which was in Ella's pocket before the party even began.'

'The other of which is this?'

'Yes. Kept for a keepsake.'

'I see.'

'Foolish, I know; but an irresistible mistake.'

My tears had gone now; and I watched my wife with sickening attention as she moved about the room with restless concentration: first to the fireplace; then to the window; then to the sofa again. The tea things lay forgotten on the table, our cups untouched. And though she brushed against the handle of the teapot as she passed it in the twilight, nearly knocking it over, she gave no sign of noticing that she had done so. Instead she talked, with mesmerizing fluency; and I listened to her and thought with dread of what she had done and of what I had yet to do. I am not, by nature, a violent man.

But Sarah talked on, oblivious to me and my thoughts; and she spoke with increasing pride in a kind of unthinking stream, her usual quiet manner completely overthrown.

'It was easy work to remove the original key from Cyril's desk for a night while I had duplicates made in London. And I wore the wig when I went into the shop to get them done because it's little touches like those that make all the difference, you know. And although it was a slim chance, I thought that if I dressed and spoke like Ella the man might recognize her from her pictures in the papers later on and come forward.'

'Which he did.'

'Yes.'

'And then there was the physical preparation.'

'Of what sort?'

'Well, Alexander was a big man and I'm not particularly strong, so I had to practise the lift to make sure I got it right. That was weeks before. And on the night of the party itself there were endless things to do. So many details; and with such time constraints. Timing was everything.'

'What did you do?'

She stopped, disorientated for a moment; and I saw that I had interrupted her flow. 'While we were all dressing,' she began slowly again, as if trying to remember it all, to leave no detail untold, 'I put a note under Ella's door asking her to meet her father secretly in his room at eight, and to wait for him if he wasn't there. I couldn't have her turning up anywhere while I was on the balcony with Uncle Alex, you see.' My wife smiled at me. 'I got him to come up by saying that the speeches were going to be made from the great hall, not in the marquee, which he thought rather a good idea. And he waited for me while I changed. I think he was quite amused by my clothes, in fact. I told him Ella and I were dressing identically as a joke.'

'Go on.'

'Well, so far so good, but the point of highest risk was still to come.' My wife looked at me; and I wondered suddenly how I could have lived with her for as long as I had done with so little idea of who she was. Our marriage, in all its wealth of peaceful detail, seemed suddenly unreal; unreal before the shining fire of Sarah's eyes.

'I couldn't be visible to everyone for too long,' she was saying. 'A moment was all right, but more than that was an unacceptable risk. On the balcony itself I stood behind him as much as I could, and I can't tell you how it unsettled me when old Lord Markham called out for Ella to show herself. I had to act quickly then.'

'So you pushed him.'

'Lifted him *then* pushed him. It was quite a complex manoeuvre, in fact. But it caught him so completely by surprise and the balustrade in any case is very low. It wasn't difficult in the end. I almost lost my nerve when he clung on like he did, though; and I thought he might scream my name or something. So I had to loosen his grip as quickly as I could.'

'That was when people thought you were helping him.'

'Yes, though I can't imagine why. It was ludicrously clear what was happening. That was the point. And as soon as he had fallen I went in and ran to my room; took off the wig and my clothes; put them in a bag and the bag into a drawer, where no one would think to look for it; put on my dress and went downstairs. No more than seven minutes, the whole thing. Oh, and on my way I liberated the note I had given Ella, which fortunately was on the dressing table in her room. It was typed, of course, so no real harm would have come of anyone finding it. The police would have thought it was a fake she had written to herself. But I was glad to get it nonetheless. And the next day, when all was quieter, I simply took the bag down to the cliffs, added a few stones, and threw it off. It was done.'

'But Ella accused you.' I had been drawn in, now; drawn in to Sarah's story in all its manic glibness. And she pounced on my observation with delight.

'Of *course* she did. I had known that she would. Being innocent herself, she was the only person who could have known – really known – the truth.'

'But you had prepared for that already,' I said slowly; and I saw the sweep of Sarah's plan with sickening clarity.

'Clever, wasn't it?'

I said nothing.

'That little monograph; my book. Everything paved the way. And when Ella was weak and stupid enough to use insanity as her excuse for ending with Charlie, the game was as good as won. You should never underestimate the power of the press. Those jurors' minds were made up before ever they walked into the courtroom; and she had lied to the family for so long that no one was really surprised by what she seemed to have done. Shocked, of course, but not surprised. She had been seeing psychiatrists for years by the time I killed Alexander. And her hysteria, however understandable you and I might know it to be, did her no favours at all. Even when she tried to tell the truth – and she told the court doctors all about her relationship with me, for instance – she wasn't believed. She was caught by then; she had nowhere to turn.'

There was silence.

'I don't believe it,' I said hoarsely.

'Yes, you do.'

But it was still with something like disbelief that I looked at her, silhouetted against the fiery last rays of the sun; and it was then that I knew that I was the last thing she had taken from Ella.

'Losing Charlie taught me something,' said Sarah softly; calmer now. 'It taught me to observe, to understand people. For the first time in my life I learned to please.'

I looked at her steadily.

'Ella had always been the charming one, you know,' she went on. 'I had never been able to compete.' She paused. 'But when she took Charlie I set myself to learn her ways. And I learned how easily men are swayed by women . . .' She stopped short, realizing what she was saying, perhaps.

And in the silence I remembered our lunch on the day of Ella's conviction and the ease with which I had fallen.

Without looking at my wife again I left the room.

34

The corridor was gloomy in the dusk; and I sat alone in the window seat at its furthest end watching the last of the day-trippers catch the last of the boats just as Ella and I – years ago though in the opposite direction – had caught the last of the boats on my first visit to this place. Perhaps I half-expected Sarah to follow me; to offer some word or gesture of regret. At the last moment I almost lost my nerve, you see; I nearly retreated in the hopes of being able to forgive.

But forgiveness was not asked, as I had known that it would not be. And listening to the breaking of the waves I sat alone, staring at the door to my wife's sitting room, wondering what right I would have had to grant it in any case. None, I knew. And so I sat, watching, as the corridor sank into darkness and filled with the first of the images I have since come to know so well again. Ella in the park, with her bitten nails: the beginning of it all. Her crumpled limbs in the sunshine of my attic. Her red eyes later, in that crowded court-room, when she was lost to me and I thought her mad and would not smile at her.

I tried not to think of her body, years after, hanging from the ceiling of her cell; I tried not to think of how I had failed to mourn her then.

Slowly I got up; and in the dark I walked towards the crack of light under Sarah's door. She was reading when I opened it; or at least sitting with a book on her lap, calm and unseeing. She did not say anything; did not seem even to notice me. She was lost in her own thoughts and did not look as I opened the bureau drawer and put on the gloves and picked up the gun. It was only as I crossed the room towards her that I saw the signs of fear on her face; the signs of fear and surprise; of shock. It was only at the last that she lost her sense of mastery; her certainty in her own success. And she had no time to struggle.

I shot her above her right ear, at something close to point-blank range.

Very deliberately, calm almost, I stepped over her body and clasped the gun in her limp right hand. Then I left the room and returned to my own, where I washed and dressed with slow deliberation; taking my time, doing things carefully. Sarah had taught me the value of detail.

The house was dark as I let myself out; only the light in my wife's window burned. And guided by its glow I took the bag which held my clothes and gloves to the edge of the cliff; to the spot – for I am sentimental, even now – where Sarah had told me of Ella's death on that blustery afternoon years ago.

The wind was calm last night; there was a full moon. I am fairly sure I found the right place.